W9-BXL-102

# A Dream of Miracles

Center Point
Large Print

Also by Ruth Reid and available from
Center Point Large Print:

*An Angel by Her Side*
*A Woodland Miracle*

# A Dream of Miracles

## An Amish Wonders Novel

# RUTH REID

CENTER POINT LARGE PRINT
THORNDIKE, MAINE

This Center Point Large Print edition is published
in the year 2016 by arrangement with Thomas Nelson.

Scripture quotations are taken from the New King James
Version®. © 1982 by Thomas Nelson. Used by permission.
All rights reserved. And from the Holy Bible, New
International Version®, NIV®. Copyright © 1973, 1978,
1984, 2011 by Biblica, Inc.™ Used by permission of
Zondervan. All rights reserved worldwide.
www.zondervan.com. The "NIV" and "New International
Version" are trademarks registered in the United States
Patent and Trademark Office by Biblica, Inc.™

This novel is a work of fiction. Names, characters, places,
and incidents are either products of the author's imagination
or used fictitiously. All characters are fictional, and any
similarity to people living or dead is purely coincidental.

The text of this Large Print edition is unabridged.
In other aspects, this book may vary from the original edition.
Printed in the United States of America on permanent paper.
Set in 16-point Times New Roman type.

ISBN: 978-1-62899-999-0

Library of Congress Cataloging-in-Publication Data

Names: Reid, Ruth, 1963– author.
Title: A dream of miracles : an Amish wonders novel / Ruth Reid.
Description: Center Point Large Print edition. | Thorndike, Maine :
Center Point Large Print, 2016. | ©2016
Identifiers: LCCN 2016009442 | ISBN 9781628999990
  (hardcover : alk. paper)
Subjects: LCSH: Amish—Fiction. | Large type books. | GSAFD: Love
stories. | Christian fiction.
Classification: LCC PS3618.E5475 D74 2016b | DDC 813/.6—dc23
LC record available at http://lccn.loc.gov/2016009442

This book is dedicated to Simon and Mary Thon, the loving couple who took me into their home, treated me like family while I attended Ferris State University, and introduced me to the Amish. As I was writing this book I was saddened by Mary's passing on June 22, 2015. I'll always remember Mary for her lively personality and unending kindness. I was blessed to have known Mary.

# Glossary

*aenti:* aunt

*boppli:* baby

*bruder:* brother

*daagdich:* scamp

*daed:* dad or father

*danki:* thank you

*Das Loblied:* Amish hymn of praise, sung in every Amish worship service

*dochder:* daughter

*doktah:* doctor

*dorstig:* thirsty

*engel:* angel

*Englischer:* anyone who is not Amish

*fashprecha:* promise

*fraa:* wife

*geh:* go

*greenhaus:* greenhouse

*grossdaadi:* grandfather

*guder mariye:* good morning

*gut:* good

*gutgckichmann:* good-looking or handsome man

*haus:* house

*hiya:* a greeting like hello

*hungahrich:* hungry

*ich:* I

*Ich liebe dich:* I love you

*jah:* yes
*kaffi:* coffee
*kapp:* a prayer covering worn by Amish women
*kinner:* children
*kronk:* sick
*kumm:* come
*kumm mitt mich:* come with me
*mamm:* mother or mom
*mei:* my
*nacht:* night
*narrisch:* crazy
*nau:* now
*nay:* no
*nett:* not
*Ordnung:* the written and unwritten rules of the Amish; the understood behavior by which the Amish are expected to live, passed down from generation to generation. Most Amish know the rules by heart.
*Pennsylvania Deitsch:* the language most commonly used by the Amish
*rumschpringe:* running-around period when a teenager turns sixteen years old
*schweschder:* sister
*sei se gut:* please
*sohn:* son
*wasser:* water
*wilkom:* welcome
*wunderbaar:* wonderful

# A Dream
# of Miracles

# Chapter One

"*Mei sohn* needs to see *Doktah* Roswell. It's an emergency." Mattie Diener stood before the receptionist's window with three-year-old Nathan on one hip, and Amanda, her eighteen-month-old daughter, teetered on her other.

The young woman looked up from her computer screen and slid the sign-in log closer to Mattie. "What's Nathan's problem today, Mrs. Diener?"

"He's *nett* himself." Mattie gently lowered Amanda to the floor at her side in order to free her hand to sign the forms. She jotted the pertinent information on the log, then handed the clipboard back to the receptionist.

Mattie cradled Nathan tighter to her chest as heat radiated from his little body. She'd given him feverfew earlier, but this time the herb did little to bring his fever down. Mattie placed her hand on his moist forehead. "He's burning up."

The woman's eyes widened as if seeing Nathan for the first time. "And I see he has a rash." She removed the headset that connected her to the telephone, rolled her chair back from the desk, and stood.

"*Jah*, it's a . . . heat rash."

The receptionist held up one finger. "Stay right

there. I'll get the nurse." She disappeared behind the partitioned wall of file cabinets.

Little Amanda clung to Mattie's legs, her round face buried in the folds of Mattie's dress. She should have asked her best friend Grace to watch Amanda. Her daughter was shy around strangers. Although not a bad thing, it did make her daughter clingy, even more so when she was overly tired. Amanda's crankiness had started last week when the temperature had risen above eighty, a record high for the second week of June in Michigan's Upper Peninsula.

Whispers spread amongst the roomful of people. Mattie glanced over her shoulder and scanned the waiting room with an apologetic smile. Doctor Roswell's office was always abuzz with patients. Well respected in Badger Creek, the country doctor took his time listening to his patients' concerns no matter how many people waited to see him.

She'd brought Nathan into the office numerous times since his birth three years ago. Doctor Roswell always managed to squeeze her son into his busy day. She studied her sleeping son. Nathan's lips were cracked, and he was panting with shallow breaths, his face blotchy with a beet-red, prickly heat rash. *Oh, please hurry.*

A few moments later, the door leading to the back hallway opened, and the nurse ushered Mattie and the children down the hall and into one of the empty rooms. "What brings you in today, Mrs. Diener?"

"Nathan's had a high fever most of yesterday and today." Mattie lowered Nathan onto the paper-lined table. He flailed his arms, but Mattie was able to settle him by gently stroking the side of his face. "I gave him feverfew, but it hasn't helped. The rash just started." Amanda tugged on Mattie's dress. She bent down and gathered her daughter into her arms.

The nurse eyed him closely. "It doesn't look like chicken pox to me," she mumbled.

Made sense why they had rushed her into a back room. Avoid the possible risk of spreading the virus. Only this wasn't chicken pox. She'd cared for her younger sisters when they were covered in spots, so she knew Nathan's was a simple fever rash. "I agree," Mattie said. "I think it's a heat rash."

"We'll let the doctor do the diagnosing." The nurse placed the tip of the ear thermometer in Nathan's ear and held it in position until it beeped. She discarded the plastic protective cap, then returned the instrument to the wall charger.

"He has a fever, doesn't he?" Mattie's dress was still damp from his sweat.

"Yes, it's 102.6." She jotted the number on the paper attached to a clipboard. "You said he's had a fever for two days. Any vomiting or diarrhea?"

"*Nay.*"

The nurse placed her hand on Nathan's wrist and monitored her watch. Afterward, she made a few notations on the form. "He isn't normally this quiet, is he?"

Mattie shook her head.

The nurse crossed the room and paused at the door. "The doctor will be in to see him shortly."

Mattie lifted her hand to Nathan's head and brushed the mop of wet curls away from his face. Bands of sweat dotted his forehead. "Lord, he's so frail. Please watch over him. *Mei* children are all I have," she whispered as the door opened.

A thirtysomething woman wearing a cranberry-colored dress under a long, white doctor's coat entered. As she crossed the room, her matching cranberry heels clacked against the laminate floor.

"I'm Doctor Wellington," she said, extending her hand.

Mattie shook the woman's smooth hand and tried to hide her surprise at how firm the doctor's grasp was for a woman. "I'm Mattie Diener. Where's Doctor Roswell? I hope nothing has happened to him."

The woman smiled. "He's on sabbatical."

Mattie crinkled her brows, unsure if that was good or bad.

"A much-needed vacation," the doctor explained, moving to the sink to wash her hands. Her friendly demeanor shifted to a professional nature once she approached Nathan. "How long has he had the red blotches on his face?" She began unbuttoning his shirt.

"They just appeared. I think the fever brought them on." Mattie scrutinized the doctor's facial expression. If the doctor was alarmed by Nathan's mottled chest, her expression didn't show it. Doctor Wellington continued the assessment, pressing her hand on Nathan's abdomen in several places. Her son's lips curled into a slight frown and his eyes opened. He stared several seconds, almost stupor-like, then closed them again.

"Is he normally this lethargic?"

"He's *nett* acting like himself, if that's what you're asking."

She scanned the nurse's notes. "You gave him feverfew?"

"*Jah.* Normally it brings his fever down in a few hours, but *nett* this time."

"How much did you give him?"

Mattie shook her head. "I didn't measure the exact amount. I made it into a broth. Yesterday he drank it throughout the day, but today he refused it."

She reviewed the chart. "No vomiting or diarrhea. How has his appetite been?"

"Other than the broth, he hasn't eaten anything since yesterday morning, and it wasn't much. Usually I can encourage him to breastfeed when he refuses everything else, but he wasn't interested."

"How often does he breastfeed?"

"When he's sick, restless. The attachment seems to calm him down."

Nathan stirred. He opened his eyes, then blinked a few times under the room's bright lights. As if focusing for the first time on the doctor, his eyes widened and he let out a shrill cry.

"It's okay. I'm right here," Mattie said in Pennsylvania *Deitsch*. She reached for his tiny hand and gave it a gentle squeeze. "This is *Doktah* Wellington."

His gaze slowly drifted to the opposite side of the table but darted back to Mattie, his face puckering with fear.

"*Bruder kronk?*" Amanda began to whimper.

"*Shh . . .*" Mattie kissed her daughter's temple. "Your big *bruder* is going to be okay."

Doctor Wellington leaned closer to him. "Can you tell me your name?"

Nathan ignored the doctor and locked his gaze on Mattie.

"His name is Nathan," she volunteered. "He doesn't know many *Englisch* words yet." She looked fondly at her son. His rosy cheeks brought out his blue eyes, the spitting image of his father, her late husband. Andy's cheeks would turn red after he'd worked outside in the cold weather and then stay that way for hours.

Doctor Wellington peered up from the chart,

16

arching her thin, penciled brows. "He's three years old. He should be talking."

"He does . . . to me." Had this doctor never treated an Amish child? They only spoke Pennsylvania *Deitsch* until they reached school age. When the doctor's brows angled in what appeared to be disapproval, Mattie opened her mouth to explain, but Nathan's moan pulled her attention back to her son.`

Nathan licked his cracked lips. Breathing out of his mouth had caused them to dry. She would dab some more beeswax on them once they returned home.

The doctor started to check his ears, and he tossed his head.

"Nathan." He stilled at Mattie's sharp rebuke. She softened her tone. "It's okay."

"His ears are clear. Can you open your mouth and say *ah?*" The doctor demonstrated by opening her mouth wide, exposing her perfectly white teeth, and sticking out her tongue. When he finally mimicked her action, Doctor Wellington's fore-head wrinkled. She leaned closer, aiming a penlight into his mouth. "How long has he had blisters in his mouth?"

"I'm *nett* sure." Such important details shouldn't come as a surprise. What else had she missed?

The physician went to the phone on the wall and dialed. "Please pull Nathan Diener's complete medical records and bring the file to me." She washed her hands again, then reexamined Nathan's mouth. "You don't know how long he's had the blisters?"

Mattie swallowed hard. The doctor's tone had sharpened, her penetrating eyes silent accusers. Mattie shook her head. "*Nay.* Until you brought them to *mei* attention, I had no idea."

A soft knock on the door pulled the doctor's attention away. The nurse entered and handed her two thick binder files. "Here's the chart you requested."

"Thank you." Doctor Wellington took a moment to scan the stack of documents.

"He's been sick a lot," Mattie said, breaking the silence. The doctor merely nodded without looking up and flipped to the next page. When she finally closed the file, her exam became more precise, less informative. Mattie chewed her lip. She wanted to ask questions, but she also didn't want to interrupt the doctor.

Nathan's whimpering at the constant probing stirred Amanda, who soon joined the chorus of sobs. Mattie rocked her daughter in her arms, trying to soothe her before the doctor suggested she take Amanda out of the room.

Doctor Wellington pressed Nathan's tongue down with a flat wooden stick, then felt his neck and under his arms. When she pinched his fingertip, Nathan retracted his hand and tucked it under his armpit.

"Let her look at you." Mattie redirected her attention from her son to the doctor. "He's *nett* like this with *Doktah* Roswell." She stroked his sweat-matted auburn locks. "We'll be going home soon."

"He needs to be admitted to the hospital for observation," the doctor said, writing something on the paper attached to the clipboard.

"I can observe him from home. *Doktah* Roswell usually gives me a list of things to watch for."

She looked up from her notes. "He's dehydrated and needs fluids."

"I'll make sure he drinks plenty of fluids." And she would bring him in to see *Doktah* Roswell once he returned from vacation. At least his exams were never abrupt. Besides, she still had a pile of unpaid hospital bills from when Andy was admitted.

Mattie lowered Amanda to the floor, then gathered Nathan into her arms. "Can you tell me when *Doktah* Roswell will be back?"

"Mrs. Diener, your son has been seen in the clinic multiple times." She motioned to the thick files the nurse had brought her. "Don't you want to get to the underlying cause of his problem?"

Mattie squared her shoulders. "Of course I do." Was the doctor suggesting Mattie didn't care for her son? She hadn't been in the room more than fifteen minutes. How could she make such accusations? "He has a weak immune system; *Doktah* Roswell knows all about him."

Doctor Wellington removed a form from the clipboard. "This is his admission orders. When you get to the hospital, you can give them to the nurse. I'll be by to check on him later."

Mattie hesitated. Her mind was going a million directions. She couldn't very well leave the horse tied up for hours in the hospital parking lot. Usually she arranged rides from her *Englisch* friend in advance. Did she even have Cora's phone number with her?

The doctor glanced at the form, then looked at Mattie, her expression hardening. "I strongly advise you not to refuse medical care for your child."

Bo Lambright loosened his tie as he entered the desk-lined office. From across the room, he nodded at his coworker, Max Roker, and lifted the fast-food bag of cheeseburgers he'd picked up at the drive-through on his way back from court. Bo's stomach had growled the better part of the morning as he waited to give his testimony. He set the fast-food bag and sodas on his desk, plunked down on the chair, and pawed through the bag of foil-wrapped burgers. He glanced at Max's hand-writing scrawled on a neon-green Post-it Note stuck to his phone. *Dinner— tomorrow. Judge Nettleton.*

Not the call he was expecting when he forwarded his calls to Max's extension, but he wasn't surprised. His mother only called to remind him of the important dinners. And lately, finding him a wife was a high priority. Or maybe she felt deprived of grandchildren. Since he turned thirty-two last month, she'd made plenty of innuendos about following the best laid plans— not his, not God's, but hers. Judge Nettleton was convinced it meant him running for political office and/or settling down to start a family. With the right wife, of course.

Bo glanced at the check marks on the wrapper of the first burger he removed from the bag. No onions. Extra mayo and pickles. He passed the sandwich to Max, whose desk butted up against Bo's.

"Thanks." Max unwrapped his burger, then lifted the bun to double-check for onions as he always did. "What do you know, they got it right today." He sniffed as he reassembled the burger.

"You still sick?" Max's sinuses plugged every spring, and for six months out of the year he talked nasally.

"Allergies." He wiped his red nose with a napkin.

Bo opened his desk drawer, then removed his tie and dropped it inside. "Did you try honey like I told you?"

"Not yet." Max chomped his hamburger.

"You're going to suffer another year?" Bo undid the top button on his shirt and rolled his sleeves mid-forearm.

"I'll pick some up."

"You need local honey. Don't buy the stuff in the grocery store or you won't build immunity to the pollen growing in this area."

"Yah, yah. Did you see the message that your mom called?"

"I don't know why she calls my cell phone *and* my work line to leave the same message." He shrugged. His mother was painstakingly thorough and bored since she retired. "I take it Josh's schoolteacher didn't call back?" The hard winter had forced the county to extend school until the end of June to make up the snow days, and Josh, one of Bo's troubled teenagers in the foster system, was in jeopardy of failing due to not showing up for classes.

"Nope. Just your mother." Max took a drink from his coffee cup and cringed. "This stuff's nasty."

"Add some ice and whipped cream and sell it for eight bucks. You'll make millions."

"We're in the wrong business." Max chuckled. "By the way, what happened in court?"

"Steinway went light on the bruiser." Bo took a bite and washed it down with a sip of cola. "I hope every time the man lights a cigarette in jail, someone shoves it down his throat for what he did to his kid." Bo thought taking lashes from a leather strap was cruel growing up, but that paled in comparison to being used as an ashtray. Judge Steinway had gone too soft on the jerk. Bo wouldn't have shown mercy. The poor excuse for a father deserved life. As it was, with the time he'd already served in jail, it wouldn't be long before the man was back at home inflicting the same pain on his kids. Bo had seen it time after time. The past always had a way of repeating itself.

Max swept his mouth with a napkin, missing some mayo on the corner. "Are you going to meet us at O'Riley's after work?"

"Nope. On call." Bo took another bite. As good as this burger tasted, he should have ordered two.

"Thought Davis was."

"We traded." The phone rang. Bo set the burger on the desk, reached for his drink, and gulped a mouthful before picking up the receiver.

"Child Protective Services, this is Bo Lambright."

# Chapter Two

Bo regretted trading being on call with Davis the moment the phone rang, summoning him to the other side of the county to investigate a complaint. The forty-five-mile jaunt turned into an all-day journey due to construction and road closures. The detours had taken him on the scenic route through the northwest Hiawatha National Forest area where jack pines, aspens, maples, white pines, and hemlocks towered hundreds of feet high. Most of the land in this area was federally owned, but a few scattered parcels were privately owned by a small Amish district. He glanced at his speedometer. Five miles per hour. His foot already rode the brake pedal in order to avoid rear-ending the buggy. This wasn't a Sunday-afternoon drive; he had things to do.

If the road wasn't so winding and the trees didn't canopy his view, he might chance a ticket and go around the buggy even though he was in a no-passing zone. Clogging up traffic like this was ridiculous. The buggy driver should know to pull over to the shoulder and allow cars to pass. Bo tapped the steering wheel. He had the patience of Job—usually. But he'd had enough of this snail's pace. Bo eased into the other lane.

An oncoming truck rounded the corner and Bo slammed on the brakes, then swerved back in place behind the buggy. His heart hammered. He wasn't a risk taker and didn't want to analyze why he was so anxious to put that buggy in his rearview mirror.

His pulse rate slowed, and he crept over the solid line dividing the lanes once again. Not seeing any traffic, he punched the Chevy Impala's accelerator. In a matter of minutes, enough distance separated him from the buggy that when he looked in the rearview mirror, the horse was a dot on the horizon. A similar image flashed in his mind of looking out the back window of his parents' station wagon fourteen years ago. The scent of cow manure engulfed his senses, only there wasn't a cow in sight. His hands moistened, and he grasped the steering wheel tighter.

Once he reached the city limits of Badger Creek, he eased off the gas. The old lumber town hadn't changed much over the years. A locally owned hardware store stood at one end and the town's only grocery store anchored the opposite end. A laundromat, bus station, bar, small-engine repair shop, and a few scattered businesses made up the remainder of Badger Creek's downtown. Hard to believe this was once a booming lumber town—a hundred years ago.

Bo followed the road signs to Community Memorial and pulled into the visitors' parking lot of the three-story hospital. Compared to the hospitals on his side of the county, this place resembled an office annex with willow trees landscaping the grounds and large clay planters filled with an array of pink and purple impatiens lining the sidewalk. Bo cut the engine and snatched his leather laptop case from the passenger seat. The summer heat blasted him as he stepped out from the air-conditioned sedan.

He glanced up at the cloudless blue sky. Should've known not to take Davis's call. Instead of peeling off his tie and rolling up his shirt sleeves, ready to kick back and relax, Bo was adjusting his collar and straightening his tie as he hiked toward the main entrance. *Lord, is it too much to ask for an easy, open-and-shut case?* He sighed. *Forget I asked.* Nothing should be open and shut about a child's safety.

The automatic glass doors opened, and Bo stepped into the air-conditioned lobby. The information desk sat a few feet away. Bo approached the gray-haired woman seated behind the desk and smiled. "Good afternoon, my name is Bo Lambright." He fished out one of his business cards and handed it to her. "I'm here to see Detective Chandler. I believe he's with Doctor Wellington."

The woman adjusted her reading glasses, looked at the card, then crinkled her brows at him. "Department of Child and Family Services?"

"Yes, ma'am." His smile wavered as the woman just stared at him. He eyed the phone on the desk long enough that she finally followed his gaze. "Perhaps the doctor has a pager you could call . . ."

She jolted. "Oh, yes." The woman dialed a four-digit number, then announced he could go to the nurses' station and proceeded to give him directions to the elevators.

Bo reached the third floor, followed the signs to a circular nurses' desk in the intersection of three hallways, and approached the first woman in blue scrubs who made eye contact with him.

Her sun-highlighted, blond hair was swept into a ponytail, and a stethoscope dangled from around her neck. "I'm Heather Merchant, the charge nurse for this unit. May I help you?"

He removed a business card from his wallet and handed it to the nurse. "I'm responding to a call initiated by Detective Chandler. I believe it's regarding one of Doctor Wellington's patients."

The nurse scanned the card and looked up. "Doctor Wellington expected you over an hour ago, Mr. Lambright. She's already made rounds and left for the day."

"I apologize for the delay." Had the nurse pushed the subject, Bo would have recited the law, which allowed twenty-four hours to begin the investigation once a complaint was filed.

Smiling warmly, Nurse Heather leaned forward and lowered her voice. "Doctor Wellington's from the city and has the patience of a woman in labor. She's filling in for one of our long-standing physicians, who I'm guessing didn't fill her in on our community hospital or small-town life." The nurse stood from the chair. "I'll try to locate the officer for you. I think he's still in the conference room talking with the hospital case manager."

A few minutes later, heels clacked against the floor. He glanced sideways at the thirtysomething woman dressed in a knee-length navy skirt, matching blazer, and bright-red shirt.

"I'm Samantha Elroy, the case manager assigned to the Diener case." She motioned to the hallway on the right. "If you would like to come with me to the conference room, we can discuss the case with Detective Chandler in private."

"Sure." Bo always tried to gather as much information as possible prior to interviewing the family. Ms. Elroy led him to a room not far from the nurses' station.

A man rose from the chair at the end of the mahogany table and extended his hand. "I'm Detective Chandler."

He grasped the detective's hand. "Bo Lambright."

"I tried to explain to the physician that your office is on the other side of the county, but apparently she had more pressing matters to attend to." He sat down, flipped open the patient's chart, then slid it in front of Bo. "I'll give you a few minutes to read the notes, then Ms. Elroy and I will do our best to fill you in on the physician's concerns."

Bo scanned the physical assessment notes, cringing when he read the section about blisters inside the child's mouth.

"Apparently the mother brought the child into the clinic earlier today lethargic, feverish, and dehydrated," the detective said. "When she failed to bring the child in a timely way to the hospital to be admitted, Doctor Wellington requested police be dispatched." He sighed. "Personally, I thought calling after only three hours was a bit premature on the doctor's part, but . . ." He shrugged. "I'm not a doctor."

Ms. Elroy cleared her throat. "The mother did bring the boy in, but I think Doctor Wellington was worried the mother wasn't going to." She rolled her eyes. "The mother does have a reputation for self-doctoring with home remedies."

"Could I speak with the nurse caring for—" Bo glanced at the chart. "Nathan Diener, please."

"I'll see if she's available." Ms. Elroy left the room and returned moments later with a young woman dressed in blue scrubs.

"Hi, I'm Camille. I was told you wanted to speak with me about Nathan Diener."

"Yes, thank you. I'll try to keep this brief," Bo said. "I usually try to speak with the physician prior to meeting the family, but from what I understand, Doctor Wellington has left the hospital. Is there anything you would like to share about the status or perhaps observations you've had about the mother-child relationship?"

Camille hesitated a moment, then obtaining a nod of approval from the case manager, proceeded. "As you've probably read in the progress notes, the boy's mouth is blistered rather severely. Doctor Wellington ruled out a host of possibilities, including an allergic reaction. However, the preliminary blood work revealed an acid-base imbalance."

"Poison?"

"That's yet to be determined. Doctor Wellington seems to believe the boy ingested either bleach or another corrosive agent. His esophagus lining shows signs of irritation and, at this point, the child is being monitored for internal bleeding."

"I take it the doctor doesn't believe it was an accidental poisoning," Detective Chandler said, jotting something down in his small notepad.

In a similar case Bo had worked on as an intern in Detroit, the child had ingested antifreeze and died after spending a week on an artificial ventilator. According to Bo's proctor, the clues were there. The mother laced the sweet-tasting antifreeze with the child's apple juice. *"Never discard the obvious,"* his proctor used to preach. "Is the child on a ventilator?"

"No, sir, at this time his condition is stable," the nurse replied.

The case manager glanced at the clipboard she held. "I noted in an earlier conversation with the mother that she claims the child is rarely out of her sight—or her care."

"She is extremely protective, and even though she's nonconfrontational, she has tried to hinder care," the nurse said. "At first, she even refused to allow the nurse assistant to change her son into a hospital gown. And when she found out about the camera monitor in the room, she covered the lens with a pillowcase." She glanced at the case-worker. "You might want to have administration talk with her about that. She's adamant about not having a camera in the room."

"I'll also mention it during my interview," Bo said. "Sometimes hearing it from Child Protective Services has a greater impact."

The detective agreed, adding, "Depending on your findings, it might be a moot point. That is, if you find it necessary to have the mother removed from the room."

"True. If she's unstable or a threat to the child's welfare, I'll petition the court to restrict her access to him." He never liked restricting parental visits with a hospitalized child, or for that matter, removing children from the home, but with even the slightest hint of abuse, he always sided on what was best for the child. Nothing would ever change that.

Once the nurse finished her report and returned

to her duties, Detective Chandler briefed Bo on the interview he had with the boy's mother. "The mother is in her late twenties, has two children. She has no prior arrests or domestic complaints on file. She acted frightened, appeared concerned, and frankly, without something more concrete such as positive test results, I don't find any reason to arrest her at this time. From the interactions I observed between the mother and child, I didn't see anything to cause alarm. After all, she did bring the child into the hospital, albeit, it took her over three hours to get here. Now, you might determine something different after your interview and if that is the situation, I will amend the case at that time." He glanced at his watch. "I have another pressing matter at the courthouse that needs my attention, so I'll leave this file pending until I hear from you."

"That's fine. I can fax you a copy of my report." He didn't have an issue interviewing the parents without the authorities present, especially in a controlled environment like a hospital. It wasn't nearly as dangerous as in a home where he'd had beer bottles thrown at him and dogs sicced on him.

Once the detective left the room, the case manager leaned forward. "If you'd like, I'll accompany you during the interview."

"Yes, thank you. It's always good to have a witness." Bo looked again at the file and read the part about the blisters. He reread the doctor's notation: *Intentional poisoning?* Sure seemed like probable cause for arrest to him. He closed the file, grabbed his briefcase, and stood. "I'm ready to interview the mother now."

# Chapter Three

Bo waited outside the patient's room as the case manager knocked on the door, then eased it open.

"Mrs. Diener?" Ms. Elroy stepped farther into the room. "I have someone who would like to talk with you." She waved Bo inside.

He blinked several times, willing his eyes to adjust to the dim light. With the window blinds drawn and a curtain divider pulled to section off the room, Bo didn't see the mother and child until the case manager slid the curtain open. Bo spotted the Amish woman sitting in the wooden rocker, two young children lying in opposite arms, and halted. This was a first. He'd never been called to investigate an Amish family. The pillowcase draped over the camera hanging on the wall facing the hospital bed made sense now. The Amish believed photographs, or in this case a video, was an engraved image and sinful.

"Hello." His voice was dry. "My name is Bo—"

"Can I take *mei sohn* home *nau*?" She jostled

the children in her arms as if getting ready to stand.

"No, ma'am. I mean, I'm—I'm not a doctor."

Her shoulders dropped and she sank back into the chair, her face drawn.

"Doctor Wellington requested that I talk with you." He motioned to a vacant chair. "Do you mind if I sit?"

"That's fine. What's this about?" The woman's bright-blue eyes darted between him and Ms. Elroy. "What did the tests show?"

"Your doctor will discuss the results." Ms. Elroy sat in the chair next to him. "Mr. Lambright is from Child and Family Services, and he would like to ask you a few questions about Nathan."

"Okay." She directed her attention to Bo. "What do you want to know?"

He reached into his shirt pocket, removed the small recorder, and pressed the Record button. "Do you mind if I tape our conversation?" He always made a point to document the interviewee's reply to his request for legality purposes.

"I'd rather you *nett*. But why do you want to?"

"I'm a slow note taker and the tape gives me something to refer back to at a later time." Bo smiled, hoping the gesture would ease some of the woman's apprehensions. He should have known it wouldn't.

She drew the smaller child closer to her chest and adjusted a lightweight blanket over her shoulder, draping most of the infant's face. Then using a similar blanket, she shielded the sleeping boy's face.

Bo had an innate ability to know when someone was lying, but that required using all of his senses. He despised note taking, especially during an initial interview when he needed time to analyze not just what the subject said but their mannerisms as well. He eyed the woman's defensive, bear-like posture. That mama bear wasn't about to release her cubs. Something told him he wouldn't be writing much. Once he started asking questions, she would clam up.

Bo clicked the Off button on the recorder. "We don't have to use it," he said, returning it to his shirt pocket. He retrieved a pen, a tablet of paper, and the clipboard with the forms from his briefcase.

"Tell me again, please, why you are here?" The woman's voice shook, and her wide-eyed gaze flitted to the case manager before steadying coldly on him.

"I need to ask you a few questions about your son." He glanced at the form. "Will you state your full name, please?"

"Mattie—I mean Martha Irene Diener."

Bo jotted her name. "And your husband's name?"

"Andy—Andrew. Diener . . . Paul. Paul's the middle name. Andrew Paul Diener."

35

"Is he Nathan's father?"

She gasped. "Of course. *Mei* daughter's too."

If she drew offense to that question, the next one would rile her as well. He was well aware that the Amish didn't believe in divorce, but he wasn't one not to follow protocol. He cleared his throat. "Does the father live in the home full-time, occasionally, hardly ever, or never?" He poised the pen, ready to circle full time.

"Never."

"Never?" he echoed.

"Andy passed away eighteen months ago."

Her mournful tone, barely above a whisper, struck a nerve in Bo. "I'm sorry." Most widowed women in their mid-to-late twenties whom he was called to interview had already moved on to another relationship, often just as abusive. That prompted him to the next question on the list— one he would rather not ask. Questioning her about live-in boyfriends, male visitors, or the frequency of male overnight guests would probably close off their communication.

*Beep, beep, beep.* The case manager glanced at her pager. "I'm sorry. I need to step out a moment and return a call." She walked out of the room, leaving the door ajar.

"Mrs. Diener, do you feel comfortable continuing or would you rather wait until Ms. Elroy returns?"

"You can continue," she said.

"Is there . . ." He stopped when the boy stirred in her arms. The pager must have awakened him. He stretched the arm the IV line was attached to out from under the blanket and nearly clipped his mother in the jaw with his hand. She leaned close to his ear and whispered something, then lifted the blanket higher on her shoulder, tenting the boy's face. Bo would have liked a view of the boy in order to observe their interactions, but he would wait. He still had a long list of questions; eventually the boy would wake again.

She shifted in the chair, slipped her hand under the blanket, and made some adjustment. Bo hadn't realized he'd been staring until she cleared her throat. "Do you have more questions?"

"I, uh . . . How old is he?" The question had tumbled out. He'd read the medical chart, knew the answer, and he mustn't let her *motherly* actions distract him again.

"He's three."

Most mothers would have their toddler weaned before the next baby arrived. Heat crept up the back of his neck. *Get back to the questions.* The topic of the child's eating, or in this case, feeding habits would come up soon enough. He studied the list. "Do you own your home, rent, or live with a relative?"

"Own."

"How many people live in the house?"

"Just me and *mei* children."

"How many children and what are their ages?"

"I have two. Nathan and Amanda." Her gaze shifted from her son to the smaller bundle in her arms. "*Mei* daughter is eighteen months."

He referenced his notes about her husband's death, then met her teary gaze. "Eighteen?"

She nodded.

*Shove the sympathy aside, Lambright.* He cleared his throat. "Other than family members, how often do you have overnight male guests?"

"Never!" Wrath replaced any hint of somberness. The sharpness in her tone indicated she was losing patience.

"What about male visitors? Father, brothers, cousins, uncles?"

She stared at him.

"Okay, we'll come back to that one." He shifted. "Does Nathan have his own room and bed to sleep in?"

Silence.

Bo looked up from the clipboard. "Do you need me to repeat the question?"

"No," she snipped. "It may be that I'm simpleminded, but will you kindly explain why it matters if I own or rent *mei* home and why *mei* living conditions are so pertinent? I don't understand what any of this has to do with *mei sohn*'s healthcare. Most of these questions have been asked already by the woman who was just

38

in here, and then again by a man . . . Detective Chandler, I think he said his name was."

"I appreciate your patience, Mrs. Diener." He kept his tone soft and even. "Yes, it was Detective Chandler who spoke with you earlier; he's with the police department. Ms. Elroy is the case manager for the hospital. I'm gathering information for the Department of Child and Family Services with the State."

"Why does the State want to know about *mei sohn*? I don't use the welfare system."

"Yes, I'm aware of that." Bo hadn't wanted to jump to this part of the interview so quickly, but judging by her growing agitation, she would probably stop cooperating at any moment. "Your doctor is concerned about the blisters in your son's mouth. Do you know how he got them?"

"*Nay!*"

He eyed her carefully, analyzing her aghast, glowering stare. She made a defensive gesture to tuck the corner of the blanket under the boy and pat his back. Natural, protective response. He went on. "So he hasn't eaten or drunk anything that would have caused his mouth to blister?"

She shook her head. "I didn't even notice them until we were in the *doktah*'s office." She grimaced, and tears—genuine—welled in her eyes. "Do you think I'm a bad mother?"

Bad mother? He'd seen plenty of newborns deposited into Dumpsters like trash and babies

39

who were born addicted to heroin. Those women were the epitome of bad mothers—not this Amish widow. *Don't let your emotions cloud the investigation . . . Read the next question.* He glanced at the form.

"You do," she said, barely above a whisper.

He lifted his gaze to meet hers and replied, "No. I don't." *Wrong. Never state your opinion.*

"I should have known something was wrong with Nathan. I should have seen the blisters."

*Don't say anything. Just listen.*

"He hadn't eaten much in days. I should have known."

How was he going to get back on track and finish this interview? Her tears had triggered something he'd never experienced in all the cases he'd worked. And he'd listened to numerous sob stories and handed women hankies to dry their tears, and all while keeping his emotions stone-cold—intact.

Bo dug into his pocket, pulled out a clean hankie, and handed it to her.

She blotted the corners of her eyes. "I'm such a bad mother," she said in a hiccupping sob.

Bo swallowed hard. Was this an admission of guilt?

She blew her nose. "Do you think Nathan is going to be okay?"

"I'm not a . . ." Ms. Elroy entered his peripheral vision and returned to her seat. He acknowledged her presence with a nod. "Only a doctor can answer that, Mrs. Diener. But I hope so."

She cried harder, her shoulders shaking. The Amish weren't ones to display emotion so easily. This woman was under a tremendous amount of stress to have crumbled like this in front of him.

Camille entered the room carrying a portable machine. She took one look at the pillowcase still hanging off the camera and frowned. "I'm sorry to interrupt," she said. "I need to check the IV fluid and take a set of vitals on Nathan." She set the machine on the table next to the rocking chair. "Have you ever used a breast pump, Mrs. Diener?"

The mother's eyes widened, her face blanched.

"If you agree, Doctor Wellington would like a sample of your milk sent to the lab."

Bo sprung to his feet. "I'll step out and give you some privacy." He would find out later if she refused the testing or not. He'd seen it before where mothers had intentionally applied poison to themselves so that when the child latched on, they ingested a toxin.

After the startled look Mrs. Diener made at the nurse's request, he couldn't even look her in the eye. The back of his neck was moist and beads of sweat were collecting on his forehead. Yes, he needed a few minutes to organize his thoughts. He'd never had such an emotional response while questioning a mother. He wasn't even halfway through the questions.

As he retreated into the hall, he overheard the nurse reprimanding Mrs. Diener for covering the camera. Bo made a mental note to explain the reason for the video. It would only serve as proof of the mother's innocence as long as her taped activity wasn't incriminating. And he couldn't imagine that being the case. Then again, something had caused the child's mouth to blister.

The case manager stepped out of the room. "Would you like a cup of coffee?"

"Sounds good." A jolt of caffeine might help him wrap up this interview.

"This way." She motioned to the right. "The coffee in the cafeteria is probably fresher than what's in the nurses' break room." She led him past the front lobby and down another short hall. The cafeteria was nearly vacant, although it was only four in the afternoon. A few visitors sat at tables scattered throughout the room, their posture weary and faces long, like they'd spent countless nights sleeping in a chair next to a hospital bed. He'd occupied an uncomfortable plastic-lined recliner once himself when his father lay dying in the cardiac intensive care unit. A physician himself, his father didn't make a good patient. He demanded to review his test results and diagnosed his own fate. *I'm dying, son. Take care of your mother."* His mother was a recently retired circuit court judge; the only way Bo found to take care of her was to entertain her newfound purpose—to find him a wife.

"Would you like something to go with your coffee?" The case manager pointed to the stainless-steel pans steaming behind the plastic window guard along the tray line.

He was starving. The hamburger he'd eaten earlier hadn't been enough for lunch, but he didn't want hospital food. Bo shook his head. "Coffee is enough, thanks." He paid for their drinks, then followed her to an empty table against the back wall. He always made a point not to discuss client information in public places, but he could see by the way the case manager scanned the area, she was about to blurt something out.

She opened the conversation the moment she sat. "I couldn't even get Mrs. Diener to talk earlier. How did you manage to get her to confess?"

## Chapter Four

Mattie clung to Nathan, the gentle movement of the rocking chair lulling them both despite the noisy activity outside the hospital room. Her eyelids were heavy, closing. A few moments later, submerged in a dreamlike state, she felt someone lift Nathan's tiny frame from her arms. She jerked awake. Using her hand to shield her eyes from the blinding overhead light, she blinked several times before she could focus. "Wh-why are you taking him?"

"He's okay," the nurse said softly. "I'm just moving him to the crib."

Eyes closed, Nathan fussed as the nurse gently lowered him onto the mattress, but quieted again by sucking his thumb.

Mattie stood. "I'd rather hold him."

"You're tired, Mrs. Diener. It'll be safer if he stays in the crib." The nurse eased up the metal railing, latching it in place. Turning, the nurse's line of vision stopped on Amanda, who was asleep on the chair next to the rocker. "Aren't you worried she'll roll off?"

Mattie stepped backward until she was up against the arm of the chair. "Amanda doesn't usually toss in her sleep."

The nurse eyed Amanda. "How old is she?"

"Eighteen months."

"She's . . . small for her age. I assumed she wasn't a year yet." Her forehead puckered. "Still," she said, lifting a stern glare at Mattie, "leaving her unattended in a chair isn't safe."

It seemed everything Mattie did was under heavy scrutiny. This nurse introduced herself less than an hour ago. Apparently she took over having already formed preconceived notions. Even her daughter's small size seemed to set off some alarm. Mattie wanted to inform the nurse of Amanda's premature birth. Maybe she hadn't made all the developmental milestones Doctor Roswell had wanted her to reach, but she was steadily growing.

The nurse shifted her attention to the untouched food tray sitting on the bedside table. "He wasn't hungry?"

Mattie shook her head.

The nurse wrote something on a piece of paper and attached it to the clipboard, which hung on the wall next to the door. "I'll leave the juice and Jell-O," she said, moving the items from the tray to the bedside table. "Maybe he will be hungry in a little while. If he wants more to eat let me know and I'll request another hot tray." She glanced again at Amanda. "If your daughter is hungry—"

"I fed her." She sounded on edge even to herself. Mattie exhaled slowly and calmly continued. "I breastfeed her and"—something registered on the nurse's face Mattie didn't like—"she eats table food too."

The nurse jotted something on the clipboard, then looked up.

"Can I get you anything before I leave?"

"*Nay*, thank you."

The nurse glanced up at the pillowcase draped over the camera and frowned. She crossed the room and hung the clipboard on a peg near the door. "I'm going to leave the door open a little so I can listen for Nathan."

The nurse's note niggled at the back of Mattie's mind. The woman was concerned about Nathan's lack of appetite. Did she think Mattie had breastfed him after being instructed not to? She went to the wall and removed the clipboard from the hook. The nurse's notation was brief: *Patient sleeping comfortably, bed railings locked in upright position. Food tray untouched. No redness noted at the IV site.*

Mattie returned the clipboard. She stood at the side of the bed. With the rails fully extended, the oversized metal crib looked more like a cage. She slipped her hand between the rails, reaching as far as possible, but wasn't able to touch Nathan's hand. He couldn't wake up behind these bars—beyond her reach—her motherly comfort. Mattie pressed against the cold rails to get closer, patted the mattress. The plastic mattress covering crunched under the sheet.

She withdrew her hand when murmuring from the nurses' station filtered into the room. Their conversation was muffled, something about the man from Child Protective Services. Mattie couldn't hear everything, but ever since the man had come into the room and questioned her about Nathan and their homelife, her nerves hadn't settled. When he'd said he would step out to give them some privacy, she had hoped it meant for good. But he returned, and with a mile-long list of questions that seemed to spotlight her inability to provide for and adequately mother her children—under State expectations, anyway.

Even after he and the hospital worker left, the nurses continued to eye her with what appeared to be suspicion. The doctor never did return to explain Nathan's test results. She still wasn't sure why she had to supply multiple samples of her milk for testing. Or why she was ordered not to breastfeed him anymore—even to pacify his restlessness. She couldn't think of anything more unnatural than to have a machine extract her milk. Her stomach soured. The man's face from Protective Services turned red and appeared mortified for her. But that didn't stop him from returning an hour later with more questions. She had avoided eye contact with him for the most part, but when she did look up, his face was as red as she imagined hers was, having to discuss such personal information.

*"Your doctor is concerned about the blisters in Nathan's mouth . . . Did you give him anything? Are you aware it took three hours from when your doctor informed the hospital about your son's admission to the time when you arrived? Did you have other matters more important . . . ?"*
A chill raced down her spine recalling the man's words. History had taught her that state workers claiming to be concerned about a child's welfare were relentless and seldom understanding of the Amish way. Several disheartening stories had

circulated over the years of various conflicts some districts had with the local government. So far her district hadn't had any major issue, but she wasn't one to trust outsiders easily. Not when it had to do with her children.

*"Do you have running water in your home? Electricity? So, do you belong to an Old Order Amish district?"* Mattie had never answered so many questions—even ones that made no sense, like what her monthly and yearly income were.

"I sell ointments and creams and special herbal blends of tea," she had explained.

The man shifted in his seat, exchanged glances with the hospital worker, then wrote something on the pad of paper.

"I have several customers who—" *buy them regularly*. They weren't listening. The horrid look on the hospital worker's face was more telling. She didn't approve. Neither of them did. They must've thought she was peddling magic potions.

The man's scrutiny made her feel as if he could read her mind, and his rapid-fire method for gathering information left her questioning her parenting skills by the time the session had ended. Though she had answered honestly, she couldn't shake the feeling that he'd analyzed her responses and found them wrong.

Mattie released the mechanism on the crib rail and lowered the side. She touched Nathan's taped hand where the IV needle was inserted, then glanced up at the half-empty bag of fluids hanging from a pole. Perspiration moistened her forehead. The man had given her his business card before he left, but that didn't mean he wasn't planning to return—question her more—accuse her of deliberately causing Nathan's mouth to blister.

*Jah*, it was time to go.

Mattie grabbed the plastic bag the nurse had given her to store Nathan's clothes and emptied it on the bed. Her hands trembled working the snaps on her son's hospital gown.

She peeled the tape from his hand. Nathan fussed. He batted his arm when she pulled the needle free. Fluid dripped onto the floor. She would clean up the mess later. "*Shh* . . . I'm taking you home where you belong," she whispered in Pennsylvania *Deitsch*.

Once she had finished dressing him, she used the hospital gown to wipe up the spill on the floor, then scooped Amanda into one arm and Nathan into her other.

The moment she stepped out of the room, a nurse at the desk spotted her.

"Where are you going?" The nurse came around the desk, brows crinkled. Another nurse came out from the adjoining room.

"Home." Mattie followed the nurse's line of vision and cringed when she noticed blood coming from Nathan's hand.

"Wait just a moment while I get a Band-Aid." The nurse disappeared into a room and came out a moment later. As she applied the Band-Aid, another nurse approached Mattie with a clipboard.

"Your doctor hasn't discharged Nathan yet," the nurse said.

"I haven't seen the *doktah* since this morning." Mattie glanced at the nurse applying the Band-Aid. "He's bleeding more than usual. How long before it stops?"

"Just a minute or so."

"I need to go. I have animals to feed . . . and supper to cook . . . and—" She stepped backward to distance herself from the nurses and almost tripped over a wheelchair parked next to the wall. Amanda wiggled and wrapped her arms around Mattie's neck in a choke hold.

"Mrs. Diener, if you insist on leaving the hospital with Nathan, we're not going to stop you. But I do need you to sign this form that states you are leaving against medical advice." She extended a pen toward Mattie.

"Okay." She would sign anything to be able to leave. She lowered Amanda, who wobbled sleepily.

Mattie took the pen and signed on the line. "Is that it?"

"Continue to monitor his temperature and please don't hesitate to bring him back if his condition worsens."

"I always watch him close." She hadn't meant to

sound defensive. The blond-haired nurse had been kind to Nathan when they first arrived. Mattie grasped Amanda's hand. "We need to go."

Mattie took a few steps down the hall, then stooped to lift Amanda onto her hip. She wanted to leave before anyone else stopped her. First, she had to find a pay phone and call for a ride. When Cora had driven them into town earlier she had said to call if Mattie needed something.

The woman sitting at the information desk in the hospital lobby directed Mattie to a courtesy phone on the wall. She set Amanda down again and jostled Nathan in her arms, then reaching into her handbag, retrieved the number. Cora answered on the second ring and assured Mattie she wouldn't be long. But with every passing minute, Mattie's anxiety mounted. Except for the elderly woman manning the information desk, they were alone in the lobby. She eased into the corner chair as tears pricked her eyes. *Get ahold of yourself.*

The woman left the desk and ambled across the room to Mattie. "Is there anything I can do for you, ma'am?"

"*Nay.*" Mattie hugged her children tighter to her chest. "Thank you, though." She glanced at the door. "In fact, I think *mei* ride might be here *nau.*" She hadn't seen any car headlights pull under the canopy in the patient pick-up area, but Mattie didn't want to wait inside any longer. Cora wouldn't be long. She hoped. Earlier in the day the temperature on the hospital sign had read seventy-four; now it flashed fifty-eight. This was too cold to be sitting any length of time on the concrete bench. She was thankful Nathan's fever had subsided. She wouldn't want him exposed to this chilly weather if he were still sweating.

A few minutes later, Cora pulled under the overhang. "Mattie, I hope you weren't waiting outside very long. You should have stayed in the lobby," she said as Mattie climbed into the car.

"I appreciate you picking us up." She leaned back against the headrest. It would feel good to get home.

It wasn't until after she'd reached the house, fed and watered the livestock, and tucked the children into bed that she sat at the kitchen table and let the soothing effects of the herbal tea settle her nerves. Nathan was home—safe in his own bed.

"You want to see me, boss?" Bo stood at the doorway of Norton Farley's office.

"Yeah, have a seat." Norton waved at one of the two leather chairs facing his desk.

"If it's about the mileage I submitted—"

"It's not." He lifted a copy of Bo's final report on the Diener case. "Since when do you close a case after one interview, Lambright?"

"You've never questioned my judgment or my thoroughness. What's up?"

"This complaint was initiated by a physician. And you only talked with the mother?"

Bo bristled. "I didn't find anything to warrant further investigation."

"Nothing?" He quirked a bushy brow, then peered down at the report.

Bo leaned back in the chair. His mother would swat him for slouching, but he was relaxed. Confident. He hadn't missed anything. The preliminary tests were negative according to the doctor's progress notes. Even the detective failed to find anything that warranted arrest. The woman was innocent.

"I think this is the first case you've closed within twenty-four hours." Norton glanced up over his wire-rimmed glasses.

"It is." Bo was one of the only investigators who kept his cases pending the full thirty days allowed. Even longer when he found reason to file for an extension.

Norton studied the report a few moments, then sighed and tossed it on his desk. "All right, if you're sure."

"My gut hasn't been wrong."

"Yet," Norton was quick to add.

Bo leaned forward. "Arrogance in check—I'd still stake my reputation on it."

"That's exactly what you're doing." He lifted the report. "You want to review it again and resubmit?"

"I'll let it sit on my desk a few days if it'd make you feel better. But I have more pressing cases to explore." He glanced at his watch. "In fact," he said, standing, "I don't want to be late for my meeting at the school or the teacher might slap my knuckles with a ruler."

Mattie stood at her kitchen sink, peering out her open window and breathing in the warm summer breeze. Alvin Graber chopped wood next to her shed. The forty-year-old bachelor was like an older brother, doing odd jobs around the farm, tilling her garden in the spring, and making sure she had enough hay in the barn and wood in the shed to last the winter. Up until recently, he'd refused to accept payment for his labor, but having suddenly acquired a sweet tooth for some of her baked goods, he rarely declined an invitation to sample a slice of pie.

The moment Alvin leaned the axe against the side of the shed, Mattie hurried to remove a mug and plate from the cupboard.

A knock sounded at the door, and Mattie straightened her apron as she headed to the sitting room. Amanda trailed her to the door. She hugged Mattie's leg and hid behind her dress.

"*Guder mariye*, Mattie." Alvin wiped the sweat from his forehead, inspected his hands, then rubbed them on the sides of his pants. "I put up another cord of firewood."

"So I see. *Danki*, Alvin." She opened the door wider and nudged Amanda to step aside. "Would you like to *kumm* in for *kaffi*? I still have a few slices of apple pie left."

"Sure, if it isn't an inconvenience." He stomped his boots on the doormat and removed his hat, exposing a head of matted curls. "Are you sure I'm *nett* a bother?"

"Of course you're *nett*." Mattie smiled. After a long night of hourly rechecks of Nathan's temperature, she would like to take a nap. Then again, she wouldn't mind the distraction.

Alvin's cheerful smile fell on Amanda, but quickly faded to a frown when her daughter disappeared behind Mattie. "She having another bad day?"

"Amanda is . . ." Mattie had used all the excuses. Sure, Amanda didn't warm easily to strangers, but Alvin had stopped in almost every day for coffee since he'd returned from the lumber camp in the spring, and they saw him at church and group functions. "She's tired." Mattie turned and headed to the kitchen, Amanda glued to her side.

"Where's Nathan?"

"He's sleeping in." The multiple needle sticks and constant parade of people traipsing into the hospital room had exhausted her boy. He'd clung to her all night, frightened by the ordeal. Mattie motioned to the sink. "You can wash up if you'd like."

55

Alvin went to the sink and rolled up his sleeves as she poured two mugs of coffee. She removed the dish towel she'd draped over the apple pie to keep the pesky flies away and cut a large slice, keenly aware of his gaze on her. Pretending not to notice, she measured a spoonful of sugar and deposited it and the spoon in his coffee.

He dried his hands on a nearby towel. "You look as though you could have used a little more sleep yourself."

Alvin wasn't normally observant, at least he'd never vocalized it. Sometimes he ate his dessert and drank his coffee in total silence. Her raccoon eyes must have prompted his comment. She handed him a fork and the pie plate, then picked up the two mugs of coffee. "Nathan and I haven't slept very well lately. He's run a fever the last few days." She omitted the part about taking him to the hospital. Members in her district already thought she was overly protective— paranoid, too, according to past whispers she'd overheard.

He took a seat at the table and stabbed his fork into the pie. Lifting it to his mouth, he paused. "You fret over that boy a lot."

Her spine bristled. "That's what mothers do when their child is sick."

"Just an observation."

One she didn't need. *Nett* from someone who had never married.

He took another bite, chasing the pie down with a gulp of coffee. "I suppose most women don't have time to hover over one or"—his gaze fell on Amanda as she sidled up beside Mattie—"two children when they have seven or eight. If you had more children . . ."

She arched a brow as much in wonderment of what he was about to say as shock the man with no kids was about to offer parenting advice.

"Well," he said, loading his fork again. "I'm sure you don't need *mei* two cents."

The sound of buggy wheels crunching over the gravel driveway caught her attention. She rose from the chair and went to the window. "It's Grace," she said, hoping he didn't hear the hint of relief in her voice. She hurried out of the room and opened the door as her best friend was tying her horse to the post. "*Guder mariye*, Grace."

Grace lumbered up the porch steps, pausing to glance over her shoulder at Alvin's parked buggy. "If this is a bad time . . ."

Mattie opened the screen door and whisked her friend inside. "It isn't."

# Chapter Five

"The *kaffi* is hot. Let me pour you a cup." Mattie shuttled Grace through the sitting room and into the kitchen. "Have a seat," she said, motioning to the chair next to Amanda's. Grace had become Mattie's closest friend when Mattie and Andy first moved to Badger Creek. She recalled how isolated the district felt tucked deep within the forest. If it hadn't been for Grace's friendship, Mattie might have gone stir-crazy that first winter not having any relatives nearby.

"I can't stay . . . long." Grace offered Alvin a nervous smile. "*Hiya*, Alvin."

"*Guder mariye.*" He gathered the last pie crumbs from the plate, then lifted his fork, only to pause it midair. "What's Ben up to?"

Mattie retrieved a mug from the cabinet and set it on the counter.

"Ben's down at the river fishing with Philemon." Grace pulled a chair out from the table and turned her attention to Amanda, who had been quietly sitting at the table munching on dry Cheerios. "And how are you doing this morning, Amanda?"

"*Gut.*" Amanda smiled and continued eating.

Mattie poured a mugful of coffee and added a

teaspoonful of sugar the way Grace liked. She hoped that since Grace's husband was fishing, she could spend a little more time with her friend. Mattie was careful not to steal Grace's time away from Ben since the men were only home from the timber camp during the few short months of summer.

"Ben would really like it if you joined them at the river," Grace said to Alvin.

"No time." Alvin drained his mug of coffee and stood. He shot a sideways glance at Mattie and offered her a brief smile. "I'll check on that lamb later this afternoon, okay?"

Mattie smiled. "*Danki*, Alvin." She had her hands full with Nathan and no time to tend sick livestock too. She crossed the room and set Grace's coffee in front of her.

Alvin grabbed his work gloves from the table, paused a second, then left the kitchen. The screen door slapped closed a few moments later.

"You have something going on with Alvin tonight?" Grace wiggled her brows.

"What makes you think that?"

"He's coming by *later* to check on the *sick* lamb. Sounds like code to me. Besides that, he's always here drinking *kaffi*, ain't so?"

"*Nay*, he wasn't speaking code. One of my lambs isn't doing well. And as for having *kaffi* with me, that's the only form of payment he'll take for his work. He's cut *mei* winter's supply of firewood for the last two seasons now. Also, he does most of the odd jobs that need attention. Alvin's helped me a lot. I wish he would take pay." Mattie sighed. "Then maybe I wouldn't feel so guilty. You heard him. He doesn't have time to go fishing or do anything he finds relaxing."

"I'm sure he doesn't mind."

"Still, there must be other things he would rather do."

Grace grinned. "I doubt it. He seems very content helping you with the chores. *Very*."

Mattie bowed her head. She would never find the same contentment with any man again. This was the home that she and Andy had made. He built it for *them* to grow old in. Andy had only been gone a year when the womenfolk started urging her to find another husband. Alvin hadn't brought anything up along the lines of marriage, but he was beginning to be more vocal about family and children.

"Hey, Mattie. Are you okay?"

Mattie lifted her head and forced a weak smile. "I'm just a little tired." *And reading more into Alvin's friendship than I should.* "I was up most of the *nacht* checking Nathan's temperature."

"Is he sick again?" Grace leaned back in her chair and looked toward the sitting room. "By the way, where is he?"

"Still sleeping. The fever really drained his

energy. I took him in to see the *doktah* when I couldn't bring his temperature down with feverfew."

"What did *Doktah* Roswell say?"

Mattie shook her head. "He's on vacation. And I don't think I like his replacement."

Nathan padded into the kitchen whimpering softly and rubbing his eyes. He crawled up on Mattie's lap. No doubt he was feeling a bit insecure after everything he'd gone through at the hospital. She gave him a gentle hug, then ran her hand over his forehead.

Grace studied Nathan. "His face is flushed. Does he have a fever?"

"*Nay.*" But on closer inspection, he did look a little red around the nose and cheeks to Mattie as well. "Maybe he was lying on that side."

Grace shook her head. "It's more than that. His eyes are bloodshot and, to me, they look glossy."

"It's probably a combination of allergies and lack of sleep." She kissed the top of Nathan's head, then turned to look at her daughter propped up on her knees in the chair beside her. Even on her knees, her little hand barely reached the table. "Will you share some of your Cheerios with your *bruder*, please?"

Amanda stretched her neck and eyed the mound of cereal, then pushed a few pieces toward Nathan, who shook his head.

"You might want to take him back into town if

the redness starts to spread. Even without a fever—"

"I'm going to make him a cool bath." She fanned her face with her hand. "Is it hot in here to you?"

"I'm *nett*," Grace said, adding, "but I'm *nett* sick either." She broke into a giggle. "Maybe Alvin will have more than a sick lamb to tend to when he returns."

"You haven't forgotten about dinner tonight, have you?" His mother's voice chimed with excitement. Hosting extravagant charity dinners was a disguise for finding him a suitable wife.

Bo shifted the phone to his other ear in order to reach for the stapler on the corner of his desk. "Would you let me forget?"

"No."

"Didn't think so." He sighed and glanced at his watch. "Tell me again what time."

"Seven. You really should put a reminder on your phone."

"Why?" He chuckled. "I have you to remind me." He stapled the pages of his monthly report and tossed it into the file folder in the bottom right drawer.

"You're hilarious."

"And to think I get my great sense of humor from you."

He pictured her sitting ramrod straight in her

judge's robe and scowling on the other end of the line. Not that she had worn her robe since retirement; it was more out of habit that he visualized her that way when she was scolding him.

"Okay, Mom, I'll see you at seven fifteen. It's just the two of us, right?" It never was.

"It's a charity dinner for the new hospital wing. Bo, I don't think you listen to anything I say anymore."

"Charity, you say. Hmm . . . Who is she?" The interoffice line rang.

"You have a lot in common with this one. She's—"

"Sorry to cut you short, Mom, but I have another call I need to take."

"Seven."

"I know, I know. I'll see you tonight." It wasn't as if he could avoid a house party. He lived with her.

"Wear something nice."

Bo groaned. That meant his tux. "Got to go, Mom." He disconnected the call, then pushed the lit button on the phone. "Lambright."

"I need to see you in my office," his boss said.

"On my way." Bo glanced at his watch. Four thirty. A new assignment this late in the day would mean missing his mother's party. Bo smiled. Entering Norton Farley's office, he shot a glance at Davis seated in the leather chair facing Norton's desk. Her long legs were difficult to miss. So was the scent of lilacs that she must have bathed in. He turned to his boss. "What's up?"

"Close the door and take a seat." Norton motioned to the empty chair beside Davis. "We need to talk about the Diener case."

Bo sat. "What's to talk about? The case is closed."

Davis shuffled some papers in her lap. "I've reopened it."

"You did?" He shot her a sidelong glare and tightened his jaw to the point his muscle twitched. She merely stared with a gloating smile, aggravating him even more.

"On my orders," Norton interjected. "Why did you fail to mention that the woman made a confession?"

Bo jerked his attention back to his boss. "Because she didn't."

"Not according to the case manager at the hospital. I spoke with her this morning," Davis announced.

The competitive glint in her eye reminded him of a peacock fanning its colorful feathers. He half expected her to rise from the chair and strut those long legs over the span of the office.

Bo rubbed his jaw and shifted his focus to his boss. "Ms. Elroy didn't hear the entire conversation. She walked into the room as Mrs. Diener made a general comment that was by no means a confession. And I told Ms. Elroy that when we had coffee." He disregarded Davis shuffling her papers—or maybe it was *his* paperwork that he'd turned in earlier—and leaned forward. "Norton, I'm not wrong about this."

His boss shrugged. "It's reopened. Apparently the woman signed her son out of the hospital AMA."

"She pulled the IV line out too," Davis added.

Bo fell back against the chair. Why in the world would the woman sign her son out against medical advice? It only made her look guilty.

# Chapter Six

Bo straightened his bow tie in the mirror. He should be used to formal dinner parties by now. He'd been summoned to enough of them during the years his mother ran for reelection. Since her retirement from the judicial system, she'd focused her efforts on two tasks, fund-raising and finding his Mrs. Right.

So far, her influence had successfully equipped the library with new computers, the county school district with more busses, and supplied a complete renovation for the women's crisis facility, but the unmarried guests she'd invited to her charity events had failed to capture his attention beyond the required meet-and-greet cocktail hour. Perhaps it had something to do with him slipping into each conversation that he lived in his mother's base-ment. The women's jaws dropped every time, and their perfectly penciled brows crinkled in puzzlement. At thirty-two, maybe he should be ashamed. But moving back home after his father had passed away seemed the right thing to do. The seven-thousand-square-foot chalet, situated on five acres of lakefront, manicured lawn, was too overwhelming and lonely for his mother to inhabit alone.

He glanced at his watch. Six forty-five. Any moment his cell would ring. He clasped the gold links on his cuffs and shoved his arms into the tux coat. At least a new children's wing was a good cause, unlike the Garden Club Cotillion where he just happened to be the only male attendee under sixty. The dinner wasn't formal— only boring. Before the evening ended, he'd heard more than he cared to know about the hundred different species of roses, how tulips could grow even after they were cut, and that roasted dandelion roots were used to make a special caffeine-free coffee. He'd stick with the fully loaded blend at the gas station.

Bo flipped off the light switch and headed up the stairs. He ducked into the kitchen, avoiding the front room where the sound of laughter mingled with a Chopin tune being played on the grand piano. Waiters from the catering service bustled around him in a flurry.

His mother's personal assistant, Rita, appeared at the kitchen entrance. "Mr. Lambright, your mother sent me to find you. Most of the guests have arrived."

He scanned the food trays lining the counter and selected a bite-size crostini piled with smoked salmon on a layer of cream cheese. "Any suggestions for how to avoid them?"

Rita smiled. "Miss Penelope Woodrow doesn't like to talk about politics or religion. She will be seated on your left."

"And on the right?"

"Sorry. Your mother handled the invitation and told me to leave a seat open next to you. But Caitlyn will be across from you. You sat next to her during the Garden Club Cotillion."

"The awkward one who stepped on my feet every time we danced?"

Rita looked down at her leather-bound note-book. "Yes, she's the one you called Tulips. If you would rather sit by"—she glanced again at her notes—"Roses, I probably have enough time to switch the placement cards."

"No." He chuckled. "You did well. I seem to recall Roses was chatty." Bo plucked a few grapes from the lattice garnishing on one of the platters and smiled at Rita. "But you shouldn't have allowed my mother to blind-side me with the mystery guest. I don't like to feel cornered." He moved toward the hallway and the whimsical sounds of laughter.

Mother approached, brushing her fingers over the front of her dress. "I'm glad you're here. How do I look?"

The glittering sequins on her gown reminded him of fish scales. He tried to recall how his father used to answer. Nothing about scaly fish. "You look . . . fancy."

She cuffed her arm around his. "I want to introduce you to some of the members on the hospital board." She led him toward the veranda where a small group of men had gathered. His mother meant well, introducing him to some of the most influential men in the county, but Bo merely obliged her. Once introductions were made, the men's conversation resumed about the conditions of the greens at Forest Hills Country Club. Bo nodded every so often, but remained mostly disengaged. He wasn't a golfer and had no inten-tions of joining the country club. His mother knew that about him sixteen years ago when she tried to get him to join the Junior League. At the time, chasing a ball across a fairway seemed pointless.

A man close to his mother's age approached the group. "Agnes," he said, smiling fondly and reaching for her hand. "I think what you're doing for the children's wing is wonderful."

"Yes, well . . ." She stammered a moment, her cheeks turning a rosy tint.

Bo cocked his head at her. Interesting. His mother never blushed.

"It's for a good cause," she said, recovering well. The pinkness vanished. "Judge Steinway, this is my son, Bo," she said with complete control of her voice.

"Willard," the judge said, extending his hand.

"It's nice to meet you, sir."

Either Judge Steinway hadn't recognized Bo from testifying in his courtroom, or he simply wanted to avoid mixing business and pleasure. Bo hadn't been keen on the judge's verdict. The lousy father had used his child as an ashtray and should have received a stiffer penalty. But his mother wouldn't appreciate Bo bringing up the case now.

"My son is an investigator for Child Protective Services."

Judge Steinway eyed him a little closer. "Tough job."

Bo nodded. "Even tougher when you have a repeat offender back in the home because the louse wasn't put away the first time." He masked his curt tone with a smile.

"Yes, I see your point," the judge said.

*Doubt it.* The man was another politician. He would say anything to appeal to a potential voter. "The percentage of repeat offenders is astronomical. It's somewhere around—"

"If you'll excuse us." His mother clasped Bo's

arm. "We should greet some of our other guests."

*Our?* These weren't people he would have invited.

She swept him across the room, chin up and smiling for the benefit of the guests.

Bo leaned closer. "I'm not a politician, Mom. I don't sugarcoat anything. Not when it comes to a child's safety."

"And you shouldn't." She patted his arm. "Now, come with me. I want you to meet Senator Delanie's daughter."

He'd met the senator two summers ago after one of his campaign speeches at the urging of his mother, but Bo didn't remember a daughter. And if the tall brunette standing with him, wearing the open-back emerald gown, was his daughter, Bo would have remembered her.

"Erica," his mother said as they approached. She didn't have to finish the introductions, for the moment the brunette turned, Bo recognized her.

"Lambright?" A warm smile overtook Davis's face.

His mother's puzzled look darted between them. "You two know each other?"

"We work together," Davis explained. She turned to the man standing beside her. "This is my father, Lionel Delanie. And, Dad, this is Bo Lambright."

"It's a pleasure to meet you, Bo." Senator Delanie extended his hand.

"Same here," he said, firming his grasp.

A waiter stopped and offered a tray of bite-sized meatballs. Erica, her father, and his mother all declined, but Bo was hungry. He stabbed one of the meatballs with the toothpick and thanked the waiter when he handed him a small napkin.

"I think now is a perfect time to make the announcement, don't you think, Senator?"

Before Bo had a chance to swallow the hickory-smoked meatball, his mother and Erica's father had walked away. He dabbed the napkin over the corners of his mouth. "I didn't realize you were the senator's daughter, *Davis*."

She lifted her wine glass as if toasting. "You didn't say anything about having deep connections with the court either. Judge Nettleton?"

"My mother kept her maiden name. She's retired." He motioned to her almost empty glass. "What are you drinking?"

"Chardonnay."

"I'll be right back." Bo tracked down a waiter who was mingling through the crowd with a tray of wine glasses and stopped him. He removed a glass for her, then made his way over to the bar and ordered a ginger ale for himself. He glanced over his shoulder at Davis. She sure didn't look like the same woman who pinned her hair into a bun for work and went head-to-head with him over the Diener case. He made his way toward her again. Wow, that evening gown was lethal.

"Thank you," she said, accepting the glass. "I never pictured you as a tux guy. You always peel off your tie and shove it into a drawer the moment you sit down at your desk. Although, I must admit, the suspenders you wear are charming."

"Surprised you noticed."

She shrugged, then turned her gaze out the window and sipped her drink.

He eyed her formfitting dress. She definitely didn't fit into the social worker's world tonight.

She glanced over her shoulder at him. "A man doesn't stare at a woman's figure that long without saying something."

His gaze met her green eyes. Bright. Confident. Bewitching. "Beautiful."

"Hmm . . ." She arched her brow. No doubt the compliment was one she'd heard many times. She didn't even blush.

"You don't seem the type to work for CPS," he said.

"True." She circled the rim of her glass with her finger. "I want field experience."

He reassessed her with hiked brows. Too spoiled—too naïve—too beautiful for the field. "You like Dumpster diving? Because sometimes that's what it feels like. You might leave a place with roaches crawling on you."

"I'm not that worried."

"You should be. I've been shot at before."

The air of confidence swarming her was that of

a newbie. Then again, perhaps her confidence came from having Norton in her daddy's back pocket. After all, Bo had taken most of the woman's calls since she started. He wasn't even sure she'd been out in the field yet.

She shrugged. "The job's temporary."

"How so?"

"In the fall I leave for Harvard Law."

"As Davis or Delanie?"

The corners of her lips curled into what appeared to be a calculated smile. Her eyes assessed him with just enough pause to send a tingling sensa-tion down his spine.

"I plan to build my reputation under Davis, but if, or I should say, *when* I need a political boost, I'll use it."

"I'm sure."

The piano music stopped and dinner was announced. The guests moved toward the dining room. Bo held out his arm. "I think you're sitting next to me."

Davis managed to manipulate the conversation during dinner. Bo didn't mind. She spared him from Tulips and Penelope. Davis was engaging, strong-minded, and dangerous. She could milk the venom from a snake and charm someone into taking a sip. A true Delanie. Even her crimson lipstick reminded him of bureaucrats' tape.

"I'd like to get some air," Davis said, weaving

her hand around his arm. "Care to step outside?"

He steeled himself from the electrified jolt of her touch. "Sure." Bo glanced at her glass. Full. "Do you need your coat?"

"I hope not." Her eyes twinkled with mischief.

Sweat moistened the back of his neck and the tight-collared shirt irritated him. He loosened his tie and unfastened the top button.

She smiled, and when her lips landed in a resting position, they were slightly parted. She could easily be a lipstick model; her glossy candy-apple lipstick had an alluring glimmer. The woman was in complete control.

This room was hot. He opened the French doors off the library, and she moved gracefully out onto the stone-covered terrace. Gas lanterns illuminated her form.

"This is breathtaking." She sipped her drink.

"I spend most of my time on the dock." He gazed at the full moon reflecting off the water. Inside the house, a storm of handclapping and cheers erupted. His mother must have announced the dollar amount raised for the children's wing at the hospital. "Maybe we should go back inside," he suggested.

"I was thinking we could walk down to the water."

He glanced at her heels. "Those spikes aren't exactly Docksiders."

She reached for his shoulder and used it for support as she removed one shoe, then the other. "Better?"

"Let's go." He took a few steps before she tugged his arm, motioning him to stop.

"Why don't you get something to drink so I don't look like a lush drinking alone?"

He shook his head. "I'm on call. Something about a family event or was it an emergency?"

"Oh, that's right." She cringed. "When I asked you to take my call, I had no idea the charity dinner was your mother's."

"I'm sure you didn't." He smiled. "By the way, I agreed to take your call with hopes I'd have a reason to be excused from the party."

"You really don't like to attend social gatherings?"

"Nope." He guided her down the limestone path. Cricket chirps filled the night air.

"May I check out your boat?" she asked once they reached the dock.

"I think you're supposed to say, 'Captain, may I board your boat,'" he teased.

She made a short bow. "May I board your boat, Captain?"

"If you'd like. But I reserve the right to toss unruly visitors over the side."

"Then I should have brought my swimsuit."

He boarded the boat, then reached for her hand and helped her across. If it wasn't so late he would walk back to the house and get the keys, but the party wouldn't last too much longer. Her father would wonder where she had gone.

Her gaze roamed the Sea Ray. "This is nice."

"Thank you."

"Can we take it out?"

"It's too late." He caught a glimpse of her pouty lips in the moonlight and for a split second was enticed to change his mind. The boat had navigation lights. He'd gone out this late plenty of times. "Sorry, I'm on call. Maybe another—"

Davis turned away. Before he could warn her about the seat possibly being damp, she plopped down on the cushioned bench. She tapped the cushion beside her, but he took the chair at the helm instead. Safer.

"Why did you make such a fuss about me reopening that case in Badger Creek today?"

"It'll be a waste of time, and we're understaffed. So while you chase down information on a case that should be closed, other children remain in danger."

"Norton gave me the assignment," she said.

"I know."

"I'm making a surprise visit tomorrow." She lifted the glass to her mouth and took a drink.

Bo stood. He reached for her hand, removed the wine glass, and dumped the contents over the side of the boat.

"Hey." She pouted a half second, then giggling, reached for the lapels on his tux and drew him closer. "I haven't gotten unruly yet." Her warm, sweet-smelling breath fanned his face.

He peeled her arms away from roping his neck. "If you're working tomorrow, you need to make decisions with a clear head." He stepped back, then offered his hand. "Come on, we should get back to the house."

"Party pooper."

"I've been called worse."

The party was in full swing when they reached the house. Well-wishers had surrounded his mother, shaking her hand, pledging their support. She glanced through the crowd as he entered the room and waved him over.

"Bo, you missed my announcement," she said. "I've decided to throw my hat into the ring for the vacant county commissioner seat."

"We tried talking her into running last term when Donaldson's seat opened," Tyler Morse, owner of Morse Sanitation, said. Several other guests agreed with him, and soon the roomful of people was chanting his mother's name, including the owner of the Colorado-based fracking company whom Senator Delanie had introduced Bo to during the meal. He'd read several controversial articles regarding the manner in which the drilling company obtained oil through a hydraulic fracturing process where high-pressure water, sand, and chemicals are used to create fractures in reservoir rock. The articles had raised concerns about potential groundwater contamination and the increased likelihood of sinkholes.

Davis sidled up beside him. "It looks as though we'll be traveling in the same political circles."

Bo tugged his collar away from his neck. "I think I'll sign up for more on-call time."

Sometime after midnight, Mattie lit the oil lamp on the kitchen table. The woodstove embers were still hot enough not to require newspaper or matches to start a fire. She added a few pieces of kindling to heat the teakettle. As the water heated, she stared out the window at the blackness.

Restless nights had become her norm despite her recent attempts to convince herself to move on with life. In minuscule ways, she *was* moving forward. The months immediately following Andy's death, she'd clung to her pillow, crying until the sun shone through the curtains. At least now, she got out of bed and made a cup of tea when sleep refused to come. That was something. Teetering baby steps, but progress nonetheless. Besides, just because Grace had encouraged her to move forward, it didn't mean she had to actively look for a husband to replace Andy. Finding someone compatible and willing to become a father to her children would take an act of God in her northern Michigan settlement where the women outnumbered the men three to one.

*Narrisch.* Mattie shook her head, discarding the crazy notion of remarriage. She was tired, overwhelmed, but not desperate. Her thoughts drifted to Andy. How he had wanted a dozen children and teased her about them all being boys. When she conceived the second time, he named the unborn baby Little Andy and used to pat her belly and talk to his son. But her husband didn't live long enough to see that the baby was in fact a daughter. Stress of his death and funeral preparations had spawned the early labor pains. While the men were covering the grave with dirt, the womenfolk were urging Mattie to push.

The teakettle whistled.

Mattie let the tea steep, then poured a cup. As she set her drink on the table, the Bible caught her eye. She flipped open to the page where she had left off earlier that evening, but couldn't focus on the message. Skimming the page, her eyes stopped on a verse in the twenty-second chapter in Psalms. *Be not far from Me, for trouble is near; for there is none to help.*

She wasn't one to believe God spoke through every scripture—not directly to her—not anymore. But something unsettled her spirit when she repeated the verse silently. Perhaps because she was alone, unable to shake her melancholic memories, she dwelled on the *none to help* part of the verse. *Trouble is near.* The forlorn words clung, impressing on her to pray. "God, I feel like the psalmist. I have no one to help. If trouble *is* near, please don't be far from me. Please."

# Chapter Seven

Bo pressed the throttle forward, and the nineteen-foot Sea Ray broke through the morning fog as it lifted off the water, leaving a spray of white caps in the wake. He breathed in deeply, taking in the dank scent of Lake Superior. Sunrise on the lake was heaven.

Once the shore was no longer in sight, Bo cut the engine. The boat dipped a few inches as though nesting into the lake and coasted to a stop. His mother harped on him for going out alone, especially when he usually left at sunrise and often wouldn't return before nightfall. But out here, in the midst of the largest of the Great Lakes, he could escape. And more and more something deep within him had been urging him to break free from the trappings of the world.

Bo moved from the captain's chair to the stern where he lounged his six-foot frame on the foam-covered cushions. Known as the grave of many sailors, Lake Superior was often unpredictable. Bo only stepped away from the helm on calm days like today and usually to fish. He tipped his face toward the sun and closed his eyes. Adrift on the lake with gentle waves lapping the sides of the boat and the *caw caw* of gulls nearby, he couldn't think of a more peaceful way to spend the day. This was much better than taking a nap in the hammock, and for once, he wasn't on call.

He let his mind go blank. Falling into the boat's lulling rise and roll over the waves, his muscles relaxed.

Moments later, he was walking over hot, dry sand. On a beach? No, he wasn't that far into sleep. He'd been here . . . before.

A long time ago.

Arid heat burned his lungs. Stretched out before him, the field of dry bones went on forever.

A shudder sped down his spine. Why here? Why the scattered bones?

Something hummed. Cadence echoes. Bright light. Clouds of white smoke dispersed, unveiling a comatose body hooked to breathing tubes. It was him.

Out of the darkness a reverberating voice called his name.

His throat was tight, paralyzed. Raspy hisses bleated from the machine, impeding his speech.

"Boaz, My child."

"Yes," he answered silently.

"Like a farmer plants seed in the ground, so I've planted you."

Planted?

His chest rose as air was pumped into his body, then fell. The voice was familiar. Why?

"Grow in knowledge. Drink wisdom as if it were a cup of cold water, for a time will come when your vines will be pruned and your roots exposed."

"When?"

"Sleep now, child. And know that I am near."

Bo shot up from the boat cushion, holding his neck, gasping for air. *Get your bearings.* Lake . . . boat . . . If he squinted, he could see the wooden lighthouse on the Grand Island East Channel in the distance. He must have fallen asleep.

*Beep, beep, beep.* He removed his cell phone from his front pocket and glanced at the screen. New voice message.

Amanda's soft cry woke Mattie from her slumber. Dazed, she lifted her head from the open Bible and straightened her posture in a slow stretch. Mattie blinked at the daylight streaming through the window.

"Mama." Amanda's whimper traveled from the bedroom into the kitchen.

Mattie pushed to her feet. No telling how late she'd slept. The children must be starved. As she started down the hallway, someone knocked on her front door. Mattie went to the door. A tall, thin man wearing a long-sleeved white shirt and tie and carrying a leather briefcase stood on her stoop. Sweat dotted his forehead.

"Can I help you?"

He pushed his black-framed glasses higher on the bridge of his nose. "Are you Mrs. Diener?"

"*Jah.*" She looked beyond the stranger to the dust-coated black car parked in her driveway.

"I'm Patrick Kline, attorney for Great Northern Expeditions." He handed her a company business card. "I'm here to make you a sizable offer on the mineral rights to your land. I'm sure you'll find the offer more than fair."

"I'm *nett* interested."

"Mrs. Diener, if I might have a few minutes of your time to explain my client's proposal. You wouldn't be selling your land, just the mineral rights. That means you'll be able to continue to use the property for crops or pasture land." He glanced over his shoulder. "Or gardens."

"I read the information packet that came in the mail a few weeks ago and I'm *nett* interested. Good day, sir." She started to close the door, but his foot was in the way.

"I'm sure you have questions you would like to ask, and I'll be more than happy to explain my client's operational process. I could go over the contract with—"

"The woman said, 'Good day.' " Alvin stood on

the bottom porch step, his face flushed from working in the heat. "We're *nett* interested in hearing about the drilling company."

The man spun around to face Alvin. "Are you Mr. Diener?"

Amanda's cry reached the sitting room. Mattie gently closed the front door, leaving the matter to Alvin, and went to check on her daughter.

Amanda's diaper was soaked. No wonder she was fussy. Guilt niggled at Mattie's conscience. She couldn't remember a time she ever slept in this late. Mattie unfastened the pins on the drenched cloth.

Amanda rubbed her eyes. "*Hungahrich.*"

"I know. I'll feed you after I get you out of these wet clothes." Mattie grabbed a clean cloth from the chest of drawers, removed the soiled one, and dropped it into the diaper pail. Lying in a wet diaper had given her a rash. Red splotches were even going down the back of her legs. She lathered the area with a paste mixture of zinc oxide, aloe, and coconut oil, pinned the new diaper in place, and changed her out of her bedclothes and into a dark-green dress.

When she checked on Nathan, he was still asleep. She would wake him once breakfast was ready. He loved oatmeal, especially when she added a dollop of honey or maple syrup. As for Amanda, she had already unfastened the flap on Mattie's dress to nurse.

Mattie settled into the wooden rocker in the bedroom to nurse Amanda. So many things to do. Closing her eyes, she compiled a mental list. Laundry. Barn chores. Pull weeds in the garden. Her stomach growled. Breakfast. Honey. She hadn't checked the hives in a while. Perhaps Alvin would collect the honeycombs. Her thoughts flitted to the unwelcomed visitor. She was thankful Alvin had been there to handle the man. She and the others weren't interested in selling the mineral rights. Once everyone received the information packets in the mail, Bishop Yoder had called a meeting to discuss the options. Though financial stability was tempting, the men voted unanimously not to accept the offer. Entering into such an arrangement would jeopardize their ability to remain separate from the world.

Her thoughts shifted to the customer orders she had to prepare. *Mary needs another batch of herb tea for her leg cramps. Ann, what was it she needed? Upper respiratory congestion or was it something for horsefly bites? And Lois, she ordered something.* The list was in the *greenhaus.* Her mind was going a million directions. Why couldn't she just enjoy a few moments of peace while she cradled Amanda in her arms? It wouldn't be long before her daughter grew independent. She had tried weaning Nathan prior to Amanda's arrival, but he must have sensed the turmoil when Andy passed away. He clung to her even more. He weaned himself a few months ago, prior to his third birthday. On rare occasions, usually late at night when he wasn't feeling well, he would still snuggle up beside her and fall to sleep nursing. He needed the closeness of his mother, and she never discouraged him.

Nathan padded into Amanda's bedroom, rubbing his eyes with his balled fists.

"*Guder mariye*," she said.

He dropped his hands and squinted.

"*Hungahrich?*" After not eating much the last few days, he should be starved.

He gestured to his tummy and turned toward the door, his backside wet.

Mattie sighed. He hadn't wet the bed in several months. "Nathan, honey, we need to get you changed first."

Amanda pulled away, satisfied and ready to get busy playing. "At least one of *mei* children will have eaten before noon," Mattie chided as she rose from the chair. His bed sheets would need laundering also. At the rate her to-do list was growing, it already felt like she was eating dust two steps behind the mule.

Bo wasn't one to grumble about being called into work on his day off. Apparently they were shorthanded. Norton's car was in the lot, and he rarely worked on Fridays. He headed into the building and went directly to Norton's office to check in.

"Only took you an hour and a half. Not bad." Davis peered over a mug of something steaming, an impish twinkle in her eyes. "Something keep you up late last night?"

"I was in the middle of the lake when I got the call." He stared at her a moment. Definitely not the fashion statement she'd made last night. She needed to let her hair down. That bun, even without a fishnet, made her look matronly. Yet her low-buttoned blouse and the string of pearls around her neck stated otherwise. He turned to Norton. "What do you need me for?"

Norton motioned to Davis. "Erica is getting ready to head over to Badger Creek. It's her first field assignment, and I thought you could ride along."

A muscle twitched in his jaw. "Is there another case you'd like me to walk her through? I closed the Diener case."

"Which is why I want you to go to Badger Creek." Norton tapped his pen on a pad of paper. "It would look better for the department if the two of your reports were in agreement."

Bo drew a deep breath and released it in a long sigh. "Fine. I'll go." But he wasn't about to compromise his integrity and change his report. Unless today's investigation gave him reason. He glanced at Davis, ignoring her pageant smile. "Be ready to go in ten minutes."

"Aye aye, captain."

Great, dragging him in today was a game to her. Bo shot a dagger at Norton, who merely shrugged. Leaving the office, he strode to his desk, logged into his computer. Perfect sunny day and he was at work. He brought up the file and printed it. He wanted a copy of the notes he'd taken from the interview and the report he had filed. No sense repeating the same questions he'd already asked the mother. He removed the warm documents off the printer and tucked them into his briefcase. Only one more thing he needed to do. He grabbed his insulated mug and went to the break room. Perhaps caffeine would take the edge off his poor attitude. He despised being manipulated. If his character assessment of Davis was correct, Norton was her puppet. Bo would be next if he wasn't careful.

He stopped in front of Davis's desk. "You ready?"

"Oh, has it been ten minutes?" She didn't wait for his response. She opened the bottom drawer of her desk and removed her purse.

They made it to the front door and Bo stopped. "You have all your paperwork?"

"Yes." She tapped her briefcase.

"Including a signed judge order?"

"No, should I get one? We'll have to stop by the golf course on the way."

"You happen to know the tee times for the judges?" *Figures.*

"One is all I need. And he happens to be playing with my father and a county commissioner or two. I think as many business deals are made these days on the greens as are in their offices. The county plans to take bids for fracking. I'm sure your mother knows about it."

"Maybe so. She does like to golf." Bo pushed the door open and held it for her. He wasn't about to chase a judge across the fairway at Forest Hills Country Club. He headed down the sidewalk toward the parking lot. "I'll let you take the lead, unless you don't feel comfortable."

She stopped midstep and swung to face him. "Bo, don't try to insult me. I have the same qualifications as you."

"Same degree, yes, but don't fool yourself into believing you have anywhere near my observation skills." He continued toward the parking lot. "You can't learn it all from a book, Davis," he said over his shoulder.

Her heels clacked behind him. She caught up to him. "You're not so perfect. Your original report had multiple holes."

"Such as?"

"You spent two hours with the mother in the hospital. You didn't even talk with the child. Or the physician. And you didn't investigate the living conditions. Maybe you should go back to following the basic guidelines in *the book*."

"Perhaps you can show me how it's done."

She tilted her face, nose up, with a convincing air of authority. "I think we should talk with the physician first."

"Okay." He doubted the physician would be available this late in the day on a Friday, but who knows, someone swayed Norton to come into the office on his normal day off.

Davis pawed through her purse, pulled out a set of keys, and jingled them. "I can drive."

He scanned the lot. "I suppose the double-parked convertible over there is yours?"

Her big green eyes sparkled. "A birthday gift from my father. It doesn't look like it'll rain today, so we can put the top down."

"Tempting, but we better take mine." He clicked the trunk release on the remote keypad and it popped open. Bo pulled out two child's car seats. He opened the back door of the sedan and fastened the first seat into the center section.

She leaned against the car. "You make installing one of those look easy. I'm impressed."

"You shouldn't be." He smiled smugly. "If you had any field experience under your belt, you would know how to install one and"—he motioned to her two-seater Mercedes—"that your little car isn't ideal for this line of work. Sometimes you have to transport multiple children from a location."

"Duly noted." She saluted.

He motioned to the second car seat. "Your turn."

"You're testing me, really?"

"Sure." He motioned to the seat again and waited.

She picked up the chair. "I, um . . . I wasn't paying attention."

He took the car carrier from her and belted it in. He would show her another time. That is, if the occasion arose. Something told him she wouldn't be taking any more field assignments. He tugged on the unit. "You always want to make sure it's secure."

"Got it."

"I hope so."

She strolled around to the other side of the car and climbed into the passenger seat.

"Another thing," he said as he clicked his seat belt in place. "Take off that necklace."

"Why?" Her hand went to her neck, her fingers touching the pearls. "This was my mother's."

"It makes you vulnerable. Most of the calls you'll get are in bad neighborhoods. Someone will take you down for it. That's after they've stripped your car while you were inside the run-down apartment building fending off a drunken parent who refuses to release their child."

She gulped.

"You sure you want field experience? You could sit poolside at the country club until you leave for Harvard and never get your hands dirty."

She sat quietly a half second, then narrowed

her eyes. "We're investigating an Amish widow. Do you think someone's going to come at me with a pitchfork?"

"No." He started the engine. "But take off the necklace anyway. You'd be surprised at the strength a panicky kid has when they're being taken away from their mother. If the string of pearls doesn't break, it'll choke you."

She worked the clasp on her necklace without success. Then shifting in her seat so that her back was facing him, she tipped her head down. "Will you help me, please?"

The sweet scent of jasmine wafted into his senses as he fumbled with the clasp. He should have rolled down the window to get a breeze or at least turned on the air conditioning. The heat index in the car had to be a hundred degrees.

"Can you get it?" She unfastened her seat belt and slid closer.

Heat pricked the back of his neck; he was keenly aware of her manipulative move. There. Free. The necklace dangled between his thumb and index finger.

"Thanks." She shot him a luminous smile. A mastered skill she no doubt practiced countless times in the mirror.

"My pleasure." Bo cranked the air on high, shifted into reverse, and backed out of the parking spot. He eased out into traffic, and the first several miles passed in silence.

"It's a nice day for a ride." She gazed out the window. "Not a cloud in the sky."

Nice day to be floating on the lake. His thoughts drifted to the dream he had earlier. It wasn't the first time he'd seen himself in the hospital bed nor felt his lungs expanded by the artificial ventilator. He'd experienced similar dreams after his accident and didn't understand them then either. The words rolled over in his mind: *"Like a farmer plants seed in the ground, so I've planted you . . ."*

# Chapter Eight

A car door slammed, then another. Mattie stopped potting the foxglove seeds and glanced out the greenhouse window that faced the driveway. She didn't recognize the silver sedan, but having unexpected customers wasn't unusual. Ever since she had hung the sign at the end of the driveway advertising herbs for sale, she'd had a steady flow of new customers.

"I'm out here," she called to the man and woman climbing the front porch steps. She probably needed another sign directing people to the greenhouse. Mattie did a quick inventory check. Rosemary. Lavender. Mint. Most of the best-sellers were on hand. Others like chamomile and echinacea were still hanging and not quite dry enough for packaging.

She glanced down at Nathan straddling the baby lamb. The two of them were inseparable. Amanda was sitting on the workbench, dirty head to toe from filling black soil into a clay pot, then dumping it out.

A woman poked her head inside the greenhouse. Dressed in cream-colored pants and a sheer blouse, she looked out of place on Mattie's farm. But so were the majority of the *Englischers* who bought herbs from her.

"Can I help you?" Mattie wiped her dirty hands on a rag.

"Are you Martha Diener?"

"*Jah.*" Mattie took a step forward, but when a clay pot shattered on the cement floor behind her and Amanda started to wail, she spun around to check on her daughter. As she did, Mattie caught a glimpse of a suspenders-wearing man holding a briefcase in her peripheral vision. Another drilling representative, no doubt. These house calls had to stop. She wasn't selling her land.

Mattie scooped Amanda into her arms. Her daughter quieted herself by shoving her filthy fingers in her mouth and sucking on them. Mattie glanced down at Nathan. "*Kumm mitt mich.*"

"*Boppli.*" He pointed at the lamb.

"Tell the *boppli* good-bye. We need to go in the *haus nau.*" She maintained a calm tone while instructing him in Pennsylvania *Deitsch.* He

94

continued petting the lamb. She supposed all children started testing authority around the age of three, but lately, Nathan had given her patience a workout. Now wasn't the time to resist her instruction. She bent down and reached for his hand. But instead of taking it, he jerked away from her and tucked his hands under his armpits.

"Mrs. Diener," the woman said, "I'd like to—"

"You'll have to wait a minute." Mattie hadn't meant to sound brash, but she had a much bigger problem to deal with at the moment. Her son couldn't get away with being disrespectful. "Spare the rod, spoil the child," she muttered under her breath as she set Amanda on the ground outside of the greenhouse. She went back inside for Nathan. Not feeling well and having been closed up in the house, she understood why he wanted to spend more time with the lamb. As difficult as it was raising him alone, she refused to give in to his disobedience just because an *Englischer* wanted to buy her mineral rights. She picked him up and held him tight as he thrashed about.

Nathan fought harder, arms flailing as they left the greenhouse, left the bawling lamb. In an attempt to wrangle him, she inadvertently butted heads with him. His forehead landed hard on the bridge of her nose. The sharp blow stole her breath and made her teary-eyed.

"You're filled with vinegar today," she rasped. No more honey in the oatmeal. She'd added extra today hoping it would entice him to eat, and now his sudden burst of energy was more than the could handle.

"*Boppli, boppli.*" He leveraged his foot against her and pushed away. Slipping from her grip, he toppled over, his face inches from hitting the gravel driveway before the man lunged forward and caught him.

The woman with him gasped.

"Settle down, son," the man said in a gentle but firm voice. He eyed Nathan carefully. "You almost cracked your skull."

Nathan stilled. So did Mattie.

Recognizing the man as the one who had spoken with her at the hospital, Mattie took in a sharp breath. She snatched Nathan from his grip. "What are you doing here?"

The woman, wearing heels that looked like they were supported by rafter spikes, spoke first. "We've come to ask you a few questions."

What more could they possibly want to ask her? She locked eyes with the man. "I answered your questions."

He nodded. "I know."

The woman swatted at a fly. "May we go inside and talk?"

Mattie picked up Amanda. She couldn't stop the state worker when he came into her son's hospital room, but this was her farm, her property. She didn't have to invite them inside her home. "I'd rather *nett.*" She moved past them and dashed toward the house.

"Why did you leave the hospital AMA?"

The woman's accusatory tone barbed Mattie. She halted in the center of the driveway and spun around. "I don't know what you're talking about. Please, will you leave *mei* family alone?"

The woman wobbled over the gravel drive, her spiked heels turning her ankles.

The man cut in front of the woman, his blue eyes radiating compassion. "Mrs. Diener, we received word that you left the hospital before the doctor discharged your son. Is that true?"

"The *doktah* never came back to see him."

His brows rose. "Usually the doctor only makes rounds once a day. They will often monitor a patient's progress remotely either through the computer or by receiving a report over the phone by the nurse. Did anyone explain that to you?"

She shook her head. "But it shouldn't matter. Nathan is fine. He hasn't spiked a fever since we left." The state workers didn't look convinced. "His face is red from the heat. It-it must be eighty degrees today. I didn't harm *mei* child. I give you *mei* word." She eased Nathan and Amanda to the ground and held their shoulders as she whispered in Pennsylvania *Deitsch* for them to go inside the house. Thankfully, Nathan

97

took his sister's hand and they both scurried inside.

The woman leaned against the man's broad shoulder. "She's talking in code," she said under her breath.

He shook his head.

"I've answered enough questions." Mattie headed toward the house, the woman practically chasing after her.

"We would like to inspect the premises," the woman said.

Mattie stiffened. *Inspect for what? Don't ask.* She proceeded up the porch steps, responding over her shoulder, "I don't invite strangers into *mei* home."

"I'm Erica Davis, an investigator for Child Protective Services, and this is my partner, Bo Lambright."

Mattie turned to face them. "*Jah*, I met Mr. Lambright at the hospital."

Ms. Davis opened her handbag and shuffled through it. "Here's my card. Feel free to call the office and validate my credentials."

Mattie raised her chin. "I don't own a phone."

"Well, it's part of our investigation to view the premises," the woman persisted.

Mattie paused at the door, her body blocking the entry from Ms. Davis, who appeared ready to barge in the house uninvited. Mattie steadied her gaze beyond the woman at Bo Lambright, who seemed more reasonable. "I answered all your questions in the hospital, Mr.—"

"Bo." He moved toward the porch. "And I appreciate your willingness to do so."

"Then why are you harassing me, at *mei* home? In front of *mei* children?"

"The investigation is incomplete," the woman answered for him. She fanned her face with her hand. "It's hot out. May we continue this conversation inside?"

"You can say no, Mrs. Diener," the man said, climbing the steps and stopping next to his partner.

The woman investigator shot him a glare, which did nothing to alter his set jaw or stony expression. Ms. Davis shifted her attention to Mattie. "He's correct. But we won't be able to close the case until we inspect the living conditions and talk with the children."

"Talk with *mei* children? *Nay*, I couldn't let you do that."

The nosy woman cocked her head. "What are you hiding?"

The man groaned under his breath. He reached for the coworker's arm. "Erica," was all he had to say for her to face him. "Let me handle this."

Ms. Davis squared her shoulders. "Good luck."

Ignoring his coworker, Bo moved in front of the woman. "You don't have to let us come in to inspect the house. But it's true. The case will remain open until we complete the paperwork."

"We'll get a court order from a judge," the woman spouted.

Court order? Judge? Her stomach roiled. "I-I don't understand."

"You're under investigation for child abuse."

"What!" Mattie's knees weakened, and she clutched the handrail.

The man's face tensed, then relaxed once Mattie had steadied herself. Ms. Davis opened her mouth, but Bo Lambright cut her off. "We're bound by law to respond when charges of abuse are filed," he said calmly. "At this point, it's still in the investigational phase."

"Is this about the blisters in *mei sohn*'s mouth? I told you I don't know what caused them."

"I've written down your statement, but we still need to inspect the living conditions and interview the children." His soft tone sounded apologetic.

Ms. Davis wormed her way closer, interjecting, "We have the authority to remove the children from the home if we deem necessary."

Mattie's gaze shot over to Bo. "Is that true?" Why was she asking the man? He'd hunted her down. Tears pricked her eyes, distorting his image.

He cleared his throat. "You have the right to have someone you trust present during the interview. Do you have a family member or friend you'd like to attend?"

Her legs wobbled again. She leaned against the handrail, thoughts swirling.

"Mrs. Diener?" He moved closer.

Her ears rang with a high-pitched squeal. She was hot. Thirsty. Her mouth coated with a metallic taste. Nothing felt real. Black spots filled her vision . . .

The woman's eyes rolled back and she collapsed before Bo could catch her. He knelt beside her. "Mrs. Diener?" He placed his hand on her shoulder, gave her a shake, then eased her onto her back. The red knot forming on her head would throb when she woke up. He gently shook her shoulder and called her name again, but she didn't respond. Now what? She'd made it clear she didn't want them inside. He should have insisted they wait for a court order. Instead, he allowed Davis's unwillingness to walk to the tenth hole in heels when a golf cart wasn't available to waste a good part of this day. He debated the ramifications of an illegal entry for half a second before ignoring the legalistic warning and gathering her limp body into his arms.

Her frailness caught him by surprise. After seeing the boy, Bo had thought the child's growth had been stunted. He'd seen it before in malnourished children living on the streets. Now the boy's size made more sense. His mother was a lightweight.

"Open the door, Davis."

Davis opened the door and stepped inside.

Entering the house, Bo located the sofa in the sitting room. He gently lowered her onto the quilt-covered cushion. "Can you find a rag in the kitchen and wet it, please?"

Davis left the room.

Bo scanned the area. Oak floors. Simple furnishings. Bare walls. Uncluttered.

"Here you go." Davis handed him the wet rag. "I would have made an ice pack, but there's no refrigerator or freezer. The stove looks to be a hundred years old, and the only things I found in the cabinets other than dishes were several jar of what looked like dried tea leaves, a package of noodles, rice, peanut butter, and a shelf full of jars marked *Honey*. That's it."

"Stop searching. We're on a tightrope as it is, entering without permission." He gingerly placed the cool cloth on Mrs. Diener's forehead. He should have been prepared to catch her. She probably wouldn't still be out cold if he had. He'd seen her face whitewash with shock. Davis needed a lesson in tactfulness.

"This room is rather drab. I'd paint it something bright. Yellow." Davis gazed at the ceiling and turned a circle. "Add crown molding and more light . . . Yes, definitely more light. This is inadequate . . ."

Bo ignored Davis's rambling and focused on Mrs. Diener.

She mumbled something and left the room,

only to return a moment later. "They really don't have electricity."

"It took you awhile to figure that one out, Sherlock."

Davis cocked her head. "Now, how would I know anything about the Amish? It's not like we attended the same boarding schools together."

Or the same political circles. The Amish didn't vote so it wouldn't matter if their lumber mill was located in her father's voting district.

She motioned with a head bob toward Mrs. Diener. "So, how's the patient doing, Doctor Watson?"

"I don't know. Sure seems like she would have come around by now." He knelt by the sofa.

Davis leaned over his shoulder. "Unless she's faking it."

"She's not faking." The woman didn't want them in her house, surely she wouldn't . . . *want them anywhere near her children.* He shot up from his knees. "I don't hear the kids, do you?"

"I'll find them." Her heels clacked against the plank floor as she left the room.

The children needed to be located, and Davis being a woman would make it less intimidating for them once they were found. A child's shrill cry broke the silence. Bo rushed down the hall and stopped at the opened bedroom door.

Davis stood with her hands on her hips and tapping her shoe on the wood floor. "They're under the bed. And you'll never guess what's in the other room." She didn't give him time to answer. "A wooden structure filled with straw. I think they have livestock in the house."

"Anything in the crate?" Bo moved closer to the bed and knelt. He spotted the children and waved. "*Hiya*, Nathan. Will you come out from under there and bring your sister, please?" Bo glanced over his shoulder at Davis's tapping shoe, then traveled the length of her legs up to her face and met her gaze with a stern look. "You think the toe tapping is helping?"

"You don't have an issue with barnyard animals living indoors?"

"What are you doing in *mei haus*?" Mrs. Diener's narrowed gaze darted between him and Davis, landing back on him. "Why are you looking under *mei* bed?"

Bo pushed off the floor and stood. "Your children are under there. How's your head?"

"You can't take them." Her eyes welled with tears.

Bo backed away from the bed. "I think we'll get going." He looked hard at Davis, who had crossed her arms and resumed tapping her foot. "Don't you agree, Erica?"

"No, I don't."

If he had to pull rank on her, he would. Bo came up beside her. "You and I need to have a word."

Davis marched out of the room and stopped

halfway down the hall. "We still have information to gather. This is an investigation."

"It's not going to happen today. She has the right to have another person present, and we're going to give her the opportunity to make those arrangements. Besides, with that knot on her head, she's in no condition to answer our questions."

"Convenient, isn't it?"

He pinched the bridge of his nose. "She's not calculating."

Davis lifted her brows. "You don't know women at all."

"I know my job." And at the moment they were breaking every rule in the book. Mrs. Diener could have his head on a silver platter.

"That's right. You staked your reputation on this case."

More than just his reputation. His license was on the line. They should have obtained a court order, or at least waited until they talked with the physician. He turned and walked back to the bedroom. Mrs. Diener was sitting on the floor clutching her two children. Bo cleared his throat. "We're going to leave now."

She ignored him.

"We'll be back on Monday around ten. You're welcome to have someone here to oversee the interview with the children." Bo's throat tightened at the sight of tears streaming down her face. He wanted to say he was sorry for putting her through this, but he couldn't. She would receive fair treatment; he would make sure of that. But he wasn't going to get attached. Not to her—not to her children.

"Well, this was a wasted trip," Davis said once they were outside. "Had I thought to call the physician's office I would have known they closed early on Fridays. And I should have gotten a court order—even if I'd had to sit in the club's lounge until nightfall to get the judge's signature."

"Perhaps." It would save him from having to answer why they broke protocol should Mrs. Diener file a formal complaint. Bo trekked toward the driver's side of the car. As for the court order, he had hoped to avoid involving a judge, con-sidered it a blessing that the judge was on the far side of the course and the carts were all taken. This case should have remained closed. An animal's cry stopped him from opening the car door. He scanned the area. The buggy horse was grazing in the field. The animal bleated again. *Baa.* This time he was sure the sound came from the greenhouse. "I'll be right back."

The greenhouse held an array of plants at various stages of growth. Clippers and tools hung on a pegboard above the wooden worktable. Other miscellaneous garden tools and watering cans were neatly placed on a shelf. He looked to the floor when he heard the lamb's cry again. The tiny creature wasn't more than a few weeks old.

"Where is your *mamm*, little guy?" Bo didn't want to leave the lamb alone with broken pieces of a clay pot scattered over the floor. He picked up the animal, and it nuzzled his ear.

Carrying the lamb inside the barn, the scent of hay filled his senses. Memories of his youth flashed before his eyes—of sweating from mucking out the horse stalls and rubbing his itchy back against the support beam to get relief from the hay dust. He passed the horse stalls, the harness tack hanging on a nail, and the bins of grain. The only empty pen was in the back of the barn. The ewe was nowhere to be found. It must have orphaned the offspring shortly after birth. Even so, the lamb shouldn't be alone. Sheep are flock animals and often become stressed when separated from the herd. Bo held the lamb a moment longer, then gently lowered it over the slat fence, releasing it on a mound of hay. Heaviness saturated his heart. It was tough to be separated from the flock—orphaned.

## Chapter Nine

Mattie spent Saturday morning washing the walls, windows, and floors. Everything had to be in order. Every nook and cranny spotless before the state workers returned on Monday. Not that her home wasn't clean already. She took great pride in keeping a tidy home. Besides, hard work gave her a new focus.

Mattie dipped the scrub brush in the soapy water and arched her back, stretching her taut muscles.

"You expecting company?" Alvin's voice rang out from the other side of the screen door.

Mattie pushed off the floor, scrub brush in hand. Her dress was soaked with mop water and soapsuds. "Hello, Alvin."

His eyes opened wide. "What happened to your head?"

She touched the knot. "I banged *mei* head on something. It's nothing."

"That's *gut*." He flipped his thumb over his shoulder. "I stopped by to check on that sick lamb, but it isn't in the barn."

Mattie met Alvin on the porch. She would have invited him inside if the floors were dry, but he didn't always kick the mud off his boots when he entered and she didn't want to have to mop a second time. As it was it would take half the day to get the wood floors ready for a new coat of wax.

"I moved Snowball into the *haus* the other day." Mattie used the front of her apron to dry her hands. "She still requires a lot of coaxing to take the bottle." And Mattie didn't like traipsing out to the barn in the middle of the night to feed the lamb.

Alvin lowered his head and shuffled his boots from side to side. "A ewe doesn't usually orphan her offspring unless the lamb is ill. Maybe you should consider putting it down."

"I couldn't do that. It would break Nathan's heart." She recalled the fit he gave her when she tried to get him to leave the greenhouse without the wooly creature.

"Sheep aren't pets." Alvin frowned. "The earlier Nathan learns he's not to become attached to the livestock, the better off he'll be. It's just a fact of life that some of the weaker ones don't make it."

*Weaker ones don't make it.* An image of Andy in his weakened state invaded her mind. The doctor had warned her his lungs were filling with fluid, but she hadn't wanted to believe he would lose his battle before he reached thirty—or before he saw his unborn child.

"Sorry, Mattie, if the news is too hard to hear."

"*Danki*, Alvin, but I don't plan on giving up on the young'un just yet."

He eyed her, his lips straight, then changed the subject. "I-I was wondering . . . since there isn't Sunday service tomorrow that maybe—maybe you would like someone to take you visiting?"

"I, um . . ." Alvin had never asked to take her anywhere before. His brows lifted, making it even more difficult to find a valid excuse. "I wasn't planning to go anywhere tomorrow. Nathan's been sick and I thought he could use another day of rest." After the cleaning frenzy today, she, too, would need a break.

"Another time?"

"We'll see." Mattie smiled nervously. This was it—starting over. She was ready, wasn't she?

The golden flecks in his eyes lit. "*Danki*, Mattie. I'll be seeing you." He turned and clambered off the porch with more spring to his step.

Bo tossed the bedcovers aside, dressed, then hiked up the basement steps. He slipped down the hall and into his father's private study. Although his father had passed away several years ago, his study remained untouched. Medical journals and old textbooks lined the massive bookshelves.

Bo lounged in the leather wingback chair behind the grand mahogany desk. *Think like a doctor.* He flipped open the laptop, typed "barnyard diseases" into the search field, and hit Enter. His father had an extensive assortment of textbooks and magazines, but Bo would rather surf the Internet instead of sift through articles. He scanned the results, particularly for diseases contagious to humans. His dream last night had been confusing. At one point, he'd been searching for a lost lamb, then the dream merged with images of Mattie and her children covered in leprous spots, hovering in the dark after being cast out of their Amish district. He wasn't sure what any of it meant, but after remembering the lamb inside the green-house, it had spawned the idea to look for barn-related diseases humans could contract. He scanned the topic index of one Internet journal, spotted an article about hoof-and-mouth disease, and clicked on that page. *Viral infection. Highly communicable. Cattle, swine, goats . . . and sheep. Thank You, Jesus.* He tipped the lampshade to remove the glare on the screen. "Characterized by fever, blister-like erosions on the tongue, lips, and mouth." Trailing the sentence with his finger, he stopped. *Not transferable to humans.*

Bo sank back in the chair. He was sure God had prompted him to get out of bed and do research, but every article he found so far was a dead end.

*Keep looking.*

He searched for other zoonotic diseases, finding related articles on sheep transmitting ringworm, bacteria causing diarrhea, and several other infectious diseases. But nothing that would explain the blisters in Nathan's mouth.

Morning rays filtered into the room when he came across the poxvirus Orf. *A study in England found 23 percent of sheep farmers had been infected . . .*

"How long have you been up?" His mother entered the room, a confused look on her face.

"A few hours."

She strolled around the perimeter of the room,

111

gazing at the numerous photographs of his father and the various orphans he'd treated through the years while on mission trips. "Martin sure had a heart for orphans," she said with a sigh. "I thought about having this room repurposed, but I could never figure out what to do with it."

Bo closed the laptop. The last time she had spent any amount of time in here, he'd found her weeping uncontrollably. Of course, she steeled her emotions immediately. The judge in her had an innate ability to suppress outward signs of weakness. Bo turned off the lamp and stood. "Are you hungry?"

"What were you doing in here?"

"Researching animal-to-human transmittable diseases. I had a hunch about a case I was called to investigate." *A hunch. Is that all it is?*

"What kind of animals?"

"Sheep. Horses." He hadn't looked up chickens yet, but he remembered a few roaming Mattie Diener's yard. "Like I said, it was only a hunch."

Monday morning Bo and Davis returned to Badger Creek, this time equipped with a signed court order to inspect the premises and remove the children if conditions deemed necessary. During the drive, Bo drilled Davis about the best ways to approach a suspected abuser, pointing out areas she could have handled more tactfully the last time. At the same time, Mattie Diener niggled at the back of his mind. Amish were meek, non-threatening—at least, most of them lived in accordance with their beliefs.

"It'd be best if you just observed," he said.

"Observe?"

"Yes." He wasn't going to run interference again.

"Norton added me to the case—"

"To get field experience, I know." He turned into the parking lot at the doctor's clinic.

"I was going to say to correct what you flubbed in the first investigation."

Bo chuckled, pulling into an empty slot. He shifted into Park and faced Davis. "Do you want to watch how it's done or sit in the car?"

She hesitated a moment, then unclipped her seat belt and climbed out. "I'm part of this investigation, Bo."

He ignored her remark and opened the clinic's door. The lobby was standing room only. Bo handed the receptionist one of his business cards and briefly explained his reason for being there without divulging any specifics of the case.

A few minutes later, the receptionist opened the door and ushered them to the office at the end of the hall. "Doctor Wellington asked that you wait for her in here." She motioned to the two chairs facing the desk. "You can have a seat."

Bo glanced at the framed certificates on the paneled walls. Doctor Roswell was certainly involved in the community. Awarded for his humanitarian efforts and for the years of service as chairman of the board for the Upper Peninsula Hands of Hope Foundation.

Doctor Wellington breezed into the room. "The best I can figure, Nathan Diener has a strep infection."

Bo exchanged glances with Davis, who appeared just as surprised by the diagnosis.

The physician continued, "I'm still not totally convinced strep was the cause of the blisters." She fidgeted with a stack of charts, straightening them, then moved them to another area of the desk. Finally, she folded her hands. "I received the final report this morning from the radiologist on the esophagus lining; it's inconclusive. In addition, the toxicology screening came back negative." She tapped her fingers on the desk. "The strep culture returned positive, that's it."

"So you don't believe Mrs. Diener abused her son?"

Doctor Wellington shook her head. "I was sure this was a Munchausen-syndrome-by-proxy case. The classic signs were there. Unusual symptoms, recurrent illness . . . The child's chart is thick. The mother signed him out AMA. Then there's the mother's past medical history to consider. According to her chart, she's been treated for depression. The last entry Doctor Roswell made in his progress notes indicated a possible bipolar disorder. I don't feel good about this case."

Bo glanced at Davis, who was nodding along with the doctor. He shifted in his chair to give the physician his full attention. "Without any medical proof . . ." He shrugged. None of these accusations would hold up in court without proof. Surely the doctor knew that. "Maybe Doctor Roswell could shed some light since he's been the one treating the family."

She shook her head. "He's on an extended European vacation. I don't have a means to contact him. What were your findings? Have you inspected the living conditions?"

"I visited the home last Friday. I didn't find anything." He glanced at Davis seated beside him. *Don't say anything.*

Davis probed him with a glare, then faced the physician. "There isn't electricity in the home. Or a refrigerator."

Bo's jaw twitched. "That's true. Old Order Amish don't believe in modern conveniences. They use horse and buggy for transportation, heat their homes with wood, grow a lot of their own food, and yes, they don't own appliances. But neither did our forefathers." He looked at Davis. "People in the 1800s didn't have any of today's luxuries, but they managed." Bo faced the doctor. "I'm sorry to get off on a tangent."

"That's quite all right, Mr. Lambright. I'm not from this area, and you certainly have more knowledge of the Amish than I do."

"There was evidence of livestock living in the house," Davis blurted.

Next time Davis was going to wait in the car. Bo stymied his agitation. "Although it should be noted, we didn't see any such animals *in* the home." He laughed lightheartedly. "I think even some celebrities have had potbelly pigs. It wouldn't be my choice of a pet, and I'm guessing not yours, Erica. But who's to say which pets can be housetrained?"

Doctor Wellington smiled. "Yes, I think I recall hearing something about George Clooney's pig."

Davis groaned under her breath. Either she was bent on discrediting Mattie or Davis was annoyed she wasn't the center of attention.

Doctor Wellington tapped the end of her pen on the desk contemplating something.

"If you're willing to support my recommendation, we can close this case," Bo said. "Unless you have more test results you're waiting to hear back on."

"Other than the results from the mother's milk, no, everything is back."

"If the milk was contaminated . . ." Bo needed to tread lightly and not step on the doctor's toes. "Of course, I'm not a doctor, but wouldn't it have shown on the boy's toxic screen?"

"I suppose there are exceptions, but I'm currently not aware of any. I'm assuming the results will be negative when the report comes back." After a brief hesitation, Doctor Wellington tossed her pen. "Okay then," she said with a sigh. "There's just one other problem."

"What's that?"

"Nathan Diener needs to start a regimen of antibiotics immediately. I have samples from the manufacturer, but the only means I have to contact Mrs. Diener is through the mail. That's going to cause a major delay in her son's therapy."

Bo smiled. "The Dieners' farm is on my way home. I'd be more than happy to deliver the medication." And the news.

## Chapter Ten

"You're pacing," Grace said to Mattie.

"No, I'm cleaning off the counter so I can scrub it." She set the cookie jar on the table, went back for the canister of sugar, then for the bread box.

"I figured as much when I smelled bleach from the front door. What are you doing, trying to sterilize this place?"

"Something like that," Mattie muttered under her breath.

"Did you say something?" Grace crinkled her brows.

"I'll put the kettle on for tea." She could use a short break. Until the water boiled, she would continue cleaning. Mattie dipped the rag into the bleach water and cringed. Her raw hands stung from the strong chemicals.

"I thought we could go into town together," Grace said.

"Can't. Nathan and Amanda are asleep." She vigorously scrubbed a small beet stain on the counter from last canning season.

Grace leaned over her shoulder. "You've tried to remove that before."

"I know." She scrubbed harder.

"When are you going to tell me what's wrong?"

Mattie gave up on the stain and moved to another section.

"I wasn't going to say anything," Grace said, reaching for Mattie's hand. "What happened to your head? It looks like you got hit with a two-by-four."

Mattie's muscles tensed and Grace released Mattie's hand. Mattie tossed the rag on the counter and touched the swollen knot on her head. Her gaze flitted to Grace who was studying her with raised eyebrows. Mattie went to the stove. "A watched kettle never boils. Who do you think came up with that?"

"Your guess is as good as mine." Grace came up beside her and wrapped her arm around Mattie's waist. "Something's wrong, Mattie. What is it?"

She half shrugged, afraid if she tried to speak,

her voice would ripple out in sobs. *Hold it together. Don't break down.*

"We've been friends a long time."

Mattie stepped away. "And you're worried I'm going to fall to pieces—again. Well, I'm *nett.*" Mattie's hands shook and to hide the tremors, she swept the front of her apron as if she'd spilled something on it. Oh, Lord, maybe she was falling apart again. *No! Not again.*

"Mattie, how did you get the bump on your head?"

She heaved in a deep breath. "I blacked out."

"What? When? Have you seen the *doktah?*"

"*Nay.* I'm fine. I was overly tired and . . . under stress." *And being interrogated by nosy state workers.*

Grace placed her hand on Mattie's arm and she jolted. "You're mighty jumpy." Grace removed her hand.

Mattie's shoulders slumped. How was she going to face the state workers' questions? She couldn't even carry on a conversation with her best friend. "I can't seem to . . . keep *mei* thoughts straight."

"Because you're sleep deprived. Just like when—"

"I know," Mattie snapped. "I won't break down again. I won't let it happen."

Grace's lips formed a tight straight line. She blinked a few times as if hurt, but said nothing.

A long moment of silence passed between them. Mattie's insides churned. Faith in the Lord should have kept her from suffering a nervous breakdown—but her faith had failed; she failed God. Postpartum depression coupled with grieving over her late husband proved to be too much to handle even with the antidepressants Doctor Roswell had prescribed to get through the so-called *normal* grieving process. Gone was the joy of serving the Lord. For that matter, joy in doing anything. Even working in the herb garden hadn't brought her much happiness. Days once spent humming as she repotted a plant were gone. She was moving forward the best she knew how—the best under the circumstances.

Steam and water erupted from the kettle spout, hissing as it pooled on the stove top. Mattie grabbed a potholder and removed the cast-iron kettle. Her hand shook as she lowered it to the wire rack.

"Let me finish preparing the tea." Grace stretched her hand out for the potholder. "You have a seat and I'll make one of Mattie Diener's cure-all concoctions to fix everything."

Grace wouldn't make those claims if she knew the extent of what needed curing. A cup of tea wouldn't stop the man from the Child Services from returning. When Grace cocked her head, eyeing Mattie with that silent instant glare of hers, Mattie relinquished the potholder. She ambled over to the table, pulled out a chair, and plopped down.

"I'm sorry for snapping at you, Grace," she said once her friend joined her. "I couldn't ask for a better confidant."

"You've seen me at *mei* worst too."

True, Grace had been born with muscular dystrophy along with having one leg shorter than the other. Her disease had wreaked havoc on her joints and muscles, and she lived with pain far worse than anyone Mattie had known.

"*Danki* for understanding. The past few days have been . . . difficult." *Downplay the state workers' looming return.* She'd worked too hard to convince the members of her district that she was stable—trusting God's will—when in reality, she had been questioning God's will since her husband died eighteen months ago. If the state workers continued to hound her with questions, what little bit of sanity she had regained would vanish once again. But bottling everything up would eventually erode her nerves. She had to confide in someone. The man had suggested having a friend or relative present during the interview. Grace had been like a sister to her, the person she trusted the most. "There's something I haven't told anyone yet." The teacup rattled as she picked it up from the saucer. *Calm yourself. Take a deep breath in . . . and exhale.*

"Please tell me you didn't sign away the mineral

rights on your land," Grace blurted. "The offer they made on our property sounds *gut* on the surface—but Ben is convinced drilling would open up a lot of problems and *nett* just from having *Englischers* roaming our land."

Light footsteps came up behind Mattie and a hand tapped her arm. "*Wasser*, please."

Mattie jumped, spilling scalding tea down the front of her dress and dropping the cup on the table. She vaulted off the chair, pulling the wet material away from her skin, and rushing to the sink. The cup rolled to the floor and shattered.

Nathan started to whimper, and Grace picked him up just as he was about to step barefooted on a piece of glass. She walked him over to the sink where she partially filled a glass with water and handed it to him to drink. "Are you okay, Mattie?"

"I will be." She blotted her dress with a dry dishrag.

"I'll put him back down for his nap, then help clean up," Grace said.

"*Danki*." Mattie held back her tears until Grace had taken Nathan out of the room. Her life felt as fragile as the teacup, and she was on the verge of shattering.

A knock sounded on the door. Mattie froze. The caller knocked a second time before she summoned the courage to answer. "God, please grant me mercy." She attempted to straighten her dress apron and took a moment to suck in a breath before reaching for the handle.

Opening the door, her eyes beheld one of the state workers. "Mr. . . ." Her teeth grated before she could find the words to greet the caller.

"Lambright. Bo Lambright."

Mattie looked beyond the man to the woman seated in the passenger seat of the silver car. Good, she would rather not deal with the brazen woman anymore. Bo was imposing enough and not just his towering stance. His daunting, pleased-with-himself grin was crooked. Under different circumstances, she might have found it boyishly cute. Mattie placed her hand on the doorframe, blocking his entrance. "This isn't a good time." He crinkled his brow and opened his mouth, but she cut him off. "Mr. Lambright, *mei* children are taking a nap, and I don't want you disturbing their rest."

"I'll keep my voice down." He lifted a small brown paper bag. "I'm making a house call for your doctor."

"I don't understand. Is *Doktah* Roswell back in town?" A thread of hope lifted her spirit, only to be clipped by him shaking his head.

"Do you mind if I come in? Not to investigate," he was quick to add. "I promised Doctor Wellington I would go over the medication instructions. I also need you to sign a paper stating you received it."

She grasped the doorframe tighter and braced. "It'll take less than five minutes."

She looked over her shoulder for Grace. Still in Nathan's room. Then, against her better judgment, she dropped her hand from the frame and stepped aside. "Five minutes, that's all."

He eased into the house. "Is there a place we can sit down so I can go over the instructions?" he whispered.

"*Jah*, this way." She led him to the kitchen.

He glanced down at the broken cup and wet floor.

"I was about to clean that up when you knocked."

His gaze lifted and for half a second his eyes seemed focused on the front of her dress. "Did you get burned?"

She wiped the wet spot on her dress with a dish towel. "*Nett* too badly." She motioned to the chair on the opposite side of the table. "You said this would only take five minutes?"

Bo sat down, opened the brown paper bag, and removed the contents: a medication bottle filled with a thick pink substance and a stack of folded papers. "Nathan received some antibiotics in the hospital, but Doctor Wellington wants him to continue the oral meds for another ten days."

"He hasn't run a fever since I brought him home," she said softly.

"That's good. But it's important that you give

him this to complete the treatment. Otherwise the illness might return. Will you do that?"

"Of course."

Bo withdrew the plastic medication dispenser out of the bag. "The doctor gave me a special measuring spoon so you'll be able to give him the proper amount. Give him 5 cc's three times a day." He leaned closer, his finger on the marking, and showed her the line for the proper dosage, then unfolded the papers. "Here's a list of things to watch for. Diarrhea is the most probable adverse effect, but there are several others listed. Do you want me to read them?"

Did he think she was illiterate? She folded her arms across her chest. "I can read."

He glanced up from the paper. "I didn't mean to offend you. I'm sorry."

Was he sincere? It didn't matter. "You said something about a paper I needed to sign."

"Yes." He flipped to the back page, then rotated the paper in her direction and placed his finger on the bottom line. "Do you need a pen?"

"I can get one." She stood, stepped around the broken glass, and retrieved a pen from the cabinet drawer. His finger still held the spot. She signed the form. "Anything else?"

"The doctor wants to recheck him in ten days."

"Okay." Hopefully Doctor Roswell would be back by then.

"Except for the positive culture, indicating a

strep infection, the other test results, the toxic screening, came back negative."

"Are you serious?" She screeched, her voice rising with excitement. "Negative is *gut* news, *jah*?"

He smiled. "I'm not able to tell you anything official about my report, but you should receive a letter in the mail that the case is closed."

"Really?" Tears pricked her eyes.

He nodded. "Now, that's unofficial. But since I'll be the one putting the final papers in the mail, I thought you might want to know."

"*Danki*—thank you, Mr. Lambright." She covered her hand over her mouth. *Danki, God.*

"Now, I just have one more question."

The air left her lungs. She should have expected a catch to this visit. "*Jah*?"

"How's your head?"

She touched the knot that took a day and a half to stop throbbing. "Fine *nau*."

"I'm glad to hear that." He stood.

She rose to walk him to the door. "Will I be seeing—?"

"Any more of me? Not unless something comes up." He reached the door and stopped. Digging into his front pocket, he removed a card. "My number is on here if you need to get ahold of me. You can call me anytime."

"*Danki*." Mattie accepted the card even though she still had the one he'd given her at the hospital.

She waited for him to step outside, then closed the door. Mattie covered her mouth to stifle a squeal. If the children weren't asleep, she would sing for joy. The nightmare had ended.

"Are you going to tell me about him?" Grace leaned against the wall, arms folded, and brows quirked.

"There isn't anything to tell." *Nau.*

"A handsome *Englischer* asks you about the bump on your forehead, and you say there's nothing to tell. Oh, and *nett* to mention the smile he put on your face. You haven't smiled like that in a long time. I hope you're *nett* fooled by his *gut* looks."

"It's *nett* what you think." Was the man handsome? She hadn't noticed.

"I know you mentioned you were ready to move on, but he's an *Englischer*, Mattie. Don't get involved with someone who might sway you from your faith."

Had any of Grace's concerns been true, her friend's reprimand would be warranted. But even though Mattie had said she was going forward, she didn't mean she would do so with an *Englischer*—ever.

"He seemed genuinely concerned about you." Grace wasn't letting the issue go.

"Hardly." Mattie handed Grace his business card, then went into the kitchen to clean up the mess on the floor.

"Child Protective Services?"

Mattie grabbed the broom from the corner. "I was under investigation. Allegations of child abuse, they called it."

"What? When?"

She swept the glass into a pile. "Nathan had been running a fever so I took him in to see *Doktah* Roswell, only he was out of town and another *doktah* was seeing his patients. This *doktah* insisted he be admitted to the hospital, then proceeded to call the police, who then called *that man* to come investigate me for child abuse. All because the *doktah* deemed I didn't bring him to the hospital in a timely manner."

"That's *narrisch*!" Grace squatted down with the dustpan and held it still as Mattie swept the glass pieces off the floor.

Mattie tossed the contents into the trash can. "None of this would have happened had *Doktah* Roswell seen him. He would have probably sent him home with a list of things for me to watch for. As it was, he never spiked another fever."

"But children run fevers all the time. Why did the *doktah* want him admitted?"

"The inside of his mouth was blistered. Apparently they thought I caused it."

Shock registered on Grace's face. "*Nay.*"

Mattie closed her eyes and nodded. "It's over *nau.* I just want to put it all behind me."

• • •

The moment Bo slipped behind the wheel of the car at the Dieners' place, Davis hit him head-on with her accusations.

"You are a manipulator, Bo Lambright."

"How do you figure?"

"You manipulated that doctor into agreeing with you just to save your reputation, didn't you?"

"First of all, I helped her come to a decision. The toxicity tests were negative. And second, I did it to save an innocent woman. The boy has a strep infection. It had nothing to do with saving my reputation." He started the engine.

"Sure."

"That's the truth." He placed the gearshift in reverse and backed up.

"You haven't stopped smiling since you got back into the car. I think you're gloating."

"Am I?" He pulled out of the driveway and headed down the rocky, narrow road, which was more of a trail blazed through the woods. Only two other Amish farms were between the Dieners' place and the main road. This district was smaller than he originally estimated. Much smaller than the settlements he was familiar with. He hit a dip in the road and Davis jostled on the seat.

"This road could use repairs," Davis said, her voice vibrating from the washboard road. "I'm glad we didn't take my car. It would have bottomed out."

"Looks like they've attempted to fill most of the holes with stones."

"I don't know why they hold so tight to this land." She gazed out the window. "I'd sell it in a heartbeat—mineral rights and all."

"The Amish aren't materialistic."

She rolled her eyes. "Everyone can be bought."

He shrugged. "You don't know the extent of their resolve."

"What are you, their spokesperson?"

He held his tongue. No matter what he said, Davis wouldn't understand. Not many outsiders did.

She sank into the seat. "Well, you worked hard enough to get the investigation closed. She must be elated with you—see you as some sort of hero."

"I wouldn't go that far." Although once he reached the other side of the county and could file his report, he would be elated to have the case closed. He'd never been so moved by a woman's emotions. She loved her children and defended them, as any mother should. Had he not left the house when he did, he might have shed a tear or two. Crazy. It wasn't like he was emotionally attached. He merely wanted to make sure she received fair treatment—and she had. His job was over. Weight he hadn't realized he'd been carrying evaporated.

"I don't think Norton will be pleased to hear you made me sit in the car," she snipped.

"Don't sulk. You tried your best to undermine me in the doctor's office. Besides, you still could use a lesson or two in tactfulness. Your approach bordered on abuse of power the other day."

"I'm practicing for the courtroom."

"That much I gathered. It might help, though, if you remember a person is innocent until *proven* guilty." He smiled. "And some cases *do* have a happy ending."

"Point taken." She settled into the seat. "Field work isn't so bad."

For her sake, he hoped Norton kept her in the office. She didn't need to be out on a call in the middle of the night on the wrong side of the tracks. If she treated someone else the way she had Mattie, Davis might find herself on the receiving end of a fist. Most people they dealt with were strung out on drugs and confrontational. Nothing like Mattie Diener.

"Well," she said, shifting in her seat to face him. "Now that we have your reputation intact, I suppose you'll want to ask me out for dinner and a midnight boat ride. A celebration of sorts."

Bo laughed. "For the record, I never thought my reputation was at risk. As I told you, my observation skills are spot-on. I'm very good at my work."

"You're full of yourself, Lambright."

"Confident sounds better." He glanced sideways at her and grinned. "Sorry, but I have to decline on dinner. I have a mountain of paperwork to finish when we get back to the office." He planned to take tomorrow off, even if it meant putting his cell phone on mute.

"That's too bad. I was going to show you how unruly I could get aboard your boat and tempt you to throw me overboard."

# Chapter Eleven

Mattie placed Amanda on the buggy bench, then helped Nathan climb inside and sit beside his sister. "I'll be right back," she told them. She jogged up the porch steps and retrieved the basket of herbal preparations and another basket with her sewing supplies. Once Bo Lambright delivered the good news yesterday, she'd had a sudden spurt of energy and was able to fill most of the herbal remedy orders. She returned to the buggy and lowered the basket onto the floorboard.

Alvin's buggy pulled into the yard as she was about to board hers. She waited until his horse came to a stop, and he climbed out.

"*Hiya*, Alvin."

"Hi, yourself. Hot day, ain't so?" He removed his hat and wiped his shirt sleeve across his forehead. "I was hoping you would be home."

She motioned to her buggy. "I was just heading

over to Grace's *haus* for the quilting bee. Was there something you needed?"

He shoved his hat on his head, pressing down his thick mop of curls over his ears. He looked at the buggy, smiling nervously at the children who had poked their heads out the window. He wiped his hands along the side seams of his pants. "I, ah . . . I guess it can wait." He motioned to the barn. "Is the lamb in the pen?"

"*Jah*." She had moved Snowball out to the barn yesterday, afraid it wouldn't look good in the report if Bo Lambright spied a barn animal living inside the house. No government authority would have understood, no matter how sick the lamb was.

"There's still some pie on the counter," she said, boarding her buggy. "Help yourself."

Alvin frowned. He scratched the back of his neck and mumbled something on his way to the barn. He was out of sorts. She'd never seen him frown at the mention of pie before.

Mattie clicked her tongue, urging the horse forward. As she pulled out of the driveway, her thoughts drifted to the conversation she had with Grace two months ago, after the men returned from the lumber camp. *"Alvin's never been married,"* Grace had said. Nothing new. Everyone in the district knew his unmarried status when he first moved to the district, and speculations were that he had chosen to relocate to northern Michigan and to their district because the women outnumbered the men three to one. But Grace went on to point out how Alvin Graber had assumed the responsibility of stocking Mattie's wood supply and hadn't missed too many days of checking in on her. Mattie's stomach roiled. Alvin Graber was like an older brother.

Mattie pulled into Grace's driveway and parked next to the row of buggies. She looked forward to spending the day with friends and helping to finish the sewing projects they planned to sell during Badger Creek's annual Fourth of July craft sale.

Grace bounded out of the house and scurried over to Mattie's buggy. "You seem chipper. Did you get caught up on your sleep?" Grace picked up Amanda.

"*Nett* a wink." Mattie hoisted Nathan into her arms.

"That's *nett gut.*" Grace scowled like an old barn cat.

"I got a lot done, though," Mattie said as they headed to the house. "I prepared a few batches of herbs. I made you another batch of poultice for your joints. You hadn't mentioned you needed it, but I figured you must be running low. How are your legs? Did I ask you that yesterday? *Mei* mind's been going a million directions."

Grace went up the porch steps, but didn't go to the door. She walked to the corner of the porch instead and turned to face Mattie. "I'm really worried about you. You can't go too many days in a row without sleep or you'll . . . hit a wall—collapse."

"I can't seem to unwind." Productive insomnia wasn't a bad thing. She'd managed to can a dozen quarts of pickled beets last night in addition to completing everything else on her list.

Grace's face crinkled.

"Don't worry about me, I'm fine." Mattie tapped her friend's hand. "Really, all is well." God had delivered her out of the hands of the enemy yesterday, clearing her from those absurd accusations. Everything was back to normal. Whatever normal was—she hadn't felt normal since Andy died. But she was getting better at hiding the pain. The members in her district believed she had accepted God's will and had adjusted. Maybe if she stopped dwelling on the loneliness she would be able to move forward.

"I'm glad you came." Grace smiled. "Remember yesterday when I asked if you wanted to go with me into town?"

"*Jah.*"

"I had a *doktah*'s appointment." A warm blush spread over Grace's face.

Mattie chuckled. "I know that glow, Grace Eicher. Have you eaten a lot of saltine crackers to settle your stomach too?"

Grace's eyes grew large, giving her secret away. "I'm three months."

"That's *wunderbaar!*" Mattie drew her friend into a hug, then feeling her stiffen, drew back. "Everything is all right with the *boppli, jah?*"

Grace's smile faded. "Ben and I had decided *nett* to have children—I don't want to pass *mei* muscular dystrophy on to—I . . . I don't want *mei* child going through what I've had to endure. What *mei mamm* went through."

"How's Ben taking the news?"

"He's ecstatic. And I am too until . . . Oh, Mattie, how can I ignore the risks? I can't." Grace turned her gaze toward the barn.

"I know the idea of having a *boppli* frightens you, but apparently God's plan differs from what you and Ben decided." Mattie forced herself to sound cheerful. In the back of her mind, she remembered how frightening it was going into early labor with Amanda during Andy's funeral. Amanda's low birth weight had Mattie a nervous wreck for weeks. God had a different plan for her as well.

The screen door opened and Grace's *aenti* Erma poked her head outside. "Is everything all right?"

"*Jah, Aenti.*" Grace leaned toward Mattie and lowered her voice. "She's hovered over me ever since I returned from the *doktah*'s office."

"Enjoy the attention," Mattie said, patting Grace's arm. "Ready to go inside?"

Once they entered, Nathan wiggled to get down.

He pointed toward the other children who had gathered in the corner of the sitting room. His rambunctious spirit was a good sign that he was feeling better. Still, she didn't want him over-doing it.

"Down." He squirmed more.

"Ask nicely, please." She wasn't about to let him make a scene like he had when he head butted her for taking him away from the lamb. Mattie hugged him a little tighter when he continued trying to worm his way out from her hold. She turned to Grace. "They say the twos are terrible, but at three he's wearing *mei* patience thin."

"*Mei* nephews were that way too."

Grace's sister-in-law Susan agreed. "Mitch still tests the depths of *mei* patience."

Nathan finally stopped fighting her and relaxed. He batted his long lashes and pointed at the other children. "*Sei se gut.*"

"That's better. *Nau*, if I put you down, do you promise to be a *gut* boy?"

"*Jah*," he peeped.

She lowered him to the floor and watched as he scurried over to where the children were building a tower with small wooden blocks.

"He's a strong-willed child. Sometimes it takes all *mei* strength to hold him down."

"A husband would cure that problem," Grace whispered. "He'd set little Nathan straight."

Two of the younger teen girls, Alice and Beth,

approached Mattie and Grace. "We'll watch Amanda so you can sew," Alice said.

Catherine Zimmerman arrived. Her two-year-old daughter, Jenny, trotted over to Amanda, and the two girls went with the teens to the back room to play with the other children.

Grace's *aenti* Erma directed Catherine, who was cradling her one-month-old son, to an empty chair at the table. "I'll bring you a cup of decaffeinated tea. Mattie, would you like *kaffi* or tea?"

"*Kaffi* sounds *gut, danki*."

Erma disappeared into the kitchen and, a few moments later, returned with the drinks.

The bishop's wife, Mary, looked up from her quilt block. "Have you decided when you're going back to Ohio, Erma?"

Erma and Grace exchanged smiles.

In unison, the women in the room stopped stitching and looked up.

Holding her hand over her belly, Grace shared her news. Congratulations and well-wishes rang out, and several of the women shared their pregnancy experiences. Mattie's thoughts drifted to when she found out she was pregnant with Nathan and then again with Amanda. Andy was speechless both times.

Mattie's throat swelled. Not wanting her melancholy to put a damper on Grace's good news, she stood. "I forgot *mei* sewing basket in the buggy." She excused herself from the table and rushed to the door. Her lungs constricted. Inhaling short gasps of air, she clutched the banister railing.

The screen door snapped. "Mattie?" Grace came up behind her and placed a hand on her shoulder. "I'm sorry. I wasn't thinking."

Mattie sniffled. "Don't make me cry, Grace. I've been so emotional lately, weeping one minute and singing and bouncing off the walls the next. Someone might think I've either gone mad or am early menopausal."

Grace laughed. "You're only twenty-eight."

Mattie wiped her eyes and chuckled. "You're probably right. I'm going mad."

"It's understandable. You miss Andy. And you've had a rough time these past few days."

Mattie took in a big breath and released it slowly. "I'll meet you inside in a few minutes."

Worry lines formed on Grace's forehead.

"I'll be all right," Mattie insisted. "I just need a minute or two. And I really did leave *mei* sewing basket in the buggy."

Grace gave Mattie's arm a gentle squeeze, then released it. "I'll see you in the *haus*."

Mattie stood, clutching the railing awhile longer. Her prayers lately about having the ability to move forward seemed to go unanswered, mere breaths in the wind, but she lifted her gaze to the blue sky. "Lord, will *mei* heart ever mend? Will I find contentment and true joy again?" She

139

watched the cottony clouds float across the pasture and sighed with the peaceful reminder that God had answered her prayer about Nathan's health, and now that he was getting the medicine, the blisters in his mouth should go away. The heaviness in her chest disappeared as she ambled across the yard to her buggy. She grabbed the sewing basket and the larger basket she had packed with herbal products and returned to the house.

Once she entered the room, the women's chatter stopped midsentence, their needles stalled mid-stitch.

"Mattie," Laura said, making a point to bring her into the conversation. "We were just discussing how pushy the drilling company has been, trying to buy our mineral rights. Have they contacted you?"

Judging by the nervousness of the bunch, that wasn't the topic they were discussing, but Mattie went along with it. "*Jah*, a representative stopped the other day, but Alvin was there to talk to him."

Several of the women's brows peaked at the mention of Alvin's name. Mattie pretended not to notice and took a sip of her coffee.

The women resumed quilting the black-and-gray log-cabin quilt.

A few moments passed before Laura started a new conversation. "Did I tell you the herbal blend you made me the other day worked wonders? *Danki* so much."

Laura had already made a point to tell Mattie last week. She wasn't sure why she was making a fuss about it *nau*. "Anytime you need more just let me know."

"Oh, I will. I told *mei* cousin in Pennsylvania how much better I feel since I started taking it, and she wants to order some," Laura replied.

Mary joined them. "I think Mattie's cure-all concoctions are such a blessing to us all."

Mattie rifled through her sewing supplies and removed a needle and spool of thread.

"Indeed, she healed *mei* gout," Emma said, pointing to her foot. "*Mei* big toe thanks you."

"And *mei* sour stomach," Sadie Knapp added. "I don't have any more acid burning the back of *mei* throat." She glanced at Wilda, who was placing a plate of cookies on the table. "What about you, Wilda?"

"Oh, please," Mattie said, putting an end to their praises. "You're embarrassing me." She didn't like to think of herself as a healer, especially since her *cure-all* concoctions hadn't helped her husband. *The herbs made him worse.*

"But you have helped us all," Sadie said.

The others were quick to agree, but Mattie's thoughts were on Andy lying sick in bed, breathing hard. Could she have prepared him something different? Mattie stood. "I should check on Amanda."

"Amanda is fine," someone said. "Have a

cookie, dear. You look a little weak in the eyes."

Mattie vaguely heard her name called, but when she turned to look at Grace, her friend's face distorted in a blur.

"Mattie?"

*Answer Grace.* But telling herself to respond and doing it were two separate things. Mattie's nerves twitched.

"Mattie, is something wrong?" Grace's voice muffled.

The tremors started. She had them before, first in her hands, then her arms. Her ears rang, drowning out the women's voices.

"Help her sit down," a distant voice said.

Hands were on her shoulders, guiding her. *Stop shaking.* She licked her dry lips. Faces blurred. The room was spinning. The women thought she was losing it—like she had after Andy died.

"Someone get her a glass of water."

"She blacked out yesterday," Grace said, snapping her finger in front of Mattie's face. Someone placed a glass in her hand, told her to drink, then guided the glass to her mouth. Mattie sipped the cold water. Her vision came back into focus and within a few minutes, her jittery nerves started to uncoil. She forced herself to speak. *"Danki."*

Grace tugged on her arm. "What happened?"

Mattie shook her head. It was difficult to keep up the pretense that all was well when no one believed her anyway.

Grace squatted in front of Mattie, eyeing her carefully. "Do you think that bump on your head has anything to do with—?"

"*Nay,*" Mattie said, cutting her friend off. "I think I just hit that wall you were talking about." She caught a glimpse of the confused expressions around her and felt obligated to explain. "I haven't slept much in the last few days."

"Weeks," Grace said. "You haven't slept through the *nacht* in weeks."

Actually, it had been months, but Mattie wouldn't argue the point.

"I get dizzy like that when *mei* sugar drops," Catherine said, pushing the plate of cookies closer.

Grace placed her arm around Mattie's shoulder. "What have you eaten?"

Mattie shook her head. She'd made breakfast for Nathan and Amanda, but only drank a cup of coffee herself.

Grace headed to the kitchen, talking over her shoulder. "I'm going to make you a sandwich to go along with the sweets."

"I don't think I could eat anything." Mattie started to rise, but the room began to spin once more and she had to sit back down.

Grace rushed to her side. "Then go lie down in one of the bedrooms."

Mattie hesitated. "I think you're right about needing sleep, but I'd rather go home and rest." That is, after she dropped off the honey jars at

Green Thumb. The jars had been in the back of her buggy for a few days now and she didn't want to chance losing the account by delaying delivery any longer. She pushed off the chair, and her legs wobbled. "Grace, will you get Nathan and Amanda?"

"I'll keep them with me," her friend said. "You need a few hours of undisturbed sleep."

"Oh, I'll be—" The roomful of women stared at her with pitied gazes. Falling apart in front of Grace was one thing. Her friend had helped her through the darkest time in her life, but Mattie didn't want the others to see her this way.

Grace touched her arm. "Mattie, you won't be able to keep up much longer at the pace you're going. You need uninterrupted rest."

"You'll watch them closely?"

Grace drew back as if offended. "Of course I will."

"I'm sorry. It's just . . ." She couldn't bear something happening to one of them. *Oh, Lord, it's happening again. I'm falling apart, aren't I? Help me, please.*

On the long drive across the county, Bo's mother conducted business over her cell phone about upcoming election strategies with her campaign manager. It didn't bother Bo. His mind was elsewhere. Lingering thoughts of Mattie Diener rattled him. Bats might as well have taken up residence in his stomach. He'd been ill ever since he sat across from her at her kitchen table yesterday afternoon and helplessly watched her tears wash over her face. He couldn't keep the confidential results of the investigation from her. She had to know right then and there the case was closed—she had to.

Why was he going over everything in his mind?

He was glad he told her.

She hadn't trusted him to begin with, but as the relief settled her nerves, color had returned to her otherwise porcelain face.

He'd done the right thing.

Next to him the one-way conversation continued about balloons and banners. Fortunately for him, his mother had a new project. Otherwise she would have sensed his turmoil. Bo hadn't been kicked by a mule in a long time, but he couldn't describe the effect Mattie Diener had on him any other way. Was it because she was an Amish widow, whom Davis had wanted to hang from the clothesline? That must be it. He didn't want the wolf devouring a lamb, and his instinct was to protect her. Yes, that would explain why he wasn't able to mentally close the case.

Bo pulled into the plant nursery and shut off the car's engine. Green Thumb had the largest selection of trees, shrubs, and flowering plants this side of the county. His mother ended her phone call and immediately engaged in another one with the nursery's owner. Her campaigning began the moment she introduced herself. In a short time, they discussed taxes, road improvements, and bringing new businesses to the area. She had the man's vote before Bo had meandered down the first row of potted fruit trees.

Another customer stole the worker's attention, and he excused himself, saying he wanted to hear more about potential fracking contracts. She already had the politician wave down and the jovial laugh.

"Should I start calling you Madam President yet?"

She touched her salon-colored, roller-set tresses and smiled. "I think I could get used to that."

He glanced at his watch. "Well, shall I suggest your first order of business be deciding what you want planted next to the carriage house?"

She eyed the selections and pointed to the impatiens. "I like those."

He stooped to pick up a flat. "How many do you want?"

"Two. But pick out the ones with the best assortment of colors." She motioned to the end of the row. "I'm going to look at the brick pavers."

Bo lifted the tray, walked it back to the counter, then selected another flat and deposited it next to the register. He craned his neck in the general direction his mother went, then hearing a horse's neigh behind him, turned around. An Amish buggy pulled up to the gate and stopped. A woman, whose face was shadowed by her black bonnet, climbed out. She headed to the rear of her buggy.

Bo scanned the area for his mother. She was busy talking with another nursery worker. He glanced at the buggy again as the woman came around the front, a wooden crate in her arms.

"Can I carry that for you?" Drawing closer, he extended his arms.

Mattie Diener's eyes widened a split second in recognition. She looked down. "I can manage."

Of course she wouldn't accept his help. He was an *Englischer*. "How are your children?"

She jerked her head up, her face ashen. "Why do you ask?"

"That wasn't an official question. I told you I was closing the case." He motioned to the crate filled with jars of honey. "Are you sure that isn't too heavy?"

"I'm sure. Thank you, though."

"Okay," he said. "Enjoy the rest of your day, Mrs. Diener."

Bo met his mother and a nursery worker near a stack of landscaping pavers.

"I can arrange delivery for the day after tomorrow, Judge Nettleton," the worker said.

"That should be fine," she replied.

The man tore off a work order. "Just hand this to the cashier and she'll take care of you." The man walked away.

Bo nudged his mother's arm. "Couldn't win his vote?"

"He's a die-hard Democrat." She shrugged. "Win some, lose some." She motioned to the register. "I'm ready to go if you are."

"Sure," he mumbled. His attention caught on Mattie Diener at the counter. He plodded along the dirt path around the cone-shaped evergreens, half listening to his mother's idea of where to build the new planters and half focused on Mattie. She didn't seem like the type of mother to leave her children with someone else to run errands.

"Are you looking forward to seeing her again?" his mother asked.

"Who?"

"Erica." Her brows crinkled.

He played it off. "I don't have much choice. We work together. Norton even assigned us to the same case."

"Oh." Her eyes lit.

"Don't get your hopes up. The case is closed."

"She's a very motivated young woman. I hear she plans to follow in her father's footsteps."

"Politics would suit her." He ambled alongside his mother down the row of rose bushes. The sweet aroma wafted his senses. Several feet ahead, Mattie unloaded the jars, then returned the wooden crate to her buggy. He caught a glimpse of her looking his direction and smiled, but she lowered her head and boarded her buggy.

"I'm sure Erica will be accompanying her father to the luncheon with the drilling executives today. Maybe you could ask her over to the house for dinner sometime next week," she said as they reached the cashier.

Mother had mentioned this afternoon's luncheon last week, but when he brought up the issue of sinkhole developments and possible groundwater contamination after drilling began, he was sure she would wish to attend the luncheon with the fracking executives alone. Hearing that Davis and the senator would be present explained his mother's insistence on him joining her. He shouldn't have mentioned anything about him and Davis working the same case. His mother had as much local power and influence as the senator. She might convince Norton to put them on more cases together.

He ignored her suggestion and directed his attention to the ponytailed woman standing behind the counter. "Did you get these?" he asked the girl and pointed at the trays of impatiens.

"Yep. Is that it?"

He selected a jar of honey and handed it to the cashier. "This too."

Mattie took a few deep breaths to settle her nerves once she was inside her buggy. She never expected to see Bo Lambright again—prayed she wouldn't. She hadn't meant to sound rude when he asked if he could carry the crate, but he'd surprised her showing up here, asking about her children.

Mattie placed her hand on her pounding chest. Other than Andy, no man had ever stolen her breath. She recalled Grace's comment about the attractive *Englischer* and chided herself for allowing her mind to wander. Bo Lambright was an *Englischer*—a government worker at that.

Her racing heart was from lack of sleep. Nothing else. She needed sleep. At least she wouldn't see him again. She tapped the reins, and the horse covered the ground quickly. A few minutes later, she entered her driveway, stopped the buggy next to the barn, and unhitched Blossom. Once she had the harness removed, she fed and watered Blossom, then checked on the lamb before going into the house.

She was more exhausted than she realized. Her head hit the pillow, and she was instantly drifting into a dreamlike state.

# Chapter Twelve

Bo's cell phone rang as he was adjusting his tie in the hall mirror. "Lambright."

"Hey, this is Josh. I thought I'd get your voice mail."

"What's wrong?" He buttoned his shirt collar one-handed.

Silence.

"Josh?" The teen had a history of skipping school and running away from every foster family Bo had placed him in. Bo had relocated him several times, but fifteen-year-olds were difficult to place.

"I couldn't stay."

"Where are you?" He strained to listen for background noises. Nothing. The last time he ran, Bo found him hanging out with thugs in the pool hall in his old neighborhood. Bo mouthed an apology to his mother who was slipping into her heels. "Josh, are you there?"

"Yup." Another long pause. "If I tell you, you're just going to pick me up and take me back."

"You know my hands are tied. We have to go through the proper channels to move you." Bo stepped away from the mirror when his mother removed a tube of lipstick from her pocketbook. She applied the mauve shade with tedious precision. Loitering, no doubt.

Josh remained silent.

Bo stepped into his father's library. "Have I ever done you wrong?"

"No." Josh exhaled a heavy breath. "But you and I both know no one wants me. The system's broken—even you said that. I just wanted to say good-bye."

"Give me time to find—Josh?" Bo glanced at his phone screen. *Call Ended.*

His mother came into the room, a tissue with a lipstick imprint of her mouth in hand. "What was that about?"

"One of the kids I placed . . ." He was probably at the pool hall again. Maybe the county park near his old neighborhood. Either place was known for dope dealing.

"You gave one of those troubled youths your private number? I don't see how that would be safe."

"He's a kid."

"A troubled kid."

Bo scowled. "I seem to remember you once had a heart for abandoned and bruised kids."

"I still do. But now I host events and write very large checks."

Bo smiled. "Yes, I know. I've attended all of your charity dinners."

"Yes, well . . ." She turned her gaze to the oversized bookshelves as if searching for a particular volume in the set of medical encyclopedias. "You're just like Martin. He would have had a houseful of children if I hadn't objected."

"He was a pediatric surgeon. I would hope he liked kids."

She turned back to Bo and smiled. "One was enough for me. You were a handful."

"Ha! I find that hard to believe."

"You're still difficult to handle. If I didn't know better, I would think this was previously arranged to get you out of lunch."

He motioned to the navy suit coat and tan trousers he was wearing. "Would I dress like this if I were planning to stay home?"

She strode to the door and looked back, her eyes scanning the interior. "I think I'm ready to remodel this room," she said, her tone melancholy. "How would you like this to become your study?"

"We can talk about that another time." He had a desk at work he wasn't fond of sitting at too long. He didn't want to disappoint his mother, but he'd rather spend his free time on the lake.

"Maybe Erica can ride along with you to find the boy. You two could always join us at the club later."

He shook his head. "The senator's daughter has no street smarts. Where I need to go—" He'd already said too much. His mother had seen plenty of delinquents in her courtroom from that neighborhood; mentioning the area would only stress her out.

Still groggy, Mattie blinked several times to focus her eyes. How long had she slept? Pulling the blanket back, she eased out of bed. She stumbled down the hall. The house was dark.

Empty.

"Nathan, Amanda?" It took a second to remember Grace had offered to watch the children.

Mattie rubbed her eyes. She hadn't slept that hard in . . . in eighteen months. But at that time it had taken a sedative to knock her out. She went to the kitchen sink and splashed cold water on her face, awakening her senses.

She paused a moment from drying her face with a dish towel from the drawer. "I'm late!" she gasped, rushing to the front door. She grabbed her shawl from the hook and swung the lightweight material around her shoulders. If she hurried, maybe she could get over to Grace's house and return home before the sun went down.

Grace and Ben's buggy pulled into the drive just as Mattie reached the barn. She turned and ran to meet them. "I was on *mei* way out to the barn to harness Blossom. I'm so sorry. I lost track of time. I hope I didn't burden you with watching them too long."

"Of course you didn't, silly." Grace looked at her husband. "We enjoyed having them over, didn't we?"

"Absolutely. This little man is going to be *mei* fishing buddy—when he's feeling better."

Mattie reached for Amanda, who had spread out her arms to be taken. Ben climbed out of the buggy on the other side, holding Nathan. "Is something wrong?"

"I tried to let you sleep as long as possible," Grace said, a hint of concern in her tone.

"What is it?"

"I don't think they're feeling well. Amanda has been cranky, and Nathan started to feel warm about an hour ago. I think he might have a fever."

Ben touched his palm against Nathan's forehead. "He has more heat radiating off him than pavement in full sun. Feel his head, Grace."

Grace rested her hand on Nathan's forehead. "He's boiling."

Mattie clutched Amanda tighter in her arms. "Bring him inside, would you, please?"

Grace hurried ahead of them and held the door open.

Mattie ran her hand over Amanda's forehead. Cool to the touch and dry. She handed Amanda back to Grace once Ben laid Nathan on his bed. Red-faced and roasting, her son barely opened his eyes to look at her. "When did you say it started?"

"No more than an hour ago."

Nathan rolled to his side, coughed hard, and vomited.

"Oh dear." Mattie helped him sit up. He vomited again. This time down the front of his shirt and onto the bedding. "Did he eat something red?" *This can't be blood. Lord, please.*

"I don't remember." Grace handed Amanda to Ben. "I'll get a wet rag and some water." She dashed out of the room.

*"Bruder kronk."* Amanda's lip puckered.

"How about we let Nathan rest." Ben left the room with Amanda, bribing her with a cookie if she didn't cry.

Nathan's face was washed out. His eyes drooped, and the corners of his mouth had blotches of red stomach contents. He heaved another time before Grace returned, this time dry. He held his stomach and cried out, heaving once more.

Grace handed Mattie the glass of water.

"Nathan, honey, can you drink some water?"

He shook his head.

"Try to take a sip. It'll help your throat." She held the glass up to his mouth.

"Beets. He ate some pickled beets at lunch," Grace said.

*Danki, Lord.* Mattie urged him to drink. He did, but after one sip, he grasped his throat with one hand and used his other one to push the glass away.

"He needs to see the *doktah*," Grace said.

Mattie set the glass on the bedside table. "It's probably the antibiotic. The instructions said it might cause an upset stomach—even vomiting and diarrhea, and—"

"*Nett* a fever, though. He needs to go to the hospital."

Mattie bit her bottom lip to stop it from trembling. *Lord, why is this happening all over again?* He'd been fever-free since leaving the hospital. She eased the soiled quilt off Nathan. He could use the blanket from the sofa to sleep tonight.

"Ben and I will go with you. Get your cloak."

Mattie's eyes burned. If she returned to the hospital, she might be accused of being a bad mother. The authorities would come knocking on her door again.

"Mattie?"

"I'll give him some feverfew." Mattie rose from the bed. "I'll be back in a minute, Nathan." His face pinched without opening his eyes. She hurried to the kitchen and opened the cabinet where she stored the herbal blends. A warm broth would help. It had to.

Grace came up behind her. "Mattie, what if this is something serious?"

"It's *nett* serious." Her harsh rebuke not only cut Grace's words off, it caused her friend to take a step backward. Mattie glanced at Amanda sitting on Ben's lap at the table eating a cookie. *Calm yourself. Take a deep breath. Inhale. Exhale.* Once she released some of the pent-up tension, she turned to Grace. "All children have coughs and colds."

Grace's face puckered with concern. "And you believe that's all this is?" Grace spoke slowly, as though deliberately choosing her words. Her friend must think she was a fragile egg about to crack.

"You know why I can't take him back to that *doktah*," Mattie said. She leaned closer and whispered, "That man was here last Friday to"— her voice wobbled—"to take Nathan away from me."

"Did he tell you that?"

"*Nay*, but you've heard the stories. The government authorities treated some of the other districts harshly. For *nay* reason."

"Mattie, we haven't had that problem."

"Yet." Mattie hardened her expression. "I won't let them take *mei* children."

"They can't take them unless they can prove you're unfit."

"The government can do anything they want."

Grace frowned.

"You don't understand. The questions the government man asked about our lifestyle, the way we live . . . he was judgmental."

Grace sighed. "None of this has to do with Nathan's fever. You said it yourself. Children get sick. It doesn't make you a bad *mamm*."

Mattie slumped into the nearest chair and buried her face in her hands. "Then why do I feel like I am? Nathan's been sickly since birth. Nothing I do helps him." Nothing she'd done for her husband helped either. He still died.

# Chapter Thirteen

Bo pulled up to the curb in front of the pool hall located on the corner of First Street and Madison Avenue. The last time Josh fled his foster home, Bo found him here at midnight, hustling a game of pool for a pack of smokes.

Bo sat with his car idling and scanned the area. Even in daylight, this section of town showed its seedy part. The windows on the liquor store across the street were barred, and gang graffiti adorned the old brick building. This side of the tracks was no place for a kid.

Bo climbed out of the car and clicked the remote door lock. Near the Stop sign, a group of teenagers shot him an over-the-shoulder glance before resuming their conversation. Bo studied them a moment, but didn't see anyone who resembled Josh. Proceeding toward the dilapidated pool hall, he spotted a gray-bearded man slumped against the clapboard siding, drinking from a bottle wrapped in a brown paper bag. Although it wasn't uncommon for the homeless to loiter in an alley, Bo continued into the building with caution.

A set of large speakers hung on the wall, vibrating to the beat of a bass guitar. No one seemed to care that the high volume of the music distorted the song lyrics. The thick haze of smoke irritated his eyes. Bo walked past a group of men, ignoring their snide comments about his suit. He headed toward the row of pool tables.

"Cop," someone called out.

Voices murmured as people shifted and faded into the background. Several youths pushed past him and bolted out the back door.

Bo spotted Josh at the far table, crouched low, a cigarette dangling from his mouth as he eyed his next pool shot. *Didn't take you long to fit back in with the crowd.* Bo strode up to the table and stopped in front of the side pocket where Josh was aiming his cue stick.

Josh pocketed the cue ball. "Thanks for getting in my shot, Bo."

"Don't mention it." He cornered the table, but as he neared Josh, two men dressed in jeans, leather vests, and sleeveless T-shirts planted themselves in his path, arms crossed. Bo had learned years ago to avoid eye contact with people bold enough to block his path. Usually they were eager to stamp out their territory, and Bo wasn't one who believed fighting solved anything. Apparently these men were not of the same belief. One jerked a cue stick from another pool player's hand. He thrust it horizontally at Bo, catching his chest and pushing him toward the wall.

"We don't like visitors in suits," the man growled.

The other man roughly searched Bo's backside with his hand until he located and lifted his wallet from his back pocket. He should have thought to lock his wallet in the car. Not that his car was any safer in this neighborhood.

"Stop," Josh shouted. "He's not a cop."

"How do you know?" The man pressed the cue stick harder against Bo's chest.

Sucking in a deep breath, Bo reached for the stick. He pushed back, reducing some of the crushing pressure on his upper body.

"He's my friend." Josh raised his stick handle. "Let him go."

"The kid's right," the darker-haired man said as he inspected one of Bo's business cards from his wallet. "He's not a cop. Investigator for Child Services."

The man holding the cue stick gave one more thrust, then twisted the stick away. Bo could breathe.

Josh tossed his pool stick on the table. "Come on, Bo. Let's go." He stormed toward the door.

Bo started to follow, then turned back to the man who still held his wallet. But the burly man tapping the fat part of the pool stick against his free hand stared with what appeared to be an eager grin to use it, so Bo pivoted around. His license and credit cards would be a hassle to replace, but even that wasn't worth being pulverized.

Footsteps followed Bo and Josh across the room.

Bo fisted his hands. *Keep walking. Don't look back.* He repeated the mantra in his mind.

Fresh air rushed into Bo's lungs as they stepped outside. He stole a glance over his shoulder. From inside the building, the man stood at the window, peering at them. Bo aimed the remote keypad at his Impala, clicked the lock release, and opened the passenger door. "Lose the cigarette and get in."

Josh hesitated.

Bo's jaw twitched. "You just called me your friend," he said, his words soaked with sarcasm.

"Duh, someone had to save your sorry—"

"Don't say it." A few hours on the street and the kid was a smart-mouthed punk again. He motioned with a head nod at the open car door. "This isn't how I want to spend my afternoon. Now, lose the cigarette and get in before I lose my patience."

Josh took a long drag off his cigarette before tossing the butt on the sidewalk. He snubbed it out with the toe of his sneaker while exhaling a cloud of gray smoke.

The kid wasn't so bad—misdirected, but nothing like the thugs with whom Josh was playing pool. At least Josh had a chance of making his life better—that is, if he stopped running away from every foster home.

Bo fastened his seat belt, started the engine, and pulled away from the curb.

"I'm starved," Josh said.

"Mrs. Walker probably saved you a plate from supper."

"Great," Josh sneered. "Have you eaten her meat loaf?"

"I can't say that I have." Bo chuckled, remembering when he had made a follow-up visit to Mrs. Walker's home to check up on the last two children he'd placed in her care. The woman was in the process of making supper, and none of the older children seemed enthused with her pot roast. Bo couldn't blame them. He'd never seen pot roast with white gravy before. When she had extended a dinner invitation to him, Bo respectfully declined, opting instead to eat a hamburger at the little diner down the road.

"Second thought, I'm not hungry. Seriously, I've eaten Spam straight from the can that tasted better."

The mere mention of food made Bo's stomach growl. He hadn't eaten anything since breakfast either. He could stop at a diner. No, that wasn't an option. His wallet was stolen, most likely his identity too. He would notify the credit card company ASAP.

He turned right onto Pine View road, which led to his mother's house. If she smelled cigarette smoke on Josh's breath, she would declare him a "juvenile delinquent" and be upset with Bo for bringing him into her home. But the kid had to eat. Besides, Josh wasn't a delinquent. He was

Bo's Little Brother. Not that Josh participated much in the Big Brother program. Every time Bo had brought up them hanging out together and shooting basketballs, Josh declined.

A short time later, he turned onto the cobblestone driveway.

Josh sat forward in his seat. "Whoa, dude." He craned his neck. "Who lives here?"

"This is my mother's place. I know you're hungry. We can get something to eat while I make a few phone calls." Bo pulled up beside the detached four-car garage and cut the engine.

"Are you calling Mrs. Walker?"

"I need to tell her you're safe. She does worry about you."

Josh rolled his eyes. "I find that hard to believe. I'm one of eight. She probably didn't figure out I was missing until suppertime."

An image of hungry children clamoring for their place at the table replayed in Bo's mind. So did the familiar sounds of his own youth come to life with chairs scraping the hardwood floor and dishes clattering. *"Wash your hands, Thomas. You weren't born in the barn. Malinda, place he potatoes next to your father's plate. Verna, check the rolls . . ."* His mother's voice echoed.

"Bo?"

"I'm sorry." Bo shook his head. He didn't need any of those issues clouding his mind. "Did you say something?"

"I asked how many people live here."

"Two. My mother and me. Well, three. She has a live-in housekeeper." He opened the car door, then glanced sideways at Josh who hadn't even unfastened his seat belt. "You coming in?"

Josh scrambled to release his buckle and climb out of the car. He walked beside Bo, his gaze climbing up the side of the house like a rose trellis. "I've never been in a house this big."

Bo smiled, recalling his first impression of the estate's enormity. The lake house was a cramped two-bedroom vacation cottage until his mother deemed it wasn't large enough to make it their permanent residence. The size of the house didn't matter to Bo; he spent the majority of his free time down by the lake.

They entered the house through the back door, wiped their feet on the rug in the utility room, then headed to the kitchen. The housekeeper, Mrs. Botello, had the day off, so the room was dark and void of activity. Bo opened the refrigerator and peered inside. He picked up one storage container and popped the lid off, but couldn't decipher what the leftover was and slipped it back on the shelf. "I hope you like ham and cheese."

"Sounds good."

"Mustard or mayo?"

"Mayo."

He set the items on the spotless granite countertop, then removed a loaf of pumpernickel bread from the bread box and two plates from the cabinet.

"Bo, I thought I heard—" Mother halted at the sight of Josh. Her posture stiffened.

"This is Josh Messer. Josh, this is my mother." She made a slight nod in the visitor's direction. "How do you do?"

"Good." Josh sported a wide smile. "How 'bout yourself?"

"Very well, thank you." Her brow quirked, then relaxed.

Bo motioned to the food on the counter. "I'm making sandwiches. Have you eaten?"

"Yes," his mother said. "I couldn't very well cancel our lunch date with Senator Delanie and the others on such short notice." She crossed the room and entered the butler's pantry.

Josh leaned closer to Bo. "She really knows a senator?"

"Yes. And the governor too." Bo slathered the dark slices of bread with mayo.

His mother returned with a bag of chips and a box of store-bought gingersnap cookies. "I offered Erica a rain check on your behalf."

Bo looked up from assembling the sandwiches and forced a smile. "Did you choose a day and time too?"

"A few dates, in fact. This Friday is the annual Hope House Charity Golf Classic. Senator Delanie and the mayor are two of the participants.

I think it would be beneficial for you to be present. I can't stress enough their influential value. Next month is the gala. Great Northern Expeditions has generously offered to sponsor the event."

"It sounds like I'm being groomed for politics."

Ignoring his comment, she turned toward Josh. "What would you like to drink? We have milk, soda, juice, or iced tea."

"What kind of soda?"

As his mother listed the variety of brands, Bo cut the sandwiches and placed them on the plates. The golf classic on Friday wasn't much time to come up with a valid reason not to attend. Perhaps he could trade his on-call time. He'd worry about the gala later.

"Bo, what would you like to drink?"

"Milk, please. But I can get it." His cell phone rang. Bo reached into his pocket, glanced at the caller ID, *Out of Area*, then pressed the Accept button. "Hello?"

"May I speak with Bo Lambright, please?"

The woman's voice was barely audible. He covered his open ear to block the clunking sounds of ice cubes being dropped into Josh's glass. "This is he."

Silence.

"Hello?" He made his way into the dining room where it was quieter. "Are you still there?"

"*Jah*, I'm sorry. This is . . . this is Mattie Diener."

# Chapter Fourteen

A sob caught in the back of Mattie's throat, and she clasped her hand over the phone in the hospital waiting room to muffle her cry. She closed her eyes and let a few seconds pass. Calling Bo Lambright was a knee-jerk decision after Grace and Ben took Amanda down to the cafeteria. "I'm sorry. I shouldn't have bothered you."

"You're not a bother. Tell me what's wrong." His soft tone was calming, tranquil.

Dare she trust him—an *Englischer* who, only yesterday, threatened to take her *sohn*? Contacting him had been a mistake.

"Mrs. Diener?"

But just this afternoon he'd told her the case was closed—unofficially, but closed nonetheless. She followed the medication instructions. Did everything he had told her to do. "I gave him that medicine. Just as you said." Her voice broke into hiccupping gasps. Her lungs tightened. *Breathe.*

*God, where are You?*

She wiped her hand over her tear-streaked face. *Calm down. Breathe.* She sounded unbalanced even to her own ears.

"Mrs. Diener, I know something has upset you. Is your son okay?"

"They—they won't tell me anything. They won't let me be with him. What did you say in your report?"

"Who won't let you be with him?"

"The *doktah*, the nurses . . . You said the case was closed."

"Are you at the hospital?"

She nodded, her voice too choked up to speak.

"Hello, Mrs. Diener? Can you hear me?"

"*Jah*," she squeaked. "I'm at . . . the hospital. I have to know what's wrong with *mei sohn*."

"Is someone there with you? Someone I can talk—"

"He's just a *boppli*. I know he's scared without me by his side." She leaned her shoulder against the concrete wall where the courtesy phone hung, twisting the long cord between her fingers. "I thought this nightmare was over—I believed you."

"You sit tight. I'm on my way."

Mattie caught a glimpse of a hospital worker in blue scrubs in her peripheral vision and hung up the phone. The nurse walked into the waiting room and circled to leave. "No, wait." Mattie rushed to the woman and clamped her hand over the nurse's arm. "How is *mei sohn*?"

"The doctor is still running tests on him."

"Can I see him?"

The nurse shook her head. "Doctor Wellington asked that you continue to wait here."

"But he needs me."

The nurse flinched and looked down at Mattie clasping her arm.

Mattie hadn't realized her grip had tightened. She released her hold. "I'm sorry. I—I'm worried. I want to know if *mei sohn* is okay. I want to see him."

"I'm sure the doctor will have news shortly." The nurse left the room.

Mattie paced to the end of the small waiting area and back. The vinyl cushioned chairs positioned along the wall were all empty. A coffee table in the corner of the room held a lamp and a stack of magazines. Nothing she was interested in looking at. Her mind was too restless, too worried. A framed picture of children flying kites on a windy day caught her eye. The children looked happy, carefree. If only her Nathan could enjoy a few blissful days. The room was quiet, the television blessedly silent. She wanted to pray. But the only word that came was *why*. Why did God allow this to happen? *Stop,* she scolded herself. If she kept asking why, what was to stop God from turning His ear from her cry?

*Don't abandon me now, please.* She closed her eyes. *Focus on praise.*

*Lord, You are kind and compassionate. Full of grace and mercy—full of wonder. There is none like You. You alone can tell the wind where to blow, command the mountains to fall down, and send rain to these dry bones. You alone can heal Nathan.*

Warm tears spilled down her face. Thankfully, Amanda was with Grace and Ben and not in the room to witness her mother's emotional unraveling. Her daughter's sensitive nature made her skittish around strangers—even church members —and more so when Amanda sensed change. If her child shut down emotionally, Mattie might too.

*Lord, where are You? Tell me Nathan will be all right.*

Mattie lapped the room another time.

"Mama!"

Mattie spun around at the sound of her daughter's high-pitched squeal. Amanda leaned out from Grace's hold, extending her little arms toward Mattie. "Mama."

A flash of guilt sped through Mattie as Grace passed Amanda to her. Her little girl needed her mother.

Grace took a seat opposite Mattie. "Have you heard anything?"

"Only that the *doktah* is still running tests. Where's Ben?"

"He's dawdling near the nurses' desk, hoping to overhear some news."

Mattie bounced Amanda in her arms. It gave her a reason to burn some energy and brought a sweet smile to her daughter's face at the same time.

A few moments later, Ben entered the room, head down.

"Anything?" Grace asked.

Ben shook his head. "They're as tight-lipped as a sealed jar of jam."

Grace leaned her head out the door and looked both ways. "I don't understand. What reason do they have to be so closemouthed?"

"They won't let me see him either," Mattie said.

Grace looked at her husband. "Can they do that? Can they keep a mother away from her *boppli*?"

"Maybe their tests are such that another person would be in the way."

Mattie hoped it wasn't something more serious. By the time they arrived at the hospital, Nathan's temperature was normal, but several places on his body had turned a dark shade of red. The emergency room doctor was alarmed enough to admit him immediately. She couldn't shake the haunting image of the doctor's stern glare after he studied the chart from Nathan's previous admission.

Mattie eased into a chair, cradling Amanda close in her arms. She gently stroked her daughter's soft cheek with the pads of her fingers. Amanda's eyelids flickered closed, then opened as she fought sleep. This unfamiliar environment and the booming voice that spoke from time to time over the loudspeaker startled her every time. Finally, her tiny frame wilted, and her heavy eyelids remained closed. *Soon we will all go home, sleep in our own beds, and everything will return to normal. I promise.*

She glanced at Grace and Ben, who were seated next to the lamp table in the corner of the room. Ben flipped through the pages of a magazine from the table, and Grace removed a ball of yarn and knitting needles from her handbag. They were good friends.

"You two don't have to stay. I'll be okay."

"We want to be here with you." Grace motioned to Amanda asleep in Mattie's arms. "If she starts to get heavy or you need to stretch your legs, I'll be glad to hold her."

"*Danki.*" Mattie gazed at her daughter, wishing she could find the same peaceful rest.

Bo reached the waiting room and spotted Mattie immediately. Holding Amanda in her arms, Mattie's head was back, her face tilted upward, staring at the ceiling without blinking. He stood in the doorway a brief moment, studying her blotchy face, her red-rimmed eyes puffy from crying. Something about her weariness wrenched his heart. At the moment, her sweet, gentle spirit and simple ways were vulnerable to a world she knew nothing about. Prompted to say something positive—something reassuring—a lump grew in his throat, blocking his ability to speak. He crossed the room in a few long strides and stood before her. "Mrs. Diener?"

Slowly, she turned her attention to him. Her bright-blue eyes, dim with despair, locked with his.

He cleared his throat. "How are you doing?" He could answer that question himself. Her eyes were glazed, and the careworn expression depicted a person who'd cried endless hours and looked near exhausted.

"I'm okay." Her weak voice said different. She sat up straighter, repositioning the sleeping infant in her lap to do so. "I'm sorry I interrupted you. I didn't expect you to come."

"You weren't interrupting anything." He motioned to the chair. "Would it be all right if I sit down?"

Mattie looked beyond him.

Bo followed her gaze over his shoulder to an Amish woman and man seated across the room. The woman's hands seemed to be frozen mid-stitch. The man, a few years younger than Bo, closed the magazine he'd been reading. An outsider asking to sit next to an Amish woman wouldn't bode well in their district. He could almost hear the chatter already. Even something as simple as wanting to help Mattie would be perceived by some Amish as detestable—evil for a woman of faith to allow an *Englischer* to sit so close. He shouldn't have put her on the spot.

"I don't mind if you sit, Mr. Lambright."

He looked behind him again at the couple. They eyed him carefully with hardened, unyielding expressions. No surprise. Of course they wouldn't appreciate an outsider conversing with their friend or maybe relative. But Mattie had called him.

Bo eased into the chair beside Mattie and turned to face her. "I take it Nathan's condition didn't get any better."

"He started vomiting. I thought it was the medicine, but his fever shot up too."

"How is he now?"

She lowered her head and fiddled with her daughter's dress, straightening the wrinkled folds in the maroon material. "I haven't heard anything."

"Still? You called me over an hour ago." Judging by the couple shuffling in their seats behind him, they didn't approve of Mattie's call. She would be in trouble with her district, no doubt. But once he recognized the desperation in her voice over the phone, he'd made arrangements with his mother to drive Josh back to his foster home so Bo could go directly to the hospital.

"All they said was that they were running tests and I should wait here." She looked him in the eye. "Why are they keeping me from him?"

He shook his head. "I don't know. What type of tests are they running?"

She shrugged. "The nurse didn't say."

Odd. Most families are encouraged to stay with their child. Especially someone as young as Nathan, who didn't speak much English. "How long have you been here?"

Mattie looked at the couple.

"Three hours," the woman said.

"Closer to four." The man stood and set the magazine on the table. "I don't have much experience with hospitals, but it seems strange for a *doktah* or even a nurse not to update Mattie on her *sohn*'s condition."

"I agree." If the child were his, Bo would stand at the nurses' station and refuse to budge until someone talked with him. He wouldn't have demonstrated nearly the patience and self-control Mattie had if the roles had been reversed. Faith was her pillar of strength. No one but God could give her such resilience.

The bearded man walked to the far side of the room and turned around. "Maybe being Amish has something to do with the worker's avoidance."

Bo shook his head. "I don't think so, Mr. . . ."

The man halted midstep and faced Bo. "Eicher." He paused a half second, and his expression softened. "But you can call me Ben." He motioned to the woman holding the knitting needles. "This is *mei* wife, Grace. We're Mattie's neighbors."

"It's nice to meet you. I'm Bo Lambright." He skipped sharing his association with Mattie. If they were a tight community like most Amish districts, they already knew his involvement. Besides, Grace looked like the same woman he'd seen at Mattie's house the day he delivered the antibiotic. An *Englischer* in her house would have brought up an arsenal of questions. More would follow gauging by the couple's initial reaction. The fact that Mattie had been bold enough to call him said a lot about her character. Although after meeting her the first time, he'd noted her demeanor wasn't as meek as he'd expected. Probably why he had a difficult time erasing her from his thoughts.

"Maybe you can get some information about Nathan," Grace said. "The staff has gone out of their way to avoid us."

"You got that right," Ben said, adding, "A nurse even turned and walked the other way when she made eye contact with me."

A coincidence? Or did it have something to do with Mattie signing Nathan out of the hospital the last time against medical advice?

Mattie, who had been silently coiling a lock of her daughter's light-brown hair around her finger, looked up when the conversation stopped. She released the tiny curl and wiped her tearstained face with her hand.

Feeling pressure to ease her bewildered expression, words spilled out of Bo's mouth. "I'll try to find out whatever I can. Although I must warn you, I don't think they'll tell me anything since I'm not here on official business."

She sniffled. "Would you *please* ask them if I can see him? I don't want him to think I left him."

Bo's heart softened to mush. A mother shouldn't be separated from her child this long. Not when there wasn't a justifiable cause. He stood. "I'll be back in a few minutes."

*Lord, give me wisdom. She's desperate, and I don't know how to help her.*

Bo headed down the hallway. A man dressed in a chef's coat was unloading food trays from a dietary cart. The scent of meat loaf teased his stomach. Mattie's call had taken him by such surprise that he left the house without even thinking about grabbing one of the ham and cheese sandwiches to eat on his way to Badger Creek. Had Mattie eaten anything all day? It was after six. He recalled as a child, supper was always on time.

A blond-haired nurse sat behind the large desk. "Can I help you?"

"Yes, can you tell me what room Nathan Diener is in?"

"Are you a family member, sir?"

"No."

"I'm sorry. I cannot release that information."

"It is visiting hours, isn't it?" His watch wasn't wrong. And the sign posted on the wall clearly stated visitation was until nine.

"I'm just going by the doctor's . . . orders—you look familiar." Her brows squeezed together. "Child Services?"

"Yes, that's right. We met the other day," Bo said calmly. "Will you check if the doctor is available to speak with me?" The nurse didn't need to know he wasn't there on official business.

"I'll have her paged." The nurse picked up the phone, dialed zero, and waited. "This is the charge nurse, Heather Merchant. Will you page Doctor Wellington to call the nurses' station, please?" She lowered the receiver. "It shouldn't be long, but if you'd like to sit in the waiting room, I'll let you know when the doctor calls back."

"I think I'll wait here, if you don't mind." Nurses were trained not to talk about patient information in public areas, but he'd overheard privileged information before by loitering by the desk.

"Can I get you a cup of coffee while you wait? I think the pot in the lounge is fresh."

"No, thank you." He strolled a few feet away, but still within earshot, and leaned against the wall. His mind began to sort the details. No visitors allowed—including the mother. The nurse hadn't been surprised to see him again. A sinking feeling washed over him. He dug his hand into his pocket and retrieved his cell phone. No messages. Maybe he was too analytical. He hadn't picked up anything suspicious from

Mattie. Worry, fear, natural signs. Bo sighed. Maybe he'd missed key clues because he'd been too consumed by the pain in her eyes to detect anything wrong with the situation.

Bo pushed off the wall. He returned to the desk. "I think I will wait in the waiting room," he said. "Will you be sure to notify me when the doctor calls?"

"Absolutely."

He took a few steps away, then pivoted around. "Sorry, I don't mean to interrupt you again, but did you know the family has been waiting for several hours to hear something?"

Her forehead crinkled and she looked in either direction. "I'm not at liberty to discuss any details," she whispered. "But yes, I'm aware."

Bo's shoulders slumped under the weight of the news. What was he going to tell Mattie? He took a few steps down the hall and stopped. A uniformed officer was entering the waiting room.

## Chapter Fifteen

*Be strong. Be still. Be faithful. God is in control.* Mattie tried to meditate on those thoughts. But despite her best efforts not to dwell on Nathan's illness, the longer she sat in the hospital waiting room without word of her son's condition, the more worry consumed her. She closed her eyes. *Worry is doubt and doubt is lack of faith. I have faith in You, Lord. I do . . . I hope—is it enough?*

An image of Nathan's frail, lifeless body floated across her mind. Her eyes shot open. Exhaling a slow breath through pursed lips, she willed her faith to stop wavering, and to focus on the blessings God had bestowed upon her. Mattie gazed at her daughter asleep in her arms. She had to believe that Nathan was resting comfortably too. Any minute Bo would return with news that her son was fine.

She closed her eyes again. *May Your will prevail, Lord. But please send Bo Lambright back with information about Nathan's condition.* Mattie needed to hear something. She would deal with whatever lot she'd been given. After all, she was expected to follow the Amish way—accept trials and tribulations. What was taking Bo so long?

A man cleared his throat. Mattie looked up fully expecting to see Bo, but instead cast her eyes on a police officer standing before her, a small black notepad flipped open in his hand.

*Nathan? Lord, no, please!*

"Are you Martha Irene Diener?"

Her throat dried.

Grace leapt off her chair. She grasped Mattie's hand, applying increasing pressure.

Mattie swallowed to wet her throat. The police officer's image blurred as tears sprang up in her eyes. "*Jah*," she rasped. "I'm Martha Diener."

"Do you live at 44801 Mulberry—"

"Is *mei sohn* dead?" *Please say no. Please say no. Please say no.*

His thin lips tightened, forming a straight line. "Ma'am, I'll need you to come with me to the police station."

Mattie glanced down at Amanda, then peered over at Grace, too stunned to speak. For some strange reason he didn't want to tell her about Nathan here. It didn't make sense.

Her friend reached down, slipped her arms under Amanda, and lifted her up. Amanda's whimper brought Mattie to her feet. She started to reach for her, but the officer stepped in front of her, blocking her path.

"Ma'am, I have a warrant for your arrest."

Despite his best effort to walk away, Bo had to find out why the police officer went into the pediatric floor's waiting room. He had a sinking suspicion that it had something to do with Nathan's hospitalization. The doctor must have involved the authorities. Had Mattie told him everything?

He headed toward the waiting room, but stopped short of going inside when he spotted Erica Davis and his boss rounding the corner from the lobby. Apparently, while he was consumed with ways to console Mattie, he'd let the truth slip past him—she *had* abused her child. Otherwise there wouldn't be a reason to call the police and social services.

His boss's eyes narrowed as he approached Bo. "Lambright, what are you doing here?"

Standing next to Norton, Davis crossed her arms. "I received a call that Nathan Diener was readmitted to the hospital."

Norton smiled apologetically. "Sorry you were called in on your day off. I'll have to do something about the slipups in dispatch."

"It's no big deal."

"Have you seen the boy?" Davis asked.

Bo shook his head. For Norton to make the forty-five-minute jaunt to this side of the county, the boy must be on death's door. *"He started vomiting; I thought it was the medicine."* Mattie's words rolled over in his mind. Bo hadn't even thought to question her about blisters inside his mouth. A sick feeling came over him.

A baby's cry stole his attention. He peeked into the waiting room, then seeing Amanda and Mattie both reduced to tears, wished he hadn't.

Her friend, Grace, tried to soothe the infant by rocking Amanda in her arms, but the bawling child held her arms toward her mother as the police officer led Mattie to the door. Bo stepped aside, and Mattie pinned him with a glare so cold it was as if another person were looking at him.

"I believed you," she said.

As the police officer escorted her down the hall, her fierce stare bore a hole into Bo's heart. Her words echoed. Bo put his chin on his chest. *Lady, I believed you too.*

The child thrashed in Grace's arms, wailing "Mama" so loudly a fleet of nurses were summoned to respond.

"Take care of *mei bopplis*, Grace."

Davis wormed between the swarm of nurses, producing the legal document from her attaché case. "This is a signed court order giving temporary custody of Martha Diener's two children, three-year-old Nathan Paul Diener and eighteen-month-old Amanda Grace Diener, to the State of Michigan Child Protective Services. I'll ask that you release the child at this time." She reached for the toddler, but the frightened child clung to Grace's neck.

Grace turned her pleading eyes at Bo. "Amanda's frightened. Couldn't I hold her for a while longer?"

"No, ma'am."

The child's arms clung to Grace's neck. Davis practically had to pry the child off.

Amanda made a piercing scream that reverberated against the corridor walls and reached the barren recesses within Bo's soul. The poor child didn't know her life was about to change.

Davis thrust the squirming toddler against Bo's chest. "I can't hold her," she said, handling

Amanda like a hot potato. He barely had a hold on the child before Davis released her grip.

"*Shh*," he said softly.

Amanda reached her arms out to her mother, now at the end of the hall.

Before turning the corner toward the bank of elevators, Mattie looked over her shoulder, her face wet with tears. "Mama *liebs* you, Amanda."

His heart was seared by the gut-wrenching scene. A mother and child's bond isn't easily broken, and he managed to get caught in the middle of this one. *Separate yourself. You're blinded by the fact that she's Amish.*

"Mama!"

Another shrill cry caused the hairs on the back of his neck to stand on end. "You're going to be okay, sweetie." He patted her back, repeating the words, reassuring the girl. If the child were older, she would have detected the apprehension in his voice. Amanda wasn't like the other at-risk children he'd rescued. This didn't feel like a rescue at all. The image of the child torn from her mother would haunt him forever.

He had to desensitize, to distance himself from this case. Not all Amish homes were centered on love. He learned that firsthand. Perspiration gathered on his brow as he jostled Amanda in his arms.

"Job getting to you?" Norton said under his breath.

"I guess." Bo tilted his face toward the ceiling hoping his burning eyes would reabsorb the developing tears. He had no sympathy in his heart for an abusive mother, so why had Mattie Diener's case affected him to this degree?

Amanda arched her back and let out an even louder scream. Maybe if he sat some place quiet, she would settle down. Bo slipped into the waiting room and took a seat in the corner. He wasn't sure what arrangements Davis and Norton had already made. But until it was time to go, he hoped to somehow settle the child. "I'm sorry you have to go through this." He patted her back, and when that didn't work, he rocked gently. The rhythmic movement eased the child's tension. She stared up at him, her big blue eyes wet with tears. Either she was beginning to trust him or she'd run out of steam. Either way, Bo was thankful she'd calmed down.

Ben and Grace approached him. "Why did the police officer take Mattie?" Ben asked.

Bo shook his head. "I don't know any of the details."

"She hasn't done anything wrong," Grace said, sniffling. "What's going to happen to her?"

Ben reached his arm around Grace's waist. "Can *mei* wife and I take Amanda home with us?"

"Please," the woman pleaded.

The transition would certainly be easier on the child. Bo's heart twisted at the agony. That wasn't

186

how the system worked. "I'm sorry. Only a judge can make that decision."

"We would take *gut* care of her," Grace said. "We've been part of Amanda's life since the day she was born. We took care of her and Nathan earlier today."

Davis raised her brow at Bo. "We need to go."

Amanda started to cry again when Bo stood.

"Please, wait." Grace followed them into the hall. "Tell us where you're taking Amanda."

"That's against policy." Davis reached for Amanda. "I'll take her now and meet you in the lobby."

Bo released Amanda, then reached into his front shirt pocket for a business card and pen. Amanda's crying echoed down the corridor as he jotted his cell number on the back and handed the card to Ben. "I can be reached at these numbers. For now, Amanda will be placed in a temporary foster home. The whereabouts is private information, but I'll make sure she's properly cared for."

"What about Mattie?" Grace dabbed her eyes with a tissue. "Are you going to tell her where you're taking her daughter?"

Bo shook his head. "Either Erica Davis or I can answer what questions Mattie—Mrs. Diener might have."

"This is exactly what Mattie feared," Grace told her husband. "Didn't she say they would take Nathan?"

Her husband nodded.

"I thought she was making something out of nothing, but she was right." Grace glared at Bo. "Why is this happening?"

For the police to take Mattie into custody, something had happened. But the pat answer he normally gave didn't seem right. They didn't deserve his typical evasive response where he deferred most questions to the state attorney. "I haven't been briefed about the situation, so I don't have an answer." Still sounded like a pat reply.

"Will they let us see Mattie at the police station?"

"I'm not familiar with their policy." His responsibility was to provide a safe environment for the children, not to visit the person responsible for inflicting the harm. "If you don't have any more questions . . ." He turned before they had a chance to respond. *Desensitize.* He took a few steps toward the door, then stopped. "Do you need a ride to the police station?" *Stupid.* He wasn't a taxi service. His job was to secure the children's safety.

"Thank you, but the station is only a few blocks from here. We'll manage." Ben directed his wife toward the elevators.

Bo followed them with his eyes for a moment. That police station would be flooded with Amish folks in a few hours. He turned and headed toward the nurses' desk.

"I'd like the room number for Nathan Diener, please."

"I'm sorry. He's not able to have visitors."

"I'm with Child Protective Services," he said.

"Can I see your ID?"

"Absolutely." He reached for his back pocket and sighed as the memory of his missing wallet flooded back. "My wallet was stolen earlier."

The nurse cocked her head.

Bo pulled a business card from his shirt pocket. "Here's my card." He craned his neck, looking for the blond-haired nurse who'd recognized him earlier.

"Without a picture ID, I'm unable to allow you to see him." She handed him back the card. "Sorry."

Bo groaned under his breath. "Is Doctor Wellington available? She's the one who requested the initial investigation."

"I believe she's already gone for the day, but I'll have her paged."

"Thank you." Bo stepped aside when another visitor approached the desk. Several minutes later, the nurse confirmed the doctor wasn't answering her page. Bo thanked her again, then headed down the hall toward the lobby.

He heard the wailing child midway down the hall. Davis was pacing the lobby, bouncing the toddler in her arms.

"What took you so long?" She strode across

189

the room and thrust the baby at him. "That child has a good set of vocal cords."

"Oh, did you hear that, darling? She likes your singing." He used a soft, cheerful tone, hoping to calm Amanda. His effort failed.

"That wasn't singing." Davis brushed a piece of lint off the shoulder of her beige linen suit coat. "Since you're here and the child seems to like you, would you come with me to drop her off at the foster home?"

"Yeah, sure." He wasn't about to leave Amanda in Davis's care.

She glanced at her watch. "Can we leave now?"

"The child senses your impatience." He spoke to Davis in the same singsong voice as he used with Amanda, which by her scornful expression had annoyed her. Perhaps Davis hadn't thought about the hair-pulling car ride ahead of them. If he didn't spend a few minutes trying to gain the child's trust, she would work herself into a full-blown panic. He learned the hard way that a child this upset could suddenly start gasping or do the opposite and hold her breath. Gaining trust was the key. "*Shh . . .* you're going to be all right, Amanda. *Ich fashprecha, engel.*"

The child stopped crying and stared at him, her long lashes glistening with tears.

Davis pivoted around to face him. "What did you say?"

Without breaking eye contact with Amanda, he replied, "I reassured her she'd be all right."

"After that. You spoke something in . . . gibberish and the child stopped crying. What exactly did you say?"

"I called her an angel." He motioned to the papers in Davis's hand. "Does your paperwork mention what home is taking her?"

"Mrs. Appleton agreed to take the child until we can establish a more permanent placement." Davis pushed up her sleeve and studied her watch. "It's after six. I told her we would drop off the child over an hour ago."

Norton ambled across the lobby toward them. Over the years, Bo had seen that solemn expression only once—restraining grave news. Bo would forever remember his first case. The sunken-eyed stare of the emaciated girl, crippled by an abusive father and lying in a hospital bed no longer fighting to live. He choked up every time he recalled the case. The system failed that little girl.

"How's the boy?" Davis asked Norton.

"Critical."

Bo stepped forward. "Did he say what happened?"

Norton shook his head. "He's sedated."

"According to the mother, the boy was vomiting," Bo said. "She thought maybe he had a reaction to his antibiotics."

Norton grimaced. "Are we talking about the same kid?"

"Nathan Diener," Bo said. "The three-year-old Amish boy."

"I don't know why she would say the medicine hurt him when the evidence shows he was beaten—nearly to death. The doctors don't expect him to make it."

"Beaten?" Bo's knees went weak. They couldn't possibly be talking about the same boy. The woman wasn't capable of inflicting that harm. Was she?

"Either that," Norton continued, "or he was trampled by horses. But the fact he has no broken bones leads the doctors to believe otherwise. He was battered nonetheless. The woman's looking at jail time—first-degree murder if he doesn't make it."

# Chapter Sixteen

The windowless room inside the police station was hot, stuffy, and smelled of stale sweat. Mattie sat in the metal chair, arms crossed in a self-hug, and shivered. Never before had gray walls looked so bleak. A metal table held the center of the room with a single chair on one side and two chairs opposing it. She lowered her head and stared at the worn spots of gray paint on the cement floor.

The day's events replayed in her mind. Allowing the hospital workers to separate her from Nathan was a horrible mistake. Calling Bo was too. She thought he would help. Wrong. He was an outsider.

Nerves had coated her tongue and throat with a bitter taste and knotted her stomach. If only she could vomit and rid her body of the sour contents.

Two men, dressed in long-sleeved white shirts, dark trousers, and wearing shoulder-holstered guns, entered the room. The door clanged shut after them. The men approached the table and sat opposite her.

The younger man placed a small recorder on the table and pressed the button. "I'm Detective Bradshaw and this is my partner, Detective Holt." He glanced at his watch. "It's 1800 hour on June 16 . . ." He settled back in his chair. "Are you ready to make a statement, Mrs. Diener?"

She looked at the gray-haired man, holding a pen poised above a pad of yellow paper, then over to the younger man who had asked the question. "I'd like to know how *mei kinner*—children are doing. Please."

A heavy pause followed. The man introduced as Detective Holt tapped the pen against the pad. Mattie's throat tightened, the hot air turning solid in her lungs.

Detective Bradshaw spoke first. "Your daughter is with Child Protective Services."

Both men eyed her hard, scrutinizing her reaction—her response.

"What does that mean?" she asked calmly.

Neither replied. The gray-haired man continued to tap his pen against the pad.

Mattie leaned forward. "Where did they take her?"

"How about you answer our questions first?"

"I have to know if she's safe." Mattie's voice cracked. "What about *mei sohn*? How is he?"

The pen tapping stopped. "Well, that's what we're here to talk about, Mrs. Diener." Detective Holt's sharp, authoritative tone sent a shudder down her spine. "Suppose you answer some questions and . . . maybe afterward, we'll make a call to the hospital for an update on his condition."

Mattie's skin tingled. The *maybe* sounded more intimidating than promising. "What do you want me to tell you?"

"What did you use, a broom handle? An iron rod? What?"

"I don't know what you're talking about. *Mei sohn* is sick. He had a fever and was vomiting."

Detective Bradshaw slid his chair back and stood. He planted his hands on the table shoulder width apart and leaned toward her. "Was he disobedient? Is that why you beat him?"

"*Nay!*"

"Do you spank your children, Mrs. Diener?"

"Sometimes."

194

The man's eyes gleamed as if what she said brought great satisfaction. "Give us an example of a time you spanked your children."

Her mind went blank. She nervously shook her head and shrugged.

"Think, Mrs. Diener. You were upset with your son. Angry he did . . . ?"

She glanced at the older detective transcribing the conversation. "It's *nett* against the law to spank your children," she said.

Detective Holt looked up from the pad. "It is if your discipline inflicts harm. The boy has bruises."

*Bruises?* "We bumped heads a few days ago. Perhaps the bruises are from that."

"The bruises I'm referring to are not on his head. You'll have to come up with another reason."

The room spun as her brain filtered the implication of what he was saying. "I don't know of any other bruises."

Both men glared.

Her mind whirled. Had Nathan fallen? Had something happened earlier? Grace would have said if that was the case. She recalled their buggy pulling into her driveway . . . Ben spoke about fishing. *"When Nathan feels better."*

"Do you have another explanation for the bruises?" Detective Bradshaw broke the silence.

"He might have fallen," she offered timidly.

"Or maybe you pushed him down a flight of

stairs? Does your home have a second story or basement?"

"A cellar, *jah*."

"Is isolating him in the cellar part of his punishment?"

"*Nay!*" Her eyes moistened with tears. "I'd never harm *mei kinner*. Never." Mattie clutched her stomach. *Churning. Churning.* She had to find a wastepaper can or . . . too late. What little substance she had in her stomach landed on the gray cement floor.

The younger man left the room as she heaved only bile the second time. A few moments later, he returned with some paper napkins and a cup of water.

Mattie drank the cool liquid. Her stomach roiled again.

"We can give you a minute or two before we begin again," the older man said.

"I-I-I think I'd like that attorney you said could be appointed."

Hours after delivering Amanda to the temporary foster care home, Bo still held the image of the child's terrorized expression in his mind. She was safe with Mrs. Appleton, although convincing a toddler of that would be impossible. The blaring TV startled the girl. So did the *ding* of the microwave when Mrs. Appleton heated a bowl of instant oatmeal. Although Davis had made it clear she wanted to leave immediately, Bo had stalled. He was glad he did. Mrs. Appleton wasn't able to get Amanda to eat the oatmeal, but she ate with his coaxing.

"You made quite an impression on her," Davis had said when they were leaving, and Amanda held her arms in the air wanting him to pick her up. Having never experienced that sort of reaction from any of the other children he'd placed over the years, his heart swelled with pride. At the same time, he hated his job. It seemed exceptionally cruel after gaining Amanda's trust to have to leave her with a stranger. But Bo couldn't take the child home with him. The image of the girl's big blue, watery eyes etched in his mind and wouldn't be fading anytime soon.

On the drive home, Davis prattled about the case. To her, it was some sort of victory. She had even suggested they go out and celebrate. Celebrate what? Didn't she know a family torn apart wasn't something to rejoice over? He declined the offer to stop somewhere and drove her straight home, then headed home himself. Only he wasn't tired. The day's events had put him on edge. He'd always been able to read people well, know if they were lying—if they were guilty. But his analysis of Mattie Diener had failed. Even the woman's friend had said Mattie expected the authorities to take her children.

The light in the library was on when he pulled

into the drive. He went through the side entrance of the house and paused at the door of his mother's library.

She looked up from a stack of papers and removed her reading glasses. "You've had a long day. I'll warm something up for you to eat." She pushed the chair away from her desk and stood.

"No, don't get up. I'm not hungry." He took a seat in the blue floral wingback in front of her desk, cupped the back of his neck with his hands, and sighed.

"I know that expression." She folded her hands as she always did, giving him time to compose his thoughts.

He directed his attention to the fireplace and studied the fake logs. He wasn't sure how much to tell her. Other cases he'd been able to talk with her on legal matters.

"Bo? Is everything all right? You rushed out of the house as though you were chasing a fire this afternoon. I thought this was your day off."

"It was." He motioned to the paperwork she'd been reading. "What has you up so late?"

"I promised to read over a few legal proposals the county attorney drew up for the ballot next fall."

"Increasing taxes again?"

"No. This should help stimulate growth in the area. More businesses, more jobs, better roads."

He chuckled. She was already sounding like a

politician. "So, in a roundabout way of saying it, you plan to increase taxes."

"More businesses and jobs will mean more taxpayers to share the burden." She sounded as though she'd rehearsed the statement.

He leaned forward. "Commissioner Nettleton, how do you plan to bring more businesses to this county?" Their area was known for tourism. Camping and hiking in Hiawatha National Forest, boating and fishing in the numerous lakes and rivers, and snowmobiling and ice climbing in the winter, but not many new people planted roots in their neck of the woods.

"Great Northern Expeditions is a fracking company who has shown interest in our area. Places where they've drilled in the past have experienced exponential growth. Many new businesses, increase in jobs . . ."

"Increase in sinkholes."

"Not always." She shrugged. "Great Northern Expeditions has one of the better track histories. They've kept extensive records."

"I'm sure." He lifted his brows. "How much have they contributed to your campaign fund?"

She straightened her shoulders. "I haven't cashed the check yet."

He pushed off the chair. "I think I will make a sandwich."

She trailed him to the kitchen. "I've arranged for Josh to come by three times a week to help

George with the grounds, on a trial basis of course. He's out of school for the summer, and he offered to wash the outside windows and trim the rose bushes. I thought his first assignment could be planting those impatiens we bought. George's knees are still giving him problems, and I know you've been busy at work. Besides, hiring a foster child looks good for my image."

"You've fostered a kid for sixteen years and have written some pretty stout checks. I think your image is pristine." He winked. "That is until you hook your name to that drilling company."

"Yes, well, fortunately for me, the area they want to drill first doesn't have many registered voters." She praised the drilling company for its history of hiring local people and remarked about the benefits for the area restaurants and lodging.

Bo removed the packages of sliced ham and Swiss and the jar of mayo from the refrigerator. Same thing he'd made to eat prior to going to Badger Creek. Untwisting the tie on the loaf of bread, his thoughts drifted to Mattie sitting in the waiting room, dabbing her puffy eyes with a wadded tissue. *"Nathan started vomiting,"* she'd said. Nothing about bruises. Nothing about him getting trampled by a horse. Did she think no one would notice? *"Doctors don't know if the boy will make it. The boy's battered,"* his boss's words echoed. *Battered.*

"What do you think about Josh painting the boathouse?"

His mother's question pulled him back to the present. "Ah, yeah, sure." He dipped the knife into the mayo, clinking against the side of the jar as he removed a glob.

"Is there something you're not telling me about Josh?"

"No. He's a good kid." He spread the mayo over two pieces of bread, then piled it with shaved ham and two slices of cheese. He would make a point to remind Josh that smoking wouldn't be tolerated, nor would the use of foul language. Now that Bo's mother had taken an interest in Josh, he wouldn't have any reason to run away or hang out with the pool hall crowd again. His mother would keep him busy manicuring the grounds.

Bo took a bite of his sandwich.

"Did Erica get ahold of you? She called shortly after you left this afternoon." She lifted her brows and paused for affect. "She mentioned something about your reputation being at stake."

"I saw her." He took another bite.

"Well?" She shifted her stance. "What did she mean?"

"I followed my gut on a case and . . . I was wrong." Snowballed was more like it, but it wasn't just his reputation at stake. According to Norton, the boy might die. Bo had the opportunity to sit on

201

the case—keep it open the full thirty days—and he did his best to persuade the doctor to drop the complaint. He wouldn't make that mistake again.

"You lost your objectivity?" She removed the milk container from the refrigerator and unscrewed the cap.

"Yeah." He snorted.

"What went wrong?"

The circuit judge came out of retirement. Not that he minded. He was used to the manner in which she helped him profile a case. She had taught him a lot. In hindsight, he should have talked with her prior to letting his gut take control.

Bo stared at the half-eaten sandwich in his hand. No longer hungry, he tossed it in the trash can. "I let my guard down. A widow with two small children . . . An Amish woman got one over me."

"I see." Her shoulders sagged like she had been given fifty-pound bags of sand to hold. She closed her eyes a half second.

"It's just that I've never had . . . I mean . . ." He was stumbling for words, and she keenly analyzed what he was and wasn't saying. This wasn't new. He was used to her tactics. She had taught him more than his college professors about interpreting hidden meaning and picking up inflections in speech and nonverbal clues. But her silence was uncharacteristic.

"I've never had to remove an Amish child from the home," he said. Whatever happened within an Amish district was kept private. The father administered discipline, and more often than not, the mother withheld any objection she might have no matter how harsh the punishment. In this case, the father was absent. Mattie Diener had the sole responsibility to administer discipline. Bo couldn't shake the doctor's comment about depression, maybe even a bipolar disorder in the woman's background.

"And there wasn't another way?"

"I don't know. Maybe." He tossed the knife in the sink. "I think I'll turn in." He kissed his mother's cheek. "It isn't anything for you to worry about. Good night." He took a few steps and stopped. "Thanks for giving Josh a shot. You'll like him."

Downstairs, in his remodeled basement apartment, he sat in the recliner and closed his eyes. The moment he did, an image of Mattie came to mind. Her wide-set blue eyes held the depth of her soul. Helpless. Afraid . . . betrayed. She'd called him for help. Why? Did she think he could get the charges dropped? The widowed mother had cracked. Even the doctor had said she was prescribed anti-depressants—why didn't he pay closer attention to the facts? Mattie's image warped into Amanda's and the same blue-eyed, frightened expression caused a shiver. He couldn't fail the child.

*God, Amanda doesn't have any idea what's happened. She's frightened. What was Mattie Diener thinking, inflicting such forceful punishment on her son?* Bo ran his hand over the scar on his upper arm. He remembered the beatings. Being punished for not working fast enough— being good enough—holy enough. Most of the time his father used a worn leather strap to teach Bo. His bruises ran in narrow strips. The beatings made it painful to sit down—sometimes to move at all. Once the end of the strap caught his ear—but only once. His fingers absently rubbed the thin scar on the side of his earlobe as if he could push the memory away.

Bo pushed off the chair. Until now he'd done well to keep his past buried—it needed to stay that way. Norton needed to hold Davis's hand through this case—not him. He rubbed the back of his neck; the corded muscles had tightened. He slid under the bedcovers, his head sank into the feather pillow, and his heavy eyelids closed.

*"Your heavenly Father loves you, Boaz."*

A reassuring calmness washed over him. He'd struggled for years to accept God's love and to understand it was not something he had to earn.

*"Feed My lambs."* The voice echoed. *"Bring My little lamb back into the fold."*

His conscience answered, *"Yes, Lord,"* as his body submerged deeper in sleep.

He was walking barefooted over barren land and kicking up puffs of dust as he went. In the place of dry bones, as Bo had come to call it, one could not see beyond the withered remnants of life. He didn't want to be here. Alone. Wandering. Yet he'd seen the place so many times, the familiarity of it held a certain amount of comfort. Hot air dried his lungs as he moved over the cracked ground in search of a place to lie down. He dropped to his knees. The palms of his hands became calloused before his eyes.

"I have not called you here to take up a place, but to lead you to the one crying in the wilderness. Now rise and walk with Me."

Bo scrambled to his feet. Turning a wide circle, he searched for the speaker.

"Do you need to see Me to know that I am with you?"

Bo stopped turning. "No." His throat quivered. He glanced around the desolate area again for which way he should go. Everything looked the same. Parched open land filled with dry bones. "Which way?"

Silence.

Bo looked upward, but a blinding light stole his sight. Disorientated, he stumbled backward.

A faint cry in the distance broke the silence.

Bo waited a moment for instruction. "I hope You still intend to lead me, Lord. My eyes feel like they have tar in them." He shuffled blindly toward the sound. Hours passed, or so it seemed. Fatigue had set in, but the child's cry propelled him forward. When he finally stopped, so did the crying.

He stood still a moment, cupping a hand next to his ear. Silence. Now he was blind and deaf. This had to be some sort of test. But what did it all mean?

"You're not blind or deaf, Boaz. You're pre-occupied with your surroundings. Now open your eyes and see why I've brought you here."

A light flashed and Boaz was no longer in the wilderness, but was standing beside a hospital bed, peering down at the purplish blotches covering Nathan Diener's body. Bo gasped. The boy looked nothing like the child he'd seen just days ago. Dark shadows surrounded his eyes. A nurse stood next to the bed, motionless, as if there was nothing more she could do.

Bo stepped closer. "What's wrong with him?"

The nurse's eyes held a vacant stare as if she were in a comatose state herself.

"Nathan?" Bo reached for the boy's limp hand. A chill rippled over the surface of

Bo's skin, sending the hairs on his arms on end. He turned his head in slow motion and peered at the statue-like nurse. But when the woman lifted her eyes to meet his, it wasn't the same person. He'd seen those eyes—blue like the summer sky. Where? "Mattie?"

The woman never blinked.

He moved closer to the bed, shielding the boy with his arm. "What are you doing here? You can't help the boy now."

"But you can, Boaz." The same inner voice that walked him through the wasteland of dry bones was prompting him once more.

Bo lifted his gaze upward. "Who am I that I can do anything?"

Shafts of blinding light danced across the room as the cool morning breeze came in off the lake and fluttered the window blinds. Bo reached down, untangled the bedcover from around his feet, and gave it a yank. Shivering, he burrowed his head under the blanket and closed his eyes, but the *clack, clack, clack* of the wind beating the wooden blinds against the windowsill prevented him from falling back to sleep. Bits and pieces of his dream flashed across his mind. Replaying the events—until he saw Mattie standing at the foot of the hospital bed. He bolted upright.

# Chapter Seventeen

Bo filled his mug with the last of the coffee and returned the empty carafe to its holder. A few coffee grounds floated to the surface. Probably should have stopped at the service station on his way into work. He sampled the heavy roast and cringed. The stuff tasted like it'd been brewed last week. He headed back to his desk, pausing next to Max's workstation on his way. "You make this stuff, Roker?"

Max glanced up from his computer. "Three hours ago."

"Tastes more like three days ago."

"Add a few tablespoons of this." Max pushed the jar of honey across his desk that Bo had given him for his allergies. "It kills the bitter taste, and I hear it boosts your immune system."

Bo eyed the thick golden substance. The simple label read Made by Mattie. He couldn't help but wonder who was checking on her bees and tending her livestock. Bo pushed the jar back to Max. "No thanks."

"Were you in court again this morning?"

"No," Bo said, pulling the office chair away from the desk. "I spent the morning disputing unauthorized purchases on my credit card with the bank. Seems the man who lifted my wallet has a taste for pricy items. He's been busy shopping online the last twenty-four hours." Bo shook his head. After receiving Mattie's call from the hospital, he'd forgotten all about calling to report his card stolen. "By the time these charges get resolved, I don't think I'll want another card."

His friend snickered. "You say that now, but we live on the cusp of a cashless society. You realize that, don't you?"

Bo took another drink of the coffee. The second sip wasn't any better. "I'd rather not think about a cashless society." It's sad that a man's word and simple handshake no longer held any power. Except amongst the Amish; they still bartered by verbal agreement. Mattie's words came back to him. *"I didn't harm mei child. I give you mei word."* At the time, Davis had scoffed at Mattie's promise—even he pushed it aside. Promises didn't hold up in court. She'd find out soon enough that she needed something more than her word to stand on. But that wasn't his problem. Other than testifying in court regarding the report he'd filed, he planned to distance himself from the case. Someone else could be assigned to follow up on the little girl he'd placed into foster care.

"Heard about the Amish case you're working on with Erica Davis." Max wagged his brows. "How did you manage to get Erica for a partner?"

Bo shrugged. The less he said, the less he would have to explain.

"Long drive through the country . . . hmm."

Bo lifted his mug to his lips, then lowered it. "The case can be reassigned if you'd like to take over." He choked down another drink.

"What do they call an Amish person who's gone off the deep end? A lost lamb or a black sheep?"

Bo's jaw muscles tightened.

"I heard she beat her kid until he was black and blue from head to toe."

"Purple." Bo's words left his mouth unchecked. Other than in his dreams last night, he hadn't even seen Nathan. The hairs on the back of Bo's neck stood on end.

"Hey." Max motioned to the lit interoffice button on Bo's phone. "You don't hear your phone ringing?"

Bo snatched the receiver. "Lambright."

"You got a minute?"

His boss really meant *Get in my office now,* but Norton seldom barked over the phone. He waited until he was face-to-face behind closed doors.

"Sure." Bo took another gulp of coffee before marching down to Norton's office. "Don't let this be about the Diener case," he mumbled to himself. How was he going to explain already being at the hospital? By now, Norton would have discovered dispatch hadn't sent Bo to the hospital.

Mattie Diener needed someone to vouch for her, and he was a sucker for a woman sobbing. He was a sucker, all right.

As Bo neared the office, he overheard his boss's muffled voice. Bo poked his head around the partially opened door. Norton waved Bo in without breaking his conversation with the caller. Inside the office a half second, Bo figured his boss's call was regarding the Diener case. He eased into the chair facing Norton's desk and studied the man's stiff jaw. His face turned redder by the second. Whoever Norton was on the phone with was doing most of the talking.

"Yes, sir. I'll look into it, sir." Norton's voice was strained. He massaged his temple.

Bo started to perspire. He loosened his tie, finding it hard to breathe in the stifling office. Budget cuts had kept the thermostat on seventy-five during the summer. The fan blowing on Norton's desk didn't offer much reprieve.

Norton hung up the phone, pushed away from his desk, and stood. He crossed the room and pushed the door closed with a thud, then returned to his chair and crossed his arms. After what felt like eternity, he said, "The doctor wants a full investigation."

"There will have to be. The woman was arrested."

"On you." Norton's tone hardened.

"Me!" Bo jumped to his feet. "Why me?"

"Apparently you coerced her into dropping the initial complaint."

He shook his head. "Doctor Wellington asked for my recommendation. And at the time, I didn't see any reason to continue the investigation." *At the time* . . . A few hours sure changed everything. Only a few days ago, Nathan was hovering under the bed with his little sister. Now he was lying in a hospital bed fighting for his life.

"Apparently Doctor Wellington feels the boy's life is in jeopardy because you dropped the ball."

"No. The boy's life is in danger because the mother's unstable. She beat him." Even as the words left Bo's mouth, an inner prompting told him he was wrong. Bo sank into the chair and lowered his head. He closed his eyes for a second and the boy's image flashed in his mind. This was insane.

"That was Internal Affairs on the phone," Norton said. "They're going to be contacting you to set up an interview."

Bo blew out a breath. "Fine."

"Until then . . . you're on administrative leave. I'll need your employee badge."

Bo snorted. "Don't have it." He slapped his legs and stood. "My wallet was stolen."

"When did that happen?"

"Sunday. I went to check on one of my foster kids and ran into some problems in the pool hall. And no, I didn't fill out a report."

Norton pinched the bridge of his nose and squeezed his eyes shut.

"I'm his Big Brother. So the call wasn't—"

"Are you talking about Josh Messer? The kid who's run away from every home he's been placed in?"

"Yes."

"That is department business." Norton's voice rose. "You're done bending the rules. You got that, Lambright?"

Bo nodded. "Yes, sir."

"I don't like receiving calls from my superior about one of my best investigators." Norton slapped his palm on his desk. "I don't like it at all."

"I'm sorry. It won't happen again."

"I need a list of the cases you're working on."

Bo opened his mouth to ask if Norton would consider holding off on reassigning Josh's case file, but decided against it. Josh had his cell number. Plus, Josh would be around the house doing odd jobs, so Bo would see him.

"Send Erica in," Norton barked as Bo reached for the doorknob.

Bo hesitated a second before exiting the office. Apparently the internal investigation had begun, Davis being the first one called for an interview. He relayed the message as he passed her desk. If she knew anything about the complaint against him, she didn't let on. Davis merely gathered a notepad and pen and rose from her chair.

Let Internal Affairs conduct their investigation. He'd acted within protocol, except for entering the Diener residence without a court order. The ruling would fall in his favor. Davis would back him up . . . wouldn't she?

Bo returned to his desk, opened the file cabinet on his right, and removed the case-pending files first. He compiled a list of names of the foster children he had scheduled follow-up visits on and those with pending court dates. He stopped on Amanda Diener's file, remembering how the frightened child had locked her arms around his neck in a choke hold. He had promised he would be back to see her again. Bo glanced toward Norton's office. The door still closed, he picked up the phone and dialed Mrs. Appleton's number. But before anyone answered, his boss's door opened and Davis stormed out.

Bo hung up the phone as she marched toward his desk.

She planted her hands on his desk and leaned forward. "I'm not going down with you, Lambright."

Bo caught a glimpse of Max in his peripheral vision, brows perked and all ears. His friend's smile widened as he shifted his attention between Davis and Bo.

"I won't let you destroy my career," she added, spouting like a kettle of boiling water.

Bo took a deep breath. "What did Norton say?"

"That our case is under investigation." She wagged her finger, the French manicured nail a blur next to his nose. "This is all your fault."

Bo nodded. "Entirely."

"Well, do something about it."

He collected the files on his desk and stood. "You have nothing to worry about, Davis."

She huffed. "Is that what you told the Amish woman too?"

He shot her an off-the-shoulder glare as he marched toward Norton's office. Bo had no more than handed him the case files when his cell phone rang. He glimpsed at the caller ID. Mrs. Appleton.

"Hello."

"Bo, this is Roberta Appleton. I know you were concerned about Amanda Diener when you dropped her off. Frankly, I'm concerned also. She refuses to eat and she's a rather fussy child."

"I'm sorry, Mrs. Appleton, but I'm no longer handling the Diener case. You should be receiving written notification within three business days with contact information of the new investigator assigned."

"Bo, you're the only one Amanda's responded to. Even the other children aren't able to get her to warm up to them. She refuses to eat."

He was afraid this would happen. The child's new surroundings were so different from everything she'd known. On top of that, Amish children didn't learn English until they were school age, another reason she should have been placed in an Amish home.

"Bo? Are you still there?"

He sighed. "Yes, I'm here. If you think it would help"—he glanced at Norton, then turned facing the wall and lowered his voice—"I could stop by in an hour or so."

"That would be wonderful. She was so distraught after you dropped her off. I've never had a toddler I couldn't convince to warm up to me."

"I know, Mrs. Appleton, and Amanda will come around too." He hoped.

Bo ended the call. As he tucked the phone into his pocket, someone behind him cleared his throat. Bo turned and faced Norton's scowl.

"Do I have to remind you that you're on administrative leave, Lambright?"

"Nope." His boss opened his mouth to speak, but Bo cut him off. "Don't ask." He headed to the door. "Let me know when Internal Affairs wants to see me."

Forty-five minutes later, Bo was standing on Mrs. Appleton's stoop. As much as he wanted to distance himself from the Diener case, he firmly believed it was his duty to help Mattie's daughter during the transitional period. After all, the child was innocent.

The front door opened wide enough for Mrs. Appleton to poke her head outside. "Have you had chicken pox?"

# Chapter Eighteen

"This is our sick zone," Mrs. Appleton warned Bo as he entered her sitting room. He scanned the room, but only spotted one child sitting on the carpeted floor playing quietly with a wooden puzzle.

"I almost didn't recognize her." Bo grimaced at the pink floral shirt and matching shorts the child had on. Amanda left the toy and tottered over to him, arms held high. He swooped down and gathered Amanda into his arms. The toddler's hot-pink outfit and rosy cheeks made her bright-blue eyes appear even larger. "I told you I would be back, angel."

"*Ich geh*," Amanda said, then pouted when Bo shook his head.

Her bottom lip protruded and Bo couldn't contain his smile. Not many Amish children would go with a stranger, yet she had become attached to him. Bo looked the child over for spots. "What makes you think she has chicken pox?"

"So far she only has a few spots on her chest and belly."

"*Ich geh*," Amanda insisted, patting his chest. Her mother would rebuke her for pouting. The Amish frowned upon strong-willed children.

Mrs. Appleton drew closer to them. "What's she saying?"

"I go," Bo replied.

Amanda wrapped her arms around his neck and burrowed her head into the crook of his neck. He pivoted to face Mrs. Appleton. "You sure it's chicken pox?"

Mrs. Appleton frowned. "She might not have a lot of spots, but I've taken care of children over thirty years. I know what chicken pox looks like."

"Do you think it's why she's been cranky?"

Mrs. Appleton chuckled. "I would say it has more to do with your absence." She gestured to Amanda snuggled against Bo's chest. "That's the most content she's been in hours."

Bo smiled. As many children as he had placed into foster homes, he'd never had one bond to him so quickly. Even Josh was standoffish at first. It took visiting the home several times before his anger subsided. Over the years, Bo had come to accept the fact that most children he removed from bad homes turned their anger toward him, which was why he made a point to follow up on their progress beyond the state requirement.

"I'm going to get her a bottle of warm milk. Maybe you'll be able to get her to drink some." Mrs. Appleton disappeared into the kitchen.

Bo eased into the rocking chair next to the sofa. In the corner of the room, *Dora the Explorer* played on the TV even though the other children were likely outside in the fenced backyard.

Bo's gaze fell on Amanda, watching two young girls combing their pony's mane in a commercial. He hoped Norton assigned someone to the case who would make it a priority to place Amanda back within the Amish community. Bo considered turning the TV off, but it wasn't his place. His chest caved with heaviness. He should be the one handling the placement, making sure they adjusted properly.

His stomach knotted at the thought of being on administrative leave. He'd heard rumors about how rough an Internal Affairs investigation could be. They wouldn't like the idea that he went inside Mattie Diener's house without consent—even though it wouldn't have been right to leave the woman passed out on her porch.

"Here you go." Mrs. Appleton handed him a bottle. "She's old enough to be drinking from a sippy cup, but that's for another day."

"Thank you." Bo tipped the bottle close to Amanda's mouth. She turned her head, batted the bottle away with her hand. Finally, after a few more tries and a little coaxing, she drank. It wasn't long before Amanda was asleep in his arms, but even in her sleep she tugged at her unfamiliar clothes. Guilt seared his heart. She should have her own clothes to wear. Not every outsider under-stood the importance the Amish placed on their appearance. Not that Amanda understood the concept either, but his conscience would be clear.

He glanced at Mrs. Appleton, sitting on the blue-and-white plaid sofa. "If I can bring you a supply of her clothes, would it be a problem to change her?"

"Not at all. I'm washing the dress she arrived in now."

"Thank you. I think she would be . . . more comfortable."

"You're probably right. She has been pulling on the shorts. I'm not sure if it's the clothing or the disposable diaper that's giving her trouble."

"I'll see if I can arrange for more clothes." He gazed at the sleeping toddler in his arms. Her light-brown hair, damp with sweat, curled into tightly coiled locks around her face. She had her mother's button nose.

"You have a gentle way with children, Bo. You'll make a great father one day."

He smiled, although deep down, he couldn't agree. The past had a wicked way of repeating itself. He'd seen it over and over in his line of work. Abusive fathers raised abusive sons. Only he refused to fall into those statistics. If he never married, never had children, then the generational curse would be broken.

"Have you someone special?" Mrs. Appleton's eyes twinkled.

"You're beginning to sound like my mother," he said. "And no, I'm not seeing anyone special."

"My niece, Helen, is a sweetheart. Now, she's a little shy, but she is such a dear and she isn't seeing anyone either. Maybe I could—"

He glanced at his watch. "Oh, wow, look at the time. I should probably be going." He eased up from the rocking chair. "Where would you like me to lay her down?"

She rose from the sofa and motioned him to follow. "I had the crib brought down from the attic last night. It's set up in the first bedroom."

He followed her down the hall and into a bedroom with pink walls. Inside were two other twin-sized beds with matching pink-and-green bedspreads and a white shaggy rug between them. Bo gently lowered Amanda onto the crib mattress, then stepped aside as Mrs. Appleton covered her with the lightweight blanket. He tiptoed out of the room, then waited in the hall for Mrs. Appleton.

Bo walked to the front door and paused. "I'll see that you get the clothes and anything else she might need."

"Come by anytime."

He turned to leave, then stopped. "One more thing," he said. "How long does chicken pox last?"

"The contagious stage lasts until the sores scab over. Several days usually, but maybe sooner if she has a mild case and no more spots erupt."

"Will you call me on my cell phone if anything changes with her condition?"

"Absolutely. She has a doctor's appointment later this afternoon, so I'll give you an update after the appointment."

"She's lucky to have you. You're terrific." Bo meant his words wholeheartedly. If Amanda were his child, he would feel safe leaving her in Mrs. Appleton's care.

"My niece is terrific too." She winked.

"I'm sure she is." He tapped the porch banister. "I'll talk with you later." He tramped down the porch steps and went to his car parked behind Mrs. Appleton's minivan in the driveway. Amanda would warm up to her soon. Hopefully, the new investigator assigned to the case would look beyond the woman's age, as toddlers were normally placed in younger families.

Bo fastened his seat belt, but before starting the engine, he checked his phone for messages. None. No news was good news, or so he hoped. He dialed the office. *Don't be a fool.* If he told Norton about Amanda's chicken pox, he would also have to explain why he'd disregarded his boss's orders.

Bo disconnected the call. He'd worked hard to become an investigator. Why would he risk throwing away his career by reporting this illness? After all, chicken pox was a normal childhood disease.

Mattie used the sleeve of the orange jumpsuit she'd been assigned to wipe the tears from her eyes. "I'm telling you the truth. I don't know why *mei sohn* is sick. Why doesn't anyone believe me?"

"You keep referring to your son as being sick, Mrs. Diener." The man, who only moments ago had introduced himself as her court-appointed lawyer, leaned forward. "He's bruised. I've seen the pictures. Now, I'm going to do everything I can to—"

"When were pictures taken of *mei sohn*? We don't believe in having our images engraved."

"We?" Mr. Lewiston cocked his head.

He didn't care. Just like the police officers hadn't last night. She tried to explain why her religious group didn't allow photographs, but these officials mocked her. It turned out being photographed wasn't nearly as humiliating as being searched with gloved hands and ordered to change into a bright-orange jumpsuit.

"The Amish. Our *Ordnung* forbids photographs."

"But you believe in the principle that to spare the rod, you spoil the child."

"Of course. Discipline teaches a child in the way he should go. So, yes, I am a firm believer of not spoiling a child. And that is based on biblical principles, Mr. Lewiston."

He frowned. Reaching into his briefcase, he

removed a large envelope. "I probably don't have to show you the marks on your son's body. But this is what the judge will look at as he considers your eligibility for bond." He slid the envelope across the table.

Mattie removed the photographs and gasped. Tears welled, blurring the purplish markings on Nathan's body. "What happened to *mei sohn?*"

The lawyer's puzzled expression barbed her with anger. "Tell me," she said. "Who did this to Nathan?"

"So, are we going for a plea of insanity?" Mr. Lewiston leaned back in his chair, folded his arms over his chest, and stared.

She studied the photos. His eyes appeared puffy, swollen. The child in the photo looked nothing like Nathan. "This isn't Nathan," she muttered.

"You don't recognize him?" Mr. Lewiston scoffed. "Or you don't remember inflicting that much force?"

Didn't the lawyer say he was there to help her? He certainly wasn't being very helpful, making her feel even worse than those police officers.

Mattie lifted her gaze. "I just want to know what happened to *mei sohn.*"

Mr. Lewiston sat forward in his chair and clasped his hands on the table next to a thick pad of paper. "As I told you earlier, anything you tell me will be kept in strict confidence. That's what is known as attorney-client privilege."

She nodded, giving the impression she understood, but she didn't. *Unless . . .* She swallowed hard *. . . Maybe he is looking for me to confess to hurting my son.*

A loud buzzer sounded. The lawyer collected the photos. "That sound means our time is up," he said.

The door opened, and a uniformed police officer entered the room. "The video arraignment is scheduled to start in ten minutes."

"Thank you." Mr. Lewiston gathered the tablet and pen from the table, shoved them into his briefcase, and stood. "Do you know who is presiding over the cases today?"

"Judge Steinway." The officer cupped her elbow, and she rose to her feet.

"That's good to hear." Mr. Lewiston turned his attention to her. "Judge Steinway is fair."

Led like a dog on a leash, she followed the officer's instructions and went with him into another windowless room. The room was crowded with other inmates wearing the same pumpkin-colored jumpsuits, many oddly at ease leaning back in their chairs, arms crossed. These weren't people she would want to drift into their settlement as two mental escapees had done almost four years ago. Now, wearing a matching colored jumpsuit and awaiting the same judge to determine her fate, she was marked as one of them. The thought roiled her stomach.

She spotted the video camera set up on a tripod facing the chairs in the center of the room, a large television off to one side, and cringed.

"The judge will appear on the television screen shortly," the lawyer said, motioning her to have a seat. "He will state the charges filed against you, ask you how you plead, and determine bail."

"Will he tell me what happened to Nathan?"

Mr. Lewiston furrowed his bushy brows. "No, this is only an arraignment. The trial will come later."

Mattie lowered her head and stared at the worn spot on the concrete floor. Between the brightness and hum the overhead lights gave off and the stench of sweat, she wanted to vomit. She needed to settle her nerves somehow. *Lord, I'm so afraid. Please have mercy.*

"All rise for the honorable Judge Steinway," the officer in the room announced.

Mattie stood next to Mr. Lewiston as an elderly man wearing a black robe appeared on the television screen. He stated the date and time, then rattled off a set of numbers assigned to the day's docket. Her case wasn't the first to be heard. By the time her name was called, her nerves were such that she only heard mumbling over the blood whooshing in her ears.

"Martha Irene Diener, you are charged with aggravated assault against a child. How do you plead?"

# Chapter Nineteen

Bo stilled himself on Mattie Diener's porch as heavy footsteps tromped up the steps and stopped behind him.

"If you're from the company that wants to drill on our land, we're *nett* interested," the man said.

Bo turned. "No, sir. I'm here to see Mattie Diener for . . . other reasons." Perhaps coming to Mattie's home was a mistake. Bo studied the clean-shaven, fortysomething Amish man who held an axe in his right hand. His sun-scorched skin wrinkled with curiosity.

"Mattie?" The man's brows jetted up.

"I mean Martha—Mrs. Diener." Bo pointed his thumb over his shoulder, aiming it at the door. "Do you know if she's home yet?"

The man eyed him carefully, his brown eyes hard. He evaluated him in the same skeptical way Bo's father used to.

"She isn't here," he finally said, lowering the axe to the porch deck and leaning its handle against the banister post. "You'll have to *kumm* back another time if you're interested in buying herbs."

"Thank you, but I'm here on other business."

227

"As I've already said, we're *nett* interested in selling our mineral rights."

"I understand." Bo extended his hand toward him. "I'm Bo Lambright. You must be Mrs. Diener's brother." Even as he said it, Bo recalled Mattie hadn't mentioned in her interview that she had relatives nearby.

The man hesitated, then reached for Bo's hand and shook it. "Alvin Graber."

On further inspection, they had no family resemblance. Mattie's button nose was small, her eyes blue, and cheekbones high. This man's nose was long and thin at the bridge, making his dark-brown eyes appear tiny and closely set.

"Do you know when you expect Mrs. Diener? I have some news to share regarding her daughter."

Alvin's eyes lit with surprise. "Is something wrong with her daughter?"

Bo glanced at the dark house, void of activity. The man probably didn't know Mattie had been arrested yesterday, which was odd given the closeness in Amish communities. "Could you tell me where Ben and Grace Eicher live?"

Alvin stood a little straighter. "What kind of news?"

Bo had already said too much. "I think I'd better wait to speak with Mrs. Diener." Bo stepped off the porch and headed to his car. He'd passed an Amish farmstead a half mile up the road. Ben and Grace had mentioned they were Mattie's neighbors. Maybe the farm belonged to the Eichers. Bo climbed into his sedan. As he turned the ignition key, he glanced over at Alvin, who snatched the axe handle from its resting spot on the porch and swung it onto his shoulder.

Bo clearly recalled the answer Mattie had given him during the interview regarding the frequency of male overnight guests. He could still hear the irritation in her voice when she responded, *"Never!"* But she never did answer the question about male visitors.

Yet Alvin Graber had spoken jointly about not wishing to sell the mineral rights when he thought Bo was a representative from the drilling company. He wasn't wearing a beard, which made him an unmarried man in the Amish settlement.

*"Our"* land. *"We're"* not interested.

Just what was Mattie's relationship with Alvin?

Bo shifted the car into reverse and slowly backed out of the driveway. The road dipped, and the underside of the car rubbed against rocks as he made his way to the next Amish farm. Bo cut the engine and climbed out of his car. Small braided rugs stretched across the clothesline, weighing down the line so the rugs nearly touched the green lawn. He knocked on the door and waited.

A gray-haired woman appeared behind the screened door. "May I help you?"

"I was hoping this was Ben and Grace Eicher's place," he said.

"This is. I'm Grace's *aenti* Erma. But she isn't home." The woman stepped out of the house and went to the porch banister. Holding the hand-rail, she rose to her toes and looked toward the barn. "I thought Ben might still be mending fences."

"Do you know when Mrs. Eicher will be back?"

Erma shook her head. "She went into town to see about a friend."

"Mattie Diener?"

Surprise registered on Erma's face. "How did you—" Her hand flew up in a flutter. "Never mind. I don't need to involve myself. I'm sorry. I didn't catch your name."

"Bo Lambright." He removed one of his business cards from his pocket and handed it to Erma. "Would you give this to your niece, please?"

Erma glanced at the card. "Lambright," she repeated softly. The sound of gravel crunching caught her attention. "Here is Grace *nau*."

Bo studied the buggy, anxious to see if Mattie would also climb out. Her arraignment would have been sometime before noon, depending on the judge. She wasn't a flight risk, so her bond, if any, would be low. Grace climbed out of the buggy. Alone. She tied the horse to the post, then, dragging her left foot slightly with each step, lumbered across the yard.

Erma met Grace at the edge of the porch. "Were you able to find out anything about Mattie?"

"They wouldn't let me see her, but I found out her bail was set. Fifty thousand."

Fifty thousand! Had the court changed the allegations from possible abuse to . . . manslaughter? Bile rose to the back of his throat.

Grace pinned Bo with a glare. "Are you here to gather more information about Mattie, Mr. Lambright?"

He swallowed hard. "Not exactly." He glanced at Erma standing next to him. Her lips were tense, drawn into a straight line. "I'm here to pick up a few items for Amanda, if that would be possible."

Grace ambled up the steps. "Where are you keeping Amanda?"

He shook his head sympathetically. "I'm not at liberty to disclose that information. But she's in a good home and she's safe." *Granted, she's not eating and she needs her family, but that's more than you need to know.*

"She has a *gut* home. Here. In our settlement," Grace said.

Bo lowered his head.

"Little children need their family, Mr. Lambright."

He nodded without lifting his eyes. "I'm sure something will be worked out soon."

"I don't understand why you had to take her away in the first place. When can I see her?"

Her question held the typical family member frustration and concern. Bo wished he had better news, but he would be surprised if he heard any updates while he was on administrative leave. "At this time"—he cleared his throat—"I'm not sure when that will happen. It's up to the judge." *And Nathan's condition.*

Grace blinked back tears, then sniffled and looked away. Erma moved closer to him, her eyes also glazed with tears. "You mentioned needing to pick up some things for Amanda."

"Yes, clothes, please, and if she has a doll or pillow she's fond of, I'll make sure she gets it. The home where she's staying will provide her with clothes, but I thought she would be more comfortable in her own dresses. Anything we can do to make the transition easier would . . ." He stared at the weathered planks, worn smooth from use.

"She shouldn't have to transition into the world," Grace said. "We've done our best to separate ourselves from it. Amanda's an innocent child. She shouldn't be forced to leave our community."

Bo swallowed hard. "I understand your frustration."

"Do you?" Grace crossed her arms. "Mattie Diener is a *gut* mother."

Erma placed her hand on Grace's shoulder. "I'll stay with Mr. Lambright while you go to Mattie's *haus* and gather a few of Amanda's things."

Grace stared at him a half second, then with

a gentle nudge from Erma, she turned and left.

Erma gestured to the wooden bench at the far end of the porch. "If you would like to sit, I'm sure she won't be long."

"Thank you." Bo ventured over to the seat and sat between the two large clay flowerpots adorning the sunny side of the porch. His gaze traveled over the lush green lawn and from one outbuilding to the next. He missed living in the country, the scent of cattle. He drew a deep breath, expanding his lungs with warm air. This was June, but the heat index made it feel more like August. A bead of sweat dripped down the side of his face. He removed the hankie from his pocket and blotted his moist forehead. "Sure is a hot summer," he said.

"*Jah.*" Erma looked toward the cloudless sky. "We could use some rain."

An image from Bo's childhood flashed before him. Barefoot, hair matted in sweat under his straw hat, and the noonday sun beating down on his face as he walked behind the team of mules. He could almost taste the field dust caking his tongue and clogging his lungs.

"Mr. Lambright," Erma said, dabbing a cloth across her forehead. "What's going to happen to Mattie?"

"Depends." He leaned forward, resting his forearms on his legs, and clasped his hands. "A lot depends on whether her son recovers."

"She would never hurt one of her children. Everyone in the settlement will vouch for her character."

Bo nodded without looking Erma in the eye. He didn't expect for a minute anyone would say anything negative about one of their own. But experience had taught him that it was rare for another member to look behind closed doors, and when they did, they seldom questioned what they saw.

"I think what's happening to Mattie has something to do with those drillers who want to take our land."

Bo shook his head. "It doesn't."

"We're *nett* wealthy people. We can't pool our money together and *kumm* up with fifty thousand dollars. They want us to sell our rights in order to free Mattie."

"No. The two are unrelated. The reason she's being held has nothing to do with selling mineral rights." Granted, the bail was high. "Really. It's two separate issues."

Grace's buggy pulled into the yard with another one behind her. As Bo stood, even more buggies came into view. In a matter of minutes, a cluster of men swarmed. A frail, gray-bearded man ambled forward aided by the man Bo had seen earlier at Mattie's house.

"I'm Bishop Yoder," the elder one said. His voice was much stronger than his wobbly legs appeared to be. "We would like to know why Mattie Diener was falsely accused, and we want to know what happened to her children."

Ben wove through the crowd and stopped beside Grace. It would have been easier to talk with Ben alone than have to address this lynch mob. Bo held on to the banister. "There isn't much I can tell you." He had a duty to uphold the confidentiality laws regarding the minor, besides the fact that Mattie had the right to some privacy. Even from her own people. The pack moved closer. He had to say something.

"The Diener children have been placed in social services' custody pending additional investigation. I can assure you that her son is getting the best care possible and her daughter is being well provided for."

The men grumbled amongst themselves. Then the bishop quieted the crowd by raising his hand. "What purpose do you have here, Mr."—he looked at the card—"Lambright? Is this part of the investigation?"

Bo shook his head. "Nothing official." He glanced over his shoulder at Erma, then to where Grace and Ben were standing on the lawn. "I thought Amanda would feel more comfortable in her own clothes." He shrugged. "But she can wear the clothes the *Englischer* provided, if you're okay with that."

Grace came forward with a brown paper bag.

"I collected a few dresses and aprons of Amanda's," she told the bishop. "She probably would feel more comfortable." The bishop muttered some-thing under his breath to her, and Grace approached the first step of the porch, her fingers fumbling nervously with the paper bag. "I'd like to go with you, Mr. Lambright. Amanda isn't able to dress herself, and our style of dress and apron can be complicated to put on."

"I'm sorry. It isn't allowed."

Bishop Yoder cleared his throat, and Grace handed Bo the bag of belongings.

"The hospital refuses to let any of us visit Nathan," the bishop said. "Why is that?"

"The last update I received, Nathan was in critical condition. I'm sure the doctor is keeping him sedated. He wouldn't be aware of visitors or even his surroundings." Or, for that matter, his mother missing from his bedside.

"And Mattie?" the man standing next to the bishop asked.

Bo gripped the banister tighter. "I'll see what I can find out."

Grace whispered something to Ben, then Ben spoke up. "Can you get the bail lowered?"

Not without a miracle. He resorted to a scripted reply. "I'll see what I can do."

"I've never asked you to intervene in a case before." Bo paced his mother's office. "But I need your help." He ran his fingers through his hair. He'd told himself when he started working as a county social worker that he would never seek special treatment for one of his clients. Amanda Diener was different. She needed her mother.

Agnes Nettleton folded the newspaper she'd been reading, placed it on the desk, and removed her glasses. "What do you need me to do?"

"Mattie Diener, the Amish woman I was called to investigate, is in jail. She's been charged with child abuse." He prayed that was her only charge. The hospital wouldn't release any information on Nathan's condition when he called. "I want Judge Steinway to reverse the bail order posted and release her on her own recognizance. Fifty thou-sand dollars seems a bit excessive considering she doesn't have a criminal history and she's well rooted in the community. Mattie isn't a flight risk."

"She can file an appeal for reduction. Who's her attorney?"

"I don't know who took the case. Whoever the court appointed, I suppose."

"It wouldn't be difficult to find out whose name is on the record. If you arrange to have a motion for appeal filed, I can talk to Willard and have the amount reduced, if nothing else."

"How long would that take?"

"Depends on how quickly you can get her lawyer to submit the motion for appeal." She shrugged. "A day or two once the file is moved to the top of the pile."

His shoulders sagged. "Can you make arrangements for Mattie to see her children? She should be granted visiting time."

She studied him a moment, nibbling on the end of her reading glasses. "Are you doing this because she's Amish?"

"Yes—no. I don't know." He walked to the window overlooking Lake Superior and pulled back the curtain. The stormy deep-blue water was marked with whitecaps. Waves lapped the pebbly shore, leaving behind a foamy residue. Any other case he would want the judge to leave the defendant locked up—separated from the minors. But no matter how hard he tried, he couldn't let this one go. He swallowed the golf-ball-size lump growing in his throat. "The little girl," he choked back. "She only speaks Pennsylvania *Deitsch*. When I checked on her, she was withdrawn, not eating, and . . . not adjusting."

"Do you need to consider relocating her to another foster care home?"

"I need emergency visiting rights established."

"I see."

Bo turned away from the window. "And I need the title for my boat."

Mattie halted midstep at the sight of Bo Lambright seated in the police station waiting room. She was told her bail had been posted, but she assumed Grace or the bishop had scraped the money together.

Bo stood and met her across the room. His eyes locked on hers. "How are you?"

If she answered him honestly, she would fall to pieces. Her throat burned and tears threatened to spill over her lids. Mattie averted her gaze. Even doing so, she could still feel his eyes on her, taking in her rumpled dress and her disheveled prayer *kapp*.

"Were you treated . . . all right?"

His voice was soft—comforting in an odd sort of way. Yet she still didn't care to answer. She wasn't treated all right. Only minutes ago she was wearing an orange jumpsuit.

"I spoke with your lawyer," he said. "Your court date is postponed until—"

"Until they know if I'll be prosecuted for the death of . . ." She blinked several times, stunned by her own words. Mattie drew in a hitched breath.

"We don't need to talk about that here." He offered an apologetic smile. "Let's get you home."

She picked at her nails. "The officer said *mei* bail was posted. Was that you?"

"I pulled some strings . . . reeled in an anchor," he muttered, then flashed a friendly grin. "You're not going to skip town, are you?"

His nervous laugh might have brought a smile to her face under different circumstances, but after spending more than twenty-four hours behind bars, she wasn't feeling amused. "No, Mr. Lambright, I don't plan to skip town. I want to see *mei* children."

His expression sobered. "I'm afraid that isn't possible."

# Chapter Twenty

Blood stilled in Mattie's veins. Bo Lambright cupped his hand over her elbow and steered her away from a staggering man in the police station lobby who was about to plow into her. She didn't like this place. The scent, a mixture of sweat, vomit, and a cleaning agent that didn't quite mask the foul odor, left her feeling nauseous.

"Let's get you out of here." Mr. Lambright guided her toward the door.

As desperate as she was to leave the police station, she wasn't convinced leaving with him was the right thing to do. He brought trouble in one form or another every time he was around. First when he showed up at her home and later at the hospital. She paused at the entrance. "Do I have to go with you?"

A hint of dejection, or perhaps confusion, registered on his face. He released her elbow. "Nope. Do you have someone to call?"

*"Jah."* She scanned the room for a pay phone, being sure to avoid eye contact with the other patrons. The tightness in her lungs eased and she exhaled slowly. The only phone was mounted on the far wall, but it was in use by a young woman wearing a sleeveless T-shirt, fringed cut-off jeans, and flip-flops. The woman's ponytail wagged back and forth as she shouted profanity into the receiver.

Mr. Lambright cleared his throat. "You can use mine," he said, digging his hand into his pocket and retrieving a cell phone. He pushed a few buttons and handed her the phone with the number pad lit. "You'll get better reception outside."

*"Danki."* She hadn't used a cell phone before. She walked outside into the blazing hot sun, staring at the number pad on the phone, unable to recall the last two digits of Cora's number.

"There she is," someone called out.

In a matter of seconds, a horde of reporters rushed toward them, snapping pictures, thrusting microphones in front of them.

"Is it true that you nearly beat your child to death?" one reporter shouted.

Mattie gasped.

Mr. Lambright clamped her shoulder with one hand, tucked her under the crook of his arm, and used his free hand to shield her face. "Don't respond."

"How do you call yourselves peaceful people?

Are the beatings everyday occurrences in your society?" One reporter edged up beside her. "At least tell us if women and children are held against their will."

"Don't listen to them." Mr. Lambright pressed her firmly against him, tucking her head under his chin.

Mattie closed her eyes and trusted her rescuer to lead her to safety. He broke through the pack, telling the reporters to step aside while keeping her under guard until they reached his car.

He aimed a clicker at his car and unlocked the door. She dropped into the passenger seat and ducked as camera flashes fired.

"I'm sorry about all that," he said, sliding behind the wheel.

They were several blocks down the road before she sat upright in the seat. "Did you know they were waiting outside the police station?"

"No." He shot her a sideways glare, brows furrowed. "I would have asked for an officer to assist us had I known."

"They asked how often I beat *mei sohn*." Her stomach sickened.

"They're just trying to flare your anger—get you riled up."

"They did!"

He glanced in his rearview mirror. "It's probably going to get worse. There's a news van following us."

Mattie craned around in the seat. "What should we do?" She turned back, wide-eyed.

"I have a full tank of gas and get better mileage than that news van." At the intersection of Colby Road and Lakeview Drive, Bo turned in the opposite direction of her settlement.

"Where are you taking me?"

He looked again in the rearview mirror. "You don't want them camping out on your doorstep, do you?"

"No, but . . ." She bit her lip.

"I'll turn around if you want me to."

She shook her head. The last thing she wanted was a mob of reporters badgering her and the other members of her settlement. "No, please don't. I suppose you're right, Mr. Lambright. Taking an alternate route is probably for the best."

"Call me Bo, okay?"

"*Mei* friends call me Mattie." She wouldn't exactly call Bo a friend, but at the moment, she had no choice but to trust him. She looked over at him. "How is Nathan? Is he out of the hospital?"

His jaw went slack. "Your son is still in critical condition."

"No one would tell me anything at the hospital or the police station," Mattie whispered. She shifted on the seat and adjusted the folds in her dress.

"He's a sick kid."

"Vomiting and fever? Maybe the medicine was wrong."

His jaw twitched and he tugged at his shirt collar. He checked the rearview mirror again. "The van is pulling off the road."

She situated herself to see out the back window. "*Jah*, they're turning around. Do you think he received the wrong medicine?"

"Are you asking if I think he had an allergic reaction?" He used a calm tone, but his wrinkled forehead said different.

"It could have been that, right?"

"Mattie"—his attention shifted back and forth between the road and her—"it's much worse. He's hurt—badly."

She listened for Bo's tone to turn accusatory as the police officer's had, but he said nothing for several miles. He turned off the road prior to the covered Waterston Bridge, taking the gravel road to the right, which led to the picnic area near the river. He parked the car under an elm tree and rolled the window down. "Earlier today it looked like it might storm."

Mattie leaned forward. Except for a red pickup truck, the lot was empty. "Why are we stopping?" Her voice quivered.

He smiled. "You don't have to worry. I just wanted to kill a few minutes to be sure the news van doesn't double back around."

"Oh." She settled against the seat.

He swatted a mosquito, then another one. After chasing another one into the crevice between the windshield and dashboard, he rolled up the window. She could have told him the river was a breeding ground for the bloodsucking insects. Mosquitoes were always bad here.

Mattie wrung her hands. She'd never been alone with an *Englischer*—at least not in a parked car at the foot of the river. She'd heard stories about some of the youth spending late hours here on their *rumschpringe*. They weren't stories she wanted her name associated with. "We don't have to stay here too long, do we?"

He smiled. "No."

"*Gut*, I need to get home to Amanda." Grace would have taken good care of her daughter, but it gnawed at Mattie how her child had witnessed the police officer taking her away.

His smile went stiff, then dropped completely. "Your daughter isn't at home." He eyed her closely. "She's been placed in the custody of Child Services."

"She's *nett* with Grace?" Tears pricked her eyes. She hadn't wanted to believe the police officer when he told her Amanda had been taken away. She thought it was their way of pressuring her into a confession—a sick tactic using her child.

"She's been placed in a foster home . . . temporarily—a good home. Didn't your lawyer tell you any of this?"

"*Nay*," she squeaked. "The police officers . . ." Her body shuddered and she wrapped her arms around herself.

He leaned forward and redirected the air vent, then lowered the fan. "The police officer told you about relocating Amanda?"

"*Jah*, but they said a lot of things that weren't true." Her voice hardened. "They said I beat *mei sohn* with a broomstick. I didn't. They twisted the words in the Bible about sparing the rod and they made me feel like I was . . . like I was a monster."

"I don't believe you're a monster." He awkwardly patted her hand, then returned his to the steering wheel. A long stretch of silence fell between them.

"How is Amanda doing?"

"She's . . ." His hand tightened on the steering wheel. "She's . . . okay."

Tears streamed down her cheeks. "You hesitated. She's *nett* okay."

"Excuse me." He leaned across her, then retrieved a small package of tissues from the glove box and handed it to her. "Your daughter is being well cared for, I promise you, she is."

Mattie removed a tissue from the container and blew her nose. "She doesn't know *Englisch*."

"I know."

"Who's going to tuck her into bed at *nacht* and rock her back to sleep when she wakes up and panics because I'm *nett* there?"

"Kids are more resilient than we think."

Was that supposed to make her feel better? She didn't want her daughter conforming to the world—not to any of it.

He turned his attention to the road. "I think it's safe to head back." He pulled out of the parking lot and stopped as a car sped past. "We'll take Waterston Bridge back to your place."

"Will you take me to the hospital instead? I'd like to see *mei sohn*."

His chest rose and fell with a heavy sigh. "Mattie, I'm working on obtaining visitation rights for you, but I haven't made headway." He pulled onto the highway.

Mattie hadn't driven under the covered bridge since it'd been restored. The bridge's wooden slats and support beams had been replaced by steel. Entering the covering, the steel grates hummed, vibrating the car as they drove through to the other side.

They reached the turnoff leading to her settlement in a matter of minutes. But once they made the turn, news vans came into view. Parked along the roadway were numerous vehicles that made it almost impossible to pass, yet Bo skillfully maneuvered the car down the long narrow driveway.

"Who gave them permission to be on *mei* land?"

"Do you have No Trespassing signs posted

anywhere?" He stopped the car next to the house.

"*Nay.*"

"I'll inform them they're on private property." He reached under his seat and removed an umbrella. "Stay put. I'll come around and get you."

Under different circumstances, she would prefer to see herself inside, but she'd already experienced how cruel the reporters' comments could be.

He opened the umbrella as he neared her side of the car, using it to shield her from the parade of questioners. This time the questions were not only aimed at her, they were directed at Bo as well.

"Mr. Lambright, what does your mother, Judge Nettleton, think about your involvement with an accused child abuser?"

"No comment."

The reporters stopped at the foot of the porch steps as she and Bo hurried up them.

Fortunately, the house was unlocked and she didn't have to fumble with keys. She turned the handle and gave the door a push with her hip. Once they were inside, she latched the dead bolt, then faced Bo. "Your mother is a judge?"

# Chapter Twenty-one

Bo went to the window in Mattie's sitting room and shut it, then closed the curtains. The room darkened like a cave. "You'll probably want to light a lamp or two," he said, moving into the kitchen and doing the same with those windows and curtains. "It's going to be stuffy in here with the windows closed, but I think you'll have more privacy."

Mattie struck a wooden match and lit the wick of the oil lamp on the table. It offered just enough light to be able to see a few feet away.

"You didn't answer *mei* question. Is it true your mother's a judge?"

"She *was*. She's retired from the bench." He hung his head. "And yes, I did ask her to pull some strings with the judge overseeing your case." Hopefully those favors were in motion prior to the media frenzy. Otherwise Mattie might not see her children for weeks if the file went to the bottom of the pile. He hadn't expected the reporters to associate him with his mother so easily since she went by her maiden name professionally. Then again, she was running for a county commission seat and that subjected her family to public scrutiny.

Mattie lit another lantern. "Did she help get me out of jail?"

"No, that was going to take too much time. I put my boat up as collateral to get you out." He smiled. "So remember, you promised you wouldn't skip town."

"You did that for me? Why?" The lines around the corners of her mouth creased slightly with a smile, but quickly faded.

He wished he understood the deeper reason why he couldn't walk away from this case—from Mattie and her children. But he couldn't shake the niggling in the back of his mind that the dreams had something to do with her. He studied her a moment. Most women in her position would crumble under the pressure. He admired her strength—her faith. He wished he could say he'd believed her all along, that he had no doubts. She'd fooled him once . . . No, he had to go with his gut. "I believe you."

Her mouth dropped open as surprise, maybe shock, registered on her face. Then she set the lantern on the table and wiped her hands on the sides of her dress. "I don't suppose you should leave right away. Unless, of course, you wish to brave the crowd."

"Not really."

"I, ah . . . I could make some *kaffi* or tea, whichever you prefer. Although I should warn you, without the windows open it'll get hot in here."

"Either would be great."

She quickly moved over to the cast-iron stove where she opened the side door, then wadded up pieces of newspaper from the stack next to the woodbox and placed them and several thin slabs of kindling inside.

He came up beside her. "Would you like me to get the fire started?"

"That isn't necessary. I do this every day." She added more wood.

He would have built the fire first before loading that much wood. When she bunched up more newspaper and jammed it between the slabs, he had to ask. "Aren't you worried about creosol buildup with so much paper in there?"

She looked up from the stove. "Like I said, I do this every day."

Bo raised his hands in the air. "Okay, it's your stove." He peered up at the smoke-stained ceiling near the pipe.

"Are you inspecting *mei haus* again, Mr. Lambright?"

"Sorry." He smiled. "And it's Bo, remember?"

Mattie pointed at the table. "You can have a seat if you wish," she said, her voice a little rushed.

Bo hadn't meant to make her nervous. He pulled a chair out from the table and sat. The topcoat of polyurethane on the oak table made it shine. It would have taken several hours of sanding to get this fine finish. Something he knew a little about—or used to. He hadn't worked on a wood project in several years. The chair felt comfortable, sturdy. In the chairs he'd built, he used dowels where these had slats for backs. All in all, this was some of the finest work he'd seen. He scanned the room. The cabinetry was handcrafted knotty pine. The wooden counter-tops weren't fancy like the granite slabs sold commercially. He liked the plain style. It reminded him of the kitchen in the house where he grew up.

Mattie adjusted the damper on the stove. The scent of burning wood stimulated memories of coming in from chores to the tantalizing aroma of fried potato pancakes cooked on a woodstove. But those days were gone. The room quickly turned hot with the windows closed. He removed his handkerchief and dabbed it over his forehead.

"Would you like honey with your tea?"

"Sure."

Mattie brought the cups to the table, then went back for the jar of honey and spoons. She sat down but only for a second before she bounced up and went back to the counter. "I'm *nett* sure how stale these are." She set the jar of cookies on the table. "I made them a few days ago."

"My *mamm*—mom—used to put a slice of bread in the jar with the cookies to keep them moist." His words ran together, seeing her brows raised and her tea bag suspended midair over her cup.

He shrugged. "I'm not sure why that is. Osmosis maybe."

She lowered the tea bag into the cup of hot water with noticeable hesitation, then with a slight shake of the head, set the spoon aside and smiled. "I'll have to try that with the next batch."

He stirred a spoonful of honey into the tea. He hadn't thought about homemade cookies in a long time. For that matter, he hadn't been jolted by this many childhood memories since the accident. He passed the jar of honey to her. "Do you make your own honey?"

"Well, the bees make it, but *jah*, I raise bees."

He reached for a cookie. "How many hives do you have?"

"Ten. What kind of strings did you try to pull with the judge?"

He smiled. "I asked for an emergency order to grant visitation with your children. I should be getting a call shortly." He patted his pocket. Empty. "Do you still have my phone?"

Her jaw dropped. "I left it in the car."

"That's okay." He pushed away from the table and stood. "I'll be right back. Don't eat my cookie." He winked.

She blushed. "I won't."

Bo readied his key fob before going outside. The reporters' questions started immediately. He opened the car door and grabbed his cell phone, jogged up the porch steps, and stopped. "If I could have your attention," he said, addressing the cluster of men and women. "You're on private property, and the owner requests you leave." He turned and opened the door.

"Thank you for saying that to them," Mattie said the moment he stepped inside.

"No problem. I'll call their corporate offices if they don't vacate the premises." He wiped his shoes on the rug, something he failed to do when he first arrived.

"Oh, don't worry about your shoes. Do you think you missed the call?" She nibbled on one of her fingernails.

He looked at the phone screen to see if he had any missed calls. "Nothing yet."

Mattie frowned.

"We'll hear something soon." He slipped his phone into his pocket. "You didn't eat my cookie while I was outside, did you?"

Her eyes widened and she shook her head, turning toward the kitchen.

Bo returned to the chair and dunked the peanut-butter cookie into the honey-flavored tea. "Mmm, good."

"*Nett* too stale?"

"Not when you dunk it." He pushed the plate closer to her. "I'll share. Have one."

"That's awfully kind of you to share."

He grinned. "You don't know how long it's been since I've had homemade cookies."

Mattie slid the plate to his side of the table and cracked a weak smile. "I won't deprive you."

He went to pass the plate back, but she held up her hand and refused to take it.

"I'm holding out for a fresh batch." She pushed back her chair and stood. "Besides, I can't eat anything. *Mei* stomach is too nervous." Mattie crossed the room to the window and pulled back the curtain. "Those news people aren't leaving," she said over her shoulder. "They're lined up by *mei greenhaus nau*."

Bo groaned as he rose to his feet and then peered over her shoulder. Sure enough, a half dozen men and women were loitering by the greenhouse. "I'll go talk to them again."

A door creaked open, then closed.

Bo glanced at Mattie.

"The mudroom," she whispered.

Seconds later, Grace bounded into the kitchen. "There's a mass of vehicles blocking the road. Is this about the *kinner*? Or"—her gaze darted between him and Mattie—"the drilling company?"

"They practically pounced on us at the police station and haven't stopped hounding us since," Mattie said.

Grace's eyes darted again. "Us?"

"Bo—Mr. Lambright and I," Mattie explained.

He stepped forward. "The reporters said some unpleasant things. I hope they weren't offensive to you too."

255

"They didn't see me. I cut through the woods." Grace drew Mattie into a hug. "How are you?"

"I'm holding up."

Grace pushed Mattie out to arm's length and studied her friend. "I'm glad they finally let you go. I spent all morning at the hospital hoping to see Nathan, but the nurses said he was too critical for visitors. Is Amanda taking a nap?"

Mattie's eyes welled. "She's—" Her voice cracked.

Grace looked at Bo. "Mattie's home. She can have her *kinner* back, *jah*?"

"It's not that simple." *If only it was . . .*

Mattie backed up and Grace's arms fell to her side. "I'm glad the reporters didn't give you a fit."

"Should I go to the mill and fetch the men?"

Bo held up his hand. "Let me see what I can do." As he started toward the door, his phone rang. He glanced at Mattie's hopeful expression as he dug his hand into his pocket.

Mattie studied Bo as he took the call. He hadn't said much since "hello" but judging by the way his nostrils flared, he wasn't pleased with what the caller had to say.

Bo cracked a smile at Mattie, then cupped the phone with his other hand, turned, and spoke in a low, growly tone. "Am I supposed to take that as a threat, Erica?"

Grace elbowed Mattie's ribs, then mouthed, *Who is it?*

Mattie shook her head, concern growing with every second.

Bo shifted his stance. "No, I will not . . . No! . . . I'm hanging up now, Davis." His shoulders lifted, then sagged as he sighed. He slipped his phone back into his pocket and faced them. "Sorry about that. I should have taken the call outside."

"That's okay. The reporters would have gobbled you up like fresh-baked cookies."

"I'm sure they'd try." He motioned to the door. "I should probably go talk to them again." He took a few steps.

"Bo?" Mattie said, stopping him before he reached the door. She wasn't one to pry, but if the call was regarding her children, she'd go stir-crazy if he didn't say so. "Is everything all right?"

"Yeah."

She'd recognized the name Erica Davis as the person who had introduced herself as his partner. "Do you need to go back to work?"

"No." He tugged on the collar of his starched white shirt and loosened his black tie. Either nerves or heat was getting to him, maybe both. One of the shirt buttons pinged to the floor. His gaze swept the area.

Mattie spotted the tiny white button near the table leg, picked it up, and handed it to him.

"Thank you. I'm always popping buttons," he

said, dropping it into his shirt pocket. He wiped his hands on his pants.

"I can brew a good tension alleviator, if you'd like something more to drink."

"It's potent," Grace added, moving to the window.

"Sure. I could probably use a cup after I deal with the media."

"We haven't had this many *Englischers* around here since the escapees from the mental hospital," Grace said, looking outside.

Bo's wide eyes steadied on Mattie. "Were you one of those hostages?"

"*Nay, nett* me." Mattie motioned to her friend. "Grace was held hostage, though. It was in all the papers."

"Yes, I remember reading about that a couple years ago."

Mattie glanced over her shoulder at Grace still looking at something—someone—out the window. It wasn't like her friend to blurt anything about that time in front of a stranger. Mattie turned back to Bo. "They gave us all a scare."

"I'm sure they did." His eyes held hers in a look filled with compassion and concern. She averted her attention. Oh, why did his stare have to be so compelling?

"I'll be back in a minute," he said and left the kitchen.

Grace spun around, the curtain swaying in her wake. "What's going on? What's he doing here?"

"He paid *mei* bail. I was going to try to get a ride home from Cora, but when I went outside to call her, news reporters surrounded me, saying awful things about me, our settlement." It might have been wrong to seek shelter with an *Englischer*, but she didn't know where else to turn.

"Did he tell you he knows where Amanda is and that he came here to get her clothes?"

"No. I mean—he said Amanda is in a *gut* home. He's trying to help me get her back."

"You believe him?"

Mattie bowed her head. Bo didn't have to bail her out of jail, yet he did. She lifted her head. "*Jah*, I do. I believe he wants to help." She went to the window. Near the greenhouse, Bo spoke to the group, his feet shoulder width apart and arms crossed over his chest, a force to be reckoned with.

When Bo turned and marched toward the house, she dropped the curtain and hurried to open the door. "What did they say? Are they leaving?"

He scratched his jaw. "They want to buy herbs."

"What!"

He shrugged. "You have a sign out front with hours of business posted. They want to buy herbs."

"I wouldn't sell them . . . a weed," she snorted.

Bo's phone rang and he quickly answered. "What did you find out?"

She appreciated the fact that he skipped the formalities and got to the point. Grace took Mattie's hand and gave it a gentle squeeze.

He closed his eyes and pinched the bridge of his nose. "What's the stipulation?"

Mattie's heart hammered. With his eyes shut, his expression wasn't readable.

"I see . . ."

He wasn't saying much and his tone stayed even, but still her insides quivered. She hung on every breath he took.

"Yes," he said, opening his eyes and steeling them on Mattie. "It'll have to work, won't it?"

# Chapter Twenty-two

"Judge Steinway granted visitation," Bo said, offering the good news to Mattie first. She leaned against the kitchen counter, hand to her chest, teary-eyed, and Grace at her side. Bo shoved his cell phone back into his pocket. "We can pick up the paperwork in an hour."

"That's *wunderbaar* news." Grace pulled a stunned Mattie into a hug. "Your *kinner* are coming home."

Mattie's gaze met his and she sobered. She stepped away from her friend and moved closer to him. "Is that true, Bo? *Mei* children are coming home?"

Bo shook his head. "No. The visitation is limited to two hours . . . a week."

She gasped. "A week?"

"I know it's not much."

She pinned him with a stare and pointed to her chest. "I'm their *mamm*. I've been with them twenty-four hours a day since they were born. Now I'm limited to two hours *a week?*"

He stepped backward, butting up against the cabinet. "It's visitation nonetheless. Two hours is better than not seeing them at all."

As the information soaked in, her shoulders wilted. She looked down. "In everything give thanks, for this is the will of God." She quoted the verse in Thessalonians, though her tone lacked conviction.

"He upholds the righteous," Bo said quietly.

Her head shot up, and she narrowed her eyes at him. "What are you trying to say? I'm walking in unrighteousness—that's why I don't have *mei* children?"

"That wasn't what I meant."

Grace stepped between them. "Mattie, focus on the *kinner*. They need you." She turned and faced Bo. "When can she see them?"

"Once we get the paperwork . . . but there is one stipulation."

"What is it?" Mattie asked.

"All visitations must be supervised," he said.

"That's fine," Grace said. "I'll go with her."

Bo shook his head. "Court-ordered supervision by either the lawyer or Child Services."

"You?" Mattie said.

"My name was listed as the original investigator of record." He hoped Norton hadn't gone to such lengths as to amend court documents at this point in Bo's internal investigation. If another investigator was listed, Mattie wouldn't see her children anytime soon. As it was, Davis found out he'd bailed Mattie out of jail. She'd tried to threaten him over the phone, telling him that she'd inform Norton and even the review board if he didn't persuade the Amish to sell their land to the fracking company. He wasn't sure why the drilling company was so important to Davis, but he wasn't about to let her leverage his job or Mattie's circumstances with property sale. He hadn't broken any law bailing Mattie out of jail, although he most likely flushed his career down the drain going against Norton's demands.

"So you might be able to arrange for Mattie to have more time with her children?"

"I can't make any promises. I need to read the paperwork." *And pray.*

Mattie motioned to the window. "Are they going to follow us into town—invade *mei* only time with *mei kinner*?"

Bo rubbed the knot forming in the back of his neck. The press would never give her a moment of peace.

"Take *mei* buggy." Grace placed her hands on

Mattie's shoulders. "Do you still have Andy's clothes?"

"Most of them. Why?"

"Bo should be dressed like an Amish man if he's going to be in the buggy."

Mattie's eyes widened at her friend.

"He has to blend in," Grace explained. "And you should probably change your dress."

"I think Grace is right," Bo said. "The reporters have already seen you in that blue dress."

Mattie eyed him head to toe, then rested her gaze on his shoulders. "I don't know that Andy's clothes will fit. He was a strong man. A lumber-jack."

Bo frowned. He worked out five days a week at the gym. He wouldn't exactly call himself scrawny.

"Well?" Grace crossed her arms.

"I put them in storage for Nathan." She buried her face in her hands, stifling a whimper.

"Mattie." Bo cleared his throat. "We can probably figure something else out."

"You'll stick out like a sore thumb," Grace said.

A few seconds followed, then Mattie wiped her eyes. "Okay." Mattie turned. "*Kumm* with me."

He trailed her to the end of the hall and into the bedroom, which also housed a small crate filled with straw. "Where's the lamb?"

"How do you know about Snowball?"

"I noticed the pen the last time I was here. I

found the lamb in the greenhouse and returned him to the barn. Did the mother abandon him?"

"*Jah*. He's sickly." She squatted beside a wooden chest and opened it.

"That's too bad. I noticed your *kinner* were attached to it."

A soft chuckle erupted as she went through the articles of clothing inside the cedar chest.

"What's so funny?"

"You said *kinner*. It sounds odd coming from an *Englischer*."

"*Jah*, I suppose it does." Bo cracked a weak smile. He'd done it again. The words had slipped out naturally.

She rose and stretched out her arms with the stack of clothing, but when he reached for them, she didn't release them immediately. Their closeness must have struck her suddenly because her face turned the color of raspberries. Mattie pushed the clothes against his chest and bolted from the room, muttering something about finding a bag for his *Englisch* clothes.

Mattie turned at the sound of the kitchen floorboards creaking behind her. Her breath caught. Bo had no trouble filling out her husband's shirt. His shoulders were as broad as Andy's. If anything, the suspenders needed lengthening and the pants were an inch too short. His fancy laced shoes would give him away, but that couldn't be helped. His feet looked big compared to Andy's.

Grace elbowed Mattie's side and leaned closer. "*Gutgckichmann, jah?*"

Mattie's face heated. Bo was only a few feet away. He might not know Pennsylvania *Deitsch*, but he certainly could figure out they were talking about him. And dressed in Amish clothes, the man was even more handsome. Mattie pinned on a superficial smile and addressed Bo. "You're a perfect Amish fit—I mean, the clothes fit—you'll blend in—to our—" The quivering inflection in her voice unmasked her embar-rassment and brought a rush of heat to her cheeks and a wider smile to Bo's face.

"Here." She shoved a paper bag toward him. "For your—belongings."

He lowered his nicely folded shirt and pants into the bag, then folded his arms across his chest, making the material taut across his biceps. "Almost like the shirt was made for me."

Mattie sobered. "*Nay*, it wasn't." She left the kitchen to change out of her blue dress. When she returned, Grace was emptying her cabinet of jars of honey, and Bo was gazing out the window.

He turned when she entered the room, a somber look on his face. "I wasn't thinking when I made the comment about the shirt. I'm sorry."

Mattie appreciated the ease with which he admitted he was wrong. At the same time, guilt niggled at her to apologize for her abruptness. "I shouldn't have replied so harshly. I'm sorry too."

Grace glanced over her shoulder. "Is this all the honey you have?"

"There's more in the cellar. Why?" This was not the time to organize her cupboards.

"I'm selling it."

"Can't this wait another day?" Mattie turned to Bo. "Didn't you say the paperwork would be ready in an hour? We need to leave for town."

"I agree." He plucked one of Andy's straw hats off the hook on the wall where it had hung since her late husband had placed it there.

Grace continued gathering the pint-sized jars of honey. "How much do you get for a jar?"

"Grace, I'll fill the orders later," she said sharply. "I want to see *mei* children."

Her friend stopped, reached for Mattie's hands, and gave them a squeeze. "I know." She redirected her attention to Bo. "I'm going to sell it to the reporters while you two sneak out the back door. *Mei* buggy is under the lean-to and the harness is hanging up in the barn."

"That's a great idea." Bo steadied his focus on Mattie. "If they see us leaving in the car, they'll follow us to the hospital. It could be tough getting through the parking lot, let alone inside Nathan's room. We don't want to give the hospital admin-istration any reason to deny visitation."

Grace turned to Mattie. "Stop by the *haus* and

let *Aenti* know what's happening. I don't want her worrying, and she'll be able to tell Ben if I'm *nett* home when he gets back from the mill."

"*Jah*, I'll be sure to let her know." Mattie still didn't like the idea of selling anything to the reporters. It would only encourage them to stay on her property.

Bo glanced at his watch. "How long does it take to get into town by buggy?"

"Thirty or forty minutes depending on the traffic. We should go." Mattie headed to the back door. "To answer your earlier question, I get three dollars a pint."

Bo chuckled. "Grace, charge twenty-three dollars a jar."

"*Ach!*" Mattie's eyes widened. "That isn't a fair price."

Bo shrugged. "Is it fair they've invaded your privacy?" He reached for the door handle. "Are you ready?"

"*Jah*." She looked back at Grace, and getting into the spirit of the game, Mattie winked. "See what herbs you can sell too."

As Grace headed out the front door with a basketful of jars, Mattie and Bo slipped out the back door. Muffled reporter voices filled the air as she led Bo through the thicket of sumac brush and into the white pine forest.

"This is beautiful country," Bo said once they were deep in the woods.

"The men planted these trees the first year we settled. They've been clear-cutting the timber across the river the past few winters and next spring intend to replant those acres as well."

"I noticed a sawmill sign off the main road. I didn't realize it was Amish owned."

"*Jah,* it's—jointly owned." She looked up, past the towering treetops to a little patch of sky. Mattie breathed in deeply, taking in the pungent scent of conifer and oaks. She loved this land and, at the same time, despised it.

Branches snapped underfoot as Bo came up beside her. "How many acres does your district own?"

She shrugged. "Collectively, I suppose it's somewhere around a thousand."

"Wow. That's a lot to timber. If you're replanting what you harvest, your district should have plenty of wood for multiple generations."

Andy had talked about the next generations, their grandchildren one day working in the sawmill. She frowned.

"Did I say something wrong?"

"I'm *nett* used to telling *mei* business to an *Englischer*, is all." She pushed a low-hanging limb aside, the prickly bristles swinging behind her slapped Bo in the chest.

"Ouch," he said under his breath. "I didn't mean to make you sad."

"You didn't."

"I hear the pain in your voice."

She stopped. "I know to an outsider, the Amish come across as stoic. And perhaps we do endure pain and hardship differently, placing our faith in the Lord . . ." But somewhere in the last eighteen months she'd lost her grip on her faith—or was only holding on to it by a thread. She looked down at the ground and pushed some loose pine needles across the sand with the toe of her shoe. "I'm sorry." She looked at him and forced a smile. "I know you're only trying to make conver-sation."

"You don't have anything to be sorry about." His deep blue eyes bore into her soul. "Was timbering how you lost your husband?"

He seemed sincere, but she didn't want to fall under his judgment about Andy's death. Mattie drew a deep breath and released it.

Bo shifted his attention to the hillside, squinting when a ray of sun shone through the branches. He adjusted the hat brim to better shield his eyes. "How much farther is Ben and Grace's house?"

She almost thanked him out loud for changing the subject. "Their pasture is just beyond that stand of birch trees. But we'll have to cut through a large patch of wild raspberry bushes to get there this way."

"Hmm. Thorns."

"The other way is longer." She pointed to the right. "And it'll mean taking the road."

Bo headed toward the stand of birch trees. He didn't want to chance being seen by anyone on the road. Besides, he hadn't had fresh raspberries in years.

When they reached the berry patch, he was shocked by how many raspberry bushes he saw. He quickly found himself in the middle of the patch, surrounded by thorny branches and not many ripe raspberries. His pant legs snagged. His forearms burned from scratches. Bo glanced behind him at Mattie tugging on her dress, her face grimacing. "You need a hand?"

"*Nay, danki.*" She plowed along in silence. After a few moments, she said, "Andy died in his sleep."

Bo faced her. "I can't imagine how painful it was to lose your spouse unexpectedly."

She turned away. "I don't usually talk about it."

Bo liked that Mattie had confided in him, but he also sensed she needed space. He veered to the left where he spotted several clusters of red berries in a sunny area. He plucked a few and popped them in his mouth. The sweet tartness melted on his tongue. He had a handful picked by the time Mattie caught up to him.

"You're bleeding." She pointed to his arm.

He turned his forearm. "Just a scratch. The berries make it worth it." If there were more, he would pick a few handfuls and put them in the bag with his clothes for later.

"They're early this year."

He opened his palm. "Would you like some?"

She took one and ate it. "They're *nett* too bad."

"Better than anything sold in the store."

"Wait another week or two." She marched ahead, climbed over the wooden fence, and strode toward a chestnut-colored horse nibbling on grass in the pasture. "Hello, Jasper," she said, taking hold of the gelding's halter.

Bo plodded alongside them until they reached the gate next to the barn. "I'll take him." He reached for the halter, but she didn't release her hold. "Grace wanted you to let her *aenti* know she was at your house, remember?"

"Oh, that's right." She left Jasper with him and headed toward the house.

Bo led the horse into the barn stall. It didn't take him long to locate the harness hanging on the wall in the equipment room. Some horses were skittish around strangers, but Jasper was calm. The horse took the driving bit without resistance and didn't jerk his head back when Bo placed the blinders or tightened the browband like many horses did. Growing up, Bo could have harnessed a horse in his sleep, but since the accident, his skills had diminished from lack of use.

Bo led Jasper outside the barn, tied the reins to the post near the lean-to, and rolled the buggy out from under the overhang. He tossed the bag with his clothes inside the buggy and finished hitching the horse. Focused on double-checking the equip-ment, he hadn't noticed Mattie until he caught a glimpse of her shadow. He glanced up at her. The sun had highlighted her form, giving her an angelic appearance.

She gasped. "What are you doing?" Then without waiting for a reply, she started to inspect the gear.

Bo stood and wiped the dust off the knees of his pant legs. "Well?"

She worked her way around the horse before answering. "Not many *Englischers* can hitch a buggy."

*Some things come back like tying a shoe.* "I can drive one too."

Mattie untied the reins from the post. "I don't know that *mei* trust extends that far, Mr. Lambright." She opened the door to the buggy and climbed onto the bench.

"Bo." He stopped her from closing the door. "And don't you think it will look odd if the man isn't driving?" He waited until she finally relinquished the reins and slid over. "I know you don't trust me—*yet*."

She pulled her dress skirt closer to her side of the bench. "You seem confident I will some-day."

"I would hope so. Trust should go both ways." He winked. "After all, I did put up my boat as collateral to get you out of jail." He clicked his tongue and Jasper lurched forward. He stole a glance at her profile. She was smiling.

Once they reached the main road, Bo patted his pants pockets in search of his phone, but then remembered Amish pants didn't have pockets. Mattie shot him a disturbed look when he reached for the sack on the floor at her feet. He extended the reins and she moved closer to take them. He fished the phone from the sack. "I just need to make a quick call," he explained, tapping the number pad. The call went straight to his mother's voice mail.

"Hey, it's me. Would it be possible for you to meet me at the hospital with the paperwork? Let me know. Thanks." He disconnected the call. "We should know something soon."

# Chapter Twenty-three

Bo spotted his mother pacing the hospital lobby, dressed in a navy business suit and carrying a large envelope in her hand. He removed the straw hat and approached her. Agnes Nettleton wasn't easily surprised, but when she saw him, she turned ashen.

"Mom, this is Mattie Diener."

His mother broke eye contact with him and pasted on a disingenuous smile for Mattie while extending her hand. "I'm Agnes Nettleton. It's nice to meet you. May I have a word with my son in private?"

"Yes, of course." Mattie crossed the room and sat next to the wall by the vending machines. Although Mattie didn't appear bothered by his mother's blunt request, Bo didn't like the cold manner in which she was dismissed.

"Is there something you haven't told me?" Mother's curt words demanded his attention.

He tugged on the suspenders. "The clothes? It's a long story." One he'd rather not discuss in the lobby.

"Yes, so I'm learning." She lowered her voice. "What are you doing, Bo?"

He glanced across the room at Mattie, then back at his mother.

"You asked me to do a favor, for someone I don't know. You didn't bother to tell me you were placed on suspension at work. How do you think bailing her out of jail looks? Or have you failed to give any consideration to your career?"

He groaned under his breath. That wasn't how he'd planned things to go. "It's just until they do an administrative review. A few days. Can we talk about this later? Please."

"Later might be too late. I spoke with Senator Delanie's daughter, Erica, on my way here."

Bo tightened his jaw. His mother didn't see Davis as the manipulator she was.

"Just because they're religious people doesn't mean they don't—"

"Don't what?"

"Abuse their children in the name of discipline. This woman you're trying to protect—"

He held up his hand. "Stop. Please."

She clamped her mouth closed and stared up at the light fixture, her nostrils flaring.

"I'm going to insist that we talk about this later."

His mother squared her shoulders. "Perhaps after you see the boy you'll think differently of what that woman—or someone in her settlement—has done. Bo, why are you not seeing this case clearly?"

He drew a deep breath. "Please don't listen to Erica. She has no experience, and she's intent on building her name. She told me so herself. Besides that, she doesn't know anything about the Amish way."

"But we both recognize firsthand what abusive power can do."

He lowered his head.

"Bo," she said, softening her tone. "I'm sure I don't have to remind you how you were treated. Your family looked straight at you and announced that you were dead."

A lump grew in his throat. "Because in their eyes, I was—I still am."

"You're not going to get back in the Amish good

275

graces by helping this woman. You don't owe her anything."

"Her name is Mattie." He motioned to the envelope in his mother's hand. "I believe you're holding the paperwork that makes me her children's advocate. May I have the documents now, please?"

She gazed at the envelope with a long face. "I hope you don't forget why you became a social worker."

He swallowed hard. "I won't."

"Bo, once Willard is made aware of the fact you are under investigation, he'll have no choice but to revoke the court order."

"I understand."

She handed him the envelope. "May I ask a question that doesn't pertain to this case?"

He shrugged. "Sure."

"Will you be home in time for dinner?"

Bo winked. "Do you have another dinner party planned?"

"No." She smiled. "Although I could probably arrange something. I know how much you love mingling with the guests." Her witty banter didn't mask her concern, but he appreciated her attempt at lightening the tension between them.

"I'll try to get home early."

"Very well then." She straightened her shoulders and smoothed the lapels on her blazer. "You probably shouldn't keep that young woman waiting any longer. I'm sure she wants to spend time with her son."

Bo looked at Mattie, sitting on the edge of the seat, nervously working her hands as if applying lotion. He tapped the envelope against his palm and faced his mother. "Thank you for this. It really means a lot to me."

"Yes, well, a mother will do just about anything for her child, even if the child is an adult." She opened her purse and reached inside. "Before I forget, Josh brought this by the house." She handed him his wallet. "He left work early. I hope he doesn't plan to make a habit of that."

"I'll talk to him." After he found out how Josh managed to get his wallet back.

Although Mattie hadn't been able to hear the conversation between Bo and his mother, their facial expressions conveyed that the discussion was heated. The stiff handshake from his mother told Mattie that she didn't approve of her son's involvement. She had clutched the envelope for the longest time as if she was reconsidering her choice to help, but Bo had it now, and that's what mattered. The wink he'd given his mother seemed to ease the tension between them and for that she was thankful. Mattie wrung her hands. Waiting was difficult, especially since every fiber of her being longed to see Nathan.

Finally, Bo walked toward her. Mattie stood

and met him in the center of the lobby. "Can I see Nathan *nau?*"

"Let's find out what this says." He opened the envelope and removed the document, then scanned the pages.

"Well?" she said after a few moments.

He peered up at her and smiled. "You really need to work more on your patience."

"Don't tease me at a time like this." She was apt to say something she would regret if she had to wait one more second.

"You have two hours." He guided her toward the hallway leading to the patient rooms. "Don't be surprised if the administration will need to verify this document before allowing you to proceed."

"What does that mean?"

"You might not be allowed in the room immediately."

Her shoulders sank. *Lord, please clear the way.*

He patted her back. "Don't lose hope. We'll cross that bridge if it comes."

Mattie forced a smile. Bo was kind and certainly attentive. She was glad he was with her, even though he was an outsider.

They reached the nurses' desk, and Mattie held her breath as Bo showed the nurse in charge the document.

"You can make a copy for your records, if you like," he told the woman in blue scrubs.

"Can I see your identification, please?"

Bo removed the information from his wallet and handed it to her.

"Thank you." The nurse disappeared from the desk with the papers.

Bo glanced at Mattie. "Have you prayed?"

"*Jah.*"

"Me too."

He drummed his fingers on the counter, humming a tune she wasn't familiar with, and every few seconds he would look at her and smile. Up until now, he hadn't struck her as the nervous type. But something in his eyes told her otherwise today. She wanted to ask if he expected trouble, but he'd already warned her the paperwork might require administration approval.

The nurse returned, handed Bo's license and paperwork back to him, then said, "You'll have an hour—"

*Two hours.* Mattie opened her mouth, but Bo's hand came up and she closed it.

"As I was saying," the nurse said, directing her comment to Mattie. "You'll have a total of two hours, however, the time will be divided into two visits with an hour in between. That will give his nurse time to attend to Nathan's needs."

"Thank you," Bo said. "What room is he in?"

"He's in our pediatric wing. I can show you the way." She came out from behind the workstation and motioned to the left.

Mattie's heart pounded with anticipation. Nathan would ask to go home and she wasn't sure how to respond. He'd also want her to stay longer than two hours. Her stomach flipped. Nathan was smart. He would see that something was wrong and she refused to lie to him. Mattie relaxed her expression. She would tell Nathan the doctors wanted him well rested.

"You okay?" Bo lifted his brows.

Kind, caring, she was beginning to see traits in him she liked. "I'm fine." They entered the children's area with colorful animals painted on the walls. Mattie read the room numbers on the doors. 2202, 03 . . .

The nurse stopped in front of 2205. "Please wait here a moment while I check to see if he's ready for a visit." She disappeared into the room and returned a few moments later. "His nurse, Jean, is inside the room. Doctor Oshay will probably talk with you after your visit."

"*Doktah* Oshay? I thought *Doktah* Wellington was treating him," Mattie said.

"She requested Doctor Oshay's consult earlier today. I'll let him know that you're here. I'm sure he'll want to talk with you."

"Okay," Mattie said.

Bo thanked her and promised to keep close tabs on the time. He opened the door to the room. It took a moment for her eyes to adjust to the dim light. She moved closer to the oversized crib, which was enclosed in a clear plastic canopy.

"It's an oxygen tent," Bo volunteered as if reading her mind.

She took a few short steps, then rushed to Nathan's bedside. Staring through the thick plastic, she gasped at the sight of his bruised body.

"Nathan?" her voice squeaked. "It's *Mamm*."

His eyes remained closed.

"Nathan?" she repeated louder. She turned to Bo on her right, tears blurring her vision. "He's—he's *nett*—responding. Something—something is—" Air depleted from her lungs in a whoosh as Bo brought her into his arms and pressed her against his chest. "Something's wrong. He doesn't even know I'm here." She sobbed.

"I know it's hard." He rubbed the palm of his hand against her back in circular motions.

"He doesn't know I'm here." She breathed in and, for a brief second, caught a whiff of Andy's woodsy scent on his shirt, and cried harder.

At a loss of words to comfort Mattie, Bo held her tighter. Now he never wanted to let go.

He looked away from the boy's bruised body. Norton's description had been spot-on. Nathan appeared to have either been bludgeoned with a blunt object or trampled on by horses. Guilt washed over him. He'd been gauging the sincerity of Mattie's tears from the time they walked into the room, and even her willingness to be held by an *Englischer*. It had to be a horse that caused these injuries—not Mattie. Surely she would know if he'd been trampled. Maybe she was covering up for someone, like the man chopping wood at her place. *Lord, help this child.*

Mattie muttered something else. Though pressed against his chest, he could only make out, "Why?"

"We're keeping him sedated, Mrs. Diener," the nurse said.

At the sound of the woman's voice, Mattie withdrew her body from his chest and averted her eyes from the nurse to Nathan.

Bo cleared his throat. "Could we open the tent zipper so his mother can hold his hand a few minutes?"

The nurse glanced at the machine next to the bed. "Sure, his vitals are stable."

Bo unzipped the tent. "Go ahead, Mattie. Hold his hand and let him know that you're here with him."

She slipped her hand inside and reached for her son's small fingers. "Nathan, honey. *Mamm*'s here." Her voice cracked again.

Bo nodded, reassuringly.

*"Ich liebe dich, sohn."*

Bo's throat tightened.

"I'm sorry about all this, Nathan," Mattie said. "I'm so sorry."

Bo fought to dismiss the declaration of guilt on

Mattie's part. *I'm sorry . . . about all of this.* The remorse was so thick it seemed to hang in the air.

Something wasn't adding up.

# Chapter Twenty-four

Mattie left the hospital room in a daze only after Bo nudged her arm and reminded her of the visitation rules. The first hour had passed so quickly. Nathan had slept through the entire visit. The image of his battered body would remain etched in her mind forever.

"Would you like to get a cup of coffee?" Bo said quietly.

She looked over her shoulder at the closed door to Nathan's room with the sign posted No Visitors. It wasn't likely the nurse would let her in before the next allotted time.

"The nurse can page us overhead if his condition changes," Bo said.

"They'll do that?" They hadn't been willing to share information with her thus far.

"I'll let them know that we're going to the cafeteria." Bo strode to the nurses' station, waited for the woman to get off the phone, then spoke to her, motioning in Mattie's direction before handing the nurse one of his cards.

"Ready?" Bo smiled at Mattie. "I gave them my cell number in case they preferred to reach us by phone."

"Did they say anything about Nathan's condition?"

"No, but I'm sure you'll have a chance to talk with the doctor before we leave." He gestured toward the elevators. "Shall we go?"

Mattie wasn't sure she wanted coffee, but maybe if they took a few extra minutes, Nathan's sedation would have time to wear off some. "Sure." She offered a tight smile, then proceeded down the hallway.

The scent of bread baking awakened her sense of responsibility as they rounded the corner of the hall. She hadn't been home long enough to prepare bread dough—to cook anything.

He directed her into the cafeteria. "It smells good, doesn't it?"

"*Jah.*" She realized then she hadn't eaten since yesterday. Not that she could hold anything down.

"Are you hungry?" He picked up a food tray. "The supper dishes aren't out yet, but it looks like the salad bar is open."

She stared straight ahead, focused on nothing in particular. It wasn't until he nudged her arm with his elbow that she responded a mechanical, "*Nay, danki.*" Grace would say Mattie's blood sugar was low, given her dazed response.

He returned the tray to its holder, then continued to the beverage area where he filled two Styrofoam cups with coffee. "You sure you don't want something to eat?" he asked before they reached the register.

"I'm sure." She hadn't felt this out of sorts since Andy's death. It had happened before, this so-called detachment. Doctor Roswell had a name for the ailment and prescribed drugs to bring her out of it—or maybe just to cope with it. Grace blamed even that on low blood sugar.

"I've never seen those bruises," she said unprompted. She would have known, even in a dazed state of mind, if she had done such a horrific thing. She was a good mother.

"I was surprised myself." Bo lifted his cup and took a drink.

She tore off the corner of a napkin and rolled it between her fingers into a ball the size of a pea. "His condition is quite serious, isn't it?"

Bo stared over the rim of his cup a few seconds, then set the coffee cup on the table. "Are you okay, Mattie?"

"Why do you ask?" *Don't fall apart. Keep it together.* She made more napkin balls.

"I'm wondering if seeing him . . . in his current condition is . . . too much to handle." His head slightly cocked.

"It's hard. Seeing him that way." She focused on the shredded napkin and willed herself not to cry, but tears welled anyway. "Now look what I've done." She chuckled nervously. "Wouldn't you know I'd start crying after I destroyed *mei* napkin. *Narrish.*"

He handed her his napkin. "Mattie," he said softly. "Prior to taking Nathan to the hospital, what had you done that day?"

He sounded like an investigator again. She turned her attention out the window. They could use rain. The marigolds lining the pathway to the fountain were drooping.

Bo tapped the table with his knuckles.

She looked at him. "I'm sorry. Did you say something?"

He smiled briefly. "Do you remember seeing me at the plant nursery?"

"Of course I do."

"Where were your *kinner*?"

She sat up straighter in the chair. "You think I left them home alone?"

He cleared his throat. "I'm just trying to make some sense of all this."

"What do you think I've been trying to do?" She sniffled and tilted her head up to keep the tears from falling.

"You said you hadn't seen the bruises before," he said. "Do you think that maybe he was pinned in one of the horse stalls or calf pens? He might have gone into the barn to see the lamb and got distracted." He took a sip.

She remained silent. Was he saying she was neglectful?

"Barn accidents are not uncommon," he said, repeating with emphasis. "*Accidents* happen all the time."

"I'm a *gut mamm* to *mei kinner*." She pushed back from the table and stood. "I thought you were trying to help me."

"I am." Bo gathered the cups and scraps and stood. He extended her cup of untouched coffee. "Will you drink this later?"

"I don't think so." She hated being wasteful, but her stomach already burned. "I'll pay you for the *kaffi*."

"That's not necessary." He tossed the drink into the trash, then glanced at his watch.

She lowered her head and studied the wood-like markings on the tile floor. His hand cupped her elbow, and she looked up.

"I know you're overwhelmed. You've had some stressful days and I'm sure you haven't slept, but please trust me when I say that anything I ask you is only to help."

*Lord, is it true? Can I trust him?*

"Mattie, I'll do everything I can for you."

She cleared her throat. "I don't deserve all this attention."

"*Jah*, you do." He guided her by the elbow out of the cafeteria, then released his hand. "They say a person can hear even when they're under sedation. Talk to Nathan. He needs to hear your voice."

If what Bo said was true, she didn't want Nathan only hearing the nurses' voices. He needed to know she was there—in the room. They walked a few minutes in silence, passing the information desk in the lobby and the drinking fountain on the wall outside the restrooms. "Grace was watching Nathan and Amanda," Mattie volunteered in response to his earlier question.

"What?"

"The afternoon I saw you at the nursery, Grace was watching the *kinner*. I had gone to her *haus* for a quilting bee and . . . well, she convinced me to go home and rest." They rounded the corner to the children's wing and Mattie slid to a halt.

Grace, along with the bishop and several other members of the settlement, were standing outside of Nathan's room.

Bo had never had so many skeptical eyes aimed at him in all his life, looking him over head to toe. He tugged awkwardly on the suspenders. The bishop was the first to turn his attention to Mattie and the others followed suit. Except Alvin Graber, the man Bo had seen chopping wood at Mattie's house. Alvin scowled. Bo reasoned the man had a right. After all, Mattie's late husband had probably been Alvin's best friend and now Bo was wearing the man's clothes.

Bo backed away from the crowd, removed his

cell phone from where he'd tucked it under the waistband on the pants, and slipped down the hall and into the waiting room. He checked for missed calls. None. At least Norton hadn't gotten wind that Judge Steinway listed Bo on the court records as the visitation supervisor. He dialed Mrs. Appleton's number. He wanted to arrange to pick up Amanda for Mattie's two-hour visitation, then call Mrs. Walker to check in with Josh. No telling how the kid managed to get Bo's wallet back. Bo wasn't even sure he wanted to know, but he had to find out if Josh was all right.

Mrs. Appleton's phone rang multiple times. Finally, on the sixth ring, the answering machine picked up.

# Chapter Twenty-five

"So what is he doing pretending to be Amish?" Alvin fumed, his face turning bright red as he cornered Mattie at the end of the hallway.

"He's helping me."

Alvin crossed his arms over his chest and snorted. "Where did he get the clothes?"

"They're Andy's."

"Andy's?" he hissed as if lending her husband's clothes were somehow sinful or immoral. Before she could form a rebuttal, he said, "And you think Andy would be okay with you giving his clothes —to an *Englischer*?"

"Bo is only trying to help."

"Bo?" Alvin flinched disapprovingly.

"Yes, and he is trying to help," she repeated with more resolve. She had to remind herself of that a few times on the drive into town. Seeing another man wearing the shirt she had made her husband had stirred painful memories she hadn't been prepared for, but Bo blending in had made it possible to avoid the reporters and that was all that mattered.

"Help?" he grumbled under his breath. "Wasn't he the one who threatened to take them?"

"Bo was the one who arranged for me to have time with *mei kinner*. *Bo* did that."

Alvin shifted his stance, irritation marring his face.

Mattie straightened to her full height and jetted her chin up. Bo had bailed her out of jail, and he'd talked to the right people to obtain visitation, something even her lawyer hadn't bothered to attempt. Bo sheltered her from the reporters, from the numerous cameras and questions. The more she tallied all he'd done, the guiltier she felt for not having trusted him only minutes ago in the cafeteria.

The longer Alvin stared at her, the more irked she became. She glanced at the wall clock over the nurses' station. Several minutes had passed and

Alvin still hadn't asked about Nathan's condition. "The man is in the waiting room *on his cell phone*." Alvin shook his head. "Talking on his phone, dressed like one of us. How do you think that makes us look? Hypocritical," he answered himself.

"I'm sure it's an important call," she said dismissively and turned to look out the window. Amish buggies dotted the otherwise full parking lot. The horses were tied to the light posts, their heads hanging low, tired. She knew how they felt.

"To be honest, I'm feeling left out," he admitted quietly. "I didn't know you were out of jail until the news people cornered me when I went over to your *haus* to check on the lamb. Then hearing the man's phone conversation that there'd been a new development in the Diener case . . . well, I guess it struck me wrong that I would have to hear the news from an *Englischer*."

"Bo said new developments?"

Alvin half shrugged. "He said he would stop by and fill *her* in."

Mattie bit her lip. Bo could have been talking with his partner, Erica Davis. But wouldn't she already know about the visitation? Were there new developments she hadn't heard about? Hope lifted her spirit.

"Well, are you going to tell me what's going on? Is Nathan really covered in bruises?"

"*Jah*, he is."

"The reporters said you did it."

"I know." She hated that so many people already found her guilty.

"Well?"

Mattie growled under her breath. *You too?*

A man dressed in a long white coat approached the group, searching their faces. "Mrs. Diener?"

Mattie's heart raced as she moved past Alvin and approached the doctor. Then Bo stepped into her peripheral vision and her pulse slowed. She'd already begun to rely on his strength. "I'm Mrs. Diener."

"I'm Doctor Oshay." He extended his hand. "I would like to talk with you about your son's condition."

Bo's heart lurched at the gravity in the doctor's tone. Mattie must not have noticed the same weightiness; she was still smiling. No doubt feeling relieved that she would finally have her questions answered.

Bo weaved through the crowded hallway despite the hard stares from the Amish members who had gathered around Mattie. He was the court-appointed advocate for the child and the self-appointed one for Mattie. He had to be near. But those surrounding her didn't budge, and Bo was forced to stop a few feet away.

Mattie stepped toward the doctor. "How is *mei sohn*?"

"He's in critical condition. I understand you've spent some time with him."

"Only an hour and he didn't wake up."

"He's—"

The crowd parted like the Red Sea for a wheelchair-bound child and the nurse rolling the IV pole behind him to pass.

Doctor Oshay glanced at the others in the hall, then turned and spoke directly to Mattie. Unable to hear the doctor from where he was leaning against the wall, Bo studied Mattie's somber expression.

Her gaze flitted toward him.

That was his cue. Bo pushed off the wall and was at Mattie's side a moment later.

"I think it would be best if we go somewhere to talk in private," the doctor said.

Mattie's eyes glistened. "Okay."

"Excuse me," Bo said, stepping forward. "I'm Bo Lambright, the court-appointed advocate for Nathan Diener. I would like to be present for the discussion as well."

Doctor Oshay eyed Bo's attire from the straw hat in his hand to his brown leather shoes with an anchor on the tongue, then replied, "I'll leave that decision up to Mrs. Diener."

"I'm okay with that." Mattie shot him a glance that said more than being okay. She appeared relieved he had spoken up. Mattie released her hand from Grace's and followed the doctor to the conference room.

Doctor Oshay took the seat at the end of the long conference table while Bo sat next to Mattie, who was wringing her hands.

"As I said in the hall, I'm Doctor Oshay. I'm one of the gastroenterologists on staff and was asked by your son's doctor to consult on his case."

"How is he?" Mattie stammered.

"I wish I had better news for you. Nathan is a very sick child."

"I didn't beat him—*nett* with *mei* hand. *Nett* with the broom handle. I don't know how he got those bruises."

"I don't believe the bruises were caused by physical trauma either," the doctor said.

Bo leaned forward. "Are you willing to tell that to the judge?"

"At this time, I would ask that we focus on Nathan's medical issues. He has a condition called idiopathic thrombocytopenic purpura or ITP. It occurs in patients who have abnormally low platelet counts and often presents as spontaneous bleeding, even bruising."

"Is it . . . treatable?" Mattie choked on her words.

Bo reached under the table for her hand and gave it a gentle squeeze.

"We're doing everything we can. But we need to discover what the underlying cause is for the platelet destruction."

She gasped. "You don't know?"

Doctor Oshay shook his head. "I was hoping you would be able to provide me with a list of everything he's ingested in the last few days. Sometimes thrombocytopenia is drug induced." He paused as if he was letting the short snippets of information absorb. "In other words," he said, "it's a chemical reaction within his body that's causing the adverse effects. It's very important that you tell me everything, even substances around the house he might have ingested . . . accidently."

Bo pinched the bridge of his nose. He could see where this was headed. Mattie might be off the radar for physically abusing her child, but fingers were wagging once again at the possibility of her poisoning him.

"Is he going to be all right? I mean, once you know what's causing . . ." Her voice trailed off and she clasped her hand over her mouth and briefly looked away.

"It's the matter of timing, Mrs. Diener. The faster you can provide me with a list of products, the sooner I can rule them out." He studied her as if he might get her to crack if he stared long enough, but Mattie just clamped her teeth over her trembling bottom lip.

"Would it be easier to write it down?" Doctor Oshay removed a blank sheet of paper from the patient chart and slid it and a pen in front of her. "It's important. Nathan could suffer spontaneous bleeding if his condition deteriorates any further." The doctor's pager beeped and he excused himself from the room.

Her eyes welled.

"Mattie?" Bo picked up the pen and placed it in her hand. "Make a list." Her stillness sent a surge of acid up the back of his throat. *Lord, I don't understand. I thought You led me to Mattie—to her son. I saw the boy in my dreams. If it's not to help him in some way, then why?*

"Rapid response room 2205." The overhead announcement repeated two more times before it registered that the room number being called was Nathan's. Bo bounded out of the chair, but Mattie beat him out the door.

# Chapter Twenty-six

Numbness spread through Mattie's body as she waited what seemed like hours for the rapid response team to leave Nathan's room. *Clank, clank, clank.* She turned to see a man in scrubs pushing what looked like a toolbox toward the room. He slipped inside without a word. Mattie craned her neck to see into the room, but with the bustle of activity at Nathan's bedside, she couldn't catch even a glimpse of her son before the door closed.

Grace sidled up alongside Mattie and drew her

into a suffocating hug. "He's going to be okay. Have faith."

Mattie's throat tightened as she recalled the words of Jesus in the gospel of John. *In the world you will have tribulation . . .* She squeezed her eyes closed, unable to recite the last part about being of good cheer. How could Jesus expect her to be cheerful over everything that had happened? *In Me, you may have peace.* She had meditated on those words after Andy died but couldn't capture the peace Jesus promised. Perhaps she hadn't meditated on them enough. It seemed God was constantly trying to teach her a lesson in letting go.

She opened her eyes when the door creaked open. A woman carrying a plastic container of blood-filled test tubes exited while another worker carrying what appeared to be blood-filled IV bags went into the room. The woman made eye contact with Mattie for a half second, then lowered her head and walked swiftly down the hall.

Mattie's gaze fell over the somber faces of those around her. Bishop Yoder; his wife, Mary; Grace; Ben; several other women from her settlement. Then she located Bo, her rock, standing off to the side, and steadied her gaze on him. He pressed a smile and nodded as if to encourage her to remain strong, but he couldn't disguise the bewilderment displayed in his eyes.

Nathan's door opened again. This time Doctor

Oshay came out of the room, his white coat splattered with blood.

Mattie moved out of Grace's embrace. "What's happening to *mei sohn*?"

"Idiopathic epistaxis—a nosebleed."

"Oh." She blew out a breath, tension draining that it wasn't more serious.

He furrowed his brows. "This isn't a typical nosebleed. He hemorrhaged. I was able to cauterize the blood vessels, but unless we identify the source of what's causing the problem, it's like putting a Band-Aid on a severed limb."

The image wasn't one Mattie wanted to think about, not with her son lying so helpless in that crib. "Can I see him?"

"Maybe once he's received the two units of blood I've ordered. He will probably require more, but I'll be monitoring his lab work closely. Once his condition stabilizes, I'd like to arrange transport to a larger facility. I can't reiterate enough how important that list is that I asked you to make."

"I'll work on it *nau*." Mattie was thankful she had something to do other than wait. *Oh, Lord, help me remember. Please.* Weakened by a medley of emotions she couldn't stave off, fear overrode her prayers. Mattie began to sob. She'd failed God.

Bo's phone buzzed. He let it go to voice mail. He was too focused on Mattie and the doctor's conversation outside Nathan's room. At the moment, nothing was more important than learning why the doctor's coat was splattered with blood and why the emergency crash cart was rolled into the room. Tears streamed down Mattie's face and tugged at Bo's heart. He wanted to comfort her, but it wasn't his place. Besides, she wasn't alone. She had her people for support.

After a few minutes, the doctor walked away and went to a cubical workstation at the nurses' desk. Mattie was immediately enveloped in Grace's arms, then another woman hugged her, then another.

Bo rubbed the back of his neck. He paced to the window overlooking the parking lot and saw the horses and buggies. Mattie had support. But that didn't stop him from gnawing away at his reserve. Finally, he pressed through the crowd.

"Mattie?" The urgency in his voice startled even him. Now he had everyone's attention.

She pulled away from an elderly woman's arms and wiped her red-rimmed eyes.

"What did the doctor say?" His words came out too fast and ran together to pass as merely inquiring for professional reasons.

"His nose started bleeding. I don't remember what he called it." She glanced at the others standing by her, but they shook their heads.

A nosebleed shouldn't summon a crash cart to

the room unless . . . "They got the bleeding stopped, right?"

"*Jah*, and the *doktah* ordered blood transfusions too."

Bo rubbed his jaw.

"I have to work on that list the *doktah* asked for."

He wanted to have a minute alone with her, and this was a good enough reason to break her away from the others. He motioned to the room. "The paper is still on the table."

Mattie made Grace promise to come get her if there was more news, then went with Bo to the conference room.

Bo closed the door behind them. Taking the chair opposite hers, he asked, "How are you doing?"

She didn't answer immediately, and when she looked up, her eyes were glossy with tears. "I'm all right."

"Sure?"

"*Nay*," she wheezed.

He reached across the table for her hand and gave it a gentle squeeze. "Nathan's in God's hands."

"I know."

She didn't pull her hand away and he didn't release his for several moments. When he did, he tapped the paper. "You should start making the list for the doctor."

Mattie jotted a few things down and paused. "I can't think."

"What do you have so far?"

She picked up the paper. "Oatmeal, honey, milk, and bread." She tossed the paper on the table. "Everything's a blur."

Bo snatched the paper and pen. "Close your eyes."

"What?"

"Close your eyes," he repeated. He waited until she finally did. "The doctor wanted a list of anything he might have ingested. Cleaning supplies. Chemicals. *Plants*. Now picture your greenhouse. You're opening the door. What do you see on the left?"

"*Mei* worktable."

"And?"

Her eyes popped open. "I don't see how this is going to help. Is this a trust thing?"

"I already know you trust me. Now, close your eyes."

She did, but more out of embarrassment. Her face was flushed, a shade of pink he'd like to see more often because of the way it intensified the simple beauty of her face. "What's on the table?"

"Potting soil and clay pots."

"What's hanging above the table?"

Her eyes opened again. "How do you know I have herbs hanging?"

301

"I've been in your greenhouse. I told you. The day I came over—the day you fainted—I heard a lamb bleating. I found him in your greenhouse and I returned him to the barn."

"Oh." She closed her eyes without his prompting.

"What herbs are drying?"

"Rosemary. Lavender. Sage."

Bo listed everything she mentioned. He walked her through the greenhouse, then the soap detergents in the washhouse, the cleaning supplies under the kitchen sink, and finally everything in the bathroom. "I think this is a good place for the doctor to start," he said, looking over the page-long list.

Her eyes lit. "I told you about feverfew, right?"

"Right." He remembered reading in the chart about her giving Nathan that herb, but Bo added it to the list anyway with a sidenote that she'd made him a broth the day he was first admitted. The doctor probably read it in the chart, but it didn't hurt to put it on the list.

"Foxglove. Add that one to the list. I have plants surrounding *mei* garden to keep the deer out and seeds in the greenhouse."

Bo jotted down the information. He would inspect the barn and greenhouse just to be sure nothing was overlooked once they left the hospital, but the current list would get the doctor started on things to rule out.

"*Danki.* I don't know that I could have *kumm* up with a list without your help."

"You're *wilkom*." He winked.

She cracked a weak smile. "Are you making fun of me?"

"*Nay*—no," he teased, enjoying her faint smile.

"Do you think I'll be able to see Nathan *nau*?"

"Let's ask." He pushed up from the chair and, as he rounded the table to her side, his phone buzzed.

"Lambright."

Mattie pointed at the door and mouthed, *I'll go out.*

Bo cupped his hand over the receiver. "Don't go. This will just take a minute."

"Hello? Bo, is that you?" The woman's frantic voice sounded muffled.

"Yes, Mrs. Walker. Is everything all right?"

"It's Josh. Have you heard from him?"

"No. How long has he been gone?"

Mrs. Walker sighed. "He was gone when I got up this morning. I kept thinking he would be back, but now it's after dinner. I'm really worried."

Bo grimaced. "Let me look into it and I'll get back with you."

"I realize he's had a troubled history," Mrs. Walker said, "but I can't have his poor behavior influencing the other boys. I can't keep him if he's going to constantly disobey the rules."

"I'll have a talk with Josh when I find him." For

the first time since becoming Josh's caseworker and Big Brother, he wanted to give the kid a good shake, but that would make Bo no better than his own father—the past would repeat itself, the very reason Bo would never marry and have children.

"Please call me as soon as you hear something."

"I will." He ended his call. "Something's come up, Mattie."

"You're leaving?" Desperation filled her eyes. "Do you have to?"

She was talking out of fear, but for a split second, he felt the urge to pull her into his arms and make promises that he could never keep. He cleared his throat. "I can come back and check on you."

She blinked a few times and fresh tears dribbled down her cheeks. "They're *nett* going to let me see Nathan again unless you're with me, are they?" She paused. "I'm sorry. I have no business asking you to stay."

He grabbed the paper on the table. "Let's turn this in and see if the doctor will make an exception about the visitation." He cupped her elbow and guided her out of the room. In the hall, the other church members met them. Bo felt the weight of all of their stone-cold stares, the bishop's in particular. For all he knew, Mattie was the bishop's daughter or daughter-in law. He wouldn't go down that road. Bo released Mattie's elbow. "You wait here while I try to make the arrangements."

Bo approached the nurse at the desk. "I have the list Doctor Oshay asked Mrs. Diener to make. I would also like to speak with him a minute if that's possible." A few moments later, Bo stood before the doctor explaining the situation.

"I can't make that decision," Doctor Oshay said in an even tone. "You need permission from either Doctor Wellington, who is the attending physician, or administration. I'll have Doctor Wellington paged."

"Thank you." Bo glanced at his watch as Doctor Oshay approached the nurses' station. Even if Doctor Wellington was available, she wouldn't allow the unsupervised visitation. She was the reason Bo was under investigation. Administration might okay the request provided a hospital caseworker was present, but Ms. Elroy had twisted Mattie's words the last time.

"Excuse me," he said, getting the attention of the nurse making the call. "I'm going to stay and monitor the visitation. I'm sorry for all the trouble."

She hung up the phone. "To be honest, it's after five and the administration building is closed for the day. I doubt the on-call administrator would have agreed to the request over the phone anyway."

"I understand." Bo pulled in a long breath and released it slowly. Turning, he spotted Mattie in the crowd. Finding Josh would have to wait. Mattie needed him more.

• • •

Mattie watched Bo the moment he turned away from the nurses' desk. She'd seen that worried look before. "Excuse me," she muttered to Grace and the others and she walked toward Bo. "Are they going to let me see Nathan?"

"In a few minutes."

"Alone?"

Bo held her gaze a half second, then averted his attention to the floor. "The nurse was going to see if the hospital case manager could monitor the . . ." He looked up. "I don't trust her."

Mattie swallowed hard. She remembered the woman from when Nathan was in the hospital the last time. She didn't trust her either. At the same time, she was still wrestling with trusting Bo despite sensing he wanted the best for her— for Nathan.

"I'm going to stay," he said.

"I thought you needed to leave. You said something had come up."

"It can wait."

His smile had a way of taking her by surprise— warming her insides. She looked down at the hem of her dress and silently chided herself for allowing a simple smile to affect her. He was an *Englischer* after all, someone she shouldn't allow to affect her in private ways. He looked beyond her and waved.

Mattie glanced over her shoulder at the nurse

leaving Nathan's room, then turned and hurried over to the woman. "How is he? Can I see him *nau?*"

"He's resting comfortably, Mrs. Diener. Has the doctor talked with you about the bleeding episode?"

Bo glanced at Mattie, then addressed the nurse. "We know Nathan's been given a couple of units of blood to replace what he lost, and that his condition is guarded."

Mattie entered Nathan's room, and seeing his ashen skin, she clamped her hand over her mouth to stifle a gasp. Her gaze traveled to a small tube that protruded from his nose and was connected to a container on the wall, which collected blood.

"Don't be alarmed by the restraints," the nurse said, drawing Mattie's attention to her son's secured wrists. "They keep him from pulling the tube out of his nose."

Mattie's throat tightened.

"The tube isn't hurting him," Bo volunteered.

"Yes, that's true," the nurse said. "We're able to monitor the amount of blood loss. We can use that information along with the lab work to determine how much blood to replace."

The container wasn't full. Mattie wanted to ask at what point they would give him more but couldn't get the words to leave her mouth. She started to tremble. First her hands, then arms, then her entire body began to shake uncontrollably.

Bo pushed a chair from the corner of the room closer to the bed. "I think you should sit down," he said, guiding Mattie into the vinyl cushioned chair.

She could only sit a moment before her nerves got the best of her. Mattie peered over at the nurse writing on a clipboard. "Has he asked for me?"

The nurse looked up from the papers. "He hasn't awakened . . . yet."

"Will he?" Her voice broke.

"Right now it's better for him to remain sedated." The nurse continued her paperwork.

Mattie's legs weakened. She took a step backward and Bo was there to guide her into the chair again. His calm, reassuring presence didn't stop her eyes from welling with tears. "He's so pale." Even to her ears, she sounded weak, frail. Hopeless.

Bo's Adam's apple bobbed down his throat in a hard swallow. He grimaced, then looked up at the light fixtures attached to the ceiling.

Mattie clamped her eyes closed. This was too much. *Lord, I don't understand why this is happening. Nathan is not responding. He doesn't know I'm in the room.*

Her time with Nathan ticked away. Before she had a chance to see his eyes open, the nurse was telling her that visiting hours were over. Mattie looked at Bo. *Ask them to let us stay longer . . . please, ask them.*

As if able to read her mind, he shook his head apologetically. "We've already stayed past our allotted time, Mattie. We need to go."

*Allotted time.* She scoffed. Her son was dying, and what time she had with him was measured in government-allowed minutes. Nathan was her son. Her responsibility. How could she wait another week to see him?

Bo slipped his hand into hers. "Let me help you up," he said, tugging gently.

She rose from the chair, her gaze fixed on Nathan. "You rest *nau, sohn.* I'll be back soon." Her shoulders sagged as she followed Bo out of the room. Soon the other members of the district, whose faces were sober, surrounded them.

"How is he?" Grace asked first.

Mattie shook her head, unable to speak.

"He's lost a lot of blood," Bo replied. "They've given him blood, but his blood pressure is low and there's still the risk of him spontaneously bleeding again."

Grace wrapped her arm around Mattie's shoulders but directed her question to Bo. "Why is he losing blood?"

Bo shrugged. "That's something they are still trying to figure out." He glanced at Mattie, then looked at Ben. "I understand the children were in your care prior to Nathan being admitted."

"Yes. Nathan had a fever. That was all." Ben's expression hardened. "Why do you ask?"

"Mattie's been asked to make a list of . . . foods and even products Nathan had access to and might have accidently ingested. Would you do the same? Any information will help."

"*Jah*, of course," Ben said. The frown softened. "Anything for Mattie and Nathan."

Bo's cell phone rang. "Excuse me." He stepped to the other end of the hall and took the call. A few minutes later, he returned, a stricken look on his face. "Mattie, can I talk with you a moment?"

She studied his grim expression. "What is it? Did you hear something more about Nathan?"

"No. I need to leave." He glanced over her shoulder at the others and shifted his stance. "I-I just wanted you to know I'm going to petition the judge to extend your time."

"Will the judge do that?"

"I don't know." He glanced at the others. "Will you be okay driving home alone?"

"*Jah*, of course."

He stared at her a moment, wishing he didn't have to leave. "I'll pick up my car later. Is that going to be an issue?" His gaze went beyond her for a brief second. "I don't want to leave without —I mean, I'll stay and explain things to the bishop if you think—"

"Everything will be fine." As much as she didn't like the thought of being the focus of gossip, she already was. But if seeing her children meant associating with an *Englischer*, so be it.

"Okay." He smiled. Bo started to turn, then pivoted back around. "I'm praying for Nathan . . . and you."

"He needs a miracle." She glanced up at the ceiling and blinked back the tears. "Please," she whispered. "Get the judge to change his mind."

# *Chapter Twenty-seven*

Bo slipped into the restroom and changed out of the Amish clothes, then neatly folded and placed them into the paper bag. In the short time he'd worn the Amish clothes, he'd felt at home in them. Of course he would never make the mistake of admitting that to Mattie again. *Made for him.* He huffed. *Stupid.*

Bo pressed the elevator button. He should have listened to his voice mail earlier. Had he been able to pick up Josh, the kid wouldn't have thumbed a ride—wouldn't have gotten into the car accident, and wouldn't have been hauled into the ER in the back of an ambulance. Bo pressed the button again. Maybe he should take the stairs.

The door opened and Bo hit the Close button a few times. Landing on the lower level, Bo followed the signs to the emergency room.

"I'm looking for Josh Messer. He was just brought in by ambulance. Car accident."

"One moment." The young receptionist picked up the phone, inquired about Josh, then lowered the receiver. "He's in X-ray. The nurse will let you know when he's back."

Bo paced the waiting room, recalling the accident he'd been in as a teen. His recollection was sketchy, the sound of a loud siren mostly. The other details had been erased along with most of his childhood memories. His case stumped a team of specialists. He answered to the name of John Doe for the better part of a year—or so he was told. He couldn't remember most of that either.

"Family of Josh Messer," the nurse standing at the entrance of the waiting room announced.

Bo stepped forward. "I'm his caseworker, Bo Lambright. Someone from here called me when he first arrived." He reached for a business card. "How is he?"

"Hello, Mr. Lambright. His injuries are minor, but the doctor wants to keep him overnight for observation. He has a slight concussion, broken ribs, some lacerations. He's going to be sore for a few days."

Bo let out a heavy sigh. "Can I see him?"

"Yes, follow me."

She led Bo to a curtained-off area where Josh was sitting on a cot, shirt off, ribs bandaged, and holding an ice pack over his right eye.

"I hear they're planning to keep you overnight," Bo said as he approached the cot.

Josh squinted. "I told the doctor I feel fine." When he attempted to move, his teeth clenched and he winced.

"Sure you do." Bo straightened Josh's pillow. "You could've been hurt much worse."

"I suppose you're going to tell me how God must have a plan for my life."

Bo shrugged. "Who knows, maybe you'll become a social worker like me."

Josh chuckled, but immediately held his ribs and grimaced. "Don't make me laugh. It hurts too much."

"Who were you riding with?"

"Friends."

"Am I going to read in the police report that you were drinking?"

"No."

"What about drugs?"

"No. What's with the interrogation?"

Bo eyed the kid hard. "Blood tests are standard procedures. You're telling me the truth, right?"

"Right," he snipped.

A redheaded nurse opened the curtain. "Are you Josh's guardian?"

"No," Bo replied. "But I've called them and they're on the way."

The redhead smiled. "If you could let them know I have paperwork for them to sign, that would be great."

"Sure," Bo said.

The nurse peeked under the ice pack. "You still have a lot of swelling." She lowered the pack. "I'll come back to get you when the room is ready upstairs."

The moment she disappeared behind the curtain, Josh snapped. "Why did you have to call the Walkers?"

"Josh, they're your foster parents."

"Well, can't you get me out of here? I don't want to stay."

Bo shook his head. "Maybe the Walkers can arrange that, but I'm not your guardian."

Josh huffed. "It's just a matter of time before they won't want me."

"Don't say that. You're the one always on the run." Bo shook his head. "You don't know how good you have it."

"I know. No one wants a teenage boy. I've heard it all before. I should be grateful."

"The Walkers are caring people. I wouldn't have placed you with them if I didn't believe it was a good home."

"You say that, but you don't know what it's like living in someone else's house—under their rules."

"I understand more than you think." He'd never shared his story with one of the kids he placed, but maybe it was about time. "I was in an accident like you. I still have the scars—"

The curtain opened again and this time Mr.

Walker entered the treatment area, a concerned look on his face. "How are you feeling, Josh?"

"Bruised."

"That's understandable." The short, gray-suited man extended his hand toward Bo. "Thanks for calling us. My wife is busy with the children." He glanced at Josh. "She wants you to know that she's praying for you."

"Thanks," Josh said and closed his non-iced eye.

The redhead returned with a clipboard in her hands, and after explaining what forms she needed Mr. Walker to sign, she announced Josh's room was ready upstairs.

"I don't know why I have to stay. I feel fine."

"It's precautionary." Mr. Walker patted Josh's shoulder. "Just think, you'll have a TV in your room. You can't get that at home."

Josh cracked a smile, then flinched. "The only time I'll probably ever have a TV to myself, one of my eyes is swollen shut, and I'm seeing double out of the other."

Bo and Mr. Walker chuckled.

A few minutes later, two workers wheeled Josh to his room on the second floor. Mr. Walker and Bo stepped out of the room while the nurse got Josh situated in his new bed.

The lines across the foster father's forehead deepened. "I'm not sure if Josh is going to work out living with us. My wife is always worrying about him."

Bo sighed. He was afraid Josh would wear them down.

"Josh doesn't seem happy with us," Mr. Walker went on to say. "I know he's only been with us a few months but . . ." He shrugged.

"Some kids take longer to adjust." Bo repeated the same thing he told the last two foster families Josh had been placed with.

Mr. Walker shook his head slowly, a perplexed look on his face.

"If you could find it in your heart to give him more time . . . I'll talk to him." *Again.*

After a long, thoughtful pause, Mr. Walker finally said, "I'll ask the wife what she wants to do."

"Thank you." Bo reached for the man's hand and shook it vigorously. "Josh is a good kid."

"Are you going to be here for a while? I hate leaving Josh alone, but I have to work in the morning."

"I'll stay with him." He made a mental note to call his mother and let her know he wouldn't be home for dinner. Hopefully she hadn't made arrangements for them to dine with anyone else.

Bo slouched on the vinyl cushioned chair in Josh's room, stretched out his legs, crossing them at the ankle. Josh's big plan to watch TV all night was short-lived. He fell asleep before the first commercial break.

Bo yawned and stretched out his arms. He made plans to pick up Amanda in the morning from the Appletons so that Mattie could spend time with her daughter. He also called his mother to inform her about staying the night at the hospital and asked her to request more visitation hours for Mattie. Two hours a week was unreasonable, at least in his mind.

As the news aired on the television, Bo fought to keep his eyes open. The announcer was saying something about a heat wave as Bo's eyes closed.

The dry bones, the people's moans, the aimless wandering were familiar to him now. A white cloud of fog settled over him and a deep reverberating voice called out.

"Boaz, My child. Draw closer to Me."

Bo shuffled toward the voice, unable to see anything before him for the blur of white was too thick. He batted away the clouds but more enclosed him.

"You have cried out for help but have not seen My hand. You have prayed for wisdom yet have not listened for My direction. Open your eyes, Boaz. Tell Me what you see."

The fog lifted. "Grass," he said. He was standing in a meadow of green grass, a gentle breeze blowing on his face.

"Listen and you will hear."

Bo stilled as a distant sound of rushing water filled his senses. Then he heard weeping and moved toward the sound. He came to the water and looked across the stream at a mother cradling a child, both of them weeping.

"What do you see?"

"A mother and child."

"Look closer."

Both the mother and child were spotted—leprosy? Bo took a step into the cold stream and immediately sank underwater. He flailed his arms. Kicked his legs. Felt the air leave his lungs, and then he was floating.

Hearing heavy footsteps tromping through the woods a few feet from her garden, Mattie looked up from pulling weeds. She squinted into the early-morning sun as Grace's husband came into view. Ben trekked across the yard, a hardened look on his face.

Mattie pushed off the ground and wiped the dirt off her dress from where she'd been kneeling.

Ben stopped at the foot of her garden, his balled-up hands on his hips and brows furrowed.

"Is something wrong, Ben?"

"You know *mei fraa* is with child and in a

weakened state. Why would you send the police to our *haus* asking questions about the day we took care of your *kinner*?"

"I don't know what you're talking about."

"They *kumm* at dawn with a search warrant. Wanted to catch us both at home, they said."

Mattie plodded barefoot over the loose soil and stopped before him. "What on earth do they want with Grace and you?"

"That's what I want to know. They told us *nett* to leave town. They might have more questions. *Nau mei fraa* is beside herself with worry."

"Ben, I'm so sorry."

"We would never do anything to hurt your *kinner*."

"I know that," she assured him.

"He wasn't bruised at our *haus*—in our care!"

Without realizing it, he was pointing his finger at her. She couldn't blame him for being angry, especially if the police ransacked their house like they had hers, scouring every inch for evidence. Her thoughts went back to what Bo had said to Grace and Ben in the hospital. *"I understand the children were in your care prior to Nathan being admitted."* Mattie's heart sank. She was the one who had told Bo that Grace and Ben had watched the children. Was that the "recent developments" Alvin had overheard Bo say over the phone?

# Chapter Twenty-eight

Bo had been awake since the nurse arrived with Josh's breakfast tray, and he still couldn't shake the events of the dream. He recalled the helpless feeling underwater, unable to reach the surface—unable to reach the mother and child.

"Would you ask the nurse for another carton of milk?" Josh said between slurps of cereal.

"Sure." Bo left the room. He yawned, then glanced at his watch. Half past eight and he was tired. Not a good way to start the day.

The nurses' station was empty. Bo wandered around the area, found an open door, and heard voices from inside the room. "Maureen called in today. Her kid's daycare had an outbreak of lice and she doesn't want her daughter to get it," a woman said.

"Sounds lame to me," another one replied.

"Oh, it's a nightmare. Combing the nits, washing the linen, spraying everything. The poor kid is a social outcast—really. It's like . . . like leprosy was in biblical times."

"Hey, did you know you could get leprosy from armadillos? You can," the younger woman said.

Bo poked his head into the storage room and

cleared his throat. "Excuse me. Can I get another carton of milk, please?"

"Absolutely." The older nurse handed the younger one a box of gloves on her way out the door. "Come with me," she said, motioning with her hand to another room a few feet away. "Do you want white or chocolate?"

"White, please."

She opened a refrigerator and handed him a milk carton. "Anything else?"

"No, this is fine. Thank you." He returned to Josh's room and handed him the milk for cereal Josh had already finished, then plopped down in the chair next to the bed.

*Leprosy.* His mind conjured up the image of the woman and child in his dream. Spots. What did it all mean? Bo rolled the words over and over in his mind until a thought sparked and he shot up from the chair. "I'll be back in a little while."

"Where are you going?" Josh said.

"I have to talk to Nathan's doctor." He sped out of the room, down the hall to the elevator, and after pressing the Up button, he decided to take the stairs. Urgency like nothing he'd experienced before fed adrenaline through his veins. He wasn't even sure why he was suddenly standing at the pediatric nurses' desk. The boy didn't have any spots.

"May I help you?" the nurse asked.

"I'd like to talk with Doctor Oshay, please. About Nathan Diener." He sucked in a deep breath and sent up a silent prayer asking God to stop him if he was wrong—if he was about to make a fool of himself. Then he whispered another prayer asking God to forgive his prideful attitude. The nurse informed him that the doctor was making rounds. She mentioned waiting for him in the waiting room, but Bo chose to loiter near the desk. After several minutes went by, he started to debate whether he'd allowed his mind to run amok—believe things unseen. The boy had no outward signs of leprosy or chicken pox. Then he rebuked the thoughts, reminding himself that faith was hope in things unseen.

A few minutes later, the doctor came out of Nathan's room.

Bo met him in the hall. "How is Nathan Diener?" The doctor's brows crinkled, and Bo quickly reminded him that he was the investigator for Child Services.

"His prognosis isn't good. His liver is beginning to shut down. I've ordered toxic screens on every chemical and plant on the list the mother provided, but everything is coming up negative."

"The boy's sister has chicken pox," Bo blurted. "I know Nathan doesn't have any spots, but I thought you should know he's been exposed."

Doctor Oshay's eyes widened. "When did the chicken pox manifest in the sibling?"

Bo shrugged. "A few days ago. The doctor the foster mother had taken her to said it was a mild case."

"That's important information, thanks," he said over his shoulder as he rushed to the nurses' station where he sat in front of a computer terminal and started typing.

Bo paced, wishing he had more information. He could search his father's library for information, but that would be time consuming, and besides, it wasn't like he had a medical background and could decipher the medical jargon.

The doctor rounded the desk. "Can I speak with you a moment?"

"Yes, of course."

"I need to get in contact with the mother. She doesn't have a phone number listed."

"The Amish don't—she doesn't have one," he said, sparing the doctor about why the Amish didn't believe in modern conveniences. "I can get a message to her to call the hospital."

"I'd rather speak with her in person," Doctor Oshay said. "The sooner, the better."

"I'm on my way." Bo hustled to the elevator. On the ride down to the first level, he typed a short text to Josh saying something had come up that required his attention. Exiting the lobby, he remembered he hadn't picked up his car from Mattie's. Bo dialed the number for a local cab company and waited near the hospital entrance.

Mattie took her frustration out on ridding her garden of weeds. If Grace lost her baby from stress, Mattie would never forgive herself. She was well aware of her dear friend's medical condition, how stress could affect her muscular dystrophy. Bo Lambright had no business involving Grace and Ben in the investigation. No business whatsoever. She reached the end of the first row of pole beans and moved over to the next one, snatching a few beans to snack on before she resumed pulling weeds.

"Mattie," a distant voice called.

She spotted Bo running up the driveway and groaned under her breath. He picked the wrong time to get his car. A tree had fallen across the gravel road leading to their district and the men figured it might keep the news vans away if they didn't rush to remove it. She pulled more weeds.

He stopped at the foot of the garden, bent at the waist, and gulped air. "Did you know your road's . . . blocked?"

"The road's blocked to keep *unwanted* people from trespassing. *Englischers* who don't belong—"

"Mattie." He gestured with an impatient wave for her to get up.

She pushed off her knees with fire in her belly. "Mr. Lambright, that includes you."

He righted himself and pinned her with a

you've-got-to-be-kidding look that added fuel to her determination to set him straight.

"You don't belong here." He'd fooled her once. She wouldn't leave herself vulnerable again. He was an investigator for Child Services, after all.

Bo stormed down the row of beans and towered over her. "I'll talk to the bishop later and clear everything up. But right now the doctor wants you at the hospital." He pointed to the road. "I have a cab waiting. We have to go."

"The doctor? What's wrong with Nathan?" She absentmindedly wiped her dirty hands on the side of her dress.

"I'll tell you on the way into town."

She looked at the dirt on her hands, her dress. "I should probably wash up, change into something . . ."

"Mattie." Bo cupped her shoulders and turned her toward him. "You don't have time." He released her and picked up the nearby watering can. "Hold out your hands."

Cold well water splashed over her hands, spilling over onto the bottom of her dress.

"Sorry, I didn't mean to get you wet." He dug his hand into his pocket, removed a hankie, and wet it.

Mattie wiped her hands on the side of her dress, then examined them. The water didn't wash away the dirt under her fingernails. Anyone would consider her unfit.

"We should go. I don't want the cab leaving without us," Bo said.

Mattie slipped on her shoes she'd kicked into the grass, then took off running.

Bo caught up to her. "I understand how the downed logs will keep the media away, but isn't the bishop worried about a fire? A fire engine wouldn't be able to get down this road."

She was too winded from running to speak. They had a system in place within their district. Should a fire break out, one of the members would direct the fire trucks from the main road down the old timber road.

Bo opened the cab door and Mattie sank into the backseat of the car, her ribs sore from breathing hard and her emotions raw from letting worst-case scenarios play over in her mind.

Bo directed the cab driver to go to the hospital, then shifted on the seat to face her. "Hold still," he said, raising the moist cloth to her face. "You have some dirt smudged here." He tipped her chin. "Are you crying?"

"That surprises you?" Her eyes watered as she spoke. Tears were something she couldn't regulate lately.

"That was a stupid thing to ask, wasn't it?" He wagged his head as if chiding himself.

"Why does the doctor want to see me? Has something changed with Nathan?"

"I told him about Amanda having chicken pox."

"What? *Mei boppli* is sick?" Mattie clasped her hand over her mouth. *Lord, this is too much. Amanda should be home with me.*

"I meant to tell you the other day, but it slipped my mind. I'm sorry," he said.

"You knew she was sick?"

"She's doing all right, though. I did stop by the foster home to see her. I got her to eat."

"She isn't eating?" Mattie wrung her hands.

"Mattie," he said, taking her hands into his. "Amanda is fine."

"And I suppose next you'll say I can trust you," she scoffed.

His eyes pierced hers. "You can."

Mattie freed her hands from his and averted her gaze out the window. She closed her eyes, picturing little Amanda covered in spots and crying for her mama. *The poor child must feel abandoned.*

Bo seemed to know she needed time alone with her thoughts. He remained silent until they reached the hospital. He didn't speak to her until they were alone in the elevator. "I'm sorry if I've caused you problems with your bishop," he said. "I'll explain everything to him."

Mattie studied him a moment. His eyes revealed a deep compassion she hadn't experienced by anyone—even Andy. She steeled herself. "Start by explaining to me why the police were at Grace and Ben's with a search warrant."

327

He shook his head, puzzled. "I don't know what you're talking about."

The elevator door opened. Two people entered, then realized it was going up and got off quickly before the doors shut. They were alone again, and Bo repeated his statement, this time with more emphasis.

"Grace is pregnant, and the last thing she needs is stress."

"If the police are investigating them, it has nothing to do with me. I didn't say anything." His shoulders rose and fell with a heavy breath. "Mattie, the police have to investigate all angles. Everyone who's had contact."

"She's pregnant and doesn't need the stress."

"It's the law." He shrugged and slapped his hands against his thighs. "Neither one of us can stop them from doing their job."

The elevator door opened again, this time on Nathan's floor. The doctor was sitting at a computer workstation behind the nurses' desk. He rose when Bo mentioned his name to the nurse and directed them into the conference room. As much as she was upset with Bo on the ride into town, she was equally grateful he was accompanying her now.

"Mrs. Diener, it was recently brought to my attention that Nathan has been exposed to the chicken pox virus, and while it's a common childhood disease that usually runs its course without issues, it can be very serious in some individuals."

A lump grew in Mattie's throat.

"I believe Nathan has an atypical hemorrhagic condition associated with the chicken pox virus. Any skin eruptions would have been masked by bruising. In other words, this form of chicken pox is more internal rather than the external kind most children experience."

Mattie wiped her eyes. "What does all that mean?"

"The virus is attacking his organs. Primarily his liver. He's in acute liver failure. I've ordered a biopsy to confirm that it is, in fact, the varicella-zoster virus. I've also ordered medicine to combat the disease. But I suspect the damage is extensive. He'll probably require a liver transplant."

The room spun. Nausea washed over her in waves.

"I didn't see any notations in the chart about him being immune compromised," the doctor went on to say. "Has he been an otherwise healthy child?"

"He's always been sickly. He catches colds easily," she said. "Doctor Roswell always thought he was small for his age. He thought maybe it had something to do with *mei* husband having German measles while I was pregnant." Mattie picked at the dirt under her nails.

"How long before we know if he needs a transplant?" Bo asked.

"I have a call into Henry Ford Hospital in Detroit to speak with a transplant surgeon. I'll know more after the biopsy is reported and I have a chance to discuss the case with the surgeon. In the meantime, I'm monitoring his liver enzymes and clotting factors." He paused a moment. "Mrs. Diener, I have to warn you. The odds of finding an organ match before his liver shuts down completely are not likely."

"Are you saying he's going to die?" Her voice strained.

"We're doing everything we can."

She closed her eyes, needing a moment to absorb the news. It all seemed surreal, like a dream. A bad dream she couldn't wake up from. Someone finally identified what was wrong with Nathan only to tell her that he was dying. Panic warred within her. Why was God allowing this to happen?

"Mrs. Diener?" The doctor's voice rose as if it wasn't the first time he'd tried to get her attention.

She glanced up, dazed and unable to form a response.

"Mattie, the doctor asked if you know what your blood type is," Bo said, concern growing in his expression.

It wasn't until he brushed his hand against her arm that she registered his question. *"Mei* what?"

"Blood type," Bo repeated.

She shook her head.

"The reason for asking," the doctor said, "is that there is a living donor procedure where a transplant can be possible through a partial organ. Depending if you're a match, you could potentially donate a portion of your liver to your son." Doctor Oshay went on to explain how the liver was an organ that could regenerate itself. In other words, grow new cells.

The news was both overwhelming and encouraging. Mattie took a deep breath and exhaled slowly. "What do I need to do?"

"We'll start with a full lab work-up." Doctor Oshay removed a prescription pad from his white coat pocket, scrawled something on it, then tore it off the pad. "Take this to the lab. We can talk more once the results are back."

"How dangerous is the surgery?" Bo broke in.

"There's always a chance his body will reject the liver." The doctor handed the prescription to her.

"For Mattie." He leaned forward. "She would be giving part of her liver, right? How dangerous is that?"

"It doesn't matter," she said appreciatively. She studied the unreadable prescription as the doctor explained how any surgery had its risks. She'd rather not be reminded at the moment. Her son's life was on the line. *Lord, please let me be a match.*

"Mrs. Diener will probably be hospitalized a

week to ten days, during which she will have ongoing blood work and tests after the procedure to be certain everything is functioning normal."

"Can I see Nathan?" she blurted.

"I would ask that you get your lab work done first, but after that, I don't have a problem with you staying as long as you wish." He turned to Bo. "Unless the court order doesn't permit such an arrangement."

# Chapter Twenty-nine

Nathan's skin was the color of a canary. Bo wished someone would have prepared Mattie for the jaundice. Her knees buckled midway into the room. If he hadn't been standing directly behind her, she would have hit the floor. He helped her into a nearby chair. "Do you need something to drink?"

She licked her lips. "I think I'm fine."

Her voice sounded weak, hoarse. She wasn't fine. The woman was crumbling, and why wouldn't she? Her child was sick—dying.

She sat a moment, shoulders hunched and head bowed, then pushed off the chair. Bo moved closer to the bed as she did, half expecting to have to catch her again.

"Nathan," she said in a broken pitch. "It's *Mamm*. I'm here." Studying the child, her face cringed. Tears streamed freely down her cheeks, falling onto the front of her dress. "I wish you would open your eyes."

Although unresponsive, the boy's expression was peaceful—hauntingly so.

In a quiet sob, Mattie's shoulders shook. "I don't see any spots."

Bo came up beside her and placed his hand on her upper back between her shoulder blades. "The chicken pox is internal." Yet, even as he said it, he couldn't tamp the image of the child covered with spots in his dream. He glanced at Mattie. She was pale, taking quick, shallow breaths, and sweat had beaded across her forehead. "Are you feeling all right?"

"*Jah*, why?"

"I just thought you might want to sit down."

"I'm fine." She continued to watch Nathan.

A sick feeling washed over him. Amanda had spots. In his dream, the mother was covered as well. "Mattie," he said. "Have you had chicken pox before?"

She shook her head. "I don't recall."

"I, um . . . I'm going to step out of the room for a few minutes." He was grateful she nodded without looking at him. Otherwise she might have noticed his fear ebbing its way to the surface. He left the room and headed to the nurses' desk where he found Doctor Oshay talking with several of the nurses. They were laughing about something. Bo wasn't sure if he should interrupt them or not, so he stood at the desk, waiting to be acknowledged.

A nurse came out of a patient's room rolling a blood pressure machine and paused at the desk. "May I help you?"

"I'd like to speak with Doctor Oshay if he has a few minutes."

"I'll let him know." She went behind the long desk, and a few moments later, Doctor Oshay approached Bo.

Without wasting the doctor's time, Bo asked, "How long does it take for someone to show signs of chicken pox after they were exposed?"

"It can take as long as a couple of weeks to develop symptoms."

"Oh."

"Is there a problem?"

"That depends. Mattie Diener has been exposed to two of the children and potentially others in her district with the virus. If she doesn't recall having chicken pox herself, will she still be able to donate part of her liver?"

"No. The risk would be too great."

That wasn't the answer Bo wanted to hear. Mattie wouldn't take the news well either.

"But we'll know more soon. The blood work isn't back from the lab yet."

"And you'll be able to tell? I mean, even if she doesn't have any outward spots? The tests will show if she has the atypical—the form her son has?"

"Yes, I've ordered varicella titers, which will show if she has immunity," Doctor Oshay said. "I've ordered a comprehensive metabolic panel as well as full red- and white-blood-cell-count tests."

Bo blew out a breath. There was still hope. "Thank you for talking with me."

"Anytime."

Bo turned away and removed his cell phone from his pocket. He had one more thing to do.

"You're perspiring."

Mattie touched her moist forehead. "It's warm in here. Don't you think?"

Bo eyed her closer. "Your face is flushed too. You might have a fever."

"Don't speak like that, Bo Lambright. I don't have time to get sick *nau.*"

His lips formed a straight line in what she had come to know as a forced smile. She turned her attention back to Nathan. *Lord,* mei sohn *needs me. I can't get sick. I can't.*

"Maybe you should drink some water. There's a fountain not far down the hall."

She shook her head, not about to leave Nathan's side.

He pushed the chair closer to the bed. "At least sit down."

She perched on the edge of the chair cushion, ready to rise should Nathan open his eyes. But her son hadn't moved a muscle the entire time she'd been in the room. Her hope was diminishing by the second, and judging by the bleak expression on Bo's face, he harbored a lot of doubts as well.

"Mattie," he said.

By the tenderness in his tone, she wasn't sure she wanted him to voice more concern. "Don't discourage me, Bo," she said, not veering her focus from Nathan. "I'm standing on what feels like shifting sand as it is."

He knelt beside the chair. "I thought we could pray for Nathan—together."

Her vision blurred as he took her hands into his.

"Father, we come to You today in need of mercy. You have promised in Your Word that when two or three are gathered in Your name, You are in the midst. We welcome Your presence and thank You for Your love. We ask, Father, that You place Your hand upon Nathan, for we know there is healing in Your command. Give Mattie peace that surpasses all understanding. We ask for this in Jesus' name, amen."

"*Danki.*" Prayers in her district were usually unspoken. Even if she tried, she wouldn't have been able to pray with the same boldness Bo had.

His eyes glazed. "Have faith, Mattie. God loves Nathan. He loves you."

"He loves you, too, Bo. You're a very kind person."

Bo gently squeezed her hand. "No matter what the doctor's report is, we stand in faith. Together."

*Together.* There truly was power in praying with another, and she knew without a doubt that God had sent Bo to her. Hope was restored. And she wasn't standing alone. Mattie bowed her head. Danki, *God. I don't have the eloquent words like Bo, but I know that You sent him during this time of trouble. Please bless Bo. He's a good man.*

Bo held tight to Mattie's hand when Nathan's door opened and two men dressed in scrubs along with his nurse entered the room.

"Ronald and Ed are here from imaging. They'll take Nathan downstairs for his biopsy," the nurse said.

One man tapped the wheel release under the foot of the bed, while the other clamped the nasal tube and detached it from the container on the wall. "You're welcome to ride along in the elevator with us," the taller one said, unhooking Nathan from the monitors.

"How long does the test normally take?" Bo asked as they walked toward the elevator.

"I'd say an hour or two," the darker-haired man said. "Is that how long you would guess, Ed?"

"That's about right." He pressed the Down button on the service elevator. The door opened immediately, and the men rolled the oversized crib inside.

Mattie chewed her bottom lip. Bo wanted to remind her about standing on faith, but decided to wait until they were alone. The imaging room was at the end of the hall in what looked like the basement. He and Mattie were stopped at the door.

"I'm sorry, but family members aren't allowed inside during testing," Ronald said. "I can have someone page you when he's back in his room."

"Yes, please." Mattie sniffled.

Once the door closed, Bo said, "Let's get something to drink in the cafeteria."

Mattie stared blankly at the door.

"Mattie?"

She snapped out of her stupor and faced him.

"We have an hour or two." He motioned to the bank of elevators. "I'm thirsty. What about you?"

At first, he wasn't sure she would leave, then she turned toward the elevator. "I'm thirsty too."

He glanced at his watch. "It's almost noon. We might as well eat lunch."

"I don't think I could eat."

He frowned. "You need your strength."

A few minutes later, they were in the cafeteria and he was coaxing her to choose something from the steaming tray line. "I'm going to pick for you if you don't select something."

"Fine," she huffed and chose an egg salad sandwich with plain potato chips.

He opted for something hot and selected the meat loaf and a side of peas. He filled two Styrofoam cups with coffee, then carried the tray over to the register and paid. They found a table near a window and sat.

Bo opened his mouth to bless the food and noticed her head bowed, eyes closed, and her mouth moving in silence. He lowered his head and prayed silently. When he looked up, she was watching him. He smiled and picked up his fork. "I hope this is good. My stomach has been growling since yesterday."

"Yesterday?"

"I was here all night." He took a bite of meat loaf and washed it down with coffee.

"Why were you here all *nacht*?"

"I got a call that one of my foster kids was in an accident. The ambulance brought him into the emergency room and from there he was admitted."

Her mouth gaped. "That was the call you received when you said something had *kumm* up and you needed to go?"

He nodded.

"Oh, I feel bad. You stayed so I could see Nathan again."

"Don't feel bad."

"How is the child doing?"

"He's going to be sore for a while. Several of

his ribs are broken, but it could have been a lot worse." He forked more meat loaf. "I plan to check on him before he's discharged."

"What's his name?"

"Josh. He's a good kid. A little wayward, but considering what he's gone through in his life, he could be worse." He pointed his fork at her plate. "You haven't eaten anything."

"So, do you keep in contact with all the kids?"

"Yes, but I see Josh more often. He tends to bounce from foster home to foster home."

Her eyes widened.

"Josh has a lot of adjustment issues."

"With the . . . foster . . ." Her face turned as white as the napkin.

All this talk about foster kids, it should have dawned on him sooner. "You're worried about Amanda, aren't you?"

"She only knows Pennsylvania *Deitsch*, and she doesn't warm up right away to strangers. Besides that, she's sick. She'll have a difficult time adjusting."

"Amanda is okay. You have to trust me."

Mattie leaned forward. "But how do you know?"

"She's one of my kids."

Mattie's brows puckered. She sank lower in the chair and crossed her arms.

"I've visited her in the home, and I call and check on her—daily." She was upset with him,

340

and he didn't like keeping secrets from her. "Amanda saw a doctor. She had a mild case of chicken pox, and from what I was told, the sores have scabbed over."

Mattie leaned forward. "I want to see her." She tapped the tip of her index finger on the table. "The court papers granted me two hours a week."

"I'm working on that." He pointed to her sandwich. "Eat. You need your strength."

"Bo, I'm serious. I have to see her."

"Then I suggest you eat." He glanced at his watch. It wouldn't be much longer before Nathan's procedure was completed and he was back in his room.

Mattie sat in the waiting room. After lunch, Bo mentioned he had to meet someone in the lobby. She didn't mind. It gave her a few minutes alone. She leaned back in the chair and closed her eyes. Perhaps a short nap would help. She'd never been this exhausted. Mattie touched her forehead and cringed. She had a fever. No wonder she was roasting hot. A pang of fear crept into her mind when her clothes felt scratchy on her skin and she began to itch. This wasn't the time to get sick. Nathan needed her.

"Mama!"

Mattie's eyes shot open at the sound of Amanda's voice. Seeing her daughter snuggled in Bo's arms, Mattie bounded up from the chair.

"How did— Where did you— Can I hold her?"

"Of course." He lowered Amanda into Mattie's arms.

Mattie hugged her daughter. *"Danki,"* she whispered to Bo.

"I'll wait in the hall and give you some time alone."

As he started to leave, Amanda called out his name. Mattie was stunned. Her daughter didn't warm up to strangers.

"I'll be back in a few minutes, pumpkin." His gaze traveled from Amanda to Mattie and he winked. "Enjoy your time."

Mattie's face heated. A handsome man hadn't winked at her in years—and an *Englisch* man at that. Bo Lambright had not only charmed her daughter, he'd charmed her.

# *Chapter Thirty*

Taking a child from her mother was never easy. Amanda was no exception. She and Mattie both bawled when he separated them. But he had promised Mrs. Appleton that he would have Amanda back by the time she finished running errands.

"It's been barely an hour," Mattie protested.

"I'm sorry. I told her foster mother—"

"I'm her mother." Mattie cried harder, which made Amanda cry harder.

Bo patted Amanda's back. Maybe this was a mistake. They were starting to draw attention from the nurses. One even poked her head inside the room to check on the commotion. "She needs a nap," he explained. He didn't like Mattie scowling at him, but it couldn't be helped. "I'll be back in a minute and we can talk about a longer visit next time."

Mattie followed him into the hall.

"Wait here, please." He couldn't allow her to follow him down to the lobby. It was against regulations for the mother to know who the foster family was. Amanda cried so hard that when he finally got her settled down, she fell asleep in his arms. She picked up her head when the elevator dinged, but then lowered it against his shoulder.

Not seeing Mrs. Appleton in the lobby, Bo strolled the area. He didn't want to wake Amanda and she seemed content in his arms. Holding her, a surge of protectiveness welled up inside him. He'd cared for several infants, but none that captured his heart the way Amanda had. She was precious, and he silently vowed to find a way to return her home.

"I hope I didn't keep you waiting," Mrs. Appleton said, entering the lobby.

"Not at all. I appreciate you going out of your way like this."

"It really wasn't out of my way. I had errands to run. I was just glad Amanda's chicken pox was scabbed over and she was no longer contagious."

"Me too." Bo slipped sleepy Amanda into Mrs. Appleton's arms just as Erica Davis and Norton Farley entered the hospital. He turned his back to his boss and Davis. "I'll call you later," he whispered to Mrs. Appleton, who thought he was doing it for the sake of the sleeping child and nodded.

He waited for her to leave, then slipped down the hall to the cafeteria. He needed a cup of coffee and Mattie would probably want one too. A few minutes later, coffee in hand, he stepped into the elevator. Remembering he'd left the bag with the Amish clothes in Josh's room, he pressed the second-floor button.

He entered Josh's room and froze. Erica Davis and Norton Farley were interviewing Josh about the accident. He glanced at the Walkers standing near the window, but couldn't get a read of their expression. Had the Walkers changed their minds about taking Josh back?

His boss glanced at Bo, then turned back to Josh. "Will you excuse me a minute, please?" Norton addressed Bo. "Lambright, we need to talk." His face was a bright candy-apple red as he marched past him.

Bo spotted the bag of Amish clothes he'd left in the room last night and snatched it from the floor. He patted Josh's arm. "Don't get into any more trouble, you hear?"

"I won't," Josh mumbled.

Bo left the room with Davis trailing behind him.

Norton's face was still sunburnt red. "What were you doing with the Diener child in the lobby?"

Bo cleared his throat. "Before you get hot under the collar, I have a court order granting the mother supervised visitation."

"You're on suspension, or did you forget that?"

"I'm also the court-appointed supervisor."

"You should have deferred it to someone else in the department." Norton spoke in a low voice, the muscle in his jaw flexing.

"It would have gotten caught in red tape." Bo glanced at Davis leaning against the wall, arms folded, a wry grin on her face. He looked back at Norton. "Time was running out. The boy's dying, and not from anything the mother did. The doctor found out today Nathan Diener has chicken pox. It's not child abuse."

"I have internal investigators breathing down my neck. And now I have a foster kid—one of yours— who ran away from home and was injured in a car accident. You knew about the accident yesterday and yet you didn't report it to the agency."

"I should have," Bo admitted.

"Yes, Lambright, you should have." Norton wagged his head in disgust, his hands on his hips. "You're going to find yourself skinned by those investigators, and I'm not going to be able to help you."

"I understand."

"Even when you go by your gut, you have to follow the rules." Norton sighed. "Let's hope this stays buried until after the review board's hearing."

Bo caught a glimpse of Davis's arched brows and had a sinking feeling none of this would stay buried.

Once Norton went back into Josh's room, Davis came up beside him making a *tsk, tsk* sound. "I think you might find your suspension extended."

"Maybe."

She lifted her hand to her chin and tapped her index finger against her jaw. "Why are you doing it?"

"To help an innocent woman. By the way, I didn't appreciate your phone call the other day. Even if I could sway the Amish, I wouldn't encourage them to sell their mineral rights."

"Great Northern Expeditions wants to buy the Amish land. They're heavy contributors to your mother's campaign as well as my father's. It's in everyone's best interest for the Amish to sell."

"I don't agree. Besides, I don't have any influence in their decisions. I'm an outsider."

She snorted. "Are you sure about that?"

He turned and stormed away. He'd heard enough. Bo was even more convinced politicians had their dirty hands in everything. He wished his mother wasn't one of them. Bo stepped into the elevator and pressed the button for the third floor. When the doors opened again, Mattie was sobbing uncontrollably, waiting to get on.

She rushed inside, and he caught the elevator doors just in time to bolt back in before they closed. Mattie sobbed so hard on the way to the lobby, she couldn't express a single discernable word. Once the doors opened, she darted toward the main entrance. Bo wasn't able to stop her until they were outside on the sidewalk.

"Mattie, take a deep breath."

She drew in a hitched breath and waved what looked like a prescription. "I . . . I-I have shingles." She motioned to a red streak that ran from her neck up the side of her face next to her ear. "I have to take medicine."

"I'm sorry." Bo didn't know what else to say. Shingles was the reactivated form of the chicken pox virus.

"Th-they said it was t-too dangerous for the patients. I'm contagious." Another wave of sobs overtook her. He helped her to a nearby bench and encouraged her to sit and catch her breath, unaware of the cameraman and news reporter approaching until they called out Mattie's name.

Bo shielded her from the storm of questions while at the same time hailing a cab that was parked near the entrance.

"They're never going to leave me alone, are they?"

Bo glanced out the back window. They weren't following yet, but they wouldn't be far behind. "We'll have to get your prescription filled later."

Mattie was silent on the ride back to her farm and Bo spent the time in prayer. When they reached the area where the trees blocked the gravel road, Mattie got out of the car and started hiking, arms swinging. He paid the driver and hurried to catch up with her. By the time he reached her, she was angry.

"You took Nathan away from me."

"You're going to get him back once everything is sorted out."

She whirled around to face him. "What if God takes him first?"

Bo swallowed hard. The same thought was in the back of his mind, and he'd been fighting to keep it stuffed away.

A news van pulled to the fallen log and parked. The reporter jumped out first with a cameraman close behind.

Mattie took off running, cutting into the dense woods and disappearing in the copse of towering jack pines.

Bo cut off the news reporter. "You're on private property."

"We just want to ask a few questions," the reporter said.

Bo held up his hand to block his face. "Turn off the camera if you want to speak with me."

The reporter signaled to the cameraman.

"I'll only talk off the record," Bo said.

"Agreed." The reporter pulled a small pad of paper and pen from his shirt pocket.

"No comment." Bo turned and walked away.

"Hey, what happened to 'off the record'?"

Bo turned. "Give me your business card. You'll get a full story—if I don't see your van around here again."

"When?"

Bo shrugged. "I'll call." He scanned the wooded area in the direction Mattie had fled. He'd give her space and stay on the road. Reaching the house before she did, he tossed the bag of Amish clothes in his car. He would wash them before giving them back. Bo plopped down on the porch step and buried his head in his hands. "Lord, this is all my fault. I should have fought harder to close the case. I should have insisted that Davis be assigned to someone else. Lord, please don't take Nathan. Please, please, please heal him."

He waited over an hour for Mattie to surface from the woods. She carried her prayer *kapp* in her hand. Her chestnut hair hung down past her shoulders, and as she drew closer, he noticed her blotchy face and swollen eyes.

"What did the news people want?" She held

up her hand. "Never mind. I don't want to know."

He stood and followed her up the steps.

"I don't feel like having company," she said, scratching the back of her neck.

"I won't stay long."

Surprisingly, she let him follow her into the house.

"You can be upset with me, but don't get angry with God. Don't lose faith."

She tossed her *kapp* on the table and went to the sink where she turned on the tap, then cupped a handful of water and splashed it over her face.

He came up beside her as she dried her face with a hand towel. He cupped her shoulder and turned her so that she was facing him. Bo tipped her chin up. "God is near to the broken-hearted."

Tears welled and her face contorted.

Bo ushered her into his arms and held her tight. "I'm so sorry this is happening, Mattie. I'm so sorry."

She clung to him several minutes, then pushed off his chest. "Have you had chicken pox?"

"Yes," he said, tucking a strand of hair behind her ear. "And I don't care if I get shingles."

She cracked a smile. "*Gut.*"

He returned her smile. "I would have guessed you'd like to see me covered in spots and scratching like a flea-infested dog."

She lowered her head, and her hair cascaded

over her face. "I'm sorry I took *mei* frustration out on you."

"You don't need to apologize."

"*Jah*, I do. You've been very kind to me. You didn't have to bail me out of jail or make arrangements for me to see *mei kinner*, but you did. It says a lot about your character. You're a *gut* man." She scratched her neck and grimaced.

"You don't have fleas, do you?"

"That's *nett* funny." She opened a kitchen drawer and searched its contents. "I should have calamine lotion in here somewhere."

"I've heard honey works too," he offered.

"So does brown vinegar, but I'd have to bathe in it."

"Oh, I guess that's my cue to leave."

She started to open the cabinet that Grace had emptied of honey and stopped. "I was hoping you would use your cell phone and call about Nathan before you left."

"I can do that." Bo removed his phone from his pant pocket and dialed the number for the hospital. He asked for Doctor Oshay, and after a brief hold, the operator returned on the line to say he wasn't answering his page. Bo asked to be connected to the pediatric nurses' station, and a moment later was told there hadn't been any change.

"No change," he repeated aloud for Mattie.

Her hopeful smile dwarfed into a frown.

"I think that's good news," Bo said. "The nurse said he was holding his own."

Mattie nodded, but Bo wasn't sure she truly agreed.

She had expected the same news he had wanted to hear: Nathan's condition had miraculously changed—he was healed—but that wasn't the case. Bo slipped his phone back into his pocket. "I'll check on him again."

"And you'll let me know?"

"Of course, and if he gets worse, I'll sneak you into the hospital to see him too. But I'm believing in a miracle."

"Me too."

He paused at the door. "Maybe we should pray again before I leave."

She smiled. "I'd like that."

"Father, we ask that You watch over Nathan. Heal his body fully. Please give Mattie peace over this situation and heal her as well. In Jesus' name, amen."

"*Danki*. You have a way of calming *mei* nerves when you pray," she said.

"Then God has answered *mei* prayer." He reached for the doorknob.

"Don't forget to let me know."

"I won't." He would give her a daily update just so he had a reason to see her. Bo told her good-bye and headed down the driveway. Then realizing he needed his car to be able to come get her for an

352

emergency, he stopped at Ben and Grace's house.

Ben came to the door, but instead of inviting Bo inside to talk, Ben stepped onto the porch. "What can I do for you?"

"I was wondering if there's a way we could move the tree blocking the road. I'd like to be able to drive my car. It's been parked at Mattie's house."

"I saw it there earlier."

"My car was there overnight, but I wasn't. I hope it didn't cause any problems with Mattie's reputation."

"What is it you want with her?"

"I'm trying to help get her children back. I'm not sure if you're aware, but Nathan was diagnosed with chicken pox. Amanda has them, and now Mattie has shingles, which is another form of the same virus."

"No, I didn't know."

"Amanda and Mattie are doing okay, but Nathan has a rare form in that the lesions develop internally. He might need a liver transplant."

Ben looked stunned. "I've never heard of chicken pox doing that."

"I hadn't either. Apparently the doctors didn't catch his symptoms and that's why they mistakenly accused Mattie of child abuse."

"So they're dropping the charges?"

"It'll take some time, but I'll see that it happens," Bo assured him.

Ben eyed him a moment. "We were going to

wait to move that big oak until after things settled down. We wanted to keep the *Englischers* off our land."

"So I was told."

Ben smiled. "But I suppose we can't keep your car ransom. I need to grab my hat and gloves, then we can hitch the team."

# Chapter Thirty-one

Over the following days Mattie had a flood of visitors stop to check on her and to drop off meals, but every time someone came to the door, she was hoping to see Bo.

"You look disappointed," Grace's *aenti* Erma said. "Don't you like split pea soup?"

"*Jah*, I do." Mattie opened the door wider and stepped aside. "I keep hoping it's Bo."

"I figured as much. Do you think that's a healthy desire?"

Heat rushed to Mattie's face. "He promised to check on Nathan and keep me updated on his condition."

Erma set the container of soup on the counter, then pulled a chair out from the table and sat. "Grace had a doctor's appointment. They're keeping a close eye on her since there's an increased risk to be exposed to chicken pox while you're pregnant."

"Is everything okay?"

"So far. She stopped by the hospital to check on Nathan."

"She did?" Mattie sucked in a deep breath.

Erma nodded. "She didn't go in to see him, but she spoke with Bo. Apparently he's been staying day and *nacht* at the hospital. I'm told he's very concerned about the boy."

Mattie exhaled. Others in her settlement would find it strange that Mattie found comfort in that information. She was grateful Bo was close by, but she wasn't about to share that tidbit of information.

"Are you sure he isn't . . . still investigating?"

"*Jah*, I'm sure. Bo knows that until I'm past the contagious stage, I'm unable to go to the hospital." She skipped the part where Bo had promised to sneak her in if Nathan's condition became worse.

"How much do you know about him?"

"Other than that he works for Child Protective Services and his mother is a retired judge, *nett* much."

Erma's forehead puckered in puzzlement. "His mother is a judge? Did he tell you that?"

"I met her."

"I see." Erma's worry lines deepened.

"Would you like a cup of tea?"

"*Nay, danki*. I can't stay." She pushed back her chair and stood. "I'll stop over tomorrow and see how you're feeling."

"*Danki* again for the soup." As Mattie opened the screen door for Erma, she noticed Alvin's buggy pulling into the yard and shot him a quick wave. He waved back, but when he got out of his buggy, he went directly to the barn. Mattie searched the containers from the womenfolk and found some peanut butter cookies. He liked pie better, but these would have to do. An hour later, a knock sounded at the door. When she opened it, Alvin had moved to the bottom porch step.

"I see the *Englischer's* car is gone."

Mattie wasn't sure she liked Alvin's undertone. "The *kaffi* is hot if you'd like a cup."

"I better not. Shingles is contagious. The lamb is doing better. I suppose you were right about not putting him down."

"*Danki* for looking after Snowball." Between resting and visitors she hadn't gone out to check on him today.

"I fed and watered the livestock. You won't have to worry about them tonight."

"Can I send you home with a plate of cookies, Alvin?"

He shook his head. "I'm eating fewer sweets these days."

She couldn't help but wonder if that was his way of making her feel guilty. After all, he'd eaten sweets daily for the past several weeks. "Well, I'm sure it would do us all some *gut* to cut back some."

●●●

Bo held a private prayer vigil for Nathan during the night. He didn't have the heart to leave the boy's room and the nurses didn't seem to mind him sleeping in the chair. That is, when he could sleep. Noises in the room, the hallway, the nurses' desk—they went on 24/7, which made sense why most hospitalized patients said they had to go home to get any rest.

His mother wasn't pleased with the decision, especially since he was missing another one of her fund-raising dinner parties for her campaign. It was just as well. After his run-in with Davis, he had no desire to sit at the same table with her all evening or listen to representatives from the fracking company talk about how their drilling would drive more local business. But at the same time, he didn't want to disappoint the woman whom he'd come to call his mother. Agnes Nettleton deserved his respect. She'd taken him in after the accident and raised him as her own. She'd done her best to introduce him to her world of influence and means. Until the dreams started reoccurring, he hadn't truly seen the trappings of the world. Perhaps all along he hadn't wanted to.

He recalled the phone conversation he'd had earlier with his mother, the inflection of desperation in her voice. "Bo, why are you ruining your career?"

"I'm not. The boy has a rare form of chicken pox. The mother is innocent."

"Chicken pox?"

"I plan to talk with the doctor the next time I see him about providing an official diagnosis to the court. How fast can you get Judge Steinway to drop the charges?"

Silence.

Bo glanced at his phone, thinking the call had dropped.

She cleared her throat. "I can see what I can do. Of course, it'll have to go through Child Services. Bo, I wish you wouldn't . . ."

"Wouldn't what? Help an innocent mother? I can't let this go until . . . until it's resolved. Besides, once Mattie is cleared, there won't be much of a case against me at the CPS."

"Yes, I see your point." Another brief silence passed before she shifted the conversation. "You have to promise you'll attend the gala next Friday. It's the most important event of my campaign and I need your support."

Was this a trade-off? Attend a dinner party in exchange for a woman's abuse charges getting dropped sooner? He wasn't about to challenge her integrity. "Yes, I'll be there," he said, sending up a silent prayer that Nathan's healing would come before then. If the boy was transferred to Henry Ford Hospital in Detroit, as the doctor had arranged, he couldn't very well be in two places at once.

Several hours had passed since his conversation with his mother and he was still pondering her motives. Bo leaned his head back on the hospital chair and closed his eyes. His eyelids felt heavy, cemented closed. His breathing slowed, his muscles went limp, and he was lost in a fog.

"Boaz, My child. Have you not found what it is you're looking for? When one sheep has gone astray, is it not true that the shepherd leaves his flock to find it?"
The fog cleared and the leprous mother and child came into view, but as he drew closer to them, the spots were no longer visible. Fog shrouded him. Once again, he was searching for the way.

The overhead light jerked him awake. He blinked several times at the stocky fiftysomething woman rolling a mop bucket into the room.
"I'm sorry. I didn't know anyone was in here," she said.
"What?" In one fluid motion, he vaulted up from the chair. "No! No! This isn't happening," he said, his mind reeling in denial. This was a dream. He looked out the window. The sky was pale blue—daytime. Nathan was gone—his bed empty.
"Excuse me?" The woman from housekeeping slanted her head slightly.
"Where's the boy?" Bo demanded.

"I was just told to mop the room." She pointed the end of her mop handle toward the nurses' desk. "You best ask at the desk."

Bo fled the room. He caught one nurse before she entered an adjacent room. "Where's Nathan Diener? The patient in room 2205."

"I'm not sure. Cindy has that room."

"Which one is she?" He scanned the other nurses in the hall, at the desk, but none of them looked familiar.

"This is shift change." The nurse craned her neck. "She must still be in report. Give her another ten or fifteen minutes and I'm sure you'll find her at the desk."

He combed his fingers through his hair. Ten minutes would feel like an eternity. How could he have slept so hard that he missed someone taking Nathan out of the room? Surely he should have heard some commotion. His phone buzzed and he pulled it out of his pocket. He wasn't in the frame of mind to talk with anyone and didn't recognize the caller ID. The buzzing stopped, then a moment later, sounded again. "Lambright," he barked.

A sharp gasp filled his ear.

"Is someone there?" he asked in a calmer voice.

"This is Cora Johnson. I'm a friend of Mattie Diener and she asked that I call you."

# Chapter Thirty-two

"Is something wrong with Mattie?" Bo's blood pressure jacked up to stroke rate with the amount of adrenaline feeding his veins. First Nathan was gone—now Mattie. This wasn't how he wanted to start the day.

"No, I think everything is all right. I didn't talk with her directly; one of her neighbors stopped at my place and requested I call you."

Bo wanted to tell the woman to get to the point, but he held his tongue.

"She's taken the prescribed antiviral medicine and her shingles have cleared up. She wants to know if she would be allowed to come back to the hospital."

His thoughts scattered. How long had it been, five days? If something was wrong with Nathan, or if he was transferred to Henry Ford Hospital, it would be easier to tell her in person.

"I would be willing to pick her up and drive her into town," Cora said.

"You don't mind?"

"No, not at all. I have a few errands to run anyway."

"Thanks, I appreciate it." He hadn't so much as hit the End button on his cell when the phone buzzed again. His work number popped up on the caller ID. *Not now, Norton.* He checked his watch. Seven thirty. The office didn't open for another thirty minutes. Bo let the call go into voice mail. He had to find out about Nathan first. He approached the only woman at the desk, her tag read *Pam, Unit Clerk.* "Could you tell me where Nathan Diener is? He isn't in his room."

"What's his room number?"

"2205."

Pam picked up a clipboard and scrolled her finger down a long list. Holding her finger on the spot, she glanced up from the paper. "He's in imaging."

"Does it say why?" Bo leaned forward, hoping to get a glimpse of the form.

"Are you a family member?"

He shook his head.

She turned the clipboard over and folded her hands. "You'll have to talk with his physician."

"Is Doctor Oshay available?"

"He usually makes rounds first thing in the morning, but I haven't seen him yet."

"Thanks." Bo strolled to the end of the hall and gazed out a window overlooking the parking lot. The morning fog had cleared and he found himself wishing he was lying on the deck of his boat, drifting with the waves. If he closed his eyes he could smell the dank air, hear the fish jumping.

His phone rang again. This time it was his mother. "Hello."

"Oh, I thought I might get your voice mail. Norton Farley called the house. Your interview with Internal Affairs is at eleven o'clock."

He groaned. "Okay, thanks for letting me know."

"Bo, I wouldn't be late if I were you."

Bo wished now that he hadn't charged his phone in the car on his drive from Mattie's house to the hospital. It would have been easier if he wasn't aware and missed the meeting. He spotted Mattie getting off the elevator. "Hey, I have to go."

"Bo?"

"Yes." He waved at Mattie walking down the hall.

"Will I see you after your meeting? Perhaps we could have lunch."

"Sure. But I'll talk with you later. I have to go." He disconnected the call and met Mattie near the waiting room. Her cobalt eyes held a shimmer similar to the deepest part of Lake Superior on a sunny day. "Well, look at you. A picture of health and—" *Beauty.*

Her face turned pink under his scrutinizing gaze. "I'm feeling better."

"So I see. That's great news."

"I can donate part of *mei* liver *nau*."

He wasn't about to remind her it had only been five days. The doctor would insist on running more tests.

"How's Nathan?"

"Let's go in the waiting room and talk."

"Why are you trying to keep me from his room?" She touched her neck. "The rash is gone. I'm *nett* contagious."

"He's not there. He's having a CT scan."

She drew in a sharp breath. "What's happened?"

"I don't know. I was asleep when they came in and took him downstairs for more tests. I over-heard the nurses say something about remeasuring the size of his liver and another biopsy." He glanced at his watch. "It's already been a little over an hour. Hopefully it won't be much longer." He motioned to the waiting room. "Let's sit in here."

She hesitated a moment, then conceded.

Bo sat where he had a direct view of the hallway. Leaving a chair between them, she sat on his right, her hand on her neck.

"Have you had a fever today?"

"*Nay.*" She stood and paced to the end of the room. "I don't like this room."

He'd forgotten this was where she was when she got arrested. "You want to go down to the cafeteria?"

"*Nay.*" She stared at a painting of children flying kites, then walked away. As time passed, Mattie grew more restless. "Why is it taking so long? It didn't take this long the last time." She wrung her hands.

Bo checked his watch. Nathan had been gone a

long time. *Patience. Lord, she needs peace. We both do.*

"Are you sure we didn't miss him?"

He shook his head. "I've been watching the corridor." She had too. They hadn't rolled Nathan past the room.

"Do you think there's another hallway?"

"No." He patted the chair next to him. "Have a seat. Let's pray."

She sat beside him and bowed her head.

"Dear Lord, please forgive us for worrying. Thank You for answering our prayers and healing Mattie. We know You are in control of this situation and that Nathan is in Your hands. Please forgive us for not totally resting in Your peace." A clatter coming from the hall echoed as he finished the prayer. He opened his eyes as workers rolled an oversized crib past the doorway.

Bo and Mattie looked at each other at the same time and leapt off the chairs.

Mattie charged into Nathan's room. His skin was the color of freshly fallen snow. Maybe too white, but that was better than yellow. "*Danki*, Father." She peered at Bo as he approached the bedside, his brows crinkled. "His skin isn't yellow," she said.

"So I see." He studied Nathan.

"That's *gut* news, right?"

"I hope so."

His tone lacked the usual optimism. What wasn't he telling her? "We prayed for a miracle. This is it, right?"

The nurse entered the room. "Mrs. Diener, Doctor Oshay would like to have a word with you."

"Okay." Mattie turned to Bo. "Will you *kumm*?"

"Absolutely." He checked his watch.

She frowned. "Do you have time? I don't want to keep you."

"Are you trying to get rid of me?" he teased.

"*Nay.*" She meant it too. He'd become her rock the last few days.

"*Gut.*" He grinned.

Inside the conference room, Doctor Oshay began the conversation. "Your son's condition has been somewhat of a medical mystery."

Mattie swallowed hard. "How so?"

"A biopsy confirmed chicken pox, and his blood work suggested acute liver failure." He tossed his hands in the air and shrugged. "But last night, instead of his liver enzymes increasing, as expected with liver failure, they decreased. His bilirubin, which had been steadily rising from less than one to five point two and the reason his skin and the whites of his eyes turned yellow, are now less than one and well within the acceptable range. His ALT, AST, alkaline phosphatase, and GGT have also dropped significantly, and the tests we use to monitor potential clotting and bleeding issues—the INR,

PT, and platelets—are back within normal limits as well. I must admit his labs are remarkable."

"So he's healed," Mattie said.

"His condition has improved. It's not safe to say he's out of the woods yet. I'll know more after I get the results of the second biopsy and can compare it with the abnormalities found in the previous one." He pushed his chair away from the table. "I wish I had more concrete news to share, but hopefully we'll know more soon. I'll send a copy of my findings to Doctor Wellington, and once I'm satisfied from a GI standpoint, she will advise you on further treatment."

"Thank you. Thank you so much." Mattie left the conference room with a spring in her step. God had answered her prayers. Nathan was healed. "I feel like a ton of weight has been lifted and I can breathe for the first time in a . . ." She glanced at Bo. He was preoccupied looking at his watch. "I haven't meant to occupy all your time. I know you're a busy man, so if there's something you need to—"

He grimaced. "I have a meeting I need to attend. If I could postpone it I would, but—"

"You don't need to explain." Then it dawned on her why his expression was glum. "I can't see Nathan without your supervision, can I?"

He wouldn't be away from the hospital too long. The meeting with Internal Affairs would satisfy formality and be over in the matter of minutes once the review board heard about Nathan's condition, or so Bo reasoned as he drove to the other side of the county. He fully expected the interview with the internal investigators to go smoothly. Unless news got back to headquarters that he'd given Mattie permission to spend time alone with Nathan. He had no power to authorize anything until his name was cleared.

Bo's assumption that the meeting would be quick proved inaccurate after spending an hour and a half answering questions hurled at him by a panel of five people. Asked to explain every minuscule detail of the Diener case and several other cases they supposedly randomly selected to review, he wasn't sure the investigation would be finished by the end of the day. Josh's file alone triggered a slew of questions. But the investigators kept going back to Mattie's case, often asking the same question worded a different way.

The only woman on the panel spoke first after everyone returned from a ten-minute break. "You entered the premises without a search warrant and after the mother refused to cooperate with an inspection. Can you explain your actions?"

"She fainted on the porch and was rendered unconscious after hitting her head. The children were alone in the house, and I didn't think it was prudent to walk away from an injured person. Not when it meant I would knowingly be leaving the children unattended. So I carried her into the house."

"Is it true that your immediate supervisor, Director Norton Farley, requested your identification when he notified you that you were the subject of an internal investigation?"

"Yes."

"And what did you say?"

"That I had lost my wallet and identification."

The man on the far left lifted a copy of Bo's identification. "Then how do you explain that it became part of the record at the hospital after the fact?"

Bo wiped his sweaty palms on his pants. "It was found and returned to me."

"Then why didn't you turn the identification in as you were instructed?"

The past few nights without much sleep were beginning to wear Bo down. He was slow to collect his thoughts, and the investigator repeated the question.

"Nathan Diener was gravely ill and because of that, Judge Steinway allowed emergency parental visitation with the contingency that it be supervised by someone from Child Protective Services, namely me, or by the child's advocate attorney. I made the decision not to hinder the mother's visitation. The hospital needed proof, and I supplied my identification."

"Do you regret your decision?"

"No," he said without hesitation.

The investigators called a ten-minute recess and excused themselves from the room. Bo remained seated. As grueling as the interrogation was going, his thoughts were on Mattie. Had she gotten any more news on Nathan's condition? When the team of investigators returned, the one seated in the center and directly across from Bo said, "At this time, we're going to delay our decision. There will be another hearing three weeks from today. In the meantime, your suspension is still in place. You will not, at any time, represent yourself as an investigator for Child Protective Services. In doing so, your license will automatically be revoked. Do you understand?"

"Yes."

"You're dismissed," the center man said.

"May I say something before I leave?"

"Yes, go ahead."

"Mrs. Diener was falsely accused of child abuse. She was arrested, humiliated, and denied visitation for multiple days. I urge you to include the recent medical findings in your report, which will show her son was misdiagnosed."

"Excuse me, Mrs. Diener," the nurse said, poking her head into Nathan's room. "You have a call at the nurses' desk."

Mattie slipped out of the room and followed

the nurse to the back corner of the workstation.

The nurse pressed the lit button and handed the receiver to Mattie.

"Hello."

"Mattie, it's Bo. How is Nathan doing?"

Mattie smiled hearing his voice. "The *doktah* said he's continuing to improve. They've lowered his pain medicine so he should be waking up soon."

"That's great news."

The relief in Bo's tone made Mattie smile even wider. "*Doktah* Oshay still wants to run more tests. He says he's never seen a case like Nathan's—it's a miracle, Bo. A true miracle." Excitement fueled her words and they ran together. "Maybe next time you see him, he will be awake—maybe home. Who knows?"

Bo chuckled.

Mattie turned when she heard someone behind her say Nathan's name. Grace's *aenti* Erma was talking with the nurse a few feet away. "I should probably go. I don't want him waking up without me in the room."

"Do you need me to bring you anything?"

*Jah*, she needed him. "*Nay*, I'm fine." She hung up the phone as Erma approached.

"How is Nathan?"

"Much better." She filled Erma in on all the good news as they headed to Nathan's room.

Erma stopped her before going inside. "Who were you talking to on the phone?"

"Bo Lambright. He called to check on Nathan's progress."

"You two have spent a lot time together, *jah*?" A motherly concern spread across Erma's face.

"He's . . . been very . . . supportive."

"So I've heard." Her expression stoic, she clasped her hands in front of her. "There's chatter among the women. It won't be long before word reaches Bishop Yoder and he'll have to address the matter."

Mattie lowered her head. She half expected uproar over the time she had been spending with Bo. After all, he was an *Englischer*—an outsider. Her faith didn't allow such involvement with a worldly man.

"Don't let your heart be deceived, child. We are to be separate from the world."

Her shoulders dropped. Everything Erma was saying was true. "Bo arranged for me to see *mei* children. When this is over . . ." She wanted to take her children and hide from the world. Avoid town. Avoid hospitals. Avoid . . . Bo.

"They said they would take the matter into consideration," Bo told his mother over dinner. He pushed his plate of lasagna aside. After rehashing the interview, he'd lost his appetite.

"I think you'll need a lawyer, and you definitely have to stay away from the Diener woman."

He wouldn't agree with that until Nathan was

released from the hospital and Amanda was back at home where she belonged. "I didn't tell you yet. God performed a miracle."

"How so?"

"Nathan Diener was in liver failure. The doctor said he needed a transplant in order to survive. God miraculously healed him."

"And the doctor said that?" She took a sip of wine.

"No, he called it a 'medical mystery.' "

"Maybe it was."

Bo shook his head. "It was a miracle. Nothing can convince me otherwise." He took a drink of water. "And while we're on the subject of Nathan, he should be discharged from the hospital soon, Lord willing. Have you talked with Judge Steinway?"

"I haven't had a chance. But I'm meeting him tomorrow for brunch."

"Nathan's been very sick. I'd hate for him to be discharged from the hospital only to be taken to a foster home. It will be better for everyone if the case is closed as soon as possible. Mattie can get back to her life and her children will have their mother."

She picked up her wine glass, brought it to her mouth, and paused long enough to ask, "And you?"

He forced a smile.

"I know how attached you become to your foster kids."

"Right."

"How about you leave the Diener children to me? I'll make sure they get home and you won't have to risk a permanent suspension."

Bo pondered her proposition. Nathan was on the mend. God would see to his complete recovery. It was best for Mattie and the children if he stepped aside and let his mother handle the legal matters. Bo sighed. "Okay."

# Chapter Thirty-three

Less than a week after Nathan opened his eyes, he was home. Mattie stood at the sink washing the morning dishes as Nathan and Amanda sat at the kitchen table, Nathan quietly drawing on a piece of paper and Amanda playing with the doll Mattie had sewn for her. She was blessed to have her children safely home. Although she wasn't thrilled about the probation, the next six months would pass quickly, or so she hoped.

Mattie missed Bo. He'd called every day while Nathan was in the hospital, but now that they were home, she hadn't heard from him. She hadn't realized just how much she had grown to need him. He'd filled a void, brought comfort during a time of emotional upheaval. Perhaps that was all Bo was meant to be—help through a difficult period, a means to propel her past grieving over Andy to being able to trust her heart to someone again. But if he was part of God's transitioning plan, why wasn't her life getting back to normal? Why did she feel displaced, as if something was missing? Home, but homesick.

Mattie shook her head. She had to stop this pondering and move forward with her life. She drained the dirty dishwater, draped the washrag over the sink, then turned to Amanda and Nathan. "I have an idea," she said with excitement. "Instead of being cooped up in the *haus* another day, let's pick some berries to make a pie."

Nathan's and Amanda's faces lit, even though Nathan probably didn't remember picking raspberries with her last year and Amanda had never gone. They scooted off the chair and helped Mattie gather the wicker basket.

Hiking through the woods in the cool of the morning proved adventurous. They spotted a few deer—which Amanda frightened with her squeal—numerous squirrels, and a woodpecker hammering on an old tree. Once they reached the berry patch, Mattie insisted they pick from the perimeter. She didn't want them tangled in the thorns. Nathan and Amanda ate more than they collected, and Mattie picked enough to make a pie for Alvin. He'd been kind enough to tend to her beehives without her even asking. He deserved something special for all his hard work.

The day was warming up by the time they

returned home. The children's faces were berry stained, their stomachs probably a little too full, and they didn't fuss when Mattie put them down for a nap.

While the children slept, Mattie processed honey. Grace had sold all that Mattie had, extorted almost three hundred dollars from the news crews. Mattie planned to drop off more jars at the Green Thumb Market later today.

Her hands were sticky with honey when a knock sounded at the screen door. She wiped her hands on a wet dishrag. The caller knocked again, harder. Catherine Zimmerman was a bundle of nerves. Two-year-old Jenny was crying and so was Catherine's two-month-old son, Mark.

"Matthew's had an accident at the mill," her friend said. "Could you watch the *kinner* a few hours while I take him to the *doktah*? I would have asked Grace, but Mark has been cranky and with the chicken pox going around—"

"Catherine, of course!" She extended her arms and Catherine handed her the baby.

"I don't know if he'll take this," her friend said, handing her a bottle of milk. Catherine bit her lip. "I hope he doesn't give you a fit. He's been irritable the last two days."

"Don't worry. We'll get along fine." Mattie rocked the crying baby gently in her arms. Mark was normally a happy baby. Perhaps he sensed his mother's anxiety.

Catherine bent in front of her daughter. "You be *gut* for Mattie. I won't be long."

Jenny hugged her doll and sniffled.

"*Danki*, Mattie," Catherine called as she hurried to her buggy.

Mattie smiled at Jenny. "Amanda and Nathan will be up from their naps soon," she said in Pennsylvania *Deitsch* as they turned away from the door. She whispered a prayer for Catherine's husband. A sawmill accident was a wife's worst fear. The fact that Catherine hadn't given any particulars was probably so she didn't upset Jenny more. "Would you like a biscuit with honey?"

The two-year-old nodded.

Mattie made a makeshift crib for Mark by placing a pillow in one of her larger wicker baskets. As she lowered him into the basket, his arms flailed in jerky motions. He cried as Mattie placed a few already made biscuits on a baking sheet and slid them into the oven to warm. A short time later, she removed the pan from the oven, and while the biscuits were cooling, Mattie placed a dollop of honey on a spoon, then dipped her finger in the honey and licked her lips. She offered the spoon to Jenny to do the same. The toddler tasted the honey and smiled.

By the time she sliced the biscuits and drizzled honey over them, Nathan's bedroom door opened. He padded into the kitchen, rubbing his eyes. A few minutes later, Amanda fussed. After a quick diaper change, all the children, with the exception of Mark, were at the table snacking on their biscuits.

Mattie warmed the milk bottle for Mark, then sat in the rocking chair next to the front, open window in the sitting room, where she hoped the summer breeze might soothe him. She offered him the bottle, but he refused. If Mark was anything like her children, at two months of age, they wouldn't drink from a bottle either; she had never needed to pump or store her breast milk. But Mattie sensed Mark's fussiness was something more. His abdomen was distended like he was bloated and gassy.

Hearing buggy wheels crunch under the gravel, she glanced out the window. Alvin climbed out of the buggy, tromped up the steps, and tapped on the wooden screen door.

"*Kumm* on in, Alvin," she replied from the rocking chair.

The door creaked open. "I thought I would—" He grimaced at the piercing pitch of Mark's cry.

She jostled the baby to her other arm. "There was an accident at the mill. I'm watching Catherine's *kinner*."

"*Jah*, I was there when it happened."

"How badly was Matthew hurt?"

Alvin curled his lip. "He severed three fingers and might lose another."

Something shattered in the kitchen. Mattie

stood up and approached Alvin. "Hold the *boppli* a minute." She handed him the baby without giving Alvin a chance to refuse.

"I, ah . . . What am I going to do with a crying *boppli*?"

"You'll be fine. He's just gassy," she said, heading into the kitchen. Nathan stood on a chair at the counter, a broken jar of honey was splayed over the floor, and Jenny and Amanda had their hands deep in the sticky substance.

Mattie grabbed Nathan as the chair he was standing on rocked. She set him on the floor away from the mess.

Alvin entered the kitchen, a look of disgust on his face. "His diaper is soiled."

"I'll get to him in a minute."

"It's diarrhea," he said. "It's on *mei* shirt. *Mei* hands. You have to take him."

He could see what kind of jam she was in. Surely he could hold the baby a few more minutes. But Mattie bit her tongue. "Can you stop the girls from playing in the honey while I clean up the *boppli*, please?"

"*Jah*," he said, holding up his soiled hands. "I need to wash up first."

She took Mark into the bedroom. In Catherine's frazzled state of mind, she'd forgotten to leave diapers. Mattie wet a warm washcloth, then laid the baby on a towel, and washed and powdered him. Before she could get one of Amanda's cloth diapers on him, he soiled himself again. The massive amount of watery stool was alarming. She cleaned him again.

When she returned to the kitchen, the children were crying, Nathan included, and Alvin was hunched over the gooey substance, picking up pieces of the broken jar. "I think they ate some of the glass."

"Did you see which one?"

"*Nay*, but they were all playing in it and licking it off their hands."

She eyed the children hovered in the corner, honey smeared on the faces and dripping from their hands, and wanted to cry along with them.

It took a little over an hour to bathe the children and change out of her own soiled and sticky clothes.

Meanwhile, Alvin, who had volunteered to take her and the children to the emergency room, waited in his buggy. He was quiet on the way into town. Mattie dreaded going to the emergency room, but she didn't have another option. She had to find out if they'd eaten glass.

Alvin stopped the buggy next to the emergency room entrance. "How long do you think this will take? I have a few errands to run while I'm in town. Do you think I should *kumm* back in an hour?"

Her jaw dropped. Didn't he think she might need assistance with four children under the age of three in a busy emergency room? "I have no idea," she snipped.

"I'll check back in an hour or so," he said, not taking the hint.

She wanted to tell him not to bother, that she would call Cora to pick her up, but she held her tongue. Alvin was a bachelor—understandably so.

# Chapter Thirty-four

Bo kept his promise to his mother and attended the gala. He even managed to force a smile through most of the event and only tugged on the collar of his tux a few times. But sitting through the gala's five-course meal with Davis, her father, his mother, and several of her honored guests—including those representing Great Northern Explorations—proved challenging. Despite his mother's nonverbal warnings from across the table, Bo couldn't resist bringing up the subject of sinkhole disclaimers with the Great Northern Explorations attorney. Bo drilled the corporate attorney with specific questions regarding ground-water contamination and sinkholes and managed to alienate himself by the time the French onion soup was served.

After a brief stint of silence around the table, Davis leaned toward him and, resting her hand on his shoulder, whispered, "Insulting your mother's biggest campaign supporters isn't helping her."

Bo raised his brows at Davis, but said nothing. He had the main course, dessert, and a few special speakers to endure and then the night would be over.

"By the way," she said. "I like your tan. Time off from work has served you well."

"I've kept busy." He'd spent most of his time outside taking care of his mother's flower garden. Josh had worked a few days with him, even though the boy's broken ribs limited what he could do.

"We've all missed you at the office," Davis continued. "I've been given another field assignment."

"Good for you." He focused on a waiter approaching with a tray of food. He shifted to one side as the server set a steak before him. Bo thanked the server and waited patiently as the others at the table received their meals. Davis made small talk about the salmon she had ordered. Bo picked up his fork and knife and cut into his medium-rare filet. He savored the juicy flavor of every bite and was too full for dessert when it came.

"The case should interest you," Davis baited. "It'll make headlines."

"Why is that?"

The speaker approached the podium. The room quieted.

"Ask me to dance when the music starts," she said.

He wasn't staying that long. Once his mother gave her speech, he planned to leave. Besides, Davis wanted to manipulate him. It wouldn't work. He'd seen Josh a couple of days ago and he was doing better at the Walkers'. His mother had arranged for Mattie to get her children back. Her file was closed. The cases he'd turned over to Norton were either closed or pending court dates.

The audience applauded as his mother took the stage. She thanked those in attendance, talked briefly about her commitment to stimulate community growth, jobs, and improve roads, then introduced the orchestra.

The music started and Davis looked his direction expectantly.

"What game are you playing, Davis?"

"It's not a game. Unless the woman you fought so hard to defend is playing you like a fool." She looked away.

Curiosity got the better of him and he rose and held out his hand.

"Don't worry," she said, taking his hand. "I won't step on your toes."

"I might step on yours. I'm not much of a dancer." He led her out to the center of the dance floor and they began to waltz. "So what news are you bursting at the seams to tell me?"

She chuckled.

He stopped dancing. "I didn't think you had anything. Good night, Erica."

"The Diener woman's children were in the emergency room—again. Along with two small children who were in her care."

He continued dancing, making a full box turn, before growing impatient. "And?"

"Apparently three of the children were X-rayed for ingested glass. The infant in her care was diagnosed with botulism. The doctor suspects Munchausen syndrome by proxy. I know it's hard to believe any mother could intentionally make their child sick, but it happens more often than people think."

He shook his head. "She loves her children. She wouldn't harm them."

"Then keep your eye on the news." Davis smiled.

Bo's stomach wretched. "You leaked the information?"

"Not yet." The song ended, and she turned to face the orchestra.

Bo joined the applause. Continuing to clap, he leaned toward her. "Why involve the news?"

She smiled. "You'll figure it out. When the time is right."

Bo glared. "Don't play games with someone's life."

"It's business. I suggest you join allegiance with those of us who support Great Northern Expediions."

Bo walked off the dance floor and continued out the door.

He needed air.

Mattie groaned under her breath at the sight of her garden. Most of the cornstalks were trampled, and deer hooves trailed a course through the cabbage. The pole beans appeared nibbled on as well. Last week she lost a complete row of carrots. Usually the foxglove she planted along the garden's borders kept the wildlife away. She would have to come up with another remedy.

Nathan and Amanda ran to the end of the row and sat down in the dirt to play. Mattie bent over and had started picking what pole beans remained when she heard a vehicle in the distance.

"Nathan and Amanda, *kumm* here. *Nau*," she said. Looking over the pasture toward the dirt road, Mattie eyed the dust storm created in the vehicle's wake. The driver was going fast considering the number of rocks and exposed roots that made up the road. It wasn't a customer. Earlier this week she'd asked Alvin to take down the Herbs and Honey For Sale sign. As the vehicle drew closer, Mattie glanced at the barn where Alvin was cleaning out stalls. At least she wasn't alone. The automobile turned down her driveway. She sucked in a sharp breath and held it until she recognized Bo's silver car.

Bo climbed out of the car and waved.

She waved back. A warm tingling sensation spread along her nerve endings as he strode across the drive, smiling. His gazed fixed on hers.

She wiped the loose dirt off her hands. "What brings you here, Bo?"

"You've been on my mind." He grinned.

He'd been on hers as well. Heat spread up her neck and infused her cheeks.

Amanda bent down, picked up a clot of dirt, and held it up to Bo.

He dropped to one knee and received the gift. "Thank you." He glanced up at Mattie and squinted. "She has your button nose."

Unsure how to respond, Mattie looked down at the ground.

"I'm sorry. I didn't mean to embarrass you." He stood up and swiped the dirt off his pant leg. "Can we go sit on the porch? We need to talk about a few things."

An image of the doctor's furrowed brows flashed through her mind as she recalled the battery of questions he'd asked concerning the glass ingestion. Mattie steeled herself. "Are you here officially?"

He shook his head. "Not exactly."

"What does that mean?"

"Mattie, it's important." He squinted. "Let's find some shade."

She glanced at the barn. The stall doors leading outside were standing open, but Alvin wasn't around. Did she want Alvin involved in this conversation? He would disapprove, lecture her about *Englischers* . . . "Let's go in the *haus*, children, and wash the beans." She caught a glimpse of Bo's frown and said, "Would you like a glass of water?"

He smiled. "I'd love one."

"We can talk while I'm washing the beans." She took the children by the hand, led them to the house and into the kitchen. She set Amanda on the counter next to the sink, then washed her dirty hands with a wet dishcloth. Bo waited patiently as she washed Nathan next. "Take your *schweschder* into the other room and play quietly," she instructed.

Once the children left the room, she filled a glass with water and handed it to Bo.

"Thanks." He studied her a moment.

"I thought you were thirsty."

"What happened the other day?"

"I don't know what you mean." She turned and put the stopper in the sink, then turned on the tap.

"Yes, you do." He leaned against the counter, legs stretched out.

She dumped the basket of beans in the water.

"You took the children to the hospital."

"Then you already know," she grumbled.

"Will you look at me?" he said softly.

She turned her head slightly and lifted her gaze to meet his.

"I want to hear what happened."

"You said this wasn't official."

"The paperwork is being processed—not by me."

"Who then?" She spun to face him. "The police?" Of course they were involved. She was on probation. "Am I going to lose *mei* children again?" For an instant she thought her only option for keeping her kids would be to leave town. She had a cousin downstate and several in Ohio.

"Tell me what happened," Bo said.

Leaving the state would be the better choice. Would they track down her relatives?

"Mattie." Bo touched her arm. "I want to help you."

Nathan padded into the kitchen. "*Wasser, sei se gut.*"

Mattie partially filled a small plastic cup with water and handed it to her son.

He slurped the liquid and handed the cup back. "*Danki.*" He ran into the sitting room.

"*Mei* friend's husband was injured at the mill. She asked if I'd watch their two children, and of course I said yes. I'd made biscuits with honey drizzled over them, and the children, except for the *boppli*, were eating a snack at the table while I tried feeding the *boppli*. He was very fussy." She went on to tell Bo how Nathan had climbed up on a kitchen chair to get the jar of honey and how it fell. How she found the children playing in the honey. "They licked the honey off their hands. They didn't know any better. I couldn't tell if they had accidently eaten any shards of glass," she explained. "I had to take them to the *doktah*." She told Bo how the baby had diarrhea at her house and again in the hospital, then how the doctor and nurses had bombarded her with questions when the baby started vomiting.

Alvin entered the kitchen. "I was here. That's what happened."

Bo tensed. "You were here?"

Alvin crossed his arms. "Stood right where you are *nau*."

Bo looked at the space between them as if silently calculating the distance. He cleared his throat. "Were you aware the baby has botulism?"

She shook her head. "The emergency room paged Catherine, the *boppli*'s *mamm*. She was waiting for her husband to get out of surgery.

"Are they going to always suspect me? They accused me of harming Nathan when I hadn't— even had me arrested." Mattie chewed her nail. She couldn't go through losing her children again.

"Has Child Services made contact with you yet?"

"*Nay.*"

Alvin stepped forward. "Are they going to? It was an accident."

"Yes, I heard they're going to. I don't know when—maybe today."

"Your partner?" Mattie said.

"She's not my partner." He bowed his head. "But she's the one who told me last night."

Feeling lightheaded, Mattie gripped the countertop. "Can't you stop her?"

Bo shook his head. "It's a long story. I think she has other motives." Bo's eyes widened as if he'd had some sort of revelation. He turned to Alvin. "I should probably talk with the bishop."

# Chapter Thirty-five

Attending the Amish Sunday service was awkward. Memories stirred within Bo that he couldn't easily suppress. Perhaps this wasn't a good idea. He pulled on the collarless shirt out of habit more than tightness as he moved to the back row of benches and took a seat on the men's side of the barn. Andy's clothes that Mattie had loaned him came in handy again today. Although the members' expressions clearly indicated he didn't belong.

He hadn't spotted Mattie yet, but that wasn't surprising. The women kept their heads down and were all wearing black dresses, white aprons, and white prayer *kapps*. Even the children

Amanda's age were dressed the same. The fact that Mattie blended into the crowd so well meant Davis wouldn't find her either, and that was a relief. Yesterday Bo had called his friend Max, who was Davis's new partner, and learned their plan to visit Mattie today. Bo had chided Max, but his friend merely boasted about looking forward to the long drive in the country with the senator's daughter. Davis was up to something. A media blitz most likely. Bo had warned Bishop Yoder to expect ruthless comments from the news crews. He even tried to convince the bishop to cancel the service, but the bishop wouldn't hear of it. Bo had to answer a slew of questions about his faith, some he hadn't thought about in years, before the bishop would allow Bo to attend the service.

The singing portion of the service began. Bo scanned the women's side of the barn, but with the married women seated in the front rows with their backs facing him, he couldn't locate where Mattie was seated. Bo glimpsed Alvin staring at him and lowered his head. Once the scriptures were read, Bo shifted his thoughts to the message. The bishop spoke about the parable of the prodigal son, and Bo was inclined to believe Bishop Yoder was talking directly to him. Bo shifted on the wooden bench. After sitting three hours without back support, his muscles had seized. He was stiff when the service ended an

hour later. Sitting four hours seemed exceptionally long, even for an Amish service. Before
the bishop concluded his message, Bo detected
engines rumbling outside the barn.

The commotion erupted the moment the barn
door opened and the members began filing into
the yard. Bo's heart pounded as he searched for
Mattie. He wanted to protect her from Davis,
who was perched in the driveway, waving a legal
document and demanding Mattie to come forward. The women held up their hands to shield
their faces and hurried across the lawn.

Noticeably agitated, Davis spoke louder,
demanding to speak with Mattie.

Bo eyed the various members of the news
crew, spotted the contact he'd arranged, then
nodded at the bishop. Approaching Davis, they
removed their straw hats and held them in
front of their faces.

"This is private property," Bo said. "You're
trespassing."

"Bo Lambright?" Davis chuckled. "I know
that's you hiding behind that hat."

"Sunday is our day of worship," Bo said. "We
ask that you leave us alone."

"You know why I'm here," she growled.
"Where are the woman and her children?"

"I'm going to ask again. Please leave the
premises."

"Oh, I get it. You're hiding behind the hat

because you're afraid the agency will see you defending the *Amish* woman. You don't want your face on TV?"

Bo held his tongue, and when she pushed his hat away from his face, he let it drop on the ground.

"Erica Delanie, I have a question for you," the local news reporter said.

Davis turned. "Yes."

"The Amish are known for their meek mannerisms. Was it necessary to knock his hat out of his hands? Wouldn't most people find that offensive given that the Amish don't believe in having their photos taken?"

"I know this person." She turned to him. "Bo, tell them you're not Amish."

Bo pivoted in the reporter's direction and lowered his head submissively. "The only statement I wish to make is that Nathan Diener was misdiagnosed. He suffered a rare, life-threatening form of chicken pox. The family is still trying to recuperate and wishes to be left alone."

He and the bishop turned and started to walk away.

Davis spoke up. "She's accused of harming her children—again."

"I'll catch up with you," Bo said to the bishop, then turned and faced her. "I find it interesting that the same doctors who misdiagnosed her son would make such a claim. They should have their facts together first. After all, the boy almost died at the hands of his doctor." He continued toward the house, anxious to see Mattie and make sure she wasn't shaken up over the matter.

The bishop had waited for Bo on the porch. "*Danki* for handling the reporters."

"Hopefully they'll leave everyone alone." By the type of questions aimed at Davis as he walked away, the reporters were going to have a field day with the senator's daughter.

"We could always drop more trees on the road," Bishop Yoder said, a hint of laughter in his voice.

Inside the house, Bo looked in the kitchen for Mattie, but didn't see her. The other women averted their eyes and scooted out of the room. Even Grace avoided him. "Where's Mattie?"

"I haven't seen her," Grace replied.

Ben rounded the corner of the kitchen. "The news vans are leaving."

"Oh, *gut*. We can eat outside," Erma said. "Will you start setting up the tables, please?"

Bo caught Ben before he left the house. "Have you seen Mattie?"

Ben shook his head.

Something was wrong. He eyed Ben.

"Sorry," Ben said, opening the door. "I have to set up the tables."

Bo approached a group of men talking with the bishop. "Have any of you seen Mattie?"

The men shook their heads, including Alvin, whose neck muscles had tightened when Bo asked.

Bo rephrased the question. "Do you *know where* she is?"

One by one, the men distanced themselves from the group, leaving Bishop Yoder, Alvin, and Bo alone.

"I know I'm an outsider," Bo began. "But I have to talk with her."

"She's gone," the bishop said.

"Mattie went home? She shouldn't be there alone. If the reporters double back—"

"She left town."

The air left Bo's lungs. "She can't disappear. The charges haven't been formally dropped. I have to talk with her."

Bishop Yoder cleared his throat. "As I said before, we appreciate your help."

Bo shook his head in disbelief.

Alvin's stoic expression hardened. "It'd be best if you walked away."

*Best for whom?* Bo wanted to ask. Instead, he drew a deep breath and released it slowly. "Mattie is still going to need help. She's on probation." They weren't listening. "Mattie has my cell number. Tell her to get in contact with me. It's important."

Neither the bishop nor Alvin acknowledged Bo. He'd never felt like more of an outsider than at this moment. A knot formed in his throat and he turned away. Bo hung his head and left the bishop's house.

He saw Ben moving a bench from the barn and set it beside a long table. He'd try one more time. "Are Mattie and the children somewhere safe?"

"*Jah*," Ben replied.

"Where are they?"

Ben hesitated. He looked at the house, then back to Bo. "I dropped her off at the bus station last *nacht*." He shrugged. "But I don't know where they were going."

Erma came up beside them with a bowl of beans in her hand. "Ben, will you bring another bench out from the barn?"

"Sure."

Erma waited until Grace's husband walked away. "I don't know many *Englischers* who know the words to our Amish hymns. '*Das Loblied*' is sung in High German."

Bo hadn't given any thought to how easily he recalled the old hymns. "Yes, I've . . . sung them before." He sighed. "Erma, I have to know where I can find Mattie."

The older woman studied him a moment. "The first time I met you, I knew there was something different about you—Boaz."

"Please," he pleaded. This wasn't the time to rehash his past.

Erma considered his request several seconds. "She's gone to Centreville, Michigan. An Amish district in St. Joseph County."

His stomach wrenched. St. Joseph County was

the last place on earth he thought he'd ever return to. Now it didn't seem like he had much choice. "Do you know where she's staying?"

Erma's mouth twisted. She looked over her shoulder, then back at him. "She's staying a day or two with her cousin, Verna Mast."

"A day or two?"

"She's going to Ohio from there."

"Thanks." Bo turned. He had to reach her before she disappeared again.

As the pot of lemony ginger tea steeped, Mattie gazed out her cousin's kitchen window. The late-afternoon sun glistened across the corn stalks, radiating a peaceful glow. Verna's corn towered over anything Mattie had ever grown. She'd have to ask her cousin the secret once she came in from talking with someone on the porch.

Mattie heard the door open and close as she poured tea into two cups.

A few moments later, Verna stepped into the kitchen, her leather birthing case in hand. "Sounds like Mary Jean is ready to deliver," she said. "I might be gone several hours. She labored over thirty-six hours the last two times."

Mattie smiled. "I understand."

"I have four mothers at full term. Depending on how Mary Jean does, I'll probably stop and check on *mei* other patients' progress while I'm out. There's fresh bread in the bread box for sandwiches and canned peaches in the basement."

"Don't worry about the *kinner* and me, we'll manage." Truthfully, she wasn't hungry. She'd made the children a late lunch and put them down for a nap a little over an hour ago, and as tired as they were from the long bus ride to St. Joseph County, she wouldn't be surprised if they slept through the night.

Once Verna left on her house calls, Mattie sat at the table with a pad of paper. She'd promised Grace she would write and let her know they'd arrived safely. Mattie started the letter by saying how much she missed her friend already. She hadn't written more than a paragraph before someone knocked on the door. *Another anxious father,* she thought as she set the pen down and rose from her chair.

The Amish man shuffled his feet on the stoop, but when he turned to face Mattie, she realized that he wasn't here to beckon the midwife.

"Hello, Mattie," Bo said.

"What are you doing here?" *Dressed in Amish clothes?*

He removed the straw hat. "Could I come in?"

She hesitated a moment. His drawn—no, betrayed—facial expression would haunt her if she sent him away. Mattie sighed and opened the door wider. "You can't stay long."

He stared at her hard as he entered, the screen door closing behind him.

"Well," she said with a wobbly voice. "What brings—" She swallowed hard when he moved closer. His determined, road-weary expression sent a shudder down her spine. "What brings you to St. Joseph County?"

"I just drove over eight hours—after sitting through a *four-hour* church service that you didn't even attend. Did you really think you could just walk away?"

"Bo, I, ah . . . You've been very kind to me, but I, ah . . ." *Can't have these feelings for you.*

"What?"

"We're from different . . ." *Worlds.*

"This isn't a social call," he said.

"Oh." Of course it wasn't. How foolish of her to think otherwise. She turned, but his hand caught her arm and bought her back to face him.

"You're not allowed to leave the county. You're on probation."

"You're hurting *mei* arm," she lied.

He loosened his grip. "Where are the children?"

"I didn't do anything wrong," she insisted.

"I know you didn't." Bo's gaze penetrated hers. "If you recall, I've been on your side since the start."

She steeled her resolve. "Then don't take them."

His expression softened. "Mattie, you know—"

Someone tapped on the door. Pleased for an interruption, Mattie scurried around Bo to answer the door. "May I help you?" she asked the younger woman on the opposite side of the screen.

"*Hiya.* I'm Verna's neighbor—"

Mattie thrust the door open. "Won't you *kumm* inside?"

The woman paused briefly to glance over her shoulder at someone else waiting in the buggy, then stepped inside. "Verna stopped by our farm and asked if I would invite your family for supper. By the way, I'm Malinda Lambright."

"It's nice to meet you. I'm Mattie, and this is—" Bo's back was to them. "Bo, we have a visitor."

Bo pivoted around slowly. "Hello." He spoke to the floor.

Mattie had never seen him act shy. *Lambright.* "Do you two know each other?"

Malinda shook her head. "I don't think so." She continued, "Verna mentioned she would be tied up this evening and our farm is just on the top of the hill on the right." Her gaze steadied on Bo. "You do look familiar."

Amanda wandered into the sitting room rubbing her eyes. "I'm *dorstig.*"

"I'll get you something to drink, pumpkin." Bo swooped Amanda into his arms and disappeared into the kitchen.

Bo's pulse raced. Malinda was seven years old the last time he'd seen her. She'd grown into a beautiful young woman. Holding Amanda in one arm, he turned on the tap and filled a glass of water with the other, then handed it to her.

He listened for Malinda to leave and blew out a breath when the screen door snapped closed.

Mattie entered the kitchen. "Her last name is Lambright."

*Please don't ask.* Bo forced a smile. "How long will it take to get your things together? I'd like to get on the road. We have an eight-hour drive ahead of us."

Mattie shifted her gaze from him to Amanda in his arms, then back to him, alarm growing in her expression. She reached for her daughter. "*Kumm* to me, Amanda."

The child handed Mattie the empty glass, then buried her face in the crook of Bo's neck.

"I think she's still tired," he said, patting her back.

Another knock sounded at the door, and Mattie groaned. "*Mei* cousin's place is as busy as a free bakery."

Amanda picked up her head when Mattie left the room but didn't cry. Instead, she touched Bo's whiskery jaw and giggled.

"You think I'm funny looking?" he said in Pennsylvania *Deitsch*.

The child giggled harder and tried to tickle him again.

"Bo?" Mattie said.

Turning, his mouth fell open.

"Boaz! *Mei* prayers have been answered. They've all been answered," his *mamm* repeated, half crying, half laughing.

"How are you . . . *Mamm*?" He glanced at Mattie, whose mouth hung agape.

"I always knew you would return." Her eyes seemed to drink him and Amanda in. "*Nau* look at you, all grown. And a family man." She tilted her face upward. "*Danki*, God, for answering *mei* prayers."

*Family man.* Bo swallowed hard.

His mother beamed when Nathan padded into the room. "A *sohn* and *dochder.*"

Had she lost her mind? Bo hadn't shaved in a couple of days, but he didn't have a beard long enough to represent having two children.

"Please," his *mamm* said, turning to Mattie. "Please, *kumm* for supper tonight. *Mei* husband will be thrilled to see Boaz again."

Bo snorted.

"We would be honored, Mrs. Lambright." Mattie smiled at him. "Wouldn't we, Boaz?"

# Chapter Thirty-six

"I'm not going there for supper," Bo said. "You don't understand. They think I'm Amish."

Mattie eyed him head to toe and crossed her arms. "You do make a handsome Amish man," she teased.

Appreciating her attempt to lighten his mood, he played along. "*Jah*, I seem to recall you and Grace talking about that." He scratched his whiskered jaw.

Mattie's face turned a blistering shade of red. "*Daagdich.*"

"I've been called worse." Truth was, he liked her teasing him. Referring to him as a scamp was a compliment.

She filled a glass with water and took a drink. "Your sister must have been young when you left home," she said, forcing the subject.

"Seven. My brother, Thomas, was twelve."

"That must have been hard leaving them."

His jaw twitched. "It was."

"Don't you think they would want to know where you've been?"

"They don't remember me." He laughed half-heartedly. "Other than maybe by 'the one who got away.' "

"Your mother remembers you. You heard her," Mattie scolded.

"Why are you taking her side?"

"Because I can't imagine what it would be like to *nett* know where one of *mei* children was. Besides," she said softly, "I think you're still . . . unsettled."

"Unsettled?"

"Someone doesn't jump the fence and *nett* wonder if they'd made the right decision."

"Mattie, stay out of this."

"Bo, your mother said she hasn't seen you in sixteen years. You can pretend to be Amish through one meal."

He scratched the prickly growth on his jaw. "My family thinks we're married." In one fluid move, he crossed the kitchen and backed Mattie up against the sink. "You're going to pretend to be *mei fraa*?"

She leaned back. "I can . . . do that."

He slid his hand behind her back and brought her closer, then slanting his head slightly, he leaned forward.

She licked her lips.

"Are you sure you want to? I'm a fence-jumper," he whispered.

She nodded.

He pulled back. "I'm still not going there for supper."

Mattie righted herself and, with a little shake

of her shoulders and arms, straightened to her full height. "I am." She marched into the sitting room where she'd sent Nathan and Amanda to play with a sack of clothespins.

Bo shoved his hand through his hair. He'd seen his mother, his sister; the only other person he would like to see is Thomas. But that wouldn't be worth sitting at the same table with his father. Bo recalled the angry—almost wild—look in his father's eyes as he whirled the leather strap Bo's direction. Bo hadn't had time to turn around and take the lashing across his backside like the other times his father wanted to beat sense into him.

He stood at the sink, the white-knuckled grip absorbing the memory of his father's wrath. Until recently, he'd kept his past buried. It would have been easier if he'd never regained his memories after the accident. Mattie's voice pulled him from his thoughts. Only she wasn't talking to him.

"Gather your things, Nathan," she whispered.

"Are we leaving again?"

*"Shh,"* she said, then whispered something Bo couldn't decipher.

Why was she whispering? It registered like a slap in the face.

She was skipping out . . . for Ohio.

Mattie had a hard time keeping pace with Bo and all she had to carry was the lantern. As adamant as Bo was about not eating supper with his family, he certainly seemed eager to go now. He'd hurried them out of the house like he had to get a dentist appointment over with. Bo carried Nathan on his shoulders and Amanda in his arms.

"We can cut through the pasture. Should be a shorter route. I think," he said.

"You think?" She remembered every inch of the farm where she'd grown up.

"It's been a long time."

"Sixteen years, according to your mother. That would make you a teen when you left home. It'd be hard to erase childhood memories even if you did jump the fence."

"It's a long story."

"Shouldn't I know these things? After all, I'm your *fraa* for the evening." The sound of being someone's wife again felt strangely comfortable. *Bo*'s fraa. She let the thought simmer on a back burner in her mind. "Well?"

"The only thing you need to know is my father isn't meek or humble. He usually isn't kind. He has a short fuse."

"I find that hard to believe. His *sohn* is the kindest man I've ever known."

He smiled, but steeled himself immediately. "I worked hard not to become like him."

"He was that hard of a man—of a father?"

Bo's brows furrowed. "It isn't a topic that should be discussed in front of the *kinner*."

As they climbed the grassy slope in silence, Mattie couldn't help but wonder about Bo's past. What made him jump the fence and move so far away from home? He had introduced the *Englischer* who had brought the paperwork to the hospital as his mother—had said she was a judge. That didn't make any sense either.

At the top of the hill sat an unpainted, rough-cut timber barn. The farmhouse had a large wrap-around porch that Mattie found welcoming. She stole a glance at Bo. His eyes seemed to dance from one outbuilding to the next. He studied the fat calico cat that followed them meowing, the large maple trees that shaded the house, and a few younger saplings near the clothesline.

Bo set Amanda on the grass next to the porch steps and lowered Nathan from his shoulders. Bo's chest expanded with a breath. "Are you ready for this, *fraa*?"

She took hold of Amanda's and Nathan's hands. "Lead the way."

He climbed the stairs and paused on the landing. "This feels strange."

The door opened and his sister greeted them with a warm smile. "I knew you would *kumm*." She glanced at the children. "I'm *Aenti* Malinda."

Bo exchanged a nervous glance with Mattie. |His face paled. Mattie mouthed, *It's okay,* but that didn't seem to settle his nerves. He wiped his hands on the sides of his pants.

407

The sitting room was scantly furnished. Two sets of matching wooden chairs faced each other with a small wooden table and lamp between each set. A wiry man with disheveled auburn hair stood next to the woodstove shuffling his feet and rocking back and forth. He lifted his hand in a short wave. "I'm Thomas," he said. "I keep the woodstove."

Mattie peered at Bo, wondering if he was thinking the same thing. This was July and too hot for a fire.

Bo strode farther into the room. "How you doing, Thomas?"

"*Gut.*" He swayed and avoided eye contact. "I *gut,*" he repeated. "I keep the fire."

"That's an important job," Bo said.

"*Jah,* important."

Malinda leaned closer to Mattie. "Thomas has a steel plate in his head."

"Do you remember me?" Bo's voice strained.

Mattie's throat tightened.

Thomas shook his head while at the same time said, "*Jah,* you're *mei bruder.*"

"That's right."

"Malinda, I found Boaz. I found *mei bruder.*" Thomas caught Bo's mother's hand as she entered the sitting room. "*Mamm,* I found him." Thomas's excitement carried throughout the house.

Until a gray-haired man, an older version of Bo, ambled through the front door. "What's the commotion about? I can hear you all the way outside."

"Bo's back. I found him," Thomas said.

"Did you *nau*?" He looked at Bo, but not like a man who hadn't seen his son in sixteen years. He made a curt nod and turned to look at Mattie, the children, then his wife. "You suppose we can eat *nau*, Doreen?" Without waiting for his wife to reply, he headed toward the sweet aroma of sourdough bread.

"Bo, it's so *gut* to have you home," his mother said, patting his arm. "You're much taller than I remember."

Bo stiffened. "Am I?"

For the first time since Mattie had known him, he looked sad. He was obviously guarding his heart, but his façade didn't fool Mattie. His pain was deeply rooted.

Bo placed his hand on Mattie's lower back. She wasn't sure if he needed her support or if he thought she was frightened by his father's gruffness.

"Something smells *gut*," Mattie said as she and Bo entered the kitchen. She sat next to Malinda and held Amanda on her lap. Nathan sat on the men's side of the table next to Bo.

"We would have slaughtered a fattened calf had we known you were coming today," Mr. Lambright said.

Bo harrumphed.

"I guess your mother's chicken will have to do on such short notice." Mr. Lambright bowed his head and everyone except Bo did the same.

Mattie eyed him hard, then lowered her head. If anyone needed to pray, it was him. The chip on his shoulder was the size of a block of ice freshly cut from the lake. *Lord, please show Bo the freedom in forgiveness. Mend his broken heart. Mend this family.* Silverware began to clatter and Mattie opened her eyes.

A bowl of mashed potatoes came to her from one side and a basket of rolls from the other. For a few minutes, the only words spoken related to the meal. "Please pass the salt, the butter, the corn." Mattie glanced across the table at Bo. Head down, he was eating like he was in a contest to finish first.

"Two *kinner*," Mr. Lambright said, sending a scrutinizing gaze from one side of the table to the other. "I don't see much beard growth, Boaz. How long have you two been together?"

Mrs. Lambright gasped. "Titus."

Mattie dabbed the corners of her mouth with a cloth napkin. "The *kinner*'s father, *mei* first husband, passed away."

Mr. Lambright's dark eyes traveled from her to Bo. "Where have you been living all these years?"

"Northern Michigan."

"The growing season is short in the Upper Peninsula. How's the farming?"

"Tree farms do well," Bo said.

Mrs. Lambright passed Mattie the bowl of coleslaw. "I can't imagine a shorter growing season. Are you able to put in a garden?"

"I start *mei* plants earlier in the *greenhaus* and transplant them after the last frost."

"I like to grow," Thomas said.

Keeping the conversation going, Mattie asked, "Anything in particular?"

"Pumpkins." Thomas smiled.

"Pumpkins," Amanda echoed.

Bo chuckled. Mattie had heard him call her pumpkin more than once.

The meal ended with hot apple pie. Mattie observed that the largest piece Mrs. Lambright served went to Bo, who didn't hesitate to dive in.

Mattie offered to help with the dishes, and Bo followed Thomas and his father into the sitting room.

Once the men left the room, his mother and sister swarmed her with questions for which she had no answers. From what Mattie gathered, his family hadn't seen nor heard from him since the day he walked out of their lives.

Bo glanced around the sitting room. The plank floor could use a fresh coat of wax, but other than that, it looked exactly like he remembered.

His father sat on the chair next to the window, Thomas on the one beside him, and Bo took a seat

411

opposite. *Mattie, don't dillydally in the kitchen.*

"Looks like you have your life together finally," Bo's father said.

Bo swallowed. Maybe he should offer to help with the dishes.

"You could have written your *mamm* a letter to fill her in on the happenings. At least about the wedding. She's your *mamm*. A mother wants to know those things about their *kinner*."

"I came back home once. Don't you remember? You looked me in the eye and said you didn't have a *sohn*."

"*Jah*, well, that was when you were in the world. It's different *nau*," his father said. "You've turned from your wayward ways."

Bo clenched his jaw. Growing up, every time his father wheeled the leather strap, he declared he would turn Bo from his wayward—or wicked —ways. Bo shook his head. His father had accused Bo of having lustful thoughts that delayed him from finishing his barn chores. Another time Bo was accused of stealing and whipped for losing a few coins on his way home from the store. His father was excessive, hard to please, and down-right mean in many cases. And Bo's mother always looked the other way.

Thomas rocked in his chair. "I waited for you to come back. Why didn't you?"

Bo *tried* to come home after the accident. Not that Thomas would have known. A year after his accident, his father met Bo at the door, sneered at the jeans and polo shirt he had on, and declared he didn't have a son.

"I waited for you, Boaz," his brother repeated.

Bo bowed his head remorsefully. Without Bo around, Thomas would have been the sole recipient of his father's wrath. Obviously, over the years something had happened to Thomas. Maybe he was kicked in the head by a horse, or perhaps his father had beaten him silly. The day Bo left home, his father was out of sorts. Thomas had spilled the milking can, and the morning supply became a bountiful feast for the barn cats. Bo took the brunt of the mishap, claiming he'd spilled the canister. That day he listened to the sound of the leather strap whirl through the air and felt the barbed sting the last time. After three lashes, one of which was misaimed and clipped his ear, Bo caught hold of the strap and raised it against his father. An old dirty rug didn't get beaten as hard as he did as a kid.

"I'm sorry, Thomas."

"That's okay." Thomas smiled. "You're home *nau*."

Nathan toddled over to Bo, crawled up in his lap, and yawned. *Perfect timing.* "It's getting late." Bo stood. "*Danki* for supper."

His father merely nodded, not bothering to stand.

Thomas bounded to his feet. "I'm glad I found you."

"Me too. It was *gut* to see you again, Thomas. You take care."

"*Jah*, I take care of the fire."

Bo smiled at his brother. Despite the circumstances, Thomas appeared happy. "That's an important job."

He headed into the kitchen to see if Mattie was ready to leave. The women were sitting at the table talking, Amanda asleep in Mattie's arms. A sudden desire for a family of his own pulled at his heart. "Nathan's ready for bed," he said.

Mattie smiled. "So is Amanda."

"I'll hitch the buggy and give you a ride," Malinda offered and scurried out the back door.

"I had a *gut* time getting to know your *fraa*," his mother said. "Will we see you tomorrow?"

Bo shook his head. "We have to get back to Badger Creek."

His mother frowned.

"Maybe you two could exchange letters," Mattie suggested.

"I'd like that," *Mamm* said.

Bo nodded. "Me too." He gave his mother a much overdue hug.

"Tell Mrs. Nettleton *danki* for all she's done," she whispered.

Bo cocked his head. "You know about her?"

*Mamm* sniffled. "She stopped to see me a few years ago. Your father had gone to town, so I invited her in for *kaffi*. That's when I learned about

414

your accident. She said she and her husband had brought you home, but . . ." She paused to wipe her eyes with a tissue.

"But *Daed* made it clear he had *nay sohn*." He hadn't meant to make her cry. The past was in the past.

"I knew you were in *gut* hands. Mrs. Nettleton promised that you would always have a place to call home."

Bo couldn't speak.

*Mamm* touched his shoulder. "Write to me when you can, please?"

"I will."

A few minutes later, they were headed back to Mattie's cousin's house. Malinda talked about the different changes in the community, people who had moved away and businesses that had opened or closed. She never mentioned what happened to Thomas. She pulled up to the darkened house and stopped the buggy. "Do you think I might be able to visit you up north some time?"

Bo wasn't sure how to answer his sister. He wasn't even Amish.

Mattie spoke up. "You're *wilkom* anytime."

He widened his eyes at Mattie but she held her smile.

His sister beamed. "I've never gone anywhere outside of St. Joseph County."

Before she started packing her bags, Bo changed the subject. "What happened to Thomas?"

Malinda sobered. "He left home to search for you and ended up in the army. His jeep turned over somewhere oversees and the military said he had a brain injury. He came home just before Christmas last year, discharged from the army and with a steel plate in his head."

*Left home to search for you* . . . Bo hated that he was the cause.

"It created an uproar in the district. Thomas had developed a *worldly* vocabulary. Our family was almost shunned. That year the crops had failed and we almost had to move away."

"I'm sorry."

"At first, *Daed* wasn't going to let him stay. But I think he felt guilty. *Mamm* sank into a deep depression after you and Thomas left. Seeing Thomas again sparked her hope that maybe she would see you again too."

Bo hung his head. "I'm glad we were able to get together for supper." He said good-bye to his sister, promising to write.

Mattie carried Amanda into the house as Bo followed with Nathan asleep in his arms. He tucked Nathan into bed. The sooner they got on the road for Badger Creek, the better.

Mattie came out of the bedroom. "Amanda is worn out."

"It's been a long day."

Mattie headed into the kitchen. "I'm going to make a cup of tea. Would you like one?"

"Is it caffeinated?" He had a long drive ahead of him.

"You're a brave soul drinking caffeine this late." She placed the kettle on the stove. "Bo, what exactly made you jump the fence?"

He thought for a moment of where to begin. "It wasn't my intention."

Her brow crinkled. "What do you mean?"

"I told you my father was a hard man to please. I still have markings from his temper. One day I'd had enough. He wheeled the leather strap and I caught it. I wanted him to feel the burn against his flesh."

Her eyes widened. "You struck your father?"

He shook his head. "I tossed it at his feet and walked off. Walked nearly five miles before hitching a ride with someone. I planned to hang out in town while my father cooled down. The next thing I remember, tires were squealing and I was tossed like a limp rag up against a car's windshield. I woke up a week later in a hospital room, my head shaved and arms restrained. Apparently my clothes were cut off me either at the scene or in the emergency room and were lost in the shuffle of being rushed into surgery. I had no form of identification to tell me who I was before the accident. What puzzled the medical staff was the fact that no one was looking for me. The surgeon, who had a heart for missions, took a great interest in finding my family. He checked with the sheriff's department for anyone searching for a missing kid and nothing ever came up. I was a mystery. The driver had died in the accident. When his family came to claim his body, they couldn't identify me either."

"What happened?"

"I became a ward of the court. Only, no foster home wanted me. I had too many health issues after the accident that required having to relearn basic tasks again. The surgeon and his wife, Judge Nettleton, took me in." He shrugged. "I underwent months of strenuous physical therapy and tutoring."

"But your memory came back, right?"

"Eventually," he said quietly. "It took a year before I could put together the flashbacks and dreams. My new parents took me back to the farm. That's when my father said he didn't have a son." Bo turned away. He'd never told anyone the story.

"So, you're *nett* a fence-jumper by choice."

He cringed. What did it matter? His father had looked him in the eye and denounced him as his son. "Can you get your things together?" Bo took a step away, but Mattie stopped him.

She placed her hand on his arm, her blue eyes intense, pleading. "*Nett* tonight, Bo, please."

"I made a few calls on my way here," he said. "Things are going to be . . ." Her grip tightened on his arm. His breathing turned ragged. "You can't . . . run . . . away." She had him floundering—underwater. Unable to think. *Focus.* Her face tilted toward his, her lips slightly parted; if he was reading the longing in her eyes correctly, she was giving him permission to kiss her. Warm breaths fanned his cheeks. "I care a great deal about . . . you." Bo lowered his mouth over hers, kissing her slowly at first, then hearing a soft moan escape her lips, he placed his hand on her back and pressed her firmly against his chest. Releasing a guttural rasp, he whispered, "You're beautiful," and he deepened the kiss. Her hands traveled over his shoulders, up the back of his neck. She twined her fingers through his hair, pulling him closer, seeking more in his kiss.

Her touch awakened every fiber of his body, and he fought to regain control. *Too far. Stop. Distance yourself.* Bo pulled back, breathing raggedly.

Mattie lowered her head. "I don't know what got into me."

He wasn't sure what happened either, but he liked it. Wanted more.

"I, ah . . ." She shuddered. "Andy's the only man I've ever kissed."

*Idiot.* He kneaded the corded muscles that were tightening in his neck. "And you feel guilty."

She looked up. "*Nay,*" she said softly. "It felt right."

He ushered her back into his arms, holding her

tight as she nuzzled her nose into the crook of his neck. She felt right in his arms. *So right.* How would he let her go? Bo kissed her forehead, then pulled back. "We have to be in Badger Creek by morning."

# Chapter Thirty-seven

Mattie's lips tingled. Her mind was numb. She had left Badger Creek to get away from the false accusations, and now she was heading home to face them again. She trusted Bo. After meeting his family and learning about the harsh conditions growing up, she understood him better. He hadn't jumped the fence in the way other youths left. But could he ever walk away from the *Englisch* world that had accepted him?

Bo turned off I-75 and stopped at a roadside park. "I know we only have a couple more hours, but I need to rest my eyes a few minutes before we cross the bridge." He turned off the engine. He dropped his seat back a few inches, leaned back, and closed his eyes.

Her nerves were wound tighter than a spool of thread. She ran her hand over the folds in her dress. "You never said how you liked the Sunday meeting."

"I tried to find you in the crowd," he said

without opening his eyes. "Whose idea was it for all the women to wear black?"

"Grace's."

"Hmm . . . That wasn't fair."

Mattie smiled. "I missed our Sunday gathering. What was Bishop Yoder's message about?"

"The prodigal son."

"Like you."

He shifted in the seat. "Aren't you tired?"

Silence fell between them and minutes turned into hours. The morning sun cast a beautiful glow over the Mackinac Bridge and Mattie waited for Bo to awaken from his slumber. His chest rose and fell in cadence with his soft breaths. She leaned against the car door, amazed at how comfortable she felt with Bo. She couldn't remember a time being more relaxed with a man she wasn't married to. A few months ago, when she told Grace she was ready to move forward, Mattie never dreamed she would give her heart to an *Englischer*. God certainly had a strange way of bringing two people together.

Vaguely aware of Mattie sitting on the passenger seat beside him, Bo's muscles went limp. He was floating through a haze of white smoke.

"Boaz, My son, open your eyes."
Obeying the Master's voice, he opened his eyes. He stood in an open meadow

that stretched beyond his depth of vision. The grassy field was soft against his bare feet as he walked toward the faint sound of a lamb's bleat. The sun shone on the wool fleece, creating a halo.

Bo knelt beside the small creature and gathered it into his arms. He looked up and spotted the herd grazing on a hillside in the distance. Bo carried the lamb to the rest of the flock, but when he lowered it to the ground to join the others, the members of Mattie's district had replaced the sheep. Bo glanced at the Amish clothes hanging on him like filthy rags.

"Bo." He recognized his stepfather's voice, but when he searched the area, Bo couldn't find him. "You promised me you'd take care of your mother."

Bo jolted awake.

"Someone's calling you," Mattie said.

Had he been talking in his sleep? Bo rubbed his eyes. A muffled ring came from the glove box.

Bo retrieved his phone but the call had gone to voice mail. He pressed the recorded message and lifted the phone to his ear. His mother had called to remind him of his appointment with Internal Affairs.

"I didn't mean to sleep so long," he said, turning the ignition key.

"You must have been really tired." Mattie glanced at the children sleeping in their car seats. "They're worn out too."

"Apparently I was. Would you like me to stop for coffee?"

"I don't need any," she replied.

If he wasn't in a hurry, Bo would have liked to stop for breakfast. But as it was, he wasn't sure if he would have time to shower and change before his appointment. He made a few turns and merged onto I-75 North. Once he was over the five-mile bridge and paid the toll, he increased his speed. Arriving at the meeting dressed in ankle-high pants, a collarless shirt, and suspenders would raise some eyebrows. He rubbed his jaw. He needed to shave.

Mattie broke the silence. "So, do you ever miss farming?"

"Sometimes." He missed milking cows and tending the horses and the hours spent alone mending fences or gathering the honeycombs from the beehives.

"What do you miss the most?"

"I used to have a small workshop where I made furniture. I wasn't very good, but I liked taking rough timber and turning it into something smooth and useful."

"Did your *daed* teach you?"

He shook his head. "My *grossdaadi*."

Mattie seemed to know he needed time alone

with his thoughts and sank against the car seat. After several minutes, she asked, "Was it difficult to adjust to the *Englisch* world?"

"I wasn't thrilled about being tutored at first. I finished Amish school after eighth grade and the thought of having four years of high school was a bit overwhelming. But it wasn't long before I discovered how much I liked learning new things. Soon I was anxious to go to college."

"Did you ever build more furniture?"

"No."

"That's a shame you let that talent go." Mattie glanced at the backseat. "I'd like to see Nathan become a carpenter."

"I'm sure he'll have that opportunity growing up working around a sawmill."

An hour later, they were on the outskirts of town. They passed the hospital on the right and Mattie frowned.

"Don't worry," Bo said. He wished the voice message from his mother included good news for Mattie instead of just a reminder about the meeting.

Mattie turned her attention out the window and sighed. "It's hard *nett* to worry."

He reached for her hand. "God performed a miracle with Nathan. He will take care of everything else too."

She glanced at their hands and smiled. "I believe He has already given me reason to hope."

Bo released her hand, using the excuse to adjust the air vent. They were from two separate worlds.

At the end of the meeting with Internal Affairs, Bo was reinstated as an investigator for Child Protective Services. He learned Davis had resigned after the press aired the debacle at the bishop's house. It seemed the senator's daughter had fallen out of favor with the public when the reporter looked into Bo's statement about Nathan's illness being misdiagnosed.

Once the members of the review board left Norton's office, Bo stood to leave.

"Stick around, Lambright," Norton said. "We need to talk."

"Sure." Bo sat back down. His mother wasn't expecting him for another hour so he wasn't in a rush.

Norton leaned against the corner of his desk and crossed his arms. "You were lucky."

Bo nodded.

"You disobeyed orders and continued to follow the case even after you were placed on suspension. That alone is grounds for termination."

"I understand," Bo said.

"You jeopardized your career for that woman."

"I had to. She was innocent."

Norton cleared his throat. "She's fortunate to have someone as loyal as you. From what I was told, you probably saved the boy's life."

He shook his head. "God performed a miracle."

His boss extended his hand and Bo shook it. "Next time you go behind my back, I'm firing you."

"Yes, sir."

Norton opened the door. "I look forward to seeing you back at your desk tomorrow."

"Thanks." Bo walked into the outer office and spotted Max filling his mug at the coffeepot and waved. He continued outside and was halfway across the parking lot when he heard his name called. He turned as Max jogged up to him.

"Hey, I hope there's no hard feelings," Max said.

"About what?"

"Bringing the reporters to the Amish church service."

Bo smiled. "It worked out for the good."

"I guess you probably heard about Erica leaving."

"I did, but can we talk about this another time? I'm meeting my mother for lunch."

"Oh, sure. I just wanted to tell you the doctor called and asked that the Diener investigation be dropped."

"Really?"

"Doctor Roswell returned from vacation and wasn't too pleased with what had happened. Just between us, I think Doctor Wellington is worried about a lawsuit."

Bo wasn't about to tell Max that the Amish

didn't believe in lawsuits. The less information Max had, the better. "So the case is closed? Totally?"

"Yep. The doctor called Norton first thing this morning. Apparently, in talking with the parents of the infant with the botulism poisoning, they discovered it was caused by honey the two-year-old sister had fed him earlier that morning."

"And the glass?"

"Another person came forward and said that it was an accident. Plus, the X ray didn't show any glass in any of their systems."

"Thanks for the update." Bo glanced at his watch. "I have to go." He'd reached his car when Max called across the parking lot.

"Hey, Lambright. That honey you gave me is working. My sinuses aren't nearly as clogged."

"Glad it helped." Bo smiled and slipped behind the driver's seat, waving as he pulled out of the parking lot. Mattie would be overjoyed when she heard the news. He wished he could tell her now, but he'd have to wait. He was late to Forest Hills Country Club.

Bo arrived a few minutes late. His mother was seated next to the window overlooking the driving range, reading a menu she'd ordered from hundreds of times.

"Sorry I'm late." He sat across the table from her.

"How did the meeting go with Internal Affairs?"

He spread the linen napkin over his lap. "I was reinstated."

"That's good news," she said. "Is everything okay between you and Norton?"

"He said not to go behind his back again." He grinned. "But he admitted to missing me around the office."

"That's wonderful that everything worked out so well." She glanced around the room, then leaned closer. "I have news to share as well."

"Oh?"

"I received a letter from Comforting Hands Missions headquarters regarding a dedication in your father's name for a new well in Africa. They requested photographs of him for their newsletter and after spending time in his study—" She cleared her throat. "I finally realized how impor-tant all those mission trips were to Martin. He wasn't just there to care for sick orphans. He funded many drinking wells." She dabbed the corners of her eyes with the napkin. "I think I was blinded by what Great Northern Expeditions could do for my campaign."

"I don't understand."

"I returned their campaign contribution. Until I see more environmental studies, I don't want my name associated with the possibility of contaminating the groundwater." She sipped her iced tea. "I'm sure it will be election suicide losing their support, but I'll sleep better, win or lose." She signaled the waiter, and once they ordered, she said, "I understand you attended an Amish church service."

"You talked with Erica Delanie?"

"I saw you on the news. I must say, it made quite the story."

"I haven't seen it yet." Bo studied the beads of sweat forming on his iced tea glass and traced the condensation with his thumb. "Mattie and her children were pawns in Erica's schemes to build her platform. I couldn't allow Mattie and her settlement to suffer."

"From what I've heard, she's on the drilling company's payroll now. They want the Amish land because of its location to state land. If they obtain the Amish property they could drill horizontally and capture the resources from the adjoining state properties too."

"The Amish won't sell."

"I assumed as much."

The waiter arrived with his burger and his mother's Cobb salad, and Bo said grace over the meal.

His mother stabbed her fork into the salad. "I know you care a great deal for the Amish woman, Bo. You have always gone beyond your duty to see that the children in the foster system were taken care of."

"It's more than that," he admitted. "I've fallen in love with Mattie." The moment he'd kissed her, he knew he would never share the same feelings with another woman.

"Has she expressed the same feelings toward you?"

"No."

His mother frowned. "You haven't told her yet, have you?"

He shook his head. She knew him too well.

"Are you worried she won't leave the Amish settlement for you?"

"I wouldn't ask her to do that." His throat swelled. Ever since he'd realized his feelings for Mattie, he'd struggled with how he would tell his mother. The Amish believed wholeheartedly in separation from the world. Some districts forbade outside contact, although Mattie had asked an *Englischer* to drive her into town on multiple occasions.

"I see." She changed the subject and talked about random things. The garden, the work Josh was doing around the house, the upcoming fund-raisers.

His eyes welled. "I want you to know I thank God every day for you. You gave me a home when I had nowhere to go. You'll always be my mother."

Tears formed on her lashes. She placed her napkin on the table and summoned the waiter. "I would like the bill, please."

Bo glanced at his plate. He had a few more

bites of his burger and she had only picked at her salad. "Are you in a hurry?"

"You are," she said. "I would suggest you wait before you make any rash decisions, but I'm sure you've given this idea of love plenty of thought."

For someone who had never been Amish, the decision would be difficult to make, but he was aware of the lifestyle differences and the sacrifice it would mean. "If I become Amish again . . ." He paused, feeling the weight of his words. "I'll have to walk away from . . . the life I have with you."

She patted his hand. "Every mother knows one day the birds leave the nest. Besides," she said, straightening her shoulders, "I'm a firm believer that there is a season for all things. A time to plant . . . and a time to uproot what was planted . . ."

She finished quoting the passage from Ecclesiastes, but Bo immediately recalled the voice in his dream. *Like a farmer plants seed in the ground, so I've planted you. Grow in knowledge. Drink wisdom as if it were a cup of cold water, for a time will come when your vines will be pruned and your roots exposed.*

"Bo," his mother said. "Is something wrong?"

"No, why?"

"You looked as if you were in a stupor of sorts. How much sleep have you had lately?"

"Not enough." He leaned forward. "I've had an overwhelming feeling of unrest for several

431

years now," he explained. "Like I was wandering through life with no direction. Mattie Diener changed that, or maybe shed a light on what my life was missing. Not that you didn't provide me with the very best," he was quick to add. "I owe you so much for all you've done for me."

"You filled a void in my life as well." She smiled. "I was too busy building my career to have children, and if you hadn't come into my life . . . well." She blotted her eyes with the napkin again and forced a smile. "Don't say good-bye—I won't hear of it—do you understand?"

He nodded. Why did this have to be so difficult?

She scrawled her signature on the bill and regained her composure. "I have Josh to watch over. He needs a little more direction than you did at his age, but I see great things in his future."

"I'm glad to hear that."

"I suppose in the near future I'll be buying my herbs and honey from Mattie. I plan to become her best customer."

Bo smiled.

"Now," she said, making a shooing motion with her hand, "I suggest you go tell Mattie the case is closed. I'm sure she's anxious to hear from you."

"You're saying he's Amish?" Grace choked on her tea. "*Aenti* Erma was right. She said he was a fence-jumper the first time she saw him."

"He's *nett* really a fence-jumper. I mean, *nett* by

432

choice." Mattie explained how Bo's father was a hard man and he was giving him time to cool off when Bo was in a car accident that caused him to lose his memory. "His father wouldn't acknowledge him after the accident, so Bo didn't have any choice in the matter."

"That's sad."

Mattie agreed. "I've been praying for his father since I met him. He still has a root of bitterness toward his son."

"Even if he's *nett* exactly a fence-jumper, he is an *Englischer nau*."

Mattie swirled her tea with the spoon. "I know."

"You've fallen in love with him, haven't you?"

Mattie nodded. "Bo's a kind man. Nothing like his father."

"He's *Englisch*."

Grace didn't need to remind her. Mattie had been reminding herself of that fact for the last few days. More so since they kissed.

Car tires crunched over the gravel drive outside her kitchen window. Mattie's pulse picked up its pace as she went to the door.

Bo was clean-shaven and wearing khaki pants, a button-down white shirt, and a dark tie. Disappointment niggled at her, even though she smiled.

"I have good news," he said, taking her hands.

Grace rounded the corner from the kitchen and glared at both of them.

Bo released her hands, stammered to greet Grace, then continued, "Your case is closed."

"It is?" Mattie put her hand over her mouth. A flood of joy hit her at once; her eyes watered with tears.

Grace wrapped her in a hug. "Alvin told the police it was his fault the jar broke."

"He did?" Mattie batted the tears off her lashes.

"He told everyone during the Sunday meal what he planned to do."

Mattie glimpsed Bo's frown in her peripheral vision. She moved out of Grace's embrace. "*Danki*, Bo."

"I knew you would want to hear as soon as possible."

She turned to Grace. "Would you go tell the others?"

Grace eyed her a moment.

Mattie dismissed the silent warning. "Please."

Grace eyed Bo with the same unspoken warning, then quietly left the house.

"Would you like a cup of tea? The water is still hot."

"I probably shouldn't stay."

Mattie understood. Their time together had ended. It was for the best, or so she tried to tell herself. "*Danki* for everything you've done."

"You don't have to thank me." He took a noticeable breath. "It was my job."

*Was it your job to break my heart? To touch a part of my soul with your kiss?*

"I'm . . . I'm going to miss you," he said.

She forced a smile. "But you'll have more women to . . . rescue in your job."

"If you need anything—anything at all . . ."

"I still have your card," she said. She was a fool to believe their kiss had meant anything to him or to hope he might consider returning to his Amish roots.

"Take care of yourself, Mattie." He placed his hand on the doorknob and paused a half second. He continued out the door.

Mattie's chest grew heavy. Falling in love with an *Englischer* was foolish. She stood at the door and watched him get into his car.

Her life could return to normal. But could his? Bo headed down the bumpy road toward the main highway. This was for the best. He'd seen the look Grace had given him. He didn't belong in Mattie's life, in their community. He wasn't Amish.

Bo passed a buggy on the road heading toward Mattie's house and sighed. Alvin. Grace must have delivered the news to him first. Bo glanced in his rearview mirror. Watching the buggy continue down the road, his stomach knotted. Alvin was part of the community. Probably the man Grace had picked out for Mattie.

435

Bo stopped the car and leaned his forehead against the steering wheel. Why did it have to be so hard to let her go?

Mattie choked back tears as Bo's car disappeared down the narrow road. Shrouded with unexplainable emptiness, she leaned her head against the doorframe and closed her eyes. An image of Bo wearing a straw hat and suspenders played in her mind. *Narrish*! She knew the day would come when Bo returned to his way of life. She wiped the creases of her eyes and was about to close the door when she noticed the puff of dust rising from the road.

For half a moment she thought it was Bo, but the sound of *clip-clopping* horse hooves became louder. Alvin pulled into the driveway and climbed out of his buggy.

She forced a smile and waved.

Alvin lumbered up the porch steps. "I just passed the *Englischer*."

Mattie nodded. "He came to let me know that the charges were dropped."

"So I heard." He fidgeted with his left suspender. "You . . . ah . . . you have any cookies or pie?"

"As a matter of fact I do." Mattie opened the screen door and Alvin trailed her into the kitchen. She motioned to a chair and went to the cupboard. "I wanted to thank you for telling the police what happened," she said as she poured coffee into a mug.

"I just told the truth."

She piled several peanut butter cookies on a plate and set them and the coffee mug down on the table before Alvin.

Amanda shuffled into the kitchen rubbing her eyes with her balled-up hands. She sidled up beside Mattie and buried her face into the folds of her dress.

A knock sounded on the door. She lifted Amanda and gently set her down on the chair beside Alvin, then went to the door.

"Bo, is something wrong?"

He rubbed the back of his neck. "Yes—no—may I come in?"

She opened the screen door and stepped aside.

"I—ah." He shifted his stance.

Something had set him off balance.

Nathan woke from a long nap and shuffled down the hall. He whimpered something about being thirsty. Amanda toddled out from the kitchen, stopped in front of Bo, and lifted her arms up to be held.

"Hello, pumpkin." He swooped down and picked her up.

Mattie smiled at how easily her daughter had bonded with Bo. She cleared her throat. "Bo, was there—I mean—did you . . ." She pressed her hands against the sides of her dress. "Why did you *kumm* back?"

He stepped toward the kitchen and groaned under his breath. Pivoting to face her, he asked, "Can we go outside?"

She eyed him carefully. His hair was askew as if he'd been combing his fingers through it. She reached for Amanda, kissed her cheek, then lowered her to the floor.

"Please," he said.

She studied him a half second more, then instructed Nathan and Amanda to play with the clothespins in the sitting room. Mattie turned to Bo. "After you," she said, motioning to the door.

Once on the porch, Bo guided her to the banister. He licked his lips. "The other night, when I kissed you . . . I told you . . . how much I cared for you."

*Remain calm.* "*Jah.*"

"I, ah . . . I care *a lot.*" His Adam's apple dipped down.

She smiled.

"Maybe more than I should—I love you, Mattie. I want you to be—"

The screen door creaked open. Alvin stepped outside and crossed his arms. "Bo, it would be best for everyone if you leave. Mattie's charges were dropped. You don't have a reason to be here."

A flicker of anger rose up inside Mattie. She

438

opened her mouth to rebuke Alvin, but Bo placed his hands on her shoulders and turned her to face him.

"Do I have a reason to be here, Mattie? Have you fallen in love with me?"

"Mattie, he's an *Englischer*," Alvin warned.

"*Jah*," she replied, her focus on Bo. "I know how he appears on the outside."

Alvin stormed off the porch.

Bo moved closer. "I love you, Mattie. I want to marry you."

Concern faded her smile. Surely he didn't think she could leave her Amish life behind as he had. "I couldn't jump the fence to be your wife."

"I'm asking you to be *mei fraa*."

A shudder tickled her insides. "Can you give up your worldly possessions and go back to a simple lifestyle?"

Bo nodded. "I've dreamt about us." He rubbed his jaw. "I had a beard and you and the children were by my side. We were married."

Her eyes misted.

Bo ushered her into his arms and kissed her softly. "I've been Amish before. I can make the necessary changes." He rested his forehead against hers. "I love you."

Joy bubbled up within her. She wanted the moment to live in her heart forever.

Bo cupped her face and held her gaze. "I believe

God has been working with me about my past—my roots. I never understood why I was in the car accident—why my *daed* rejected me."

"But you know *nau*?"

He smiled. "God planted me for a season as an *Englischer*. Then you came into my life, and I no longer belonged in the world."

Tears blurred her vision. God had sent Bo to help clear her name, to pray for Nathan's healing . . . to hold her steady when her world was falling apart.

"Mattie," he said. "I'll talk with Bishop Yoder. I'll explain why I became *Englisch* and I'll ask to join the church. I love you. I love your *kinner*."

"I love you too," she whispered.

"Will you marry me?"

The screen door opened, and Amanda and Nathan toddled outside. Amanda went to Bo and lifted her arms. Nathan hugged Mattie's leg.

"I asked your *mamm* to marry me," he said, swooping Amanda into his arms.

Tears of joy streamed down Mattie's face. "Yes, Boaz. We'll all marry you."

# Reading Group Guide

1. Bo felt God's direction through his dreams. Have you ever felt like God provided you with a solution to a problem by way of your dreams? Can you think of three instances when dreams played a critical role in the Bible?

2. Alvin Graber helped Mattie around the farm after her husband died. Do you think that Mattie would have pursued a future with Alvin if she hadn't met Bo? Would it have been a good match? Why or why not?

3. Do you believe Doctor Wellington was out of line to suspect Mattie of child abuse?

4. When the bruising on Nathan showed up, did you have any idea what might be causing his illness? Were there points in the novel when you questioned Mattie's innocence?

5. Honey plays an interesting role in the story. Can you think of two ways that honey was used as a means of healing? Of harming?

6. Nathan and Amanda are timid children, wary of strangers, and perhaps overly attached

to their mother. Is Mattie raising her kids to behave this way or do you think she's responding to their natural temperaments?

7. How did it make you feel to know that Bo would have to almost entirely cut his ties to his foster mom, Judge Nettleton?

8. In one of Bo's final dreams, he hears his stepfather's voice reminding him that he promised to look after his mother. What role does Josh play in this?

9. Of all the characters in the story, who did you find the most frustrating? Why?

# Acknowledgments

This book would not be possible without the support of my husband, Dan, and our children, Lexie, Danny, and Sarah. I'm blessed to have your encouragement and love. Thank you!

Thank you to my publishing family at HarperCollins Christian Publishing. My editors, Becky Philpott and Natalie Hanemann, are the best! Thank you to Jodi Hughes for typesetting and to Kristen Golden for the outstanding marketing work she does on every book.

It's wonderful coming from a small town. I want to say a special thanks for the support I received from the following businesses of Onaway, Michigan, who helped promote my book signing at the Onaway Library:

Awakon Federal Credit Union
Brian's Auto Shop
Cable TV (local news)
Citizens National Bank
Custom Embroidery
Doll House
Ellenberger Lumber
Family Dollar
Farmers Insurance

Lynn Street Manor
Manzana Grill
Marathon Gas Station
Onaway Baptist Chapel
Onaway Chiropractic Center
Onaway High School
Onaway Laundromat
Onaway Tire
Parrott's Outpost
Presque Isle Electrical and Gas Co-op
Red Oak Furniture
Sally's Beauty Salon
Shell Gas Station
Subway
Sunoco Gas Station
The Cabinet Shop
The Flower Shop
The General Store
Tom's Family Market
Woodwinds Restaurant
211 Outpost
Bundy's Party Store (Tower, Michigan)

A huge thank-you to Pastor James and Cozee Warner of Onaway Baptist Chapel for printing the flyers that went into every shopping bag at Tom's Family Market.

All of this wouldn't have been possible without Joy Elwell's and Ella Roberts's diligence in asking the area businesses to post the flyers.

I'd also like to thank Kathy, JoLynn, and Beth, the staff at the Onaway Library, who worked hard to provide the perfect setting for me to talk about my books and provide coffee for the wonderful people who attended.

Wow! My hometown is the best! Thank you all. God bless you!

# About the Author

Ruth Reid is a full-time pharmacist who lives in Florida with her husband and three children. When attending the Ferris State University College of Pharmacy in Big Rapids, Michigan, she lived on the outskirts of an Amish community and had several occasions to visit the Amish farms. Her interest grew into love as she saw the beauty in living a simple life.

*Visit Ruth online at* ruthreid.com
*Facebook:* Author Ruth Reid
*Twitter:* @authorruthreid

**Center Point Large Print**
600 Brooks Road / PO Box 1
Thorndike, ME 04986-0001 USA

(207) 568-3717

**US & Canada:**
**1 800 929-9108**
www.centerpointlargeprint.com